THE PRICE OF REVENGE

A NOVEL

BY

RITA M. BOEHM

This is a work of fiction. Names, characters, places, and incidents either are the product of the author's imagination or are used fictitiously, and any resemblance to actual persons, living or dead, is entirely coincidental.

Printed in the United States of America

Independently published

ISBN: 9798847707633

Follow author on Facebook @ Author Rita Boehm

Website: www.ritamboehm.com

OTHER BOOKS BY RITA M. BOEHM

FICTION

MISSING ON MAPLE STREET

The SECOND CHANCES trilogy:

- SECOND CHANCES
- BEYOND SECOND CHANCES
- ANOTHER CHANCE

CHILDREN'S PICTUREBOOK

BLUEBIRDS IN THE GARDEN

NON-FICTION: WWII MILITARY

ONE SOLDIER'S WAR: In His Own Words

The deeper that sorrow carves into your being,

the more joy you can contain.

The Prophet, Kahlil Gibran

PART 1

CATHY DIAL

1

PINE VIEW, NJ - LAS VEGAS, NV
1986

Cathy Dial blew the hair out of her eyes as she sank onto a stool at the Pine View Diner's worn counter. She stared down at the gravy stains splattered across the front of her uniform and shook her head in disgust.

"Looks like you had a tough morning."

Startled, Cathy turned to her left, surprised to see Pine View's police chief standing next to her. His usually stern expression was replaced with a broad grin that accentuated the deep lines in his face.

Police Chief Frank Peters was a big deal in Pine View. He made a lot of people nervous, but not Cathy—at least not so much anymore. He was almost always at the diner, always seemed to be there when she was on her lunch break or at the end of her shift. Somehow she'd fallen into the habit of making him dinner once a week, although she couldn't quite remember how that had happened. He'd become a father figure—of a sort.

She glanced back down at the globs of brown gook. "Yeah, you could say that. The kid responsible for this mess will either be an abstract artist or a serial killer when he grows up. The jury's still out."

Chief Peters laughed—a hearty, throw-back-your-head kind of laugh. Cathy offered up a weak smile in response. Her comment hadn't been all that humorous, but then again, he *was* the police chief. Maybe he thought serial killers were funny.

"Maybe this will help."

He reached into the inside pocket of his jacket and retrieved an envelope, presenting it to her with a flourish. Cathy gazed in confused silence at the words 'Pine View Travel Agency' emblazoned across the front of the envelope now in her hand.

Still grinning, Chief Peters eased himself down on the stool next to Cathy's. He turned to face her boss who was standing behind the counter, order pad in hand. His next words, although phrased as a question, were actually more of a pronouncement. "You can do without Cathy for a few days, can't you, Marge? We're leaving next Tuesday for a little vacation in Las Vegas."

Shocked, Cathy stared dumbly at Frank. Marge was well-known for her hot temper. In the two years Cathy had worked at the diner, she'd witnessed Marge lose it on a number of occasions—fortunately, never at her. She was on the schedule to work next Tuesday and Wednesday and messing with Marge's sacrosanct work schedule ranked only slightly behind stealing to incur Marge's wrath.

Cathy waited expectantly—hopefully?—for Marge to react. She expected her to say, "Hell no, Frank. I can't do without Cathy on such short notice."

Instead, after an uncomfortably long silence during which her boss nervously tapped her pen on the counter, Marge just shrugged and said, "Sure, Frank."

And that was that.

~

Four hours later, her interminable diner shift finally over, Cathy trudged up the backstairs to her apartment, clutching two grocery bags in her arms. As she fumbled with the key, her purse fell, dislodging an envelope from its cluttered interior. The words Pine View Travel Agency shouted at her from the otherwise blank envelope lying on the floor at her feet.

Cathy rebalanced the grocery bags and unlocked the door. Part of her wanted to leave the envelope, to allow it to get blown away by the wind. "Fat chance," she muttered after shaking her head. After bending to retrieve the unwelcome gift, she pushed open the door and flung the envelope on the kitchen table without a further glance.

Too exhausted to focus on anything but the simplest of tasks, she put the groceries away, peeled off her stained and sweaty uniform, and retreated into a hot, welcoming shower. The pulsing water washed away the day's sweat and grime—and some of her exhaustion.

Once she was comfortably attired in an oversized tee shirt and shorts, Cathy stretched out on the sofa in her cozy apartment, her sore feet resting on a pillow. She purposely avoided the kitchen and the envelope waiting for her on the table. Out of sight, however, didn't mean out of mind.

Should I call Jean?

She debated the question in her mind.

Jean would know what to do. Jean always knows what to do.

Jean Donahue and her husband John had always been there for her, even before her father's death. Proof of their kindness and generosity shouted at her from every corner the apartment Cathy had called home for the past two years.

As soon as she'd called Jean to share her exciting news, to tell her that Doc and Betty Waldron had solved her obnoxious college roommate problem, Jean had started talking about paint colors. She and John had arrived, paint rollers and paint cans in hand, as if the two-hour trip from Harmony Farm was a mere ten minutes away.

The following weekend, they'd arrived with their truck and horse van filled with furniture and kitchen utensils. "Just stuff we had in storage, and here and there." Jean had said, as Cathy stared in wide-eyed surprise while John and a friend maneuvered the furniture up the outside staircase to the apartment over Doc Waldron's vet clinic.

Jean's dismissive comment about the history of the new-looking furniture was typical of the Donahue's casual generosity. They were always there to solve her problems—without fanfare or comment. They filled the empty place in her heart where family belonged.

No, Jean's done enough. I can't always be running to her.

Cathy continued her internal argument as she focused on the colorful Turkish rug she'd purchased at an estate sale. The rug, along with the plants, bright throw pillows, and her watercolor paintings on the walls, made the apartment her own. She'd created a home, a refuge from a world she often found overwhelming and more than a little daunting.

I can't be running to Jean all the time. I'm twenty-one years old. I need to stand on my own two feet.

The envelope stayed on the table—just below the phone hanging on the kitchen wall. Cathy drifted off to sleep on the couch. She didn't call Jean.

2

LAS VEGAS, NV

Cathy's fingernails dug into the armrests of her seat as the wheels of the plane slammed down on the wet tarmac at McCarron International Airport in Las Vegas. She was scared, and not just because of the plane's hard landing. She turned her head and stared at the middle-aged man snoring in the seat next to her.

What am I doing here?

She'd had her summer activities all planned out. Marge had agreed to increase her waitressing hours at the diner. Doc Waldron had offered to pay for a week-long vet tech clinic. She was looking forward to going home for a few days to see Jean and hang out with the horses at the farm. If she had time, maybe she'd even get started on an art project for next semester. A trip to Las Vegas wasn't on the list, not even at the bottom. Yet, here she was.

She sighed and shook her head. This was her own fault. As the plane taxied to the terminal, and Frank slept on in spite of the turbulence and hard landing, she continued to beat herself up—and to worry. *How on God's green earth did I end up on a plane to Las Vegas with Frank Peters?* The more she thought about it, the more she realized that she'd never actually agreed to the trip. When Police Chief Frank Peters wanted something, nothing stood in his way, and he'd apparently wanted to go to Las Vegas—with her.

Everyone in the diner, at least everyone sitting at the counter, had heard Marge give her the time off to make the trip. How could she say no? Frank would have been upset and humiliated. If Marge, who'd known him forever, couldn't say no to Frank Peters—how could Cathy?

Now, as the plane approached the terminal, Cathy nervously gnawed on her lip. Part of her was excited about the adventure, about spending time in glamorous Las Vegas. The other part of her, the nagging part that sometimes kept her awake at night, was afraid she didn't really know who Frank Peters was, or how she'd become such a big part of his life.

She enjoyed Frank's company, at least most of the time, and his paternal good-night kisses suited her just fine. He could be funny and entertaining, and he was certainly more interesting than the immature college guys she knew. She didn't have to fend off the sweaty groping that was part of any date with guys her own age. Frank was always a gentleman—except, of course, that one time...

Her stomach clenched as she remembered the night three months earlier when he'd shown up at her apartment in a drunken rage and almost raped her. She pushed the memory aside. He'd apologized more than once for his behavior. He'd confessed that the horrific things he'd witnessed in Vietnam gave him nightmares and sometimes made him drink too much. She couldn't even imagine how terrible the war must have been. So she'd forgiven him—and he'd barely touched her since.

The plane came to a stop and the flight attendant made a final announcement. "Welcome to Las Vegas, folks, and thank you for flying American Airlines. Be careful when you open the overheads. Those vacation clothes may have shifted during the flight. We're hoping to see you on your next flight, so try not to lose too much money." The passengers laughed right on cue.

Cathy had no more time to ponder the details of her odd and sometimes frightening relationship with Frank Peters. Next to her, Frank stretched and yawned. She watched as he glanced around at the departing passengers and then turned to face her. His eyes were bloodshot and a bit of drool pooled in the side of his mouth.

She forced a smile. "We're here, Frank."

He flashed her a quick smile of his own before he stood, popped open the overhead compartment, and extracted their two carry-on bags.

∿

By the time they'd collected their luggage and taken a taxi to the Tropicana Hotel, Cathy was exhausted. The meal on the flight from New Jersey had been neither tasty nor filling, but she was past being hungry. All she wanted to do was sleep—in her own room, as Frank had promised. She didn't think he'd lie about their sleeping arrangements, but she was still a little nervous.

After wending their way through the brightly lit and noisy casino, they found the hotel's registration desk. When the desk clerk handed them key cards—to two separate but adjoining, rooms, Cathy relaxed. She was ready for bed. Unfortunately, Frank had other ideas. He insisted on showing her the sights.

The cacophony of slot machine bells, music, and garish neon lights overwhelmed her senses. This was nothing like Atlantic City—although she'd only been there that one time five months earlier on her twenty-first birthday. An earlier surprise from Frank. Now, he propelled her down the Las Vegas Strip, surrounded by noisy crowds of happy, drunken revelers, past myriad casino hotels with their bright, blinking neon signs,

Men accosted them, or rather they accosted Frank, constantly handing him flyers with pictures of exotic dancers and naked women. Radiating energy, Frank's wide, full-toothed grin was one she had never seen before. "Isn't this exciting, Cathy?" He hadn't bothered to face her when he'd asked, so he couldn't have noticed that her response was a weak, unenthusiastic smile.

He dragged her into a small casino, past the slot machines and into a noisy dark room that reeked of sweat and stale smoke. Men were hooting, yelling, and stomping their feet. As she peered through the crowd, Cathy saw big-breasted dancers gyrating to the pulsating music with nothing on but tiny string bikini bottoms. She turned away in disbelief and embarrassment, but Frank wasn't paying attention to her.

After locating an empty table, Frank motioned for her to sit. When a cocktail waitress approached, he ordered himself a scotch and Cathy a rum and coke without raising his gaze from the young waitress's ample breasts. When he said, "You've got quite the rack there, sweetheart," Cathy squirmed in her chair, mortified by his behavior. The waitress just winked before sashaying her way back through the crowd.

Frank laughed. His mood soured abruptly when he turned and noticed Cathy's disapproving expression. "Don't be such a prude. Why do you think she wears that skimpy outfit?"

He turned back to face the stage, his body leaning forward to better leer at the dancers. Cathy was grateful the crowd blocked her own view of the show. She drank the rum and coke and focused her gaze on the people around her—almost all of them men. Other than the waitresses, she saw only one other woman. When their eyes met, the woman shook her head and shrugged. Cathy offered the woman a tight smile and a shrug of her own.

The waitress brought them a second round of drinks. "Keep them coming, sweetheart," Frank said as he tucked a twenty dollar bill into the waistband of her hot pants.

Cathy nursed her second drink. She was exhausted and embarrassed, but there was no way she could convince Frank to leave, even if she had the nerve to try. As she watched him down yet another drink, she tried to quell her uneasiness by rubbing her thumb over the key card in her pocket. She had her own room. She'd be fine. Then her thoughts began to jumble and slow. The alcohol went to her head, and the fatigue claimed her.

~

"Cathy, wake up. It's time to go."

She heard Frank's voice through the fog of sleep. Her head jerked up, and she opened her eyes, confused and frightened until she remembered where she was. She looked around. The dancers were gone, and the crowd had thinned.

"The show's over. Let's head back to the hotel. I can't believe you fell asleep."

He didn't say much on their walk back to the hotel. She wondered if he was annoyed with her for falling asleep. She didn't have the energy to ask.

When they reached their rooms, Frank waited until she unlocked her door. "Get some sleep. After breakfast, we can hang out at the pool if you want." Then he turned away, entered his own room, and shut the door behind him.

Cathy stepped into her room, switched on the lights, and pulled the door shut. After engaging the security lock, she rummaged through her opened suitcase for her pajamas and began to tug off her clothes. On her way to the bathroom, she glanced at the door separating her room from Frank's. When she noticed there was no security lock, she was too exhausted to worry about it.

3

LAS VEGAS, NV

With her eyes half open and unfocused, Cathy stretched across the bed to grab for the phone, anxious to silence the head-splitting noise. "Hello," she mumbled into the receiver while she assessed the unfamiliar room.

"Good morning, Cathy!" Frank's surprisingly upbeat voice reminded her of where she was—and with whom. Her pounding head reminded her that she was a light-weight drinker.

How can he be so cheerful—and so loud?

Her weak attempt at matching Frank's upbeat tone resulted in a mumbled, "Good morning, Frank." When she heard him chuckle, she realized that not only had she failed at sounding upbeat, she'd barely managed to sound awake.

"It's time for lunch—we already missed breakfast. Trust me, some food will clear your head. I'll meet you outside your room in a half-hour." His pronouncement was followed by a firm 'click' as he ended the call.

Cathy hung up the phone and staggered out of bed. Frank would expect her to look nice. She had thirty minutes to shower, unpack her suitcase, and make herself presentable. Her fresh-faced college girl look and long blonde ponytail wouldn't cut it in glitzy Las Vegas.

Twenty minutes later, she was still struggling with the final touches on her make-up. Her eye-liner was straight, her eye-shadow unsmudged, and her long lashes coated neatly with mascara. Somehow though, even when covered with concealer, the freckles on her forehead stood out too much.

She grimaced when she rummaged through her suitcase and saw the wrinkles in her new clothes. There was no time to iron them. So, she pulled on the tight, white slacks and form-fitting blouse and hoped for the best, breathing easier when she saw the wrinkles disappear. As she tugged the blouse down, she couldn't help but compare her cleavage—minimal, even with a push-up bra—with the massive, double-D breasts Frank had been leering at the night before.

Although there was no time to muse about the oddities of male behavior, she couldn't stop herself from imagining how hard it would be to avoid smacking yourself in the face with those mammary monstrosities if you were riding a horse. With that thought in mind, she smiled and hurriedly hung the rest of the clothes in the closet.

She thought of the items in her vacation wardrobe as 'Frank's clothes', since he had insisted on paying for them. "Listen," he'd said with his usual bluntness, "you don't exactly have the right clothes for a fancy hotel in Las Vegas, and those outfits your friend Jean bought you for Christmas won't work for Las Vegas in June. It's no big deal. Take the money."

So, she did. She accepted his money—and she'd followed his instructions and spent it at Monique's. The boutique was in a part of town she rarely frequented, next to the Pine View Bowling Alley and across the street from a place that advertised X-rated videos. She hadn't even known the store was there. The tight-fitting, colorful slacks and tops they sold were a world away from her usual jeans and tee shirts.

She slid into her sandals and picked up her purse. As she reached for the door, the image in the full-length mirror stopped her. She was stunned. She looked nothing like herself, nothing like the Cathy Dial she knew, but she didn't have time to think about whether or not she liked her new look. Frank didn't like to be kept waiting.

The next two days disappeared in a blur of shopping, gambling, drinking, and night clubbing. The excitement and glamor of Las Vegas was way beyond anything Cathy had ever experienced—or imagined.

Since her father's Army assignments had often taken him away from home, there'd been no formal family vacations, even when she was little, even before her mother died. They'd mostly stayed in the little German town where they lived or took a day trip to other places in Germany. After she and her dad moved to New Jersey when she was fourteen, there'd still been no time for vacations—at least not with her father who was often away on Army assignments. She'd spent all her free time at the Donahue's

Harmony Farm. Her idea of a vacation was sketching and grooming Jean's gorgeous Arabian horses.

Las Vegas was nothing like hanging out at the farm. Everything here was new and exciting—like the Neil Diamond concert Frank took her to. She hadn't expected to enjoy music she considered more appealing to a middle-aged crowd. Yet as she watched Neil Diamond perform up close from her second row seat, it was impossible not to absorb the excitement and energy.

"Isn't he wonderful?" An older woman in the next seat, her eye make-up smeared by joyful tears, excitedly grabbed Cathy's arm before returning her attention to the stage. Swept up in the excitement, Cathy stood with the crowd and sang along to *Sweet Caroline* as loudly and lustily as Diamond's die-hard fans. Frank even stood and sang along, although they both laughed when he messed up the simple words.

The following evening's entertainment was different, but no less exhilarating. Once again seated close to the stage, Cathy was enthralled by the magic show at the Mirage. Perched at the very edge of her seat so she wouldn't miss anything, she slipped forward and would have landed on the floor if Frank hadn't grabbed her. Even Frank seemed impressed by the illusionist's act, especially after the man's scantily clad assistant disappeared from the stage and magically reappeared at the back of the theater.

They were enchanted, fairy-tale evenings, or at least they would have been if they'd ended after the concert and the magic show—but Frank's appetite for entertainment had been barely whetted.

He dragged her to seedy venues that reeked of sweat and booze. While he ogled the naked performers, his breathing became so rapid and shallow that Cathy was concerned he'd have a heart attack. She knew better than to bother him, and she had no desire to view the lewd performances, so she mentally replayed the evenings' earlier G-rated entertainment.

When the shows were over and Frank had finally had enough, they stumbled back to their hotel. As they rode the elevator up to their floor, Cathy's self-preservation worries managed to finagle their way into her alcohol-fogged brain. A variety of frightening questions and 'what-if' scenarios played themselves out.

What if Frank pulled her into his room? What if he followed her into hers? He was paying for their rooms, had paid for the trip, for her clothes, for their entertainment. Was she stupid to think the trip was free? What would she do—what could she do—if he demanded payment?

Both nights, she'd held her breath as they walked down the long, plush-carpeted hallway to their rooms. She tried to appear relaxed though her hands shook, and she fumbled with her key card. Frank stood in front of his own door—and waited. None of her frightening 'what-ifs' were realized. No payment was demanded. She began to relax. Maybe all he wanted was her company while he enjoyed the exotic dancers and X-rated entertainment?

~

Day three was to be their final full day in Las Vegas. She turned down Frank's offer of a bus tour to Boulder Dam and Lake Mead. The tour sounded interesting, and she would probably have enjoyed it, but she preferred staying indoors until the sun went down. She'd learned to love the wet, steamy heat of summers at the Jersey shore—but the intense, blast-furnace heat of the Las Vegas desert sapped her strength and took her breath away.

Instead of the tour, Frank insisted on taking her on a shopping spree— in air-conditioned splendor. She was overwhelmed and discomfited by his generosity, but he kept pulling out his credit card. He wouldn't listen when she said no. After lunch, he surprised her with a spa afternoon that he'd already paid for—leaving her no out but to accept. "Enjoy yourself. You're on vacation! We'll have a drink in my suite before dinner. In the meantime I'll be winning at the craps table." He'd winked and walked off.

Three hours later, feeling pampered and glamorous, she met him for a drink, surprised to see that he actually did have a suite, and a sitting room. Then she returned to her own room to change for dinner. When he knocked on the adjoining door to her room less than an hour later, she pulled the door open wide, eager to show off. "What do you think?" She giggled and twirled around, stumbling before regaining her footing. "I don't look like the old me at all!"

Cathy was wearing one of the new dresses he'd insisted on buying her. It was red, low-cut, and tight—a wrap-around dress that showed off her still woefully under-endowed cleavage.

He beamed down at her. "You look ravishing, Cathy! Better than any of those topless dancers."

Flattered by his attention and approval, she surprised herself with her response. "You look pretty good yourself in your spiffy suit and tie." She clapped her hand over her mouth. *He did look pretty good, clean-shaven and nicely dressed, but where had that come from?* She wondered just how much rum he'd mixed in her drink. She was already drunk, and the evening hadn't even started.

Frank laughed and bowed in an exaggerated manner. "Well, thank you, Ma'am! Ready for dinner? I can't wait to show you off." He opened the door to the hall and gestured for her to leave before him.

Feeling a bit like Cinderella going to the ball, Cathy giggled again. She smiled and floated out the door.

~

A waiter showed them to a table set with sparkling wine goblets and an array of shining silverware. Cathy couldn't hold back her excited, "Wow!" Dinner in the fancy French restaurant in the opulent Caesar's Palace hotel was just one more in a list of overwhelming and impressive experiences.

Frank ordered for both of them. A variety of courses arrived at their table, brought by several waiters who hovered over them. Terrified she'd do something stupid, like spill the fancy sauce on her new dress, Cathy only nibbled at her meal. Her head was spinning as much from the glitz and glamor as from the bottle of champagne Frank ordered.

After dinner, as competing scents of expensive perfume wafted around them, they joined the throng of excited, party-goers wandering through the noisy, vibrant casino. Frank handed her a one hundred dollar token and pointed to a giant wheel of fortune. She slipped the token into the slot and held her breath as the wheel spun. It stopped on the number 500.

"Oh my God, five hundred dollars!" She shrieked in excitement before spontaneously throwing her arms around Frank in a bear hug. Her worries about this unexpected vacation evaporated. She was having fun.

They stopped at the craps table where Frank said he'd won 'big' earlier in the day. Cathy watched the other players while Frank played.

"Hey, sweetheart, when it's my turn, how about blowing on my dice for good luck?"

She hadn't noticed the man next to her until he'd spoken. She smiled uncertainly, but felt a tight grip on her arm before she had a chance to answer him.

"She's with me." Frank's voice was low, a warning growl, leaving no opportunity for the intruder to misunderstand.

"Sure, man. No problem." The younger man stepped away and disappeared into the crowd.

Frank rounded on her, his expression fierce, his dark eyes blazing. "Why were you flirting with that asshole? Haven't I done enough for you?"

Cathy shook her head, confused. Only moments earlier, they'd been laughing. "I...I didn't. Frank, I didn't even know he was there until he started talking."

He relaxed his grip and exhaled. The anger faded from his eyes. "Okay. I guess he was just a jerk."

~

Frank kept his arm around her waist and nuzzled her neck as they walked outside and wandered down the Strip. She was too drunk to be concerned. Her skimpy dress provided little protection from the cool night air, so she leaned into the warmth his body offered. They stopped at another casino for yet another drink. Cathy lost track of just how many drinks she'd had. Her mind was fuzzy, and her steps uneven. She was so out of it that she stumbled when they continued their walk.

Frank supported her as they progressed further down the Strip. They stopped at a cute, little building that kind of looked like a church. Cathy's fuzzy mind was still trying to process the meaning of the words on the door when Frank ushered her inside the Little White Wedding Chapel.

4

LAS VEGAS, NV AND PINE VIEW, NJ

She woke naked, alone and confused in a sunlit hotel room. A jackhammer pounded in Cathy's head with enough force to split her skull, and her mouth felt like she'd swallowed a desert's worth of sand. She gasped in pain when her sensitive nipples chafed against the sheet, and she became aware of an aching soreness between her legs.

What happened to me?

Vague images of flowered arches and muttered words drifted through her mind, but she couldn't focus. Panicked, but in desperate need of the bathroom, she stumbled from the bed, noticing that the furniture arrangement was different from her room, and a man's suit jacket was thrown across a chair.

Where the hell am I?

As she passed the bureau, a legal document propped against the lamp caught her attention. Shocked, she clamped her hand against her mouth, the urgency of her bathroom needs forgotten. Leaning forward, she focused on the signed Nevada marriage license displayed next to a smiling picture of her and Frank standing under a flowered arch in a wedding chapel.

Cathy stared, transfixed. She peered more closely at the picture. Her expression seemed more dazed than happy. Frank was smiling broadly enough for both of them. As she reached for the picture, the glint of a plain gold band on the ring finger of her left hand came into view—further proof of a reality her mind was struggling to process.

What have I done?

Shaken, she stepped back and sank onto the rumpled bed, refocusing when she heard the click of the door announcing that a key card had been inserted. Suddenly aware of her nakedness, she jumped up from the bed and rushed into the bathroom, closing and locking the door behind her.

"Cathy, are you awake?" Frank called out. "I brought you some coffee. Our flight's in three hours. Time to get up."

Ignoring Frank, she splashed cold water on her face, purposely not meeting her own gaze in the mirror. Her head was pounding so hard she would have eagerly traded one of her kidneys for two aspirin. Since that option wasn't available, she chugged three glasses of water, but still couldn't come close to quenching her thirst. She sank down on the toilet and buried her head in her hands.

What do I do now?

Frank had surprised her with a vacation in Las Vegas—and now she was married to him? No engagement ring, no wedding dress, no horse drawn carriage to the church, no reception at Harmony Farm—none of the things she had always imagined for her wedding.

She'd never even had a chance to tell Jean and John she was getting married, let alone invite them to the ceremony. They may not be blood relatives, but they were her family, her only family, and their beautiful farm had been her home since even before her father's death. They should have been a part of her wedding.

Questions pounded with each hammer blow of her hangover. Had Frank planned this all along? Is that why he'd asked her to help him pick out new furniture for his house? Was it the reason he'd been so generous about buying her things? How was it possible that she could get drunk enough to blindly follow him into a wedding chapel and get married? Had he slipped drugs into her drink?

She began to retch, not sure if her sudden nausea was brought on by her alcohol consumption, the water she'd chugged, or the hopelessness of her situation. A few slow deep breaths helped settle her stomach, but not her mind.

She had no answers to her questions, but as she began to conquer the initial panic, other thoughts floated through her mental confusion. Would being married to Frank be such a bad thing? True, she didn't love him, and it wasn't something she'd ever considered, but could it maybe work?

When he's not drinking, he can be a pretty nice guy. He says he cares about me. Isn't that what I always wanted, someone to care about me? Someone who won't leave me?

"Cathy?" Frank knocked on the bathroom door. "You in there?"

"Yes." She murmured, her voice a whisper. She took a deep breath and answered in a louder voice. "Yes. I'm... I need to take a shower." She turned on the shower faucets to demonstrate her intention.

The hot water pulsed over her body, helping to clear her head, but not by much. Frank, her husband, was just outside the door. As much as she might want to delay seeing him, she couldn't stay in the shower forever. Resigned, but still without a real plan, she turned off the water, exited the shower, and toweled herself dry. Wrapped in the generously sized bath towel, she opened the door.

Frank was sitting on the unmade bed dressed in a polo shirt and pressed black slacks. She brushed the wet hair away from her face and tucked the towel more tightly around her, feeling vulnerable and afraid. When he met her gaze, Frank's smile was guarded and uncertain, as if he was unsure what she would say or do. She didn't expect his uncertainty. It made him seem less frightening. The tight knot in her stomach loosened slightly.

"Good morning, Cathy." Frank held the coffee cup out to her without moving off the bed. "How are you feeling this morning?"

His words were so normal, so matter-of-fact, that Cathy had difficulty making sense of things, especially with her hangover headache. She didn't answer him. Instead, she turned her gaze from him to the marriage license and back.

Unasked questions hung in the air between them.

The silence built until Frank spoke. "You were having such a good time last night, I guess you drank too much. You do remember the wedding though, don't you?" He pointed at the documents and the picture and raised his eyebrows in question.

Not waiting for her response, he rose from the bed, placed the coffee cup on the dresser and approached her. She stiffened when she felt him wrap his arms around her, but when he patted her back in an almost fatherly way, she relaxed.

"I think the door between our rooms is locked from your side. Let me check to make sure the coast is clear and then you can go back to your room to get dressed. I have some aspirin that will help your hangover. We'll have more time to talk on the plane."

That was it. They were married. There was a marriage license to prove it. Cathy might not remember the ceremony beyond some vague images, but the photograph and her signature on the license were certainly proof enough of the event.

Clutching her clothes and purse, Cathy allowed Frank to usher her out the door and into her own room. She still hadn't uttered a word. As she blew her hair dry and made a half-hearted attempt to style it, she considered her options. She had read about movie stars getting quickie Las Vegas divorces. But she had no money for a lawyer and no place to stay.

Even if she could find the money, did she want to make a big scene with Frank? Could she confront him and accuse him, of…what? Forcing her to marry him? Drugging her? He was a police chief for God's sake. Who would believe her? Could she ever go back to Pine View if she attempted such a thing?

She stared into the mirror as she applied her eye make-up. Then she stayed her hand and stepped back to fully focus on her image. After blowing out a long breath, she shook her head and communed with the confused young woman in the mirror.

Maybe it was meant to be. We've spent a lot of time together, and I did come to Las Vegas with him. I could do a lot worse than

Frank Peters, couldn't I? Maybe I can learn to love him. It isn't like I have anyone else...

Resigned, she went back to applying her makeup.

As soon as she was dressed and packed, they checked out of the hotel and took a cab to the airport. While they waited to board their plane for the flight home to New Jersey, the aspirin and a light lunch helped cure the worst of her hangover. She still felt off, like she was in a dream—or maybe she just hoped she was.

She dozed on the plane until Frank made an announcement that shocked her fully awake. "When we get home, you'll need to tell Marge that you're quitting your job at the diner. I don't want my wife busting her butt waiting on Pine View's riff raff. You'll have plenty to do at home."

She bristled at his words, and if she'd been feeling better she might have reminded him that he was part of that riff raff. After all, he practically lived at the diner. People joked—never to his face, of course—that the Pine View Diner should be renamed the Pine View Police Annex.

Her slow mental reflexes allowed her time to reconsider her initial reaction—and save herself from Frank's ire. Maybe it wasn't such a bad idea to quit her job at the diner. If she wasn't waitressing, she'd have time to focus on her art and her college classes.

Cathy accepted his pronouncement without argument. "Okay. I need to give Marge two weeks' notice, though. It wouldn't be fair to leave her short-handed."

Frank nodded his agreement.

Relieved, Cathy took a breath and asked a more important question. "I can still work at the vet clinic, though, right?" Her time spent at the clinic with Doc Waldron and his four-legged patients was precious to her. "It's only a couple of afternoons a week, and I really love it."

Frank smiled indulgently. "Sure. If you like cleaning up dog shit, go for it. Just make sure you don't bring any fleas home with you."

5

PINE VIEW, NJ

The first night she spent in Frank's bed, Cathy didn't sleep much. She hadn't meant to flinch when he touched her, but her nipples were still sensitive, and she couldn't help but stiffen when he pushed himself inside her already sore body. He hadn't been pleased, but after murmuring something like, "It's okay. You just need some time," he'd given her a quick hug before turning away and falling asleep.

While he slept, Cathy lay next to him, staring at the ceiling of a bedroom she had never imagined would be her own. When she turned on her side away from her husband, a murky twilight in the unfamiliar room allowed her to make out the dim outline of a large chest of drawers. She smoothed down the fabric of the black silk nightgown Frank had given her as a wedding present—but she couldn't get comfortable, couldn't find sleep.

Unbidden, a tsunami of memories flooded her mind. Vignettes of her sexual awakening with Mike appeared, as if she was flipping through a video diary. Sweet memories of shared experiences between two young people who had planned to spend their lives together—until Mike's passion for music trumped his passion for her, and turned their plans to dust.

Truth was, she hadn't been important enough. She'd never been important enough. Not for Mike. Not for her parents. They'd all left her. Lying in a strange bed, facing an uncertain future married to a man she hardly knew, Cathy had no room in her heart to forgive her parents for dying. Her mother chose suicide instead of taking care of her little girl.

Her father chose the dangerous military career that took his life. Mike chose his music. They had all made choices. They had all left her.

She finally slept, her arms wrapped tightly around a pillow soaked with her silent tears.

~

Frank made breakfast in the morning, although he made it clear it would be her job from that point on. Cathy didn't mind. She liked to cook, and she liked Frank's kitchen. It was the only room in his house where she felt comfortable.

"I'm going to head into the station for a couple of hours. Give you some time to drive over and talk to the old vet to tell him you're moving out of the apartment." Frank was standing by the front door while he made his announcement. "I'll meet you there around eleven to help you move your stuff. There are some boxes in the garage you can use. Then we can swing by the diner and share the good news with Marge over lunch."

Cathy smiled and nodded. Her opinion didn't seem to matter, and Frank's plan was as good as any.

~

Less than an hour later, she parked in the driveway of a modest two-story home, one with yellow clapboard siding, white shutters, and window boxes overflowing with bright red geraniums. Doc and Betty Waldron's home, a place she'd come to know well.

In a reflective mood, she didn't get out of the car right away. She thought back to the afternoon two and half years earlier when she'd banged on the locked door of a vet clinic in the middle of a rainstorm. A white-haired vet with a lined face and kind eyes had opened the door and invited her in. Soaked to the skin and dripping water on the linoleum floor, she'd clutched the whimpering puppy she'd found lying on the side of the road. "Please help him," she'd begged.

Doc Waldron had done more than help. He had tended to the puppy's wounds, set his broken leg, and then he and his wife Betty adopted the little mixed-breed terrier Cathy had named Buddy. They'd pretty much adopted her, as well. Betty became the grandmother she'd never had. Doc became her boss and her mentor.

Cathy took a deep breath and stepped out of the car. The sticky heat of a New Jersey summer enveloped her as she trudged up the cement walkway toward the house. Her surprise at seeing a dandelion poking through the otherwise manicured lawn was fleeting, pushed aside by more weighty thoughts. She wasn't looking forward to sharing her news with Betty and Doc. They'd never actually come out and said anything bad about Frank, but there was always an undercurrent, always something left unsaid whenever his name came up.

Both Betty and Doc had made a point of telling her to have fun, enjoy her college years, and spend time with friends her own age. Those suggestions seemed to come up whenever she mentioned Frank. "It's never easy to make friends, Cathy. Maybe you just need to give the other young folks a chance to get to know you," Betty had advised.

"I never feel like I fit in. Maybe I'm too serious," Cathy offered as an explanation for why she hadn't made friends. She reminded Betty that she'd moved out of the college dorm to avoid the incessant partying. "I came to college to learn, not to party. I don't know what I would have done if you and Doc hadn't offered me the apartment over the clinic. Besides, with my two jobs, I don't really have much extra time to spend on campus."

Although she felt comfortable talking to the older woman, Cathy hadn't explained about her failed adventures in bar-hopping with some of the other waitresses. While they got drunk, she'd sat on the sidelines trying to find nice ways to tell loud-mouthed guys with sweaty, groping hands and foul mouths that she wasn't interested.

She'd always been different, especially in high school, where being different wasn't a good thing. Being different, which in her case meant being quiet, introverted, and a recent immigrant from Germany, made her an outsider. Until she'd met Mike, another newcomer, another loner, just like herself.

Mike had been her best friend and confidant long before he became her boyfriend, long before they'd learned about sex together. When he'd quit college to follow his music dreams to California, he took more than his guitar. A huge part of her heart went with him.

~

The sound of riotous barking greeted Cathy as she approached the Waldrons' front door. She smiled, pushing her morose thoughts aside. Excited to see the exuberant little dog, she lifted her hand to ring the bell. When the door opened, thirty pounds of canine joy bolted out.

Cathy crouched on the front stoop as Buddy wriggled around her feet, excitedly licking her face and trying to climb into her arms.

"Good morning, Cathy. What a nice surprise!" Betty Waldron smiled down at her. "I didn't expect to see you so early. Did you have a good time in Las Vegas?" The older woman's warm, welcoming words held a hint of curiosity.

Cathy stood. Betty held the door open wide so she and Buddy could enter. The dog bounded ahead until they reached the living room with its comfortably worn sofa and matching easy chair. Cathy plopped down on the carpet in front of the sofa to allow the excited pup to show her just how much he'd missed her.

"I tried to tell Buddy you'd be back, but he didn't believe me." Betty's smile broadened. "The little guy sure loves you."

Fighting back tears, Cathy pushed herself up from the floor. This was going to be harder than she'd thought. Not only did she have to tell Betty and Doc that she'd married Frank Peters and would be moving out of the apartment over the vet clinic, she'd have to say goodbye to Buddy. She'd no longer be living around the corner, able to take him for long walks a couple of times a day. Now, she'd be living clear across town.

She took a deep breath and eased herself onto the sofa as Buddy sighed contentedly and stretched out on the floor at her feet, resting his head on her foot.

"Is everything all right, dear?" Betty perched on the easy chair next to the sofa, an expression of concern etched in her kind face. "You seem upset." She looked toward the kitchen. "Doc's just finishing his breakfast. Did you want something to eat? It won't take but a minute to make you something." Betty stood and started to turn toward the kitchen.

Cathy shook her head. "No, please. I'm fine. I just had breakfast. I just needed…" She stopped. Then, after exhaling and attempting to swallow the huge lump lodged in her throat, she continued speaking, "There's something I have to tell you—and Doc."

"I see," Betty answered, although it was obvious she didn't. "I'll get Henry."

As Betty hurried away, Cathy knew she'd upset the slight woman with the caring heart. Betty Waldron only referred to Doc by his first name when she was upset.

While she waited, Cathy glanced at the family photos displayed on the mantel. Most were of the Waldron's son, Kevin. He'd been dead for four years, yet Cathy knew his suicide remained a raw wound in his parents' hearts. Doc never spoke about it, but Betty did. When she bragged about her only child's high school achievements and his college awards, her voice would break. She'd go on to explain how the war wounds the young man had experienced in Vietnam had gone deeper than a lost arm and a scarred face.

"You and Buddy have been a blessing, dear," Betty had told her more than once. "I don't know how I'd have managed these last couple of years without either of you."

Cathy turned away from the photos, away from the pain they represented. She bent down to pet Buddy's head while she waited for Betty to return with Doc.

~

Her news didn't go well. Doc winced as if he'd been hit. "You're married...you married Frank Peters." He repeated her words in a tone that suggested he was hoping his ears had betrayed him and that he hadn't properly heard what she'd said.

She hadn't expected them to be excited for her. After all, Doc had once commented on the age difference between her and Frank. At the time, she'd explained that Frank was just a friend. Doc had started to say something more, but then he'd stopped and let the subject drop.

Now, Doc and Betty exchanged wide-eyed looks—then they neutralized their expressions and responded to her news. They seemed...upset? As if trying to counter her husband's response, Betty hugged her and offered congratulations—although Cathy could sense her heart wasn't in it. "You'll still come by and spend time with Buddy, won't you? He'll miss you if you don't." Betty's voice quavered, making it clear it wasn't just the dog who would miss Cathy's visits.

"Of course I'll come by," Cathy promised. "And not just to see Buddy." Cathy returned Betty's hug and did her best to hide her own tears.

She stepped away and glanced toward the front door. "I have some boxes in the car," she announced. "I was going to move my stuff out of the apartment…" Her voice cracked. She loved that apartment, and now she had to leave it.

Betty smiled, if a bit tremulously. She patted Cathy's arm. "It'll be okay dear. Change is never easy." She spoke the words without conviction, as if she had searched deep in her brain for something positive to say, and could only come up with this one trite cliché.

Too upset to speak, Cathy hugged them both and headed toward the front door. Buddy's sharp bark stopped her. His expressive eyes, so filled with love, tore into her heart. She knelt down to hug him, then rushed out the door.

6

PINE VIEW, NJ

"Cathy? Honey, are you ready?" Frank stuck his head through the open apartment door. "What're you doing in here?"

"I'm packing my stuff." Cathy swiped at her tears as she carried a box from the bedroom. If Frank noticed the tears or the sadness in her eyes, he ignored them.

"Is this all of it?" He gestured to the boxes piled in the living room.

She attempted a tentative shrug of her shoulders. "Yeah. It's all my stuff. School stuff, art stuff mostly. I don't have all that much, really. Just a few things."

"No, I guess you really don't have all that much. We'll find a place for it. Don't worry." He pulled her close to him and ran his hands down her back until they cupped her rear end. "You have the cutest ass. Have I ever told you that? I'm a lucky man, Cathy, a lucky man."

She offered a weak smile as he stared down at her. His probing eyes expected a response. "Thanks, Frank. I'm pretty lucky, too."

"Did you tell old Doc that you were moving out, that you're a married woman now?"

His tone confused her. *Is that pride I hear in his voice? Or...what? Smugness?* Struggling to find the right way to answer him, she tried not to overanalyze his words. "Yeah....yeah I told him. I...I think he and Betty were a little surprised...."

"I'll bet they were!"

His reaction, his upbeat voice and the gleam in his eyes, reminded her of a kid who just reeled in a big fish or scored tickets to a World Series game. *Is that what I am to him? A prize?*

She pushed that thought aside, still searching for a way to explain. "Well, I've never really told them much. I didn't even tell them we were going to Las Vegas until the last minute…and it wasn't like we had planned the wedding or anything. I can understand…" Her words trailed off.

Frank's posture stiffened. His excitement disappeared and his piercing gaze held her captive. When he spoke, his words took on a challenging tone, "Having second thoughts, Cathy?"

"No!" Her immediate response left no room for misunderstanding, although she had to work harder to find the right words to continue her explanation. "It's…it's just a little hard to adjust to everything. I…I never thought….I guess I'm a little nervous. I've never been married. I'm not sure I know what I'm supposed to do." Overcome with uncertainty, she stared down at the floor, her eyes filling with tears.

Frank lifted her trembling chin with one hand while he pushed her long hair away from her eyes with the other. His gesture was gentle and unexpected.

"You'll do fine, Cathy. You'll do just fine. I guess I should have given you an engagement ring and let you tell your friends and plan a wedding. But it's not like you have any family to invite."

His words stung. *Is he being intentionally hurtful, reminding me that I have no family?* She searched his face but found nothing in his benign expression to feed her concern.

She considered his words. It was true that both of her parents were dead, that she had no family, but she had Jean and John Donahue. They were her family. They'd been a part of her life as long as she'd lived in the States. Some of her happiest memories were tied to their farm. Jean might not be her real mother, but she was close enough. Cathy opened her mouth to explain, but thought better of it. Frank wouldn't understand.

As Frank pulled her to him in a hug, she allowed herself to be comforted by his gesture.

"We okay, now? Do you want me to start bringing these boxes down to the car?"

"Yeah, please. Thanks, Frank."

It didn't take long to move out of the apartment she'd called home, a place where she'd felt like she belonged, maybe for the first time in her life. Frank put the boxes in his police SUV. All her clothes fit in the back seat of her car.

She left the furniture. Each item had been donated by people who cared about her, but she had no room for it now. She made a mental note to ask Jean if she wanted any of it back. She left her paintings, too—all except for Buddy's portrait. Now that there'd be no more daily walks and romps, she'd have to settle for the painting that captured the lovable likeness of the puppy whose life she'd saved.

After staring long and hard at the framed poster of Mike and his rock band, she decided to leave that, too. Mike might have been her first love, but he was a part of her past, of her childhood. Besides, Frank wouldn't understand.

∼

When they reached his house, Frank unloaded the boxes and stacked them in the bedroom, their bedroom. When would she begin to think of it as her house, too? She began to unpack her clothes.

"A penny for your thoughts?" his question surprised her.

She turned away from the bureau where she was arranging her clothes in the unfamiliar drawers of the heavy, colonial-styled bureau.

He was standing in the doorway watching her. "Worried about there being enough room for your clothes? I can clear out more bureau drawers if you need them."

"No, I don't need any more room. I don't have enough stuff to fill the space you've already given me." She stood next to the open bureau drawer, feeling like a trespasser—wondering how long it had been since his dead wife's clothes had filled the same drawers. Cathy had once tried to ask him about his wife, but his terse response that she'd died 'a few years ago' made it clear it was a subject he didn't want to discuss.

When she looked up and met his gaze, his eyes were thoughtful, watchful. She felt herself blushing, embarrassed that he might have read her thoughts.

"This is your home now, Cathy. You can relax. It's not like you've never been here before."

She attempted a smile. How could she explain? Before last night, she'd never been in his bedroom, never even been on the second floor of the house. "I know I'm being silly. It just takes me a while to adjust to new things. I've always been that way. I'm fine."

His grin emphasized the deep lines around his eyes and reminded her of the huge difference in their ages. "I know one room you've always been comfortable in. How about making us some dinner, and then we can have dessert."

He stepped into the room, slipped his arms around her, and pulled her toward him. His hands rested on her rear end, and he kissed her with an aggressiveness she still wasn't used to. She could feel his arousal as he pulled her tight against him.

When he broke away, his laugh was throaty as he whispered in her ear, "Can't wait for that dessert."

When he slapped her on the butt, she giggled. She always giggled when she was nervous.

7

PINE VIEW, NJ

Cathy slowly adjusted to the reality of her life as the wife of Police Chief Frank Peters. A couple of days after their return to Pine View, he took her to a fancy restaurant and made a big show of pulling out her chair. She'd blushed at the unexpected attention when he made a point of telling the waiter that she was his new bride.

When they were at home, he seemed to go out of his way to make her feel comfortable, to convince her that his house was now hers too. He took her shopping and helped her pick out new curtains and a comforter for the bedroom. They even purchased a comfortable easy chair for the corner of the room. The heavy colonial-style furniture was still not something she'd have chosen, but with the softer fabrics and the new chair, the room seemed almost inviting—except when she thought about what went on in the bed with her new husband.

A week went by, then two. Things seemed almost too good to be true. Frank was almost too nice. Sometimes she felt almost happy. Not over the moon ecstatic and in love kind of happy, maybe more like content. That was okay. She could live with being content.

So then, what's the problem? What am I worried about? Why haven't I called Jean?

The summer was slipping away. She hadn't spoken to Jean in almost a month. She knew Jean would be worried about her. Why was she afraid to share her news with the woman she loved like a mother?

Late one afternoon, Cathy rushed into the house with her mind focused on the meal she needed to prepare for dinner. She dropped her oversized purse on the edge of a kitchen chair. Unbalanced, it slipped to the floor with a thump. As Cathy bent to pick it up, her thoughts reverted to the Christmas morning two years earlier when she'd received the expensive and beautifully styled bag as a gift from Jean.

With that memory in mind, Cathy found the courage to pick up the phone to call the woman who had never once let her down. With every ring, she felt more and more eager to speak to Jean.

"Hello?"

Cathy smiled at the familiar brusqueness and impatience she heard in Jean's voice.

"Hi." Her own voice was uncertain.

"Cathy? Honey, is that you? We've been so worried about you! I know you left me a message saying that you were going away on vacation, but I thought you'd be back by now. We were hoping you'd spend some time with us before classes started...."

She stopped. Cathy heard her chuckle.

"Well, would you listen to me? Sorry. I guess you can tell I've missed you. As we both know, prattling is one of those woman things I can't abide. Now, it seems I've caught the bug. How are you, honey?"

Cathy's eyes filled with tears. How could ever have worried about calling Jean, about sharing her news with Jean?

"I'm fine, really good actually. I'm sorry...I'm really sorry I haven't called. I...we..."

She took a deep breath and then blurted it out. "I'm married, Jean. Frank and I got married in Las Vegas."

There, she'd said it.

Her announcement was greeted with a prolonged silence at the other end of the line. Finally, she heard Jean's voice. "Married? Did you say you got married?"

"Yes. It wasn't really planned. We didn't invite anyone. I would have definitely invited you and John if we'd...."

Jean interrupted. "Congratulations, Cathy! We would love to have been there, but as long as you're happy, that's all that matters. That's all that has ever mattered. You know you don't have to stand on ceremony with us."

"Thanks, Jean. It means a lot that you're happy for me. I'd still like for you to meet Frank. I know it didn't work out the last time I tried. But now that we're married, I'll invite you over for dinner soon. Frank has a nice house. I mean, we have a nice house. I think you'll like it. We just bought new furniture and everything."

She didn't know what else to say. It used to be so easy to talk to Jean. This was the woman who had helped her deal with her father's death, with Mike's abandonment, with all the uncertainty in her life.

Now, Cathy struggled to find words to fill the silence. "How's John? Are the horses okay? Are you okay?"

"We're all fine, Cathy. Everyone's fine. John will be sorry he missed your call. We'd love to see you, and we are definitely looking forward to meeting Frank. We'd love to visit you of course. But while you're getting settled, we'd love it if the two of you could come here. We're free most weekends. If you'd like to stay over, you know we have plenty of room. The horses would love to see you, too—especially Buster. He'll find a huge mud puddle to roll in, just so you can brush him."

They shared a laugh. Cathy had spent hours grooming the gorgeous, dappled gray stallion. He loved to be groomed, almost as much as he loved to roll in the mud.

"I'd love to come visit. I'll have to ask Frank, though. Sometimes his schedule isn't very predictable, being the police chief and all."

"I understand. If it's easier, we can come there. We miss you, Cathy."

"I miss you, too," Cathy answered. And she meant it.

Cathy had a smile on her face as they said their goodbyes. Her smile faded as she considered her husband.

Would Frank be willing to visit Harmony Farm? Would he be angry when she told him she'd invited the Donahues for dinner?

Her happiness faded with her smile.

8

PINE VIEW, NJ

After kicking aside the newly fallen autumn leaves, Cathy unlocked the back door and entered the dark kitchen. She shrugged out of her jacket, idly wondering why Frank hadn't turned on the lights. His police car was in the driveway. He had to be home. After three months of marriage, Cathy had his schedule down pat.

"Frank, are you in here? You can really feel a chill in the air. It'll be pumpkin time soon."

She chattered on excitedly. "Did you get the message I left on the answering machine? Professor Steen invited the class to his home and I got to meet Ann Sheridan, the artist I told you about. She was so nice to everyone! She gave me some tips about …"

Cathy pulled up short after she entered the den and reached his chair. The television screen was dark, and even though the lamp wasn't on, the outside street light projected just enough illumination for Cathy to see the tight set of Frank's jaw. Her excitement turned to something closer to fear. She shuddered involuntarily as she processed the thrum of tension in the air.

"Ummm." She cleared her throat and continued. "I took chicken cutlets out of the freezer before I left this morning. I can have dinner ready by eight."

He didn't answer her. He sat stock still in his recliner staring at the blank TV screen, an empty scotch glass on the table next to him. Her stomach clenched. Unlike the first few weeks of their marriage when he seemed to be purposely avoiding alcohol, he'd been drinking a lot lately.

Has he been drinking since he got home?

She swallowed and forced out more words. "Frank? I'm...I'm sorry I wasn't here. You did get my message though, didn't you? It won't take me long to make dinner..."

He lifted his head and turned to face her, staring through her as if she wasn't there.

Her voice trembled with uncertainty. "I'll...I'll go make dinner."

She turned away. Before she could take a step toward the kitchen, Frank reached out and extended his right arm to block her exit. Shocked, she turned to him, just as his other hand reached up to clamp a tight hold on her long hair. She sucked in her breath, fell back against his chair, and slid to the floor.

"You little slut!" he growled while he pulled hard on her hair. Even though his tone was low, she processed his words as a shout. "You think I was born yesterday? You're off balling some college punk while I'm sitting here waiting for you. I deal with the dregs of society all day, and you think I'm going to sit here and take it?"

Tears filled her eyes. As he tightened his grip, the pain in her scalp became excruciating.

"Answer me!"

She was too terrified to speak.

The force of his unexpected punch to her gut knocked the breath from her lungs. She couldn't answer him—even if she could find the words to do so. She doubled over and clutched her stomach.

Still, he held on to her hair. He jerked her head up. "Look at me!"

She stared into the rage-filled eyes of a stranger and breathed in the fetid odor of the alcohol on his breath.

"Listen to me because I'm only going to say this once. I don't ask a lot. Your job is to take care of this house and have my meals on the table when I get home. If your school shit gets in the way, then you'd better kiss it goodbye. Do you understand?"

He tightened his grip. Her head was on fire from the pain.

She nodded even though it hurt to move her head.

"Answer me!"

"Yes....Yes, Frank. I understand."

"Good. Now get your ass out to the kitchen and make dinner. We'll put this little episode behind us."

Cathy rose on shaky legs and stumbled into the kitchen. She held one hand against her stomach as she opened the refrigerator. Trembling, and with her vision clouded by tears, she reached inside for the chicken. When her unsteady hand brushed against the carton of milk, it slid forward, fell through the open door, and exploded on the floor at her feet.

She stared down at the mess. Overwhelmed by fear and a sense of helplessness, her legs gave out, and she collapsed on the floor. She wanted to get up, wanted to run away, wanted to forget she had ever met the crazed man in the next room. Instead, she lay huddled in a fetal position in the middle of the puddled milk.

"Oh, for Christ's sake. Look at this mess."

His voice was calmer now, more controlled. Cathy was too afraid to look up.

"Here, let me help you up."

She flinched when he touched her.

"I'm not going to hurt you. Come on, you're covered in milk. I'll help you clean this up, and we'll order pizza. I don't know why you get me all spun up like that. You should know better than to come prancing in here from play time at school after I've had the day from hell."

She was on her feet now, her eyes wide with fear when she turned to face him.

"Stop. Stop looking at me like a terrified puppy. You're okay. I'm not going to hurt you. Go change your clothes. I'll find the mop and clean this up. Do you think you can manage the pizza order, or do I have to do that, too?" His tone was that of a parent speaking to a young child of limited intelligence.

She nodded. "I can do it." *Where had his anger gone? Why was he suddenly acting like nothing had happened?*

"Good. Order a large pepperoni pizza and tell them it's for Chief Peters. Maybe that way we'll get it sometime before tomorrow morning."

Still muttering to himself, he opened the door to the pantry to retrieve the mop. Cathy struggled to compose herself as she dialed the phone to order the pizza.

~

Frank ate his pizza in front of the TV and fell asleep watching a hockey game. Cathy didn't eat. She didn't like pepperoni pizza. She sat in the kitchen staring into the brown depths of a cup of herbal tea searching for answers that weren't there. When the sound of Frank's loud, uneven snoring broke through her mental fog, she pushed herself up from the chair and turned out the kitchen light. Then she tiptoed past the den and climbed the stairs.

The master bedroom was at the end of a short hall past the two other bedrooms. The door to the room Frank used as an office was kept closed. Frank had made it clear that this was his domain, his personal space. She didn't have an invitation to enter. The other bedroom was for guests, although Cathy couldn't imagine who they might invite to visit. As far as she knew he had no family or close friends, and he hadn't been receptive when she mentioned inviting Jean and John for a visit. Somehow, he also hadn't found the time for a trip to Harmony farm, and Cathy didn't dare ask if she could go alone.

The massive colonial-style furniture in the master bedroom was from Frank's past life, but in selecting the soft burgundy bedspread, matching drapes, and an upholstered chair for the corner, Cathy had put her stamp on the room. It had become her refuge, even though she tried to forget some of what went on in the king-sized bed where she'd spent the last three months as Frank's wife.

The warm room enveloped her, and she allowed herself to exhale. She pushed the door almost closed, leaving at least six inches of open space. Frank didn't like it when she shut the door. She dropped her shoes next to the closet door and continued on into the bathroom to turn on the bath water. She ignored the reflection of her naked body in the large mirror over the double sink as she undressed. The mirror wasn't her friend. Who would have thought that skin could turn so many shades of yellow, pink and blue? Frank was always telling her she bruised too easily.

As she sank into the hot soapy water, she let her mind retreat to reminiscences of her childhood, to the sounds of laughter in an alpine meadow, her mother's voice reading her favorite bedtime stories.

The cooling water brought her back to the present. Cathy dragged herself out of the tub, toweled dry, and pulled a nightgown over her head. She didn't much like nightgowns, especially the skimpy things Frank insisted she wear, but Frank didn't like pajamas. He said they made her look like a boy, and he was too much of a man to want to fuck a boy.

She turned out the light, pulled back the comforter, and slid into bed. As she lay on her side with her knees drawn up to her chest, she prayed that Frank's last scotch would keep him on the couch until morning. The pain in her stomach reminded her of the previous night's humiliation. She stuck her hand between her thighs and squeezed them tight as she relived the shock of waking up with him on top of her, once again tasting the scotch and feeling his rough hands kneading her breasts.

She had gotten used to being called names while he pumped away at her. Whore and bitch rolled off his tongue the way some men probably whispered honey and darling. When he was finished, he rolled over and fell asleep. She felt nothing—except emptiness, pain, and self-doubt. *Was it all her fault, like he said it was?*

A little voice in the back of her mind fought against the self-blame. She hadn't come to Frank's bed a virgin. The insistent voice reminded her of how it had been with Mike. They had learned about sex together, and they'd both enjoyed the discovery. Those were good memories, until she remembered that Mike had chosen his music over her.

She rubbed at her eyes with the edge of the sheet. It didn't much matter whose fault it was. Mike was gone, and only Frank's opinion mattered.

She hugged the pillow to her chest and wished for sleep, but scenes of her initiation into sex with Frank flashed into her mind. He'd been patient with her at first, until it became obvious that she didn't know how to please him. When his patience had run out, he began to call her a frigid bitch. Lying there next to her husband, she felt lonelier than she'd ever felt sleeping alone.

He told her to drink more, to loosen up, but she never got quite drunk enough. She'd been humiliated the first time he'd pushed her down on her knees naked in front of him and told her what he expected. He'd laughed when she'd gagged, but there'd been no mirth in his words when he told her she'd better learn to love it.

The memories ran in a constant loop in her brain. She sobbed and wondered, for at least the hundredth time, how this had happened. She'd wanted to go to college and be an art teacher. How had she ended up married to a man who controlled every second of her life? She had no answers—and there was no way out. He was Police Chief Frank Peters. She was nobody.

Exhaustion finally gave her release—and she slept.

~

It was still dark when she woke. Next to her, Frank was snoring loudly. Grateful that he'd apparently been too drunk to reach for her when he'd come to bed, she dragged herself out of the bed and stumbled down the stairs. He'd want his breakfast on time. She turned on the night light over the stove to allow her eyes time to adjust. Frank had promised to install a dimmer switch on the kitchen lights, but she didn't hold much hope that he'd keep his promise. The light didn't bother him.

She measured out the Maxwell House coffee and turned on the coffee maker. The comforting aroma of brewing coffee and frying bacon helped her relax, but she maintained her vigil at the stove. When she heard his footsteps on the stairs, she cracked the eggs into the hot frying pan. Frank didn't like cold eggs.

As she heard his footsteps get closer, she reached for the kitchen light switch and blinked twice to adjust her eyes to the bright light. He walked into the kitchen still buttoning his uniform shirt.

"Good morning, Frank." She glanced over at him as she placed his plate of bacon and eggs next to his coffee and toast.

He stopped in the doorway and appraised her without any warmth in his eyes. She was suddenly self-conscious of her ratty terry-cloth bathrobe, messy hair, and swollen eyes.

"You look like shit. I've got enough of a headache, I don't need to look at the bride of Frankenstein first thing in the morning."

He shook his head in disgust and sat down at the table, reaching for the newspaper she had placed next to his plate. She turned away to put the frying pan in the sink, so he wouldn't see her tears. She held her coffee mug in two hands and took a long sip, enjoying the warmth, but knowing she'd pay for it later with an upset stomach. There didn't seem to be much her stomach could handle lately.

She didn't have to see her reflection in the mirror, or hear his insults, to know she was losing weight and was no longer pretty. No wonder he didn't want to look at her. When tears pooled in her eyes, she left the room not wanting him to see her shame.

9

PINE VIEW, NJ
6 MONTHS LATER

Cathy slumped in a chair at the kitchen table, her head in her hands and her long, unwashed hair curtaining her face. An April breeze fluttered the curtains at the open window in the spotless, silent kitchen.

"Cheriup, Cherri, Cherrup".

Her back straightened, and a hint of a smile played on lips that had been compressed and tight. Cathy stood and pushed the chair back to get a clear view of her visitor. Her lips finished the smile when she spotted the red-breasted robin serenading his mate from a perch on the branch of an old oak tree.

She pushed the hair out of her eyes and allowed herself to absorb the richness of the serenade while she breathed in the earthy scent of spring. She used to love this time of year, loved seeing how the tiniest hints of green blossomed to reveal the full promise of rebirth and renewal. But now…her smile faded, and she shook her head. The ravens would probably kill the baby robins in their nest. Sometimes even the promise of nature was a lie.

Her life had developed a rhythm of sorts over the previous months. Two days at the vet clinic, one morning at the college. She wouldn't graduate any time soon but that wasn't important now. Her job and her art class were proof that the world could be a sane place. The rest of her time was spent worrying about which version of her husband would come home on any given night. She never knew. The uncertainty was eating away her insides, as was the knowledge that there was no way out.

Even her relationship with Jean was no longer any solace. Frank hadn't exactly threatened Jean and her husband, but Cathy knew him well enough now to understand his implied message when he made vague comments about the folks he knew up in the Tinton Falls area—which just happened to be where Harmony Farms was located.

Recently, he'd been less vague. After checking the phone messages and finding yet another message from Jean, he'd slammed his fist on the table and muttered under his breath, "Your old friend Jean just won't leave us alone." Then he'd turned and skewered Cathy with an intense, hard gaze. "She places a lot of store in those nags she raises, doesn't she?"

Cathy was too shocked to even attempt an answer. Besides, she doubted he'd even tolerate one. He wasn't actually asking a question. He'd held her gaze with a flinty, challenging stare. Then he'd turned and sauntered away chuckling to himself, as if he'd shared nothing more than a funny comment about the weather or a sports score.

Alone, Cathy had begun to shake uncontrollably. Her stomach retched, and she barely made it to the bathroom before vomiting up the little she'd eaten for lunch. She couldn't take a chance that Frank would hurt Jean's beloved horses. Swiping away tears, she erased Jean's message on the answering machine. She wouldn't be calling her back.

She cursed herself for being so stupid, for missing all the signs. How had she not understood that fear was the reason the other waitresses, and even Marge and Doc, had always shied away from the topic of Frank Peters?

Everyone in town was afraid of her husband—the police chief and Vietnam War hero who had always had a mean streak. Since their marriage, she'd gathered bits and pieces of information from fellow students who had grown up in Pine View. Since she saw no reason to share her marital status, they hadn't minced words. She'd put the details together on her own. Anyone who crossed Frank Peters paid for it—in spades. Unfortunately, she'd been too naïve—and maybe too needy—to figure that out before marrying him. And now it was too late.

~

As the robin finished his serenade, Cathy returned to the present, to her dinner chores. She gave the clock over the sink a nervous glance while she prepared the pork chops. After Frank had finished watching some noisy sports event on TV a few minutes earlier, she'd heard him drunkenly lumber up the stairs to his office. Soon he'd be heading back down those stairs, expecting his dinner.

A shouted curse commanded her attention, and her hand stopped with the breadcrumb can in mid-shake. She sucked in her breath as she heard Frank's feet pounding hurriedly down the stairs. Her heart pounded with fear as his heavy foot falls grew nearer.

Did I forget to hang up his shirt? Did I leave the closet door open?

She swallowed the lump in her dry throat and turned to face the insane man who inexplicably was also her husband.

His fleshy face was flushed and contorted with rage. "What were you doing in my office?"

She struggled to reply, her voice barely a whisper. "I...I needed an envelope for the paperboy..."

The fury in his dark eyes hit her like a palpable force. The breadcrumb container began to slip from her shaking hands. Without turning, without taking her eyes from Frank's face, she slid the container onto the counter behind her and gripped the edge to quiet her hands.

"You lying bitch! You didn't need a fucking envelope. You thought I wouldn't know you were going through my things. You thought you were smarter than me, you stupid cow!"

"No." The word was more of a plea than a statement. She felt herself shrivel inside. "I didn't touch anything, Frank. I swear. I just took an envelope, I swear."

"You useless, lying piece of trash. You think I'm stupid?"

She hugged herself, sucked in her breath, and felt the sweat bead on her skin as she tried to control her shivering. Although she hated herself for being so weak, she hated him even more.

Time was suspended. The seconds dragged. She knew what was coming. She almost welcomed it. The beatings were never as bad as the anticipation.

This time she was wrong. She wasn't prepared for the ferocity of his attack. The impact of his open-handed smack lifted her off her feet. Her arm knocked over the container of breadcrumbs as she fell. Her head snapped back and glanced off the ceramic knob on the cabinet door as her body slid to the floor.

She lay in the middle of the bread crumbs, afraid to move, her senses alert—attuned to her surroundings like a cornered mouse waiting for the next move of the ever-patient cat. She sensed his approach before his feet moved into her line of vision.

"Get up."

He grabbed her hair and yanked her to her feet.

"At least if you were good in bed you'd be worth something, but I might as well fuck a log. I work all day dealing with the scum of the earth, only to come home to an ugly piece of worthless, trash who has the fucking nerve to go through my personal files."

He was beyond angry.

"What were you looking for? Who asked you to spy on me?"

His lined face was inches from hers. She inhaled a mixture of scotch and decaying teeth. How could she have ever believed he cared about her? She was only twenty-two years old—and she was going to die.

The punch to her stomach dropped her to the floor. Curled in a fetal position, she whimpered as his heavy work boot connected with her ribs. She tasted the blood in her mouth and smelled the onions sautéing on the stove. She felt the gritty bread crumbs embedded in her face. There was a deafening ringing in her ears. Just as she slipped into unconsciousness, her mind searched for a memory and focused on a laughing little blonde-haired girl skipping through a flower-filled alpine meadow, holding her father's hand.

10

PINE VIEW, NJ

Cathy woke in darkness—with no idea of the time of day, or where she was. The only sounds were of the heating system clicking on, and a branch scratching against the window in the wind. Dizziness overwhelmed her when she lifted her head, the intense throbbing settling to a steady drumming when she lowered her head back to the floor and closed her eyes.

As she slipped in and out of consciousness, she struggled to recall what had happened. Finally, her memory returned, and she once again shivered in fear. She had been sure Frank was going to kill her. But somehow she was still alive and was lying on the bedroom carpet with no idea how she'd gotten upstairs, or how long she'd been lying there.

Finding it too painful to stand, she crawled into the bathroom and felt her way in the dark to the sink. In spite of the pain, she pulled herself up and then leaned against the bathroom wall to catch her breath. Her face was throbbing, and she could feel the caked blood above her eye. Groping for the sink, a quick turn of the faucet provided a stream of cool water. She cupped the water and splashed it onto her face before dipping a nearby facecloth into the sink and patting the sore and bloody places.

Through the open blinds of the second-floor window, a narrow beam of street light guided her as she dragged herself from the bathroom, to the bureau, to the footboard of the bed, and then a few unsteady steps across the open floor to the bedroom door. As foggy as her mind was in her pained stupor, she wasn't surprised when she turned the knob. The door was locked.

She rested her face against the cool wood and let her body slide to the floor. There was no way out. She couldn't even call 911. The police were his. She had no one, except... maybe Jean. She lifted her head, focused on the night table, and managed to crawl halfway to the bed before she realized there was an empty place next to the lamp where the phone had been.

She was a prisoner. Her husband was a madman who was going to kill her, and there was nothing she could do. Closing her eyes and giving in to defeat, she leaned her head against the soft bedspread and escaped into unconsciousness.

~

The bright sunlight woke her where she lay curled in a fetal position on the deep pile carpet next to the bed. She held her breath, listened, and exhaled when she was sure of the depth of the silence. From where she lay, she could see the open bedroom door. When she lifted her throbbing head, she saw Frank's clothes draped across the chair. The rumpled unmade bed announced that he had slept there. She closed her eyes and leaned back against the bed to think.

What now? What would happen now? The pain in her damaged body pushed the questions out of her mind. Instead, she attempted to concentrate on taking an inventory of the areas that hurt most. Pain wracked her body when she tried to move her legs. A sharp stab to her ribs punished her attempts to take a full breath, so she focused on shallow breaths that didn't satisfy but kept her lungs pumping.

Her inventory only half complete, the sound of footsteps on the stairs refocused her thoughts. Panicked, she pressed herself against the bed and stared at the floor by the partially opened bedroom door. As the door was pushed fully open and she saw Frank's steel-tipped black work boots, her arms tightened over her broken ribs.

"Cathy?"

She stared at the boots as they came closer.

"Cathy? Look at me." His voice was low, controlled, and insistent.

She looked up. She had no other choice. Her gaze scanned the jean-clad legs, stopping at the heavy metal belt buckle partially hidden by Frank's tee-shirt clad protruding gut. Her pain was intense, but she forced herself to tilt her head further back until she saw the face and intense black eyes, beefy nose, and fleshy lined face of the man who was going to kill her.

He held out his hand.

She shrank back further against the bed and hugged herself tighter.

"I'm not going to hurt you. I just want to talk. Let me help you up."

When he reached down again and touched her shoulder, her overfilled bladder reacted, sparking something akin to rebellion in her brain. Even if he was going to kill her, she wouldn't let him reduce her to peeing on herself.

She took a ragged breath, stared at the floor, and found the words. "I have to use the bathroom."

Without waiting for Frank's permission, Cathy turned her body toward the bed and pulled herself up. As she clutched her abdomen and leaned against the bed for stability, Frank backed away. The large bureau provided support as she struggled across the bedroom. Each small step was a trial—and an accomplishment.

She'd barely made it to the toilet before her bladder let go. It was a victory, however small, for her pride—until the nausea hit her. Still on the toilet, she dropped her head to her knees and gasped in pain as her ribs revolted against the sudden movement. She sat until her head cleared.

Grasping the sink, she pulled herself to standing and slowly dragged herself back into the bedroom. Frank was still standing near the door.

"Sit down. We need to talk." His voice was calm and controlled. Was there just a trace of apology in it?

She inched her way to the chair and sat on the edge, careful not to disturb the clothes he had draped over the arm.

Frank walked around the bed and sat across from her. She wanted to back up, to put more distance between them, but fear froze her in place.

He ran his fingers through his short hair and shook his head, a prelude to the exasperation that came through in his words. "I didn't mean to hurt you. You push my buttons sometimes, you know? I told you not to go in my office. You should have known better."

As he often did, he spoke to her as if he was reprimanding a child, a young, not so bright child.

She nodded, afraid to meet his eyes.

"What am I going to do with you? Have you seen yourself?"

Knowing he'd be upset if she didn't do so, she forced herself to make eye contact. She shook her head. No, she hadn't had the nerve to look at herself.

"You can't go out like that. I don't know if I can trust you anymore, Cathy. How can I trust you?"

It seemed like a rhetorical question. She didn't even try to find an answer.

They sat in silence until he let out a loud sigh and announced his decision, a judge handing down a verdict to which there could be no appeal "Okay, here's how it's going to be until your face heals. When I'm home, you can come downstairs. When I'm at work, you'll stay here in the bedroom. In the mornings, when you go downstairs to make breakfast, you can also make yourself something for lunch.

"I'll call the old vet and tell him you're sick and won't be in this week. We'll see how it goes. Maybe next week, if the bruising isn't so obvious, you can go out again. Meanwhile, no phone."

He was police, judge, and jury—and Cathy had received her sentence. "Cathy?"

Was it her imagination or had the tone of his voice changed?

She turned to him and saw the steel in his eyes.

"You'll behave, right? You won't do anything stupid and make me angry again, will you?"

She shook her head.

He smiled and reached forward to caress her face with the back of his hand.

She flinched at his touch.

He pulled his hand back, his smile gone. "I told you I wasn't going to hurt you. Did you think I was lying?"

She could sense the change in him. "No. No. You wouldn't lie."

His face softened. This time when he caressed her face, she forced herself not to move, forced herself to think of something happy and safe, so he couldn't read the fear in her eyes that called him a liar.

"That's a girl." With his hand now cupping her face, he repeated his earlier demand. "Now, promise me you won't do anything stupid."

"I promise, Frank."

"Good. That's good. Why don't you get yourself cleaned up, and I'll make you some breakfast. Would you like that?"

"Yes, Frank. Thank you."

She spent the day locked in the bedroom, locked in the purgatory that was her new life, grateful for the pain pills she'd found in the medicine cabinet that helped her make it through the day.

~

That night, the rain woke her, or maybe it was the pain. During her mostly sleepless night, her mind had alternated between hopelessness and fury, between the construct of a plan for freedom and revenge—and the fear that one day Frank might actually kill her in one of his drunken furies.

She turned her head just far enough to see the clock on the night stand. It had been five hours since she'd taken the two Tylenol with codeine, and every move, every breath, was agony. She only had eight pills left from when she'd had her wisdom teeth pulled. She had to make them last.

With her brain still foggy with sleep, she inhaled deeply, or tried to. Her gasp as the pain ripped through her chest and stopped her breath was loud enough to wake Frank—or to at least disturb the regularity of his snores. She froze until he rolled over, and she once again heard the rhythm in his breathing.

She glanced again at the clock. It was five am. The alarm wouldn't go off for another hour. She had sixty endless minutes to reflect on what her life had become: the pain, humiliation, and endless fear. But among all those feelings, another one fought to find space. When she recognized this new feeling as rage, she embraced it.

11

PINE VIEW, NJ

Cathy shut off the alarm just as the numbers on the clock clicked to 6:00. She stared at the time, watching as more minutes slipped by. She had to get up, had to make Frank's breakfast, but movement seemed beyond her ability. At 6:15, it was the fear of Frank's wrath that forced her to move, to lever herself into a sitting position. The intense pain of that small move took her breath away. She gritted her teeth, slowly placed her feet on the floor and stood.

The pain pills are only a few feet away.

With that as her mantra, she stumbled across the room and into the bathroom. After swallowing the blessed pills, she was faced with yet another painful task—forcing her arms into the sleeves of her terrycloth bathrobe. Praying for the pills to do their job and sweating from the exertion of completing once-simple tasks, she dragged herself down the stairs.

Food held no attraction for her battered body, and drinking coffee on an empty stomach was out of the question. Instead, Cathy nibbled on a piece of dry toast and sipped herbal tea as she fried eggs and bacon for Frank.

She wasn't frightened when she heard Frank's slow plodding steps on the stairs—a far cry from the previous evening when his alcohol-fueled rage had propelled his rapid descent. This morning, Frank's energy would be focused on nursing his hangover. As long as his breakfast was on the table, she was safe.

In the past, she could also expect him to show contrition for his actions—for allowing her behavior to upset him enough to lose his temper. Not this time. She didn't expect contrition this time. Something had changed, and she felt the change—like a tectonic plate shift altering the landscape of their relationship.

"Don't forget to make yourself a sandwich."

She hadn't expected "good morning", so Frank's gruff first words didn't come as a surprise.

Without turning to face him, Cathy answered in a meek tone. "I won't forget, Frank."

She turned away from the stove and carried his plate to where he now sat at the table. Setting the plate in front of him, she announced, "Here's your breakfast," with a forced pleasantness.

Cathy didn't join him at the table. They rarely ate breakfast together, and she certainly didn't expect to do so this morning. Not after last night. She could sense a distancing in him that hadn't been there before. The weight of that knowledge settled on her, increasing her fear.

Standing at the sink, staring out the kitchen window into the dim light of early morning, Cathy waited, listening to the sounds of Frank's breakfast—his knife and fork scraping against the plate, and the newspaper's pages being folded back. When she heard the legs of his chair scrape against the floor, she turned to face him.

Newspaper in hand, he stood and announced, "I'm out of here in ten minutes. Get your stuff together."

Cathy nodded, even though Frank hadn't bothered to look at her when he spoke. She retrieved his empty plate and quickly rinsed it in the sink. Then she picked up the insulated bag she'd filled with a small thermos of coffee, some crackers, a can of ginger ale, and a sandwich.

By the time she'd completed her labored trip up the stairs, Frank was waiting at the top impatiently tapping his foot. She shuffled down the hall to their bedroom, Frank behind her. Once inside, she heard the door close and the awful sound of a key turning in the lock. Retreating to the unmade bed, she curled into a fetal position, whimpering as much from hopelessness as from pain.

The cramps hit soon after. This added pain was almost too much to bear, but it wasn't as if she'd been given a choice. She struggled to the bathroom, swallowed two more pills, and collapsed onto the toilet. She hadn't wanted to believe she was pregnant. The signs were obvious, but she hadn't wanted to face the impossible dilemma. How could she have Frank's baby? How could she bring a child into the hell in which she lived? Would Frank even allow it? Now, as she writhed in pain, she realized that Frank's attack had solved her problem.

Dizzy and weak, she dragged herself back to bed. At noon, eager for some relief from both her emotional and physical agony, she downed two of her last four codeine pain killers, and anxiously waited for them to do their job. At last, she drifted into a heavy, dreamless sleep, waking with barely enough time to pull on a pair of sweat pants and a roomy cotton shirt before Frank unlocked the bedroom door.

It was time to prepare dinner.

There was no talk of her transgressions when they sat at the dining room table for dinner, the one meal where her presence was demanded. There was no talk at all, except Frank's request for another piece of chicken, and his after-dinner pronouncement. "After you clean the kitchen, you can do whatever else you do down here. At eight o'clock, you'll have to go back upstairs."

He reached across the table and clasped her arm in a firm grip. She was forced to make eye contact with him, something she had been avoiding. His gaze held the coldness of glacial ice when he continued. "I'm not sure I can trust you enough to leave you alone while I'm watching TV." He shook his head and snorted. "I don't think you're stupid enough to try anything, but you never know. You actually might be that stupid…"

His unspoken threat hung in the air, but the threat wasn't needed. Cathy had neither the strength nor the inclination to run away or to call someone, even if there had been someone to call. She certainly couldn't call the police—his police. And she couldn't take a chance on reaching out to Jean.

Her reticence had nothing to do with her shame at ignoring Jean's recent calls and letters. Jean would forgive her for that. No, she couldn't call Jean because she was afraid Frank would make good on his barely veiled threats. His own hands would stay clean, but Cathy had no doubt he'd destroy the lives of people she loved, just to make her suffer.

~

By the end of the second day in her bedroom prison, Cathy was growing restless. Her pain had only minimally improved, but the four walls of the bedroom were beginning to close in on her. She read a little, but not even the Agatha Christie mystery could hold her interest for long. She sketched for a while, but mostly she tried to nap. Sleep was her only real escape.

As days three and four churned slowly by, she yearned for rain, something gloomy to match her mood. Yet each day dawned bright and sunny. When day five presented another cloudless blue sky, she also had to contend with the relentlessly joyful song of a mockingbird. The perky fellow perched in an oak tree across the yard from her open bedroom window and sang his heart out.

Annoyed, she approached the window, intending to chase the bird away. She was instead mesmerized by the sheer determination of the long-tailed songster. As she listened, she felt her face relax. Then, focused on the bird's dedication to its musical repertoire, she smiled. Some of the fog lifted, taking with it the worst of her depression.

"I can do it. I can get away." She whispered the words so she wouldn't frighten the bird. It didn't matter that it could neither hear nor understand her. She was really talking to herself.

She turned away from the window and faced the room, seeing with clear eyes the untidy bed, Frank's clothes strewn across the chair, and the layer of dust on the bureau. Not even the fresh air from the open window could fully dispel the odor from the full hamper of Frank's sweaty clothes. Later, she'd ask Frank to carry the heavy laundry hamper downstairs to the laundry room. Such feats were beyond her now.

Needing to stay busy to avoid sinking back into depression, she put Frank's clothes away, dusted the bureau, and made the bed. Then she looked around for something else to work on. The open closet beckoned, offering up its rows of clothes and untidy shelves.

Dragging the clothes out of the walk-in closet and spreading them neatly on the bed aggravated her sore ribs and depleted most of her energy. She rested while she ate her lunch and gazed longingly out the window at newly leafed trees and fluffy white clouds skittering across a blue sky. When she felt the fog of a black mood begin to claim her, she went back to work.

Using the small step stool Frank kept in the closet, Cathy slowly removed each of the items on the shelf above the now empty clothes rod.

Once emptied, the shelf revealed something previously hidden from view—something wedged behind the far corner of the shelf beyond the illumination range of the closet light.

At first, it appeared to be a piece of stray paper, maybe a dry cleaning receipt. In deference to the painful stretch she'd have to endure to reach the paper, she almost left it there. Curiosity won out over discomfort. Using a wire hanger as a tool, she jabbed until she knocked the item free. A tight rectangle of folded paper landed on the floor with a soft thud. Definitely not a dry cleaning receipt.

Unsure of what she'd found, Cathy slowly unfolded the secreted pages. Neat, precise handwriting covered every available surface of the sheets of white notepaper. Lowering herself to the floor before her shaking legs could give out of their own accord, she began to read.

Fighting to control her trembling hands as she held the pages, Cathy focused on the carefully scribed words written by Frank's second wife, Amy.

I'm not sure why I'm writing this, why I took the risk that Frank might catch me stealing the paper from his office, or worse—that he might find what I wrote. There is a good chance no one will ever find these pages and that no one will ever know what happened to me. I have no close family and no friends in Pine View. Frank saw to that. But I can't bear the thought that I'll just disappear and no one will ever really know who I was.

He's going to kill me. I don't know when, but I know he will and there's nothing I can do about it. All I can do is write my story and hope someone will find it someday and they'll know who I was—a young woman with silly dreams who was naïve enough, at least for a short time, to believe that the vicious monster who killed her had once actually loved her.

Amy's short, sad story told about a twelve-year-old girl's idyllic world exploding in a car wreck that killed her parents. She mentioned the kind relatives who took her in and the rebellious streak that made her declare her independence when she turned eighteen. Always unlucky in love and attracted to losers, Amy was sure her luck had changed when the handsome police chief asked her out. He'd been a regular and a generous tipper in the Atlantic City cocktail lounge where she worked. He'd courted her and made her feel safe and special—until their wedding night.

The words blurred under Cathy's tear-filled gaze, matched by the wavering lines of Amy's handwriting as she described her humiliation and degradation at the hands of the man she'd loved.

Clutching the paper to her heart, Cathy leaned back against the wall of the empty closet. She closed her eyes and cast her mind out across the ether, hoping to somehow connect with the young woman whose pain was so vividly recounted on the pages Cathy held in her hands.

The last page of Amy's story was far different from the earlier pages. It was obvious some time had passed. The hand-writing was shaky and there were missing words and erratic thoughts.

Amy knew she was going to die.

It's all over. He bragged about killing Helen. His first wife—dumped her body somewhere. Now he has to kill me. Not tonight. He's too drunk. Soon. No one will ever know. No one.

The pages fell from Cathy's hands. In spite of her pain, she hugged her knees to her chest to control her shaking as the shock of what she'd read washed over her.

The truth of her own relationship with Frank became as clear as a headline printed in bold across the front page of her life. He had stalked her because she fit the profile—just as Amy had, and maybe his first wife, too. He had used her just as he had used them. And he would discard her just as he had discarded them.

I'm just like Amy. No family. No one for him to answer to. No one to care.

She sat for a long time on the carpeted closet floor, shocked into immobility. Until she'd read Amy's story, she'd worried that Frank might kill her in one of his drunken rages. Now she was certain he would—he was already a murderer.

When she finally raised her head and forced herself to take a deep breath, she inhaled the scent of starch permeating the closet—the scent of Frank's cleaned, perfectly pressed, perfectly starched clothes. The smell overwhelmed her, reminding her of his constant demands for perfection. She unconsciously rubbed at the scar on her arm, her punishment for scorching one of his shirts. As she retched from the smell, the pain in her ribs ripped through her middle and took her breath away.

After exhaling a shaky breath and swiping at her tears, Cathy fought to push the worst of her pain and fear aside. The orphan wives of Frank Peters were her family now. She'd escape, and she'd avenge their deaths. She might die trying, but she'd make him pay. Somehow, she'd make Frank pay.

She picked up the precious pages, convinced they were a special communication from Amy meant just for her. Then, after refolding them with care, she considered where to hide them. Stretching to wedge them back behind the shelf was out of the question. Instead, after crawling across the closet floor to the farthest corner, she pried a corner of carpet up, slid the pages underneath, and pressed the carpet back in place.

After checking the clock, she hurriedly returned the clothes to the closet. Frank would be home soon. She had a purpose to her life now, and it had nothing to do with cleaning the closet.

~

Over the next few days as her injuries slowly healed, Cathy plotted and planned. There seemed to be no way out. No way to escape Frank's reach. But she'd find a way. She had to find a way, before he killed her, too.

Ten days after his vicious attack, Frank announced over dinner that her forced isolation was over. "I hope you've learned your lesson, Cathy." His words startled her. She was used to silence during dinner while he read the sports section of the newspaper, and she pushed the food around on her plate. It was impossible to digest her food in his presence, but she made a show of eating to avoid upsetting him.

She looked up. He was focused on her with an implacable intensity, the way she imagined he'd face a crime suspect. "Starting tomorrow, you're free to go back to work for the senile old vet, and since I've already paid for school, you can finish that silly art class you were taking."

He stopped speaking and stared at her. She was confused by his silence until she realized he was waiting for a response—for her gratitude. She was happy. Damn, she was thrilled! But she wasn't grateful. How could she be grateful for her freedom when he'd had no right to take it away in the first place?

Although she wouldn't let him see her happiness, she couldn't afford to let him see her resentment. She still had to play the game and bide her time. So she forced her lips to expand into a smile. Then she responded with downcast eyes in what she hoped was an appropriately obsequious manner. "Thank you, Frank."

"Look at me." His voice was clipped and stern.

Her eyes flew to his as she fought to hide her fear. *Did he see through my pretense?*

"What are you planning on telling the old vet?"

She rushed to reassure him. "Nothing, Frank. I won't tell him anything."

"What if he asks? The meddling old fool might ask a lot of questions."

"I'll tell him I had the flu, like you said. He won't ask. He's old, and he'll be busy with the animals, Frank. He's just my boss. He won't ask." She was lying. She was becoming good at lying.

~

Cathy returned to the vet clinic the following day. She doubted that Doc believed her story about the flu. The look on his face said as much. But she was glad he didn't challenge her. She wouldn't have been strong enough to hold on to her lie, and telling him the truth wasn't an option— at least not yet. Not until she had a plan, a way out. Until then, she had to keep up the pretense. It was the only way she could protect herself, and Doc, from her husband's wrath.

Two days later, she returned to school with an appropriately believable story about the flu and a promise to her instructor that she'd make up her missed assignments. Pretense was easier at school. No one really knew her there.

Even though she had no real friends at the college, she'd heard some of her fellow art students brag about going to pill doctors for drugs. She approached one of them and was rewarded not only with information about a couple of doctors who asked few questions, but also with the name of someone who sold fake college ID's.

A plan was forming.

Obtaining the fake ID was easy enough. All it took was a quick visit to a guy looking to make a few easy bucks using his father's printing equipment. With her new college ID in hand, she slipped into a sleazy office in a strip mall and told the doctor she'd hurt her back in a fall down some stairs. A few minutes later, she walked out with a prescription for painkillers made out to Sandra Brown, a young college student with a striking resemblance to Cathy Dial, the name still on her real college ID. If she needed more pills, there were always other doctors, and some campus pushers, as well.

She had no intention of taking the drugs herself. She had fought through her depression and won. Though staring at the bottle of drugs in her hand, she was glad she didn't have them a few weeks earlier. Then, she thought, she might have taken them—*hell, who am I kidding? I would have. I would definitely have taken my mother's way out.* No longer. Now the drugs were a way to keep her safe while she finalized her plan for escape and revenge.

She would continue to play the role of submissive wife even as she laced Frank's food with drugs. Since she wasn't sure how the potent pain killers would interact with alcohol, she'd take it slow. She'd allow his drunken mauling to continue until she was able to calibrate the dosages.

Her goal wasn't to kill him, just control him. At least for now...

12

Cathy sat in the passenger seat, distractedly gnawing on her lip while Doc Waldron drove them into Manhattan. Part of her wanted to tell him to drop her off at the Port Authority Bus Station, so she could hop a Greyhound bus to some anonymous far-away place. The other part, the realistic part, acknowledged the futility of that desire. Frank had power—and he had the means, the money, and she was sure, the desire to track her down. Running away would only work if he couldn't find her, if it was impossible for him to even try.

So instead of hopping on a bus, she was on her way to meet some guy named Gino Valenti in the back room of an Italian restaurant. Scenes from old gangster movies played in her mind. None of those stories had ended well. But Doc had assured her that this guy would help her. She trusted Doc. Still, the skin on the inside of her lip was raw from her nervous chewing.

"Why are you helping me, Doc?"

Either he hadn't heard her or her blunt question caught Doc Waldron off guard. Cathy continued gnawing on her lip, waiting for a response as Doc maneuvered the station wagon into the lane for the Lincoln Tunnel. When it appeared that he either had no intention of answering her, or hadn't heard her question, she spoke up again.

"Doc?"

"I heard your question, Cathy. I was trying to find a way to answer you." He patted her leg, his touch gentle, the same way he handled the frightened animals in his care. Then he returned his hand to the steering wheel. When he continued speaking, the warmth and caring in his voice reminded her of why she trusted him, why even the most skittish of animals trusted him.

"You know, most people wouldn't have asked that question. Most people would assume they deserved to be helped, but you're not most people, are you Cathy? Why wouldn't you wonder? After all, you've always had to find your own way."

He exhaled audibly and settled the car into the middle lane of crawling traffic before he continued. "Why am I helping you? I guess there are a lot of reasons, the simplest of which is you deserve to be helped. No one should live the hell I know you're living, even though you've never confided the details."

After a few moments of silence, he shook his head. This time when he spoke, Cathy heard anger in his voice. "I feel so damned impotent, Cathy. I should have said something when I saw you getting involved with him. It's my fault. You had no one else. I had hoped Marge might say something, but it was up to me. I should have warned you about Frank Peters."

He made quick eye contact with her to make his point before once again focusing on the traffic. "The man makes my flesh crawl, always has. I've known him since he was a teenager. Since he and my son were in high school together. I saw him change from a high school jock and an arrogant bully to something much worse when he came back from Vietnam and joined the police force."

He blew out his breath and once again shook his head. Cathy saw the deeply wrinkled face of the elderly man settle into a grimace as he pronounced, "I was afraid of him. What sort of man lets a young girl sacrifice herself because he's afraid?"

She could hear the distress in his voice and see it in the stretched skin of his veined hands as his fingers tightened on the steering wheel. It wasn't right that he should feel guilty about her mistakes.

"No, Doc! It's not your fault. Do you think I would have listened? Do you think I could have even comprehended…?"

She shuddered. Her voice trailed off as she reflected on the depths of pain and degradation she couldn't have imagined a year ago. Even if she was somehow able to get away, she would never be able to escape the memories, or the scars.

Sometimes, when she needed something less painful to focus on, her thoughts drifted to Mike, her first love. But that memory had an abrupt dead end—and left a different kind of pain. When Mike chose his music dreams over their love, he slammed the door shut on the life they'd planned together.

Her future, if she had one, belonged to someone new, someone without a past. That was her only way out. Cathy Dial Peters needed to disappear forever.

She turned to face Doc.

"I'll never be able to thank you enough for helping me. Even if…even if it doesn't work out the way I've planned, I'll still always know someone cared enough to help me. You can't possibly understand how much that means to me."

She took a deep breath and turned back to the window, ignoring the tears tracing their way down her cheeks. She rested her head on the cool glass and let her mind wander.

It had been over two months since Frank had kicked her into unconsciousness on the floor of the kitchen. Her body had healed, except for the occasional twinge in her ribs. Of course, there were always new bruises, but nothing that came close to the day she'd thought she was going to die.

After finding Amy's story, her entire focus had changed. She knew she would need evidence to destroy Frank—more evidence than just Amy's pained written words. To get that evidence, she needed to take risks. And so she had.

On day seven of her imprisonment, after she'd made Frank's morning coffee, beaten the eggs for his breakfast, and listened for the water running in the shower, she'd tiptoed into the den. As she reached for his Polaroid camera with shaky hands, she memorized its exact location on the bookshelf. Her heart had pounded with fear, and with every creak of the old house, she had been sure Frank was sneaking up behind her. But she'd stared down her fear and picked up the camera.

Once in her hand, she'd fought an urge to smash the clunky camera that had spewed out instant pictures portraying the depths of her degradation. Just holding it made her cheeks burn with shame. Soon, she'd thought, soon she'd destroy the pornography Frank had created and locked away in his desk. Soon, but not yet

On that auspicious morning, she'd used Frank's camera to bear witness to her abuse. After slipping off her bathrobe, she'd captured vivid evidence of her battered and bruised body. Her task completed, and her robe back on and tied tight around her waist, she'd replaced the camera exactly where it had been. Then with the pictures safely stowed in her bathrobe pocket, she'd returned to the kitchen just as she'd heard Frank's steps on the stairs.

~

Lost in her daydreams about her small victory with the camera, and with her head still resting on Doc's car door window, Cathy laughed. The brittle, cynical sound surprised her—sounding embittered and world-weary. But maybe that wasn't too far off. Thanks to Frank, she felt ancient and worn, decades older than her years.

A touch on her arm suddenly jerked her out of her reverie. Frightened, Cathy lifted her head and snapped around to confront her attacker.

Doc jerked his hand back, his expression registering concern. "Is everything all right, Cathy? Are you okay?"

She exhaled, forcing a weak smile. "I'm sorry, Doc. I was drifting there for a while. Forgot where I was. I'm fine." It was her turn to reach out. She patted his arm, making amends.

He nodded and refocused his attention on the road. She turned away and once more allowed her thoughts to wander.

Doc's voice brought her back. "Cathy, we're here."

She watched as he expertly guided the big car into a tight parking spot on the busy street. Once parked, he turned to her and pointed through the front window, "Claudio's is about a block up on the right. You can't miss it."

She nodded, trying hard to hide her nervousness, but her clenched hands and deer-in-the-headlights expression must have given her away.

"You'll be fine, Cathy. Just ask for Gino Valenti and remember to say that Tony Romano sent you. Okay?"

She nodded again, but didn't move

"Do you want me to come with you?"

Cathy turned to face him. Worry was written across his deeply lined face. Knowing he was in her corner gave her the courage she needed.

"No. You've done enough." She squeezed his arm. "Thanks." Nodding again, she added, "I'll be fine. I'll meet you back here, okay? I don't know how long..."

Doc smiled. "No worries. I'll be here."

She slipped on her sunglasses and tugged a baseball cap on over her long hair. Then she opened the door, slid out of the car, and closed the door behind her. Moments later, in search of her future she joined the throng of pedestrians on the crowded sidewalk.

~

A little less than an hour later, Cathy returned to Doc's car and greeted him with a broad smile.

"Everything good?" Doc asked, his bushy white eyebrows raised in question.

"Yeah, Doc." Cathy shrugged and grimaced. "It was a little shaky at first. I was so nervous that when I asked for Gino Valenti, I forgot to tell the burly man up front that Tony Romano sent me."

Doc's eyes grew wide.

She laughed to reassure him. "Yeah. It was tense for a bit." She smiled. "He stared right through me and I got even more nervous. Then I finally remembered what you'd said. Once I mentioned Tony Romano, everything was fine. The guy's whole expression changed. It was like I was suddenly his daughter's best friend or something!"

Doc looked relieved. "Good. You had me a little worried there."

"Mr. Valenti was wonderful, Doc. He insisted I have something to eat. I told him someone was waiting for me, but he said I had to at least have a slice of pizza and a Coke. I didn't want to seem ungrateful, and it was more of a demand than a question anyway, so I just sort of nodded. The pizza was really good. I was so nervous I had a hard time swallowing it, though."

Doc was grinning now. "Did you get everything you needed?"

"Yes! Well, sort of." She hesitated a moment. "I have another favor to ask, Doc. I need to be back here in two weeks to pick up the IDs and stuff.

Can I impose on you again? Is there some other trip we can plan? I hate to ask..."

His response was immediate. "Of course, Cathy. Whatever you need. We'll drop off these cages I'm donating to the Humane Society so that our alibi holds for today, and then, let me think for a minute..."

After a short delay, he nodded as if confirming his thoughts. "In two weeks, we can pick up some supplies one of my vet friends ordered in bulk to save me money. I'm such an old guy, I'll need you to help carry the boxes." He smiled and winked conspiratorially. "Will that work?"

She nodded, her tentative smile turning into a broad and appreciative grin. "Thanks. I hate that you have to make up stories for me. I know Becky and Robin have worked for you for a long time. Maybe I'm just paranoid, but...."

He shook his head. "You're being smart, not paranoid."

"Thanks for understanding. I don't want to take any chances."

She glanced down at her watch, the humor gone from her expression. "We should get going now. I need to be home by four o'clock. Wouldn't want my caring husband to worry about me, would I?" Her words dripped with sarcasm and simmering anger. "It might take me a few minutes to get back in character, especially after today."

She reached out and touched Doc's arm, hoping he could see the gratitude in her eyes. "Thank you, Doc."

He squeezed her hand in response.

Cathy leaned back in her seat, getting comfortable for the drive home. As Doc maneuvered the car through the city traffic, she asked the question that had been on her mind since he'd first mentioned the New York 'connections' that might help her escape. "You never did explain how you know these people, Doc. Is it a story you can share?"

He nodded. "It's a long story, but we have the time."

His expression softened and his lips curved in a slight smile as he began his story. "I grew up in an Italian neighborhood in Newark. I may not look it," he gestured to his deeply lined fair skin and mane of thick white hair, "but I'm half-Italian. The neighborhood I grew up in is still one of the safest areas in Newark." He turned to her, raised his eyebrows apparently requesting her acknowledgment of some unspoken statement.

When she didn't immediately respond with a knowing laugh or nod, he shrugged. "I sometimes forget you didn't grow up around here. There are areas in the city, this city…" He gestured out the window at the residential New York City street they were driving down, "and other cities, like Newark, that are safe because of who lives there. There are a lot of euphemisms: the mob, the Mafia, Cosa Nostra. Whatever you call them, there is no denying that they are extremely protective of their families, and they don't depend on the police to keep them safe.

"A lifetime ago, when I was still in veterinary school, I was visiting my mother…" He paused and even though he was staring ahead at the traffic, Cathy could sense that his mind had traveled back in time. "I had just said goodbye and was about to get in my car when I heard the rumble of a city maintenance truck that had just turned the corner of our narrow street. I looked up and saw a little boy, not much older than a toddler, run into the middle of the street—right in front of the oncoming truck. I acted instinctively when I ran out and grabbed him. I certainly wasn't trying to be a hero."

He turned to her and when their eyes met, he shook his head, his expression indicating that even after all these years he was still surprised about what he was about to share. "The little boy was Frankie Romano, son of Big Tommy Romano and brother of Tony. The Romano name may not mean anything to you, but let's just say it's well known to law enforcement. I knew Tony from the neighborhood, although he was a couple years younger than me. Even back then he was being groomed to take over for his father.

"Tony and his family were, of course, overjoyed that I had saved the child's life. Tony told me with great sincerity that his family would never forget the debt they owed me. I didn't take it seriously. I had never considered a situation where I might need the kind of help they could provide. I'd actually forgotten all about it.

He chuckled. "We don't exactly run in the same circles, so over the years I rarely saw any of the Romanos." He continued in a more somber tone. "Unfortunately, funerals brought us together a couple of times in recent years. Our mothers were friends, and they both lived well into their nineties. I attended his mother's funeral, and when my mother died, I appreciated that he made the time to attend her funeral."

He paused in his story as a blocked traffic lane forced him to squeeze over into an already packed middle lane. Cathy used the time to reflect on what he'd told her, and to think about the man sitting next to her, a man she'd trusted from the first time she'd met him more than two years earlier. The day she'd shown up on his doorstep in the pouring rain with a puppy she'd found hurt on the side of the road. Both she and Buddy had found a friend in Doc Waldron.

Once the car was again moving in free-flowing traffic, he continued his story. "Some might say it was a coincidence that I ran into Tony two weeks ago when I went back to finalize the sale of my mother's home, but I don't believe in coincidence.

"When I left the house, I didn't even notice the black limo that had driven past until it pulled over to the curb. Tony Romano climbed out of the car followed by a young man I didn't know. I was surprised that Tony'd stopped and even more surprised when after we'd exchanged greetings, he instructed the young man to shake my hand. He said, 'Doc, this is my brother Frankie's son, Joseph.' Then he turned to his nephew and said, 'Joey, shake Doc Waldron's hand.'"

Doc laughed as he recounted the story. "The confused kid shook my hand. I was equally confused, but I went along with it. I have to admit, Cathy, I wasn't prepared for what Tony said next."

Cathy leaned toward him, eager to hear the rest of the story.

"I had long forgotten the incident with the truck, but Tony hadn't." Doc's expression registered disbelief and surprise when his eyes met Cathy's for a long moment, before he once again focused on the road. "Tony said, 'If it wasn't for this man, you wouldn't be here, Joey. He saved your father's life.'

"I was still processing this information when Tony turned back to me and said, 'That was over forty years ago, Doc. I remember it like it was yesterday. Now Joey here's all grown up. He made the family proud, just graduated from Columbia University. Can you believe it?' Tony looked at the young man with obvious pride before he waved him away. As the boy walked back to the car, Tony said to me, 'We still owe you, Doc. That kid and Frankie's other three kids owe you, too. They wouldn't be here if it wasn't for you. Anything you need, anything at all, you just let me know.'"

Doc flicked the turn-signal on to exit the turnpike. As he slowed the car for the exit, he once again looked over at Cathy. "As I said before, I don't believe in coincidences, Cathy. As soon as Tony said that, I thought of how I've watched a pretty young girl turn into a frightened shell of herself.

"Tony is an astute observer of men. I guess he has to be in his line of work. Maybe it was because I didn't immediately respond, or maybe he saw something in my expression, I don't know. All I know is that he hesitated a moment. Then he asked, 'Is something wrong, Doc? Is there something I can help you with?'"

They turned off the turnpike. After Doc paid the toll, they drove on in silence for a few minutes. "You know the rest, Cathy. You'd finally confided in me. We'd talked about how you might escape, how a new identity might help. Then, Tony was there. He gave me the name of the man you met with today and, after he helps you, Tony's debt—one that I never believed he owed—will be paid in full."

He sighed and added in a low voice, "I just hope I did the right thing."

"You did, Doc. Please believe me, you did." She wouldn't allow him to second guess himself. "Whatever happens now, I'll always be grateful for your help." She didn't want to put him in a situation where he might have to lie for her. So she wouldn't share the actual details of her plan, or her new identity. He'd done enough.

They were silent for the rest of the drive home.

A car accident just outside of Pine View caused a massive traffic jam that tested Cathy's new-found confidence. She rushed through the kitchen door at 4:05, just in time to answer the phone on the fourth ring and, in as a calm a voice as she could muster, tell Frank what she was making him for dinner.

When she hung up, she exhaled deeply and collapsed onto a kitchen chair. *What am I thinking? How can I ever pull this off when the mere thought of his anger turns my legs to jelly?*

She hugged herself as her mind replayed the beatings and the constricted definition of her life. Then she thought about Amy, of the terror and pain that bled from the pages of tight pencil script the young woman had written. Her resolve firmly cemented, she opened the refrigerator door and began dinner preparations. A quick check of the pill bottle hidden in the back of the junk drawer reminded her that she was running out of pills. Tomorrow she'd limp into the pill doctor to get more.

~

The next two weeks were especially difficult. She could almost taste freedom, but she couldn't afford to let her guard down. She forced herself to cater to Frank's every whim. Staying one step ahead of his flashpoint anger left her feeling like her nerves were daily fed through an industrial paper shredder. She had no idea what would cause him to explode, or when—but she knew he would.

She dreaded the nights when he went out with the guys, knowing he'd come home in a drunken rage and stumble up the stairs to take his anger out on the useless whore piece of trash trembling in his bedroom. As much as it made her flesh crawl, she sometimes flirted and played the whore to entice him to stay home, a place where she had control, where a light dusting of pharmaceutical spice in his dinner would keep him asleep on the couch, instead of abusing her in their bed.

The rigid exercise regimen she had started as soon as her ribs healed, and the disciplined development of each minute detail of her escape plan, helped her stay sane as the days slipped away, as more time passed in purgatory, where she lived on the edge of hell. Patience. She whispered the word to herself often during the day as the fourteen days clicked down. Just a little more time, her inner voice encouraged. 'Soon you'll have all the pieces to your freedom plan.'

She needed to learn more about the neighbors—none of whom had been very neighborly. Her attempts at friendly conversation with the middle-aged couple in the house next door, the elderly woman across the street, or even a nod or wave to folks walking down the street, had been met with either barely polite head nods, or outright hostility. It was as if Frank had dug a moat around the house and filled it with piranhas.

Frank unwittingly assisted her escape plan when he stomped into the house one evening, ranting about a neighbor who'd snubbed him as the man walked his dog past their house. "What do the Feds know about the bullshit I have to go through every day? That FBI prick, Wilson, thinks his shit doesn't stink; thinks he's better than the real men who face the worthless scum on the streets every day." She nodded in agreement, and half-listened to the rest of his rant, but she turned away so he couldn't see the hint of a smile on her face. An FBI agent lived only two houses away.

She watched the neighborhood, paying careful attention to the neighbors' routines—noting that the FBI agent's wife walked their German shepherd at precisely 3:45 each afternoon. One warm afternoon, just before that time, Cathy strolled down the driveway to Frank's mailbox—she always thought of it as his, not theirs. She neither looked at nor acknowledged the older woman walking the dog toward her along the sidewalk, even though she was only a few steps away. Instead, she reached into the mail box and allowed the mail to slide from her fingers onto the ground.

When she bent to pick up the scattered letters, she allowed her short tank top, purchased from a second hand store just for this occasion, to slide up and expose the huge yellowing bruise on her lower back. The recent bruises on her upper arms stood out like matching black and blue bracelets on the fair skin of her bare upper arms.

She wasn't always able to control Frank's moods, and at least once a week she provided a convenient outlet for his anger over some real or imagined slight. It didn't matter who had slighted him, she paid the price. Now, feigning embarrassment, Cathy made furtive eye contact with the dog-walking neighbor before turning and rushing back up the driveway and disappearing into the house.

She hid behind the drapes to gauge the woman's reaction. She wasn't disappointed. Peggy Wilson didn't move for a long while. She stared at Frank's house, frowned, and then shook her head before continuing her walk. Frank may own the local police, but he didn't own the FBI. Cathy was pretty sure Mrs. Wilson would share the story of their encounter, and her bruises. Without knowing it, the woman had become a part of Cathy's escape plan.

~

After another quick trip to the city, Cathy had everything she needed to carry out her plan for escape and revenge. Yet, she hesitated. She stalled for days, then a full week went by while she waited for a sign—for some event, some thing, some feeling—to tell her it was time. When she finally received that sign, it arrived from an unlikely source.

She had been sitting at a traffic light, a bag of groceries on the seat next to her, when she noticed two chestnut foals racing across a lush pasture. Without planning or conscious thought, she pulled over to the side of the road to watch them. She smiled as they nipped at one another and jumped in the air with all four of their little stick legs coming off the ground at the same time. She giggled at their silly antics, and then she laughed out loud. That one act, that one simple laugh, was all it took to break through the sturdy fence she had built to corral her feelings.

That was the sign, an unwanted reminder of how far she'd fallen, and how hopeless her life had become—a realization that she didn't remember the last time she had laughed.

13

PINE VIEW, NJ

The first event in the final act of Cathy's life as Mrs. Frank Peters was mostly symbolic. She removed the painting of Buddy from the wall of the bedroom she shared with Frank and replaced it with another of her water color paintings. She doubted Frank had even noticed the painting was there.

After carefully placing Buddy's portrait on the backseat of her car, she drove crosstown to the vet clinic. She pulled into her old parking spot, the one closest to the apartment stairs. Then she sat in her car, fighting back tears, remembering how much she'd loved the small apartment—in some ways, her first real home.

Stop it!

She tightened her lips and admonished herself as she got out of the car and slammed the door shut. This was not the time for nostalgic trips down memory lane. Her self-pity was replaced by the nervous sweat beading on her forehead. She swiped it away as she approached the clinic door and squared her shoulders.

Showtime.

She opened the door and stepped inside. "Good Morning, Becky." Cathy forced an upbeat tone to her words as she nodded at the receptionist and smiled at the elderly woman in the waiting room sitting beside her panting Boston terrier.

So far, so good. Now comes the hard part.

After inhaling a deep breath, she pushed open the door to the examination room. When she heard Doc speaking to someone on the phone, she exhaled a sigh of relief. The longer she could postpone interacting with her boss, the better.

No one, not even Doc, could know this was her last day working at the clinic. She desperately wanted to say goodbye, to say thank-you and tell Doc not to worry about her. She wanted to take Buddy for one final walk and cry her goodbye into his fur.

Most of all, she wanted to call Jean. She wanted to explain, and she wanted to beg forgiveness. Her disappearance would devastate the woman who had loved her like a daughter. And not just Jean, her husband John, as well. He'd been the one who'd helped her through her father's death, who'd arranged the funeral at Arlington cemetery, who'd asked the hard questions of the Army. They both loved her. They'd grieve for her—but she couldn't explain. They couldn't be part of her crime.

Her life had been full of painful goodbyes. Her mother. Her father. Mike. They'd all vanished from her life. This time was different. This time, she would be the one who'd disappear. The one who'd cause the pain.

Even though she wouldn't be able to say goodbye, she couldn't leave Doc without a farewell message, however cryptic. Buddy's picture was that message. Doc had refused to take back the keys when she'd moved out of the apartment eleven months earlier. He'd said, "It's your apartment, Cathy. You were the first person to live in it since Betty and I moved out years ago. I've no intention of renting it out again, and I don't need the storage space. Keep the keys for now."

He'd known then what she was getting into by marrying Frank Peters. He'd known, and he'd felt responsible for her bad decisions. Perhaps he'd hoped the apartment would give her a place to run to, but there was no place in town to hide, not from the reach of the psychopath she'd married.

On her lunch break, Cathy retrieved the painting and quietly scurried up the stairs to the apartment. She propped it up on the kitchen table so that Buddy's alert, friendly eyes would be the first thing Doc saw when he entered the kitchen. He'd be drawn to the apartment, she was sure of it. That's when he'd see Buddy—Cathy's goodbye message, and her thank you to a man who'd been more of a father to her than her own father had ever been. The portrait wasn't much. It had to be enough.

An emergency surgery and the resulting backlog of patients eliminated the conversational pressure that had concerned Cathy. With no time for chit-chat, the day flew by. There was a noticeable end of day silence after an excited little boy thanked Doc for saving his dog's life and then followed the pup out the door.

Cathy glanced at the clock on the wall. It was 4:30, time to leave. She opened the file cabinet and removed her purse. As she did so, she repeated one thought in her mind like a mantra.

Don't lose it now. This has to be like any other night.

Her resolve faltered when Doc looked up from his desk. As their eyes met, Cathy's "good night" caught in her throat. No words came out. Doc nodded as if in acknowledgment of more than just her unspoken words. She stared back at him, certain that her eyes reflected the pain of a final goodbye. She rushed out the door before he could see her tears.

When she arrived home, her actions were mostly on auto-pilot. She prepared Frank's dinner, enhancing the chicken gravy for his portion with a delicate sprinkling of drugs from her stash. She poured his first glass of scotch with a light touch, knowing he'd pour generously for his second, and third—if he didn't fall asleep first.

The strain of trying to act normal throughout the evening resulted in a pounding tension headache which two aspirin did little to keep at bay. She breathed a sigh of relief when Frank finally headed to the den, knowing he'd soon be asleep in front of the TV. Thirty minutes later, she heard the first snore. Grateful the evening was over, she climbed the stairs to bed.

Hours later, she woke to feel Frank squeezing her breast. She cursed herself for using too light a hand with the drugs. As he grabbed and poked and grunted his way through his one-sided sexual gratification routine, she focused on a happy childhood memory. She'd become good at disassociation, at leaving her body and finding somewhere else for her mind to dwell. She'd had a lot of practice.

Early the next morning, the alarm woke her from a restless sleep full of half-remembered nightmares. The soreness between her legs brought back a nauseating memory of a faked orgasm and left her with a strong desire to take a hot shower.

Her discomfort was soon forgotten. As the fog of sleep lifted, she remembered what day it was. Thursday, July 23rd was forecast to be a sunny, oppressively hot and muggy day. But it was much more than that to Cathy. For her, it was New Year's Day, Easter, Christmas, and July 4th all rolled into one. It was liberation day.

She kissed Frank goodbye when he left for work, leaving him with just the hint of a promise about a new sexual adventure to celebrate their eleven-month anniversary that evening. He smiled and promised to be home on time—either a credit to her acting skills or an ego that made him too easily convinced of his allure. She tried not to shudder when she read the desire in his eyes.

Running on a vast store of nervous energy, she mentally reviewed each minute detail of her plan as she vacuumed and dusted every corner of the already spotless house. At precisely five o'clock, she began final dinner preparations for one of Frank's favorite meals: salad, followed by garlic bread and spicy lasagna filled with sausage, chopped meat, and lots of cheese. She smiled as she put the small pan of lasagna in the oven.

There hadn't been much religion in her family other than occasional church visits on Christmas and Easter. She was a bit of a cynic when it came to thoughts of God and church. So she didn't view it as particularly sacrilegious to think of the evening's upcoming events as her own version of the last supper, followed by her very own resurrection.

She had spent weeks timing each part of her version of the passion play, even staging a dress rehearsal of sorts a week earlier, lasagna and all. The pros and cons had long since been mentally charted and the risks analyzed. She deserved a future, and there was only one way she could have one. Nor could she forget her promise to Frank's other wives—Amy and Helen deserved justice.

There was no hesitation, no second-guessing as she set the dining room table with taper candles and the best china. Soft, romantic music played on the stereo in the living room, and she turned the lights down low before greeting Frank at the front door dressed in a slinky black dress—one of his many "I'm sorry" gifts. When she handed him his drink, the smile on her face was genuine. She was in control. She reminded herself not to get cocky.

As they sat down at the candlelit table for dinner, she noticed that Frank's eyes were focused on the low cut bodice of the skimpy dress. He was practically licking his lips in anticipation of dessert. She read the expression on his face, and it chilled her. She couldn't afford for him to get too aroused, not now, not yet.

While Frank picked at his salad and enjoyed his second drink, she slipped back into the kitchen, removed the lasagna from the oven, and sliced it into rectangles that oozed with cheese, sausage, chopped meat, and a thick tangy marinara sauce. She put a portion on one plate and set it aside. With a quick glance over her shoulder, and her heart beating a staccato rhythm in her suddenly too-tight chest, she slid a large portion onto Frank's plate.

Biting her lip in concentration, she pulled the lasagna layers apart. She held her breath and listened for the sound of movement from the dining room. Hearing nothing, she exhaled, slipped a small bottle out of the back of the silverware drawer, and sprinkled its crushed pill contents liberally over the ricotta cheese and meat mixture before adding extra sauce and a sprinkling of fresh Parmesan cheese. With shaking hands, she placed the bottle back in the drawer, forced a smile on her face, and carried two plates into the dining room. She presented Frank's meal to him with an exaggerated flourish.

He laughed, clearly enjoying the special attention. "Why thanks, honey. This looks delicious."

She raised her wine glass in salute. "*Bon appetit!*"

As she sipped her wine, picked at her meal, and tried to feign a relaxation she didn't feel, she was sure her heart was pounding loudly enough to drown out the music, sure its staccato hammering would give her away. She waited, concerned that Frank would notice the slightly bitter flavor of the extra dose of drugs, but he chewed away, seemingly unaware.

While he ate, Cathy entertained him with a story about one of the neighbors who'd backed his car into his mailbox. She forced the words out in a steady conversational tone while her thoughts did double-time in her brain. He laughed and shoveled more food in his mouth.

When his plate was empty, he belched in appreciation and asked for seconds. She was out of her chair before he finished the request. Her mouth dry and her hands shaking, she pulled the pan out of the warm oven and inhaled the aroma. She almost giggled from nervousness at the silly idea that lasagna smelled like freedom.

She slipped the spatula under the chunk of layered pasta, lifted it from the pan, and slid it onto the plate. Then she stopped and listened but heard nothing but the music and the wind. Again, she opened the silverware drawer and removed the little brown pill bottle.

As she held the bottle over the lasagna and emptied the rest of its crushed contents into the cheese and sauce, her hand shook more violently, and she was overcome with lightheadedness. She stopped, took a deep breath, and thought about Amy. She was doing this for Amy. With that thought as her comforting refrain, she carried the plate into the dining room.

"Here you go, Frank. I saved the last piece for you." She was too nervous to sit. "I'll get you another drink."

Afraid he would sense her nervousness, she took her time getting the ice and pouring the scotch. By the time she returned, he had consumed more than half of his second helping—and he had stopped eating. He was staring down at the plate. Her heart stopped. She took a deep breath and exhaled slowly as she approached the table.

"Here ya go, Frank. Here's your drink. I'd better finish my own dinner before it gets cold."

She sat down and smiled at him across the softly lit table. She picked up her fork, willed her hand not to shake, and speared a chunk of lasagna. After shoving it into her mouth, she chewed loudly for effect.

"Damn, that's good, even if I do say so myself."

She giggled as a million butterflies did acrobatics in her stomach. She forced herself to swallow even though her throat was closed, and she was afraid she'd choke. As she reached for her glass, she focused on steadying her hand and then took a sip of water to help swallow. As she watched, Frank picked up his fork and began eating again—but more slowly now. His plate was nearly empty. His motions were slowing. He seemed confused.

"Frank, is something wrong?"

He stared at her as if he wasn't sure who she was.

"Frank?"

The fork slipped out of his hand.

"Here, let me help you into the living room. Maybe you just ate too fast and need to lie down."

Did she imagine the suspicion she saw in his eyes?

"Do you think I should call the doctor, Frank? Is it your stomach?"

She pulled his arm around her neck and half dragged him into the living room. When they got to the sofa, she let him go. His bulk pulled her down with him, and she struggled to get out from under the near dead weight of his arm. She took a deep breath and pushed his upper body back so his head lolled against the cushion.

"Let me take your shoes off and loosen your shirt. Are you sure you don't want me to call the doctor? Maybe I should, you don't look so good."

His eyes rolled back in his head, and he slid sideways on the sofa. As he lost consciousness, she panicked. Her hand began to reach for the phone to dial 911. She forced herself to relive the pain of the last time he'd raped her. With renewed determination, she pushed herself up from the couch and hurried back to the kitchen. There was still much to do.

After pulling on a pair of latex gloves, she scrubbed everything that could have been tainted with the drugs: his scotch glass, his salad and dinner plates, his fork and knife. She dried each of them with a clean dish towel and returned them to their respective places in the immaculate, well organized china cabinet and tidy silverware drawer. She wiped her finger prints off the empty pill bottle and put it in her pocket, grateful she'd remembered to remove the label. Nothing would tie her or her fake college persona to the drugs.

After collecting her own plates and silverware from the dining room, she scraped her mostly uneaten lasagna into the garbage can under the sink and wiped the edges of the dinner plate with a dish cloth. She stacked this single place setting haphazardly in the sink next to an empty scotch glass and turned to survey the kitchen. The unwashed lasagna pan on the top of the stove was a nice touch. Even middle-aged, murderer cops knew how to heat food. She nodded and checked off a box on her mental to-do list: stage set.

She was halfway through the living room on her way to the stairs before she turned to look back at Frank. His head lolled at a slight angle off the sofa pillow. His breath was shallow and with his eyes closed, his lined face and slack jaw made him appear old and impotent. There was no danger from him now. She swallowed and fought back unexpected tears of regret. This wasn't how it was supposed to be. She shook her head to clear it, to remind herself—he had left her no other choice.

Her footsteps were light as she ran up the stairs and continued down the hall to Frank's office. She had long ago discovered the reason for his paranoia and the violence of his reaction when he'd thought she'd been snooping. Still wearing the gloves, she un-taped the key to the file cabinet from the back of the desk drawer where an earlier clandestine visit had located it. She opened the file cabinet, knowing there would be money.

Her dedicated housekeeping, especially her committed dusting of the china closet directly under the heating vent in his office, had provided all the information she'd needed about the drug and protection money. Frank and his sleazy detectives had no idea their conversations could be overheard.

She expected there to be money, but she wasn't prepared for the amount. She gasped when she saw the stacks of fifties and hundreds, recoiling as she imagined the human misery the money represented. After selecting two thick stacks of hundred dollar bills and one of fifties, she closed the drawer, leaving the rest.

She placed the money, her freedom dowry, on top of the desk and returned to the file cabinet for the strong box. Even knowing what she'd find inside didn't stop her hand from shaking when she opened the lid. A sob escaped as she picked up the pictures and stared down at the disgusting proof of her shame and degradation. Turning her head aside, she rapidly tore up the photos. She grabbed the money and on her way down the hall, stopped in the guest bathroom just long enough to flush the torn photos down the toilet.

In the master bedroom, she got down on her knees behind her night table and pulled up the plush carpet. There, between the carpet and the padding, she'd hidden a small manila envelope, a tiny Plasticine packet, Amy's pages, and a small stack of Polaroid pictures. Her pictures.

She sat back on her heels and stared at the proof of her husband's violence. The bloody cuts, the swollen eye, the burns, and the masses of multi-colored bruises evoked a different kind of shame. She wiped her eyes and stood up. With her head held high, she marched down the hall and placed the pictures in the top drawer of Frank's desk.

After stepping out of the sexy black dress, she smoothed out the wrinkles and hung it in the closet next to a similar one in red crepe. Her jaw tightened when her mind flashed back to the last time she'd worn the red dress. The words "never again" forced their way out of her mouth and helped her focus as she pulled on the jeans and tee shirt that had been neatly folded on the floor next to her sneakers. The worn jeans came with memories that helped calm her, helped remind her of who she used to be.

She picked up her purse from the bedroom chair, opened her wallet, and gave Cathy Dial Peters' driver's license a final goodbye glance before placing the wallet, along with her car keys and assorted other personal items, in a shoe box on the top shelf of the closet behind some old clothes. It wouldn't take a good detective long to find them. The empty purse joined others lined up on a lower shelf.

Next, she pulled a blood-stained nightgown and tee shirt from her lingerie drawer. The blood on both items came from a recently self-inflicted wound, but memories of other nightgowns, and other wounds, remained vivid. As she backed out of the bedroom, she gave one last reflective glance at the room that had been both her prison and her refuge.

Carrying a small backpack along with the bloody clothes, she tiptoed down the stairs, hesitating before she turned the corner. *What if he's awake? What if he tries to stop me?* She sucked in her breath and dared a peek into the living room. Frank's body had slipped further sideways on the sofa, his breath barely audible now. Steadying her own breath, she crossed the living room. She was almost done, almost gone.

She pushed the bloody nightgown to the bottom of the bag of garbage under the kitchen sink. Returning to the living room, she retrieved Frank's gun from the hall closet and laid it next to him on the cushion. As she perched on the edge of the sofa, she carefully slid the silk flower arrangement off the decorative mirror on the coffee table, picked the mirror up in her latex-clad hands and pressed Frank's fingers onto its edges before placing it back on the table.

The illegal drugs came next. Cathy shook her head, still amazed at how easy it had been to buy cocaine on campus, even for someone like her who wasn't part of the drug scene. She removed the small Plasticine envelope from her pocket, sprinkled the contents on the mirror, and separated it into two careful lines with the razor she'd hidden in the side of the flower arrangement. After placing a thin straw next to the lines of coke and sprinkling a bit of the drug on Frank's pant leg and hand, she retrieved the small pill bottle out of her pocket, wrapped Frank's lifeless fingers around it, and let it fall.

Ever the artist, she turned on the lamp next to the sofa and stepped back to appraise the scene. Was it too much? Too staged? She glanced down at her watch. It was already ten o'clock. There was no time for second guessing.

After peeking through the blinds to check out the street in front, she adjusted the angle of the slats to allow a sight line from the front porch for someone who was just curious enough to want to look. She stood for a moment longer, closed her eyes, and ran through her mental check list one last time. More hopeful than confident that there was nothing she had missed, and with her eyes focused on her unconscious husband, she backed out of the living room.

"Bye, Frank," she whispered under her breath before she tiptoed through the darkened kitchen and slipped out the back door.

14

PINE VIEW, NJ

Creeping around the side of the house, Cathy was guided by the light of a hazy half-moon and the filtered beam of a streetlight in front of the house next door. She fought to stifle a sneeze as the pungent smell of a neighbor's recently tilled garden assailed her nostrils.

As she rounded the corner to the front yard, a noisy rustling in the overgrown bushes a few feet away froze her where she stood. Heart pounding, she slapped a hand over her mouth to muffle a scream. *It's just a squirrel or a rabbit. Nothing to be afraid of.* She waited. After a few moments of silence, the only sounds she heard were of the wind and a dog barking on the next block.

With cautious steps, alert for the sound of footsteps or a car engine, she stole forward toward Frank's police vehicle in the driveway. The latex gloves still on her hands, she opened the driver's side door and jammed her bloody tee shirt under the front seat. Then she slid onto the seat, disengaged the parking brake, put the car in neutral, and whispered a thank-you to an unnamed deity for the steep driveway grade.

She cranked the wheel to the left and placed her foot lightly on the brake, allowing the car to slide backward down the small hill. The corner of the back bumper came to rest against the mailbox post with the rear end slightly canted out into the road. At some point during the night, someone, most likely a neighbor—hopefully the FBI agent—would notice the odd situation. Maybe they'd peek through the front window. More likely, they'd call the police station. She doubted they'd knock on the front door.

Cathy had struggled with giving Frank this out, this chance to live. In the end, she decided that a prison sentence—at the very least for his larceny, but hopefully, with the help of the evidence she'd planted, for the death of his missing wife—would have to be enough revenge. There was no certainty that someone would find him before it was too late, but leaving him this serendipitous chance at survival was more than he'd granted either of his other wives, and it was enough to allow her the moral high ground.

Moments later, she was walking down the street with a backpack looped over her shoulders and her blonde ponytail hanging out the back of her baseball cap—just another college kid. She picked up the pace as she turned the corner onto the main road. As she jogged, she pulled off the latex gloves and stuck them in her back pocket. Taking a shortcut through a few backyards, it was less than three miles to Doc's clinic—a not overly-difficult run even with the backpack. She could almost taste freedom in the hot humid air.

~

The sweat that soaked Cathy's tee shirt when she unlocked her old apartment door and stepped inside was as much from fear as from the heat. She leaned against the wall to refocus and catch her breath. With the streetlight at the corner of the parking lot providing the only illumination, she picked up a Boston College sweatshirt, another pair of jeans, a couple of clean tee shirts, and some underwear from where she'd left them neatly folded on a kitchen chair. After tucking the items into her backpack, she blew a kiss to Buddy's picture without allowing herself to acknowledge the action as a final goodbye. Then she turned away.

A small smile curved her lips as she rolled the almost-new bicycle through the open doorway and locked the door behind her. She slipped the key into the potted plant on the landing and carefully rolled the bike down the stairs. Buying the bike had been easy, almost too easy. At the end of the spring semester, a freshman at the college had been glad to sell it for fifty bucks. Getting it to the clinic and up the stairs without anyone noticing had been tricky, but not impossible.

It was a six-mile ride to the New Jersey Turnpike entrance, and the closest turnpike rest stop. Half of the trip was on a narrow road with no shoulder. Twice her tires skidded on gravel, and she fought to gain control of the bike. Cars squeezed by close enough to touch, and she gripped the handlebars so tightly her hands became numb.

Finally, with the Turnpike in sight, she breathed a sigh of relief and dismounted. She bent deeply at the waist with her hands on her thighs to catch her breath, glad to have survived what should have been an easy ride. The bike was useless to her now. She leaned it against a tree, a gift for a stranger.

Thankful for the light of the half moon, she skirted the toll-booths and hugged the tree line as she followed the lights along the Turnpike. She stumbled on the uneven ground and an unseen piece of tire rubber almost brought her to her knees. When she finally saw the building through the mist, the haloed lights of the Edison Service Plaza looked other worldly. Her eyes filled with tears.

Can my plan really work?

The lights turned into welcoming beacons and soon Cathy's shaky legs were propelling her across the parking lot passed the gas pumps and toward the building. It was eleven-thirty, but there was still a steady stream of travelers, and at least ten long-haul tractor trailers in the parking lot. She stood off to the side and waited until a family with a crying baby and two whiny children came through the doors. Then she slipped inside and made her way to the ladies' room.

Once there, and grateful that no one else was about, she entered the handicapped stall, stripped off her wet tee shirt and discarded it in the waste bin. After patting herself dry with paper towels, she pulled her thrift store finds out of her backpack. She tugged on a Disney World tee shirt, draped a Boston College sweatshirt over her shoulders, took a deep breath, and headed out. The air was so heavy she could taste the moisture in it.

Standing in the shadow of the building, she nervously chewed her lip as she assessed each of the truckers leaving the restaurant. One of their big, growly trucks was her magic carpet to the future. One of them would take her to her new life. She stood for nearly an hour, watching—and waiting. Then she saw him, an older man with graying hair and a potbelly.

"Excuse me."

The trucker turned. Cathy stepped out from the shadows and approached him. She hoped he'd assume she was a just a college kid.

"Excuse me." She repeated in a tentative voice as she looked up at the man she'd guess was probably in his fifties. She'd picked him because he reminded her of Doc Waldron. He was paunchier and younger, but there was something about him—maybe it was the way he walked, or the gray hair. He looked...kind.

She stared at the ground and dug the toe of her sneaker into the gravel as she spoke. "I'm sorry. I've never done this before, but...I need a ride. I've got to...I've got to get to my grandmother's..."

His response was firm and immediate. "Listen, Miss. I'm sure you're a nice kid, but I don't pick up hitch-hikers. Why don't you call your parents and go on home. I'm sure that whatever you did, they'll forgive you."

"Please. You don't understand. I..." Her voice broke. She stared up at him, sure that even in the dim light the trucker could see her tears. She wasn't acting. The adrenaline high that had carried her through the long day was gone. She was desperate and running on empty. The tears were real.

She hesitantly touched his arm. "I don't have any family here. I need...I have to..."

He stepped back. "Listen. I'm sorry, but..."

Don't fall apart now. You're too close to freedom. She took a couple of measured breaths, trying to calm her racing heart and control her frantic thoughts. Somehow, she needed to make this man understand.

"Please. I won't be a bother. I promise." She kept her hand on his arm. She stared into his wary eyes and continued. "Please. I'm scared. My boyfriend..."

She gazed down at her feet again and whispered the rest of the story, alternately glancing up and then back down, unable to keep eye contact as she wove her tale, skirting around the edges of the truth. "My boyfriend told me if I ever left him he'd kill me. I thought he loved me. Now he's doing drugs, and he wanted me to...he wanted me to sleep with some guys so he could get more."

She looked up. The details of the story may have been a fabrication, but her fear was real. Frank *would* definitely have killed her. And now, if Frank was dead, she was a murderer.

"Please," she begged.

"What'll you do if I don't take you?" The man's voice was gruff, but even in the gruffness, she could sense that his resistance was faltering.

Before she could answer, two young truckers came into view. One of them, a well-built, blond guy with a dragon tattooed around one of his biceps, was gesturing as he spoke. "You should have seen the jugs on her! Best lay I've had in a while, and trust me, I've had some hot ones." His buddy laughed and slapped him on the back. Their conversation became muffled as they entered the building and the door closed behind them.

Cathy swallowed. She turned back to face the trucker. "I don't have a choice. I've got to get away." She glanced toward the door where the two men had been. "Someone will take me."

"Why me?" The trucker asked. His voice no longer quite as gruff.

"You remind me of someone I used to know, someone I trusted—someone who never let me down."

"You didn't ask me where I was going."

"It doesn't matter. Where are you going?"

He smiled and shook his head. "Kansas. Wichita, Kansas."

"That's fine. That's good," she answered. It was far away from New Jersey. "It's close to Colorado. My grandmother lives in Colorado." She added this last part after doing a quick geography review, envisioning the puzzle she'd had as a child where all the states were laid out in different colors.

He stared down at her for a long while. Then he chuckled and again shook his head. "I must be getting soft in my old age. I hope I don't regret this. Okay, let's go."

When they reached his truck, a shiny green and silver sleeper cab with the words 'Road Warrior' painted in fancy script on the door, he stopped and turned to face her

"If we're going to be spending the next couple of days together, I guess we should introduce ourselves. I'm Pete. Pete Connelly." He held out his hand.

She shook the large calloused hand with as much strength as she could muster. Her voice was low and tentative when she introduced herself. "My name is Cassie." Then she exhaled, stood up straight and announced in a stronger voice, "Cassie. My name is Cassie Deahl."

Cathy Peters was dead.

PART 2

CASSIE DEAHL

15

CROSS COUNTRY TO WICHITA, KS

"Cassie? Wake up. Cassie!"

Her eyes snapped open. She was strapped into a seat in an over-warm truck cab, facing a rain splattered windshield. For a moment, frozen in fear, she stared at the slapping windshield wipers and listened to the rumble of a diesel engine.

Where the hell am I?

Terrified and confused, Cassie turned, wide-eyed, to face the man who'd shouted at her. He had shaggy gray hair, a prominent nose, and stubble on his cheeks. He didn't look dangerous—but neither had Frank.

The truck driver kept his hands on the wheel as his head swiveled back and forth between her and the road. "Cassie? Are you okay?" His voice, although unfamiliar, sounded concerned. He was no longer shouting. "Do you remember where you are? I'm Pete Connelly, the trucker giving you a ride to Wichita. Do you remember?"

She stared at him, her breath held, while she processed his words. As she came fully awake, the remnants of a horrifying nightmare faded. She remembered what she had done, and why she was in Pete Connelly's truck. She blew out her breath, her thoughts in a whirl.

Did I kill Frank?

Cassie sat up straighter. She inhaled another lungful of the warm air and pushed the question aside. She was free, and she was on her way to Wichita, Kansas to start a new life. That was all that mattered now.

After attempting a tremulous smile for the truck driver, she shrugged and stated the obvious. "I guess I was having a nightmare."

He smiled in obvious relief. "You were crying in your sleep and fighting the seat belt. I was worried."

"I'm sorry. Thanks for waking me. I'm fine, now." *Thanks to you.*

He didn't respond.

She stared out the window at the wet, black strip of highway and watched the giant windshield wipers rhythmically swipe back and forth. Periodically, the CB radio crackled and the voice of another trucker intruded into the dark silence of the truck cab. Cocooned in the warm cab, sleep once again claimed her.

The cessation of movement woke her. This time, although the cab was still dark when she opened her eyes, she didn't panic. "Where are we?" she asked as she stretched and rubbed her eyes.

"We're in eastern Ohio. We've been on the road for about five hours since I picked you up. We'll stop here to get something to eat, and so I can get some sleep in the back." He gestured to an open area behind the seats that she couldn't see. "Are you hungry?"

She nodded.

"Well then, let's go eat. I hope you're up for hearty fare. I didn't get this gut eating salads, and these places cater to my kind!" He laughed at his own joke. Cassie surprised herself by laughing along with him.

"I'm pretty hungry, too. I could use some hearty fare," she said with conviction. She couldn't remember the last time she'd actually eaten a full meal—certainly not sitting across the table from Frank.

They ate in companionable silence in the garishly lit truck stop restaurant. Cassie, deep in thought about her future, almost forgot Pete was sitting across from her. When he finally spoke, she glanced up from picking at the remains of what had been a hamburger platter and noticed his plate, once filled with meatloaf and mashed potatoes, was clean.

He said, "I'm afraid you'll have to entertain yourself while I get a little sleep. This place has an arcade and an area where you can sit and read..." He stopped, apparently unsure about what to say next.

She rushed to reassure him. "I'll be fine." Although, after a quick look around at their mostly empty surroundings, she had a slight feeling of unease. "I'll get a cup of tea and read for a while." She pulled a thick paperback book out of her oversized purse. She'd jammed the leather bag Jean had given her into her backpack, even though it limited the clothes she could bring. It was the only link to her past, one not easily identifiable, and she'd been determined to keep it. She held the book up for him to see. "Ken Follett and I have a date that will last for quite a while. Don't worry about me."

"Do you have money?" He stood up from the table and reached into his pocket.

Cassie fought back tears at the kindness of this unexpected gesture, then quickly nodded her head and responded "Yes. Yes, I have money. Thank you. Thank you for asking. It was nice of you to pay for my dinner. Don't worry. I'll be fine."

She attempted a lighthearted joke with a serious undertone. "You won't leave without me though, will you?"

He smiled and shook his head. "I promise. I won't forget you. I'll see you in about four hours." He glanced up at the clock on the wall. "We'll be back on the road about nine. Meanwhile, you get to watch the sun come up."

~

As promised, they pulled back onto the interstate just before nine. Five hours later, they were sitting in yet another truck stop restaurant. When she looked up from her tuna salad sandwich, Pete was staring at her with his head cocked to one side and an odd expression on his face.

"You remind me a lot of my daughter, Julie." He spoke in a quiet voice, and then, perhaps embarrassed to have shared this bit of information, he focused his attention on picking up a French fry and dipping it in ketchup.

Cassie put down her sandwich and sat quietly, watching him, waiting for him to say more.

"Julie's nineteen now," he continued, his gaze locked on something just behind her, or maybe on nothing at all. "She left home last year, after she finished high school. She wanted to see the world. Wichita wasn't big enough for her. She said college wasn't her thing." He shrugged. "I couldn't talk her out of it. We argued before she left."

Cassie wasn't quite sure what to say, but she felt some response was expected, so she asked, "Do you hear from her? Do you know where she is?"

He shook his head. "She called for her mother's birthday in April. We haven't heard from her since. She was in Los Angeles then. Said she was working as a waitress…" His voice trailed off.

"It must be hard for you and your wife…not knowing," Cassie offered.

Pete didn't acknowledge her comment. He refocused, and when their eyes met, he said, "When you asked me for a ride, I thought of Julie. I thought you could be her. Every day I pray that God will take care of her, that when she needs help, someone will be there to help her. Most of all," he paused and cleared his throat as if fighting to control his emotions, "I pray she'll come home to us."

He pushed himself up from the table without making further eye contact. He glanced at his watch and announced, "Truck leaves in twenty minutes." Then he headed toward the men's room, leaving Cassie with a much better understanding of the kind man who'd saved her.

~

The steady rhythm of the truck, and her emotional need for rest and escape, kept Cassie asleep for much of the trip. They stopped at regular intervals for food, and so Pete could rest. She picked up travel brochures and read whatever she could find about Kansas, and she updated and rearranged the details on her to-do list.

As they neared their final destination, Cassie was too excited to sleep. She was wide awake when they arrived in Wichita at nine o'clock on a Monday morning. In the preceding hours, she'd encouraged Pete to tell her about his hometown. He was looking forward to seeing his wife and son, and he was happy to talk about the city his family had called home for three generations. Cassie had a good feeling about Wichita.

Pete pulled the truck to the curb across the street from a Holiday Inn at the edge of the downtown area. The bus station was a block away.

"Are you sure this is where you want me to drop you? This isn't the nicest part of town. Do you have enough money?"

Cassie smiled at the concern in his voice. "Yes. I'll be fine. I want to get some clothes and make myself presentable before I head to Colorado. I'll get a room here. You already told me a lot about the city, and it sounds like it'll be easy enough to get around."

She opened the door. When she turned back, she could barely see him through her tear-filled eyes. "Thank you," was all she could manage before her voice broke. She reached over to hug the man who'd turned from gruff stranger to guardian angel.

"Take care, Cassie," Pete said as he returned her hug.

She slid back across the seat, opened the door, and climbed out.

16

WICHITA, KS
1987 – 1989

With her backpack slung over one shoulder and her sweatshirt loosely tied around her shoulders, Cassie watched until Pete's truck and its load of manufacturing equipment turned the corner and disappeared from sight. There were cars driving by, people walking on the sidewalk, others entering and leaving the few small stores on this side of the street. But for the first time in her life, a life where she had often felt abandoned, Cassie understood what it truly meant to be alone.

"Excuse me." A mother with a giggling, blonde-haired, little girl in tow jostled her on the sidewalk. "I'm sorry," the young woman said with a hint of exasperation as the child pulled her forward toward the door of a bakery. "My daughter is on a mission." She laughed and rolled her eyes. Cassie smiled, nodding her acceptance of the apology.

Grateful to the woman and her child for interrupting a pity party that could have easily spiraled into depression, Cassie exhaled and relaxed the tension in her shoulders. She crossed the busy street and checked into the Holiday Inn. Her room was uninspired, but clean. It would do. She stripped off the clothes she'd lived in for the past two days and eagerly approached the shower. The cascading stream of hot water was her baptism, washing away more than just travel grime.

As she pulled her last clean tee shirt over her head, she reminded herself that clothes shopping was the second item on her to-do list. The first was finding a bank. Thanks to Frank's criminal enterprises, she had plenty of money. And not unlike the little girl dragging her mother down the street, she too was on a mission—one just a bit more important than a bakery cookie or a toy.

She needed to create a life and a future for a woman named Cassie Deahl. To do that, she needed to find a bank, establish a checking account, and rent a safe-deposit box. Fortunately, there was a bank only two doors down from the hotel.

The bank manager was helpful, if a bit officious and stuffy, and within an hour she had established her account and found a home for a large portion of the money she'd liberated from Frank's ill-gotten gains—over twenty thousand dollars. Once the money was tucked inside the vault, along with Amy's precious pages and a few other items, she breathed easier.

She spent the entire next day creating her new persona. Cathy Peters was a college student with long blonde hair and twenty-twenty vision. Cassie Deahl would share none of those traits. A quick trip to a hair salon was followed by a visit to an eyeglass store to purchase a pair of glasses with non-prescription lenses. A drug store near the hotel provided shampoo-in hair dye. She nervously waited the requisite time after applying the hair dye, then showered it off and blew her hair dry. Her transformation complete, she took a deep breath and stared into the bathroom mirror at a stranger.

A woman with short, fluffy brown hair and tortoise shell glasses stared back at her. Cassie Deahl wouldn't look out-of-place working in a library, or sitting in front of a typewriter in an insurance office. She looked nothing like a blonde, long-haired college student named Cathy Dial Peters.

Thankfully though, Cathy provided some transferable skills—like waitressing. The next day, when Cassie wandered into a busy diner with a Help Wanted sign in the window, a harried, over-worked manager hired her on the spot.

With her new identity firmly established, she allowed herself time to focus on determining the answers to two important questions: *Was Frank alive? Did the police believe Cathy Peters was dead?*

Cassie spent a portion of each day in the periodicals room of the Wichita Public Library scanning the New York newspapers looking for answers. Four days after arriving in Wichita, her diligence paid off. A short article in the New York Daily News reported on a Pine View, New Jersey police chief recuperating in the hospital from a possible suicide attempt while the police searched for his missing wife. Cassie breathed a sigh of relief. So far, so good.

Meanwhile, Cassie continued to build her life in Wichita. The Holiday Inn remained her home for a week until her daily perusal of the classified ads paid off. After a friendly meeting over tea, an elderly woman agreed to rent Cassie a comfortably furnished apartment on the second floor of her home. Cassie checked one more item off her to-do list.

While she juggled orders at the busy diner, Cassie deflected stories about her past. When a persistent waitress kept pushing, Cassie shared the same painful story she'd created for Mrs. Allison, her landlady. In a strained voice she confided that her parents had died in a car accident in upstate New York while she was away at college. Only sad memories remained in the little town where she'd grown up. So, with no siblings or close family, and with no desire to return to college, she'd decided to head west. She only had to tell the sad story once. None of her co-workers peppered her again with questions.

While she was working—smiling at customers' stories, taking their orders, listening to the other waitresses complain about their love lives— she almost felt normal. Not quite happy, but not overwhelmed by sadness or fear. Not so at night when her mind was free to roam and too often took her to places she'd rather not go. She'd wake, gasping for air, sobbing into her pillow, grateful her landlady was hard of hearing.

She picked up the phone a dozen times to call Jean, desperate to speak to her but terrified she'd answer the phone—thrilled just to listen to her voice on the answering machine.

Cathy Peters' disappearance touched off a national media storm. At first, Cassie was surprised by the attention, but then she understood. Why wouldn't the country be enthralled with a story about a middle-aged police chief whose young wife vanished under suspicious circumstances?

The media tempest reached epic proportions when Frank was charged with her murder. The newspapers presented a variety of theories, but the scenario presented by the District Attorney was the only one that mattered: Frank Peters' abused young wife had uncovered proof of his illegal activities. Peters was afraid she'd use that information to destroy him, so he killed her.

In support of his position, the DA presented the array of circumstantial evidence Cassie had carefully laid out—the pictures of her bruised and battered body found in Frank's desk, the bloody tee shirt hidden under the car seat, the blood-spattered nightgown in the bottom of the garbage bag, and the driver's license and college ID found hidden on a top shelf in the closet. Frank's suicide attempt was painted as a guilty man's reaction to the murder of his wife.

Cassie shook her head in surprise and disbelief as she read the news articles day after day. Unbelievably, it had all played out exactly as she'd hoped, exactly as she'd planned.

Frank's life story also played out in the newspapers and on TV. The stories focused on a high school football star, an Army soldier and Vietnam veteran, and Frank's years on the police force, culminating in his position as police chief of Pine View, New Jersey. The major news outlets focused on the more positive aspects of his past, while posing questions about where he'd gone wrong. The tabloids speculated about the deaths of Frank's first two wives, and presented unsubstantiated rumors about dirty dealings.

Interviews with wary Pine View residents, including Marge at the diner, provided little in the way of significant information about Frank Peters. When people spoke about the police chief, it wasn't respect or friendship Cassie saw in the eyes of the interviewees, spouting platitudes and bland niceties. It was fear. Why hadn't she noticed that before she'd married him?

The media storm waned after Frank's indictment, leaving Cassie totally unprepared when the start of Frank's trial reinvigorated a media storm three months later. As she unloaded her grocery cart at the checkout line in the supermarket one afternoon, she gasped in surprise. Frank's angry face stared at her from the cover of a *Newsweek* displayed in the magazine rack in front of her.

As she stood gaping at the picture, her hand unconsciously squeezed the milk container she'd been placing on the conveyor belt. The container split, presenting a cascade of white liquid over everything in its wake.

"Miss? Miss, are you okay?" A concerned cashier swiped at the mess with a wad of paper towels.

Cassie mumbled an apology and allowed the cashier to take the container. Red-faced and embarrassed, she paid for her other groceries and hurriedly left the store.

The following week, an idle glance at a newsstand on her way to work nearly brought her to her knees. She grabbed a nearby light pole for support and sucked in her breath while she stared unblinking at *PEOPLE* Magazine.

A picture of Cathy Peters, taken on what had turned out to be her Las Vegas wedding trip, was on the cover. The buxom blonde with big hair and heavy make-up bore little resemblance to Cassie Deahl, yet Cassie still glanced furtively around her. For days afterward, she expected someone at the diner to remark about how much she looked like the woman in the magazine. No one did.

The magazine coverage rattled her, but the *60 Minutes* segment on TV came close to destroying her. Cassie sat on the floor in her dark apartment, knees pulled up tight to her chest, as she watched the show on her small TV. Spellbound, she listened to Morley Safer interview Doc Waldron. Had Doc's comment about her painting of Buddy been a message for her? Had he understood that she'd left the pup's picture as a goodbye?

She hugged herself tighter and sobbed during the wrenching interview with Jean and John Donahue. Their obvious pain and the sorrow in Jean's voice wracked Cassie with guilt. She hadn't wanted them to suffer, but there was no way she could have shared her plans with them. They, like everyone else, had to be surprised by her disappearance, had to believe Frank killed her.

She reached for the phone to call Jean, to tell her it was all a lie. The phone rang twice before Cassie hung up and cursed her own stupidity. John was an attorney. As he had once explained to her, that made him an officer of the court. He had an obligation to uphold the law. She couldn't put John in the position of knowing that Frank was innocent of her murder—even if he was guilty of two others.

Though she knew she had no real options, Cassie still agonized over what to do. The Donahue's loved her. They were her family. Maybe John would keep her secret. But wouldn't her telephone call leave a trail? What if the police arrested her for framing Frank? He'd surely find a way to kill her then. After all the agonizing, she acknowledged the truth she had known all along. She couldn't call Jean.

Two weeks later, she was half listening to the late night news when the verdict in Frank's murder trial was announced. She stood wide-eyed, her breath held and her eyes locked on the screen, as the newscaster announced: "After two weeks of deliberation, and based on circumstantial evidence that even the prosecution admitted provided more questions than answers, the jury returned a guilty verdict in the second degree murder trial of disgraced former Pine View New Jersey Police Chief, Frank Peters. The body of his young wife, Cathy Peters, has not been found. Peters' attorney issued a statement repeating his claim that Peters was framed. They will appeal the conviction."

Transfixed, Cathy watched as a slide show of her life flashed on the screen. She saw the shy smile of a self-conscious girl in a high school year book, a laughing teenager with a playful horse tugging on her pony tail, a sophisticated young woman standing confidently next to Mike at the senior prom.

She wasn't prepared for those memories. She covered her mouth to keep from crying out in pain, but couldn't stop her body's violent shaking. When the tears started, she couldn't stop them.

Cathy Dial Peters was officially dead.

Cassie crawled into bed and huddled under the covers. She cried for her mother and ached to hold the treasured picture book that held her mother's cryptic suicide note, her goodbye message to Cassie's ten-year-old self. She had kept nothing of her childhood, or her past. When she walked out of Frank Peters' house and became Cassie Deahl, she'd left it all behind, everything that had defined Cathy Peters' life.

The unexpected slide show of the happy moments in her life, a life before Frank Peters, sliced through her heart, leaving it in bleeding slivers. The loving homage someone had put together to honor the too-short life of Cathy Dial Peters filled her with grief and guilt—and completed the downward spiral into the depression that had been gnawing away at her.

She found it impossible to drag herself out of bed the next morning, other than for a short trip to the bathroom and a call to her boss at the diner to say she was sick. She retreated to her bed where the closed blinds kept the sunlight at bay. Her mind was foggy and unfocused, her limbs heavy, and her body depleted of energy as if she'd run the Boston marathon in record time.

Waking in a dark apartment hours later, her mind barely registered that an entire day had disappeared. After first dragging herself to the bathroom, she wandered into the kitchen for a glass of water and some crackers before climbing back into bed and burying herself under the covers once again.

She was awakened the next morning by the sound of a tentative knock on the door, followed by more persistent and louder knocking.

"Cassie? Cassie dear, it's Mrs. Allison." The hesitant voice of her elderly landlady intruded through the fog in her mind.

Even with her mind infused with darkness, she couldn't ignore the woman who had always been kind to her. Cassie trudged to the door. As she turned the lock and opened the door, she caught sight of her reflection in the mirror hanging over a small table. She barely recognized the swollen-eyed person with the blank expression staring back at her. A vague swipe at her tangled mass of matted hair did little to improve its appearance.

"Cassie dear," Mrs. Allison said, making no comment about Cassie's disheveled and distraught appearance. "Cassie dear, if it isn't too much of an imposition, I was wondering if you could drive me to the doctor's office this morning. I hate to bother you while you're resting, but the road seems a little slick, and I get so nervous when I drive these days."

Cassie stared down at the tiny woman and forced her mind to register the request. How could she say no to the caring old woman?

She nodded, all the time wondering why Mrs. Allison hadn't commented on how horrible she looked. Was her eyesight an issue? "Sure. Sure I can. Ummm..." she paused and fought to focus on what needed to be done. "I need to take a shower and...and get dressed."

"No problem, dear. We don't have to leave for close to an hour. Thank you, Cassie." Mrs. Allison smiled and patted Cassie's arm. "You're a life saver. I'm so glad you're here, dear."

Cassie showered and dressed, then drank a cup of tea and nibbled on some toast before heading downstairs to help Mrs. Allison out to the car. As they left the house, she noticed that the sun was shining. The roads were barely wet from an earlier rain shower. They were certainly not slick.

Her thoughts were refocused by a greeting from the next-door neighbor. "Good morning, Cassie." Mr. Raleigh, the friendly, retired school principal, called to her from the front porch of his house. "How's that old car running for you? You let me know if you have any problems, you hear?"

Cassie smiled at the elderly neighbor. He'd insisted on selling her his old, gently driven, Chevy after noticing her walking home from the bus stop in the dark shortly after she'd moved in to Mrs. Allison's place. The price was more than fair, and he'd even taken it to his mechanic for a tune-up and oil change before he transferred the title.

"Good morning, Mr. Raleigh. The car is running fine. I still can't thank you enough for selling it to me. How are you doing?"

"I'm well, young lady. Thank you for asking. It's nice having a pretty, young girl like you in the neighborhood. You've livened things up for us old folks. Isn't that so, Amanda?"

Mrs. Allison nodded and patted Cassie's arm. "Yes, John. Yes, that's certainly so."

Did she imagine the look that passed between her landlady and Mr. Raleigh? Had they been talking about her? A variety of questions chased themselves around in Cassie's mind. Was Mrs. Allison as wise as she was caring? Was her hearing more acute than Cassie had thought? Had she been worrying about her? Cassie's questions were never asked, nor did the answers matter. Helping Mrs. Allison forced her to move forward. Her tentative steps became more solid as the days progressed.

She later wondered what would have happened if her landlady hadn't knocked on her door that morning. Would she have found her way back on her own, or would she have taken her mother's way out? She had no answers. Determined not to get that close to the darkness again, she faced her days with a new energy and focus—and devoted her free time to learning how to protect herself.

~

When she wasn't at work, Cassie was at a martial arts school learning self-defense and karate. The school was in a sketchy part of town, but after a few weeks she no longer noticed the cracked sidewalks, closed stores, and occasional vagrant. As she walked to her car late one night, her mind was replaying her last kicking drill when someone stepped in front of her.

"Wanna party?"

Cassie froze. The stench of alcohol overwhelmed her, taking her back to a place she'd rather not be, to memories always close to the surface no matter how hard she tried to bury them.

She cursed herself for letting her mind wander, for letting her guard down—for becoming complacent. Yet when the man grabbed her arm, the anxious, frightened young woman disappeared. New instincts, new muscle training, took over. Within seconds, the man's arm was twisted behind his back, and she'd flung him to the ground.

After eighteen months of training, she still only had her blue belt in karate. Although her sensei had praised her steady progress, she wouldn't be happy until she'd achieved her black belt, until she was a karate master. Her limited self-defense skills had served her well, though. Or so she'd thought.

"What the..." Momentarily dazed, her would-be attacker lay where he'd fallen. Then he began to push himself up from the ground. Even in the dim street light, she could see the anger and alcohol-fueled hate in his eyes. Once more she froze, seeing the rage-filled eyes of the man who'd made her life a living hell.

"Cassie? Cassie are you okay?"

The sound of hurried footsteps approached from behind her. Cassie exhaled, the spell broken. Dale, her instructor, the sensei who had taught her all she knew about self-defense and karate, arrived at her side. It didn't take him long to assess the situation.

Grabbing the drunk by his collar, he shouted directly into the man's face. "IF I EVER SEE YOU AROUND HERE AGAIN, YOU'LL WISH YOU'D NEVER BEEN BORN. DO YOU HEAR ME?"

The man seemed to shrink in size. He looked down and mumbled his response. "Yeah."

Dale pushed him away. "Get lost and don't forget what I said."

Student and teacher watched as the man stumbled away down the dark street.

"Are you okay?" Dale turned to Cassie and asked in a concerned tone, "Do you need to sit down for a while?"

She tried to steady her voice as she answered, although she was still shaking inside. "I'm fine. Thanks to you." She patted his arm in gratitude. Then she climbed into her car and drove home.

The next day, she stopped at a local gun store. Wide-eyed and overwhelmed, she hesitated as she entered the store. Staring at the scary array of firearms, she remembered her conversation with Gino Valenti, the man who'd provided her new identity. His question, "Do you need a gun?"

had been asked conversationally, as if wasn't a big deal. At the time, she'd been shocked and had hastily said no. She'd been wrong.

The clerk in the gun store never even asked her name. He answered her questions and accepted her money. With her new pistol and ammunition safely stowed in a case, she left the store and headed for a local shooting range. Once there, determined to add one more layer of self-protection, she signed up for shooting lessons.

The range competed with the martial arts dojo for a claim on Cassie's free time. As she worked on her shooting skills and progressed toward her black belt, her self-confidence grew. She'd always have to look over her shoulder, but she was no longer the meek young woman who'd married a monster.

~

The months flew by. One day she glanced at the calendar and realized she'd been in Wichita for two years. She shook her head, remembering the early August morning when she'd climbed out of Pete Connelly's truck to face the future alone. Now, her two years were up. It was time to move on. She almost talked herself into staying longer. There was no magic in the two-year rule she'd established as part of her survival plan. She liked Wichita. Mrs. Allison treated her like family, and she'd begun to make friends at the diner.

A front page article in the Wichita Eagle changed her mind. Next to a picture of a smiling, dark-haired woman was the headline, "Local Nurse Murdered". The article described how the woman's ex-husband had tracked her down and knifed her to death in front of her apartment in Wichita.

Cassie's hand shook as she placed her coffee cup on the table next to the newspaper. Frank might be in prison, but she wasn't naïve enough to believe he was without the resources to track her down. A long-buried memory came back to her, a memory of two teenagers standing in a barn talking about family and roots. She had envied Mike's roots even while he chafed at them.

She left Wichita the next day, having learned a painful lesson. Two years was too long to stay in one place. It made leaving too hard for someone who couldn't afford to plant roots—and survive.

17

MONTANA
1999 - 10 YEARS LATER

With one hand on the steering wheel and the other resting on the open window frame, Cassie sped down the highway, putting miles between herself and her winter job waitressing in Bozeman. She smiled as she breathed in the fresh Montana air that still held a taste of winter. The blankets of wildflowers in the meadows and the ragged white-capped peaks in the distance were a balm for her winter blues.

She slid one of her favorite flea market finds into the tape deck and sang along with Kris Kristofferson and his gravelly voiced rendition of "Me and Bobbie McGee". She belted out the lines about freedom being just another word for nothing left to lose and thought about the words of the melancholy ballad.

She was free—the opposite of the life she'd dreamed of as a young girl yearning for family and roots. She had grown accustomed to facing the world alone, wary of people, especially men. And always, the specter of Frank Peters haunted her.

More than twelve years had ticked down on her freedom clock. Unless a parole board released Frank early—her nightmare scenario—she had another thirteen years of freedom. Once Frank was out of prison, all bets were off. She shivered, fighting back the fear she had mostly learned to deflect.

She took in a deep breath and refocused her thoughts to reflect on her ten-year odyssey, an exercise she used when thoughts of Frank Peters threatened to overwhelm her.

From Wichita, she'd headed south to Tulsa. Tulsa hadn't felt welcoming, so she'd continued south and spent a year wandering through Texas, picking up waitressing jobs and living in cheap apartments or motels.

After a while, the towns all seemed the same—backwater places time had passed by. Her only criterion before she'd call any of them home, even for a few weeks, was that they have a karate school.

Within twelve months of her tearful good-bye to Mrs. Allison, she'd achieved her goal—her black belt in karate. Her reward? Giving up the dark hair and glasses. Cassie Deahl became an older, wiser version of Cathy Peters.

Silence in the truck brought her back to the present. She changed the cassette. This time, the sweet, country sound of Dolly Parton allowed for a more upbeat mood as she returned to her reflections.

She had enjoyed her yearlong sojourn as a cook at a small ranch in Santa Fe. When she wasn't working, she spent long hours enjoying the unique palette of colors that defined the New Mexican desert. Some day she would paint it all from memory. When she moved on, she headed north. As always when she moved, she left no forwarding address—and no friends who would miss her.

Her pick-up truck, purchased new three years earlier while working on a ranch in Colorado, was as close to a permanent home as she had. She traveled light. Although her saddle took up a significant chunk of the back seat's real estate, there was still room left for all her belongings. There were no fancy clothes, just a few pairs of Levi's, some tee shirts, long sleeve cotton shirts, a down parka for the winter, and a cowboy hat.

Now, she raced down the highway toward her new ranch job, excited at the prospect of spending the next six months in the saddle. The sweat, the long hours, the aches and pains at the end of the day, she embraced it all. The horses accepted her at face value. They didn't care who she was— or what she was running from.

She was singing along with Johnny Cash and Waylon Jennings when she saw the sign for the Bitterroot Ranch. Smiling in anticipation, she turned off the paved road and started down the two-mile-long dirt track that would take her to the ranch.

A lean man, his ruggedly handsome face leathered by years in the sun, welcomed her with a warm smile as she climbed out of the car. She responded with a smile of her own. "Hi, I'm Cassie Deahl. I'm looking for Luke, the ranch foreman."

"I'm Luke," he said by way of introduction as he held out his hand. "Welcome to Bitterroot Ranch, Cassie." He hesitated for a beat while they shook hands, then he added, "I've got to warn you up front that the boys weren't so happy when they heard I'd hired a..." He cleared his throat. "Um, a woman..."

Cassie responded with a small laugh. Grateful for his willingness to address the issue head on, she helped him out. "I have a feeling they didn't use the word woman when they reacted to your announcement, Luke. 'Girl' 'broad', 'chick' come to mind as the nicest of the words that might have been used." She shrugged. "As I told you on the phone, I've been doing this for a long time. I doubt there's anything the guys can do or say that would surprise me. Over time, I'll win some of them over. Others not. I'm not looking to make friends—or enemies. I'll get by just fine."

Luke nodded, his eyes casually appraising her, though not in an uncomfortable or sexual way. "John told me as much when he recommended you. He said you performed magic with his young stock horses, and that you could take care of yourself."

Then, as if to contradict his words, the creases around his eyes deepened and his expression reflected discomfort and uncertainty. "I don't want to say something out of line, Cassie, but John never said a word about..." He raised his hands, gesturing toward her. "Umm." He seemed truly uncomfortable. "I guess I made some assumptions about how you'd look."

Cassie had no idea where this was going. "How I'd look?"

Once again, Luke cleared his throat. This time he also shuffled his feet. Finally, he exhaled and his words rushed out. "I wasn't expecting you to be so pretty."

Relieved and somewhat embarrassed, Cassie threw back her head and laughed. She covered her mouth and turned her laugh into a smile. "I'm sorry. I had no idea where you were going with that comment. Thank you for the compliment, I think. I have a feeling you were trying to say something more. Perhaps that you're concerned my 'looks' may cause problems?

Luke smiled and seemed to relax. "Yeah. I guess that's it."

"Like I said, I've been doing this for a long time. I can handle whatever the crew has in store for me. It may take a while, but eventually I'll just be one of the guys."

Luke nodded. "Okay," he said. "I'll take your word for it." His tone indicated that he wasn't convinced. "I'd thought about giving you my old room in the bunk house. It provides some privacy, but you'd have to share a bathroom and trust me, I'm not the tidiest guy at my best, but even I didn't like sharing a bathroom with some of those guys. Fortunately, Mrs. J solved the problem. You'll have a room off the kitchen in the big house. It has a separate bathroom."

"Thank you. I don't expect special treatment, but I appreciate the added privacy."

"Since you'll be starting the young stock in addition to being a ranch hand, it doesn't count as special treatment. The guys are okay with it."

~

A room in the big house was more than she'd anticipated, providing an indication that the owners would be more welcoming than she'd dared hope. Luke instructed her to park in the driveway near the back of the house. He cut across the pasture and met her by the back porch.

"The Johnsons are lookin' forward to meeting ya," Luke said as he opened the door. He gestured her forward to precede him into the house through a mudroom, where jackets and boots were neatly arrayed along the wall and floor, and then into a spacious kitchen where her hosts were waiting.

"Cassie Deahl, I'd like you to meet Carl and Maryann Johnson, Bitterroot's owners and the nicest folks you'll ever work for." Luke grinned and raised his hand to present the older couple standing in front of him.

Carl Johnson was an affable-looking, older man wearing worn jeans and a faded work shirt. His laugh filled the room as he reached out to shake Cassie's hand. "Welcome, Cassie. Luke's been here long enough to be family, and I think he's just a bit prejudiced in his opinions." He gestured to the petite, silver-haired woman at his side. "This here's my wife, Maryann, the matriarch of Bitterroot."

Maryann Johnson welcomed Cassie with a warm smile. Her slacks and blouse looked expensive but comfortably worn, and their wearer seemed comfortable in both her clothing and her skin. The hand that shook Cassie's was freckled with age spots, and the woman's fingernails were short and unpolished. "I'm glad to have you here with us, Cassie. I've been looking forward to having another female around the place. Too much testosterone around here if you ask me."

She rolled her eyes, but her smile and the affectionate glance she gave both her husband and Luke said that her comment was merely an attempt at humor. "Let me show you your room. I hope you'll like it. I couldn't abide the idea of you being out there with the boys. They're a nice enough lot, but I'm afraid their mamas didn't teach them much about cleanliness." She made a tut-tut sound and ushered Cassie forward toward a door at the far end of the large kitchen.

"Angelita, our cook and housekeeper, has a family now, so she and Carlos and their two little ones live in a house on the property. This used to be her room." She opened the door to a comfortably furnished room bathed in afternoon sunlight. A plush chair was positioned in the corner. A double bed with a dark wood framed headboard and a brightly patterned quilt sat in the middle of the room with matching tables on either side.

Cassie was overwhelmed. She had gotten used to small 'make-do' rooms partitioned off the corner of a bunk house that provided her just a bare measure of privacy. Even when she'd had her own space, it had been Spartan at best. This was like a fancy hotel. She stammered her thank-you. "This is beautiful, Mrs. Johnson. I don't know what to say. It's certainly more than I expected. I…"

Mrs. Johnson raised her hand to stop her. "Call me Maryann, dear. I've spent my life on a ranch, including a few years in the saddle, chasing cows with Carl in the early days. Sometimes I kind of miss it, but then I remember how hard it was!" She laughed and shook her head. "We're Carl and Maryann. No need for formalities. I'm glad you like the room. I kind of like it myself. The bed frame and tables belonged to my parents." She sighed and gave a slight shake of her head. "Long time ago."

Her smile firmly back in place, she beamed up at Cassie. "Now, you get yourself settled in. Bob and I have a meeting in town, so we'll be leaving in a few minutes. Angelita will have dinner ready in about an hour. Everyone tends to eat when they have time, so the meal will be set out in warming trays for a couple of hours. Luke'll show you where the food is served and introduce you to any of the hands that are around. The others you'll meet in the morning. Make yourself at home."

~

After a satisfying dinner of hearty ranch food, followed by a good night's sleep, the next morning Cassie arrived in the stableyard twenty minutes early. She was the last one to arrive. Not a surprise. The crew were curious. They wanted to see the chick—and test her.

The head wrangler led a plain-looking, dun-colored, cow pony over to her and announced, "This here's Dusty."

The guys sniggered and elbowed each other as she accepted Dusty's reins. She was pretty sure Dusty had some issues, but she was used to having to prove herself. It helped that she had a way with horses.

She didn't crowd the horse. Instead, she stayed a few steps away and proffered her hand for him to sniff. He was intrigued by her and took a step forward. She rewarded his brave act by taking a small step back, giving him space. After a few minutes, the guys wandered off, but she knew they'd keep her in view. She ignored them as she worked with Dusty. When he finally relaxed, she took the reins in her left hand, put her left foot in the stirrup, pulled herself up, and then softly lowered herself onto the saddle.

She felt Dusty's body tense in anticipation of her spurs. She waited, keeping her spurs away from his sides. When he exhaled, she clucked, and he moved forward. Once they were clear of the other horses, she clucked again, and the horse picked up a rhythmic lope. She circled around a few times, gently reined him in, and walked back to the corral.

At least ten cowboys were staring open-mouthed at her, kind of like wide-mouth bass she thought, but she didn't laugh. First battle won. Dusty hadn't bucked her off, and at least some of the boys would be impressed. She nodded at them, patted Dusty on the neck, and turned to the wrangler.

"He'll do just fine. Thank you."

She heard a soft chuckle as she passed a tall cowboy standing off by himself.

"That was quite a show. Good for you."

She smiled as she glanced down into the cool, gray eyes and rugged face of the stranger. He didn't offer any other comment and didn't quite smile in return, but his look was respectful, if somewhat distant.

"Thanks." She sensed that she had found an ally. She wasn't looking for friends, but it was good to know there was someone who might be there to watch her back.

As the other ranch hands mounted up, she spent more time working with her horse, getting a feel for his responsiveness.

"Guess you're stuck with the old guy," Gray-eyes said as she passed him.

Cassie glanced around. The other guys had all paired up. Gray eyes was the odd man out. He looked down at her from the saddle. His tone was casual, his expression hidden by the brim of his hat.

"I guess you're stuck with the chick," she replied. "Sorry."

"No matter to me. Looks like you can handle yourself. The name's Cliff, and this here's Rocky." He motioned to the strawberry roan gelding he was riding.

"Hi, Cliff. I'm Cassie, and I'm pretty sure we both know why they call this guy Dusty, and I doubt it's because of his color." Cassie smiled as she spoke, but she didn't laugh at her own joke. She was sure they'd given her the meanest, rankest horse on the ranch, expecting him to buck her off into the dust. She'd passed the first test. There would be others.

~

She and Cliff developed a rhythm as they worked together over the next few weeks. Neither of them were talkers, and they accepted without question the long silences some would have sought to fill with senseless chatter. After the excitement of the round-up, after the young calves had been branded and castrated, life settled in to a routine. Although most of the cattle ran free on government land, some areas were fenced. Part of their job was to check the fence lines, stopping when needed to fix a break in the barbed wire or reset a fence post.

Each day merged seamlessly into the next. In the evenings, the guys played cards or swapped stories. Some of them drove into town for drinks. Cassie never joined them. She kept to herself, choosing to read or sketch a scene she especially wanted to remember. Her dream, if she ever allowed herself to admit she had such a thing, was to someday settle in one place long enough to paint again. The sketches would help her remember the details of the incredible places she had called home during her wandering years.

~

On a mid-afternoon in late August, she relaxed in the saddle and gazed at the mountain vista, breathing in the beauty she challenged herself to remember. When Dusty's nicker interrupted her musings, Cassie followed his gaze and watched as Cliff and Rocky approached at a slow lope. A strong wind was blowing, and Rocky's hooves kicked up a cloud of dust.

Cliff reined his horse in next to her at the crest of the ridge. "Looks like a storm's comin'."

She nodded. Storms came quick in the mountains. She knew how powerful and dangerous lightning was at this altitude and how fast a picturesque mountain stream could become a roiling torrent of deep water.

"Yeah. I guess we should be heading back."

Moments later, the first clap of thunder sounded and lightning ripped through the sky. The dark clouds spewed their contents and within seconds they were drenched. Cliff pointed to the west and turned without waiting for Cassie's response. She urged Dusty into a jog, careful to keep Cliff and Rocky in view as they picked their way down the side of the ridge. She knew where they were heading, a cabin they'd passed many times about half a mile down the mountain

The going was tough. A too-close-for-comfort lightning strike spooked her horse. Dusty reared and spun. Cassie fought to stay in the saddle and only her years of experience kept her there. Muttering, "It's okay, it's okay, Dusty," as much to calm herself as the horse, she managed to get him under control as they made their way to the cabin set in a small, protected meadow.

Cliff was dismounting as she arrived. They pulled the saddles and bridles off their horses before turning them loose in the small, attached corral. The storm raged around them as Cliff pushed open the cabin door. They stumbled in and dropped their saddles on the floor.

"Whew! I wasn't sure..." Cassie pulled off her wet hat and bent at the waist, breathing in huge gulps of air.

Cliff nodded as he struggled to catch his own breath.

The worst of the storm passed within thirty minutes and settled into a steady rain. However, the deluge had created impassable streams with swift moving currents where earlier there had been mere trickles of water.

As the afternoon light weakened into dusk, they stood in the open door of the cabin, staring out at the darkening sky. Cassie turned to Cliff with a shrug. She spoke with weary resignation in her voice. "We'll never make it back down the mountain. Guess this is home for the night."

Cliff blew out a breath and nodded in agreement.

They turned to scan the simple, one-room cabin that others had used for refuge for close to fifty years. There wasn't much—a couple of cots, a fireplace with a stack of dry firewood next to it, a small, rough-hewn table, and a couple of benches pushed up against the wall. A kerosene lamp sat on the table, and a handful of canned goods were stored on a shelf along the back wall. A ten gallon, metal bin of oats sat in the corner. It would do for the night.

Cliff fed the horses while Cassie heated their one-pot dinner of beef stew mixed with beans. The warmth from the crackling fire relaxed them and the hot food took the edge off their hunger. A welcome find of a bottle of Jack Daniels loosened their tongues. Cassie didn't drink much, even when she was bar-tending or waitressing. She'd learned her lessons about liquor the hard way.

After weeks of constant company, she and Cliff were used to long silences between them. That night was different. They sat on the rough-cut benches with their backs up against the wall and swapped stories about their cowboying adventures and the characters they'd met. They debated whether the word cowboy was a generic term that should cover women, since Cassie thought the word cowgirl was too frivolous.

Cliff tossed out terms like cowhand and ranch hand. With her eyes closing, and the Jack Daniels making her silly, Cassie surprised herself by giggling at the word cowpoke. She took that as a sign it was time for bed. First, she had to address her near bursting bladder. She pulled open the cabin door with reluctance and muttered a curse. Then she sidled outside and leaned against the cabin wall for balance while the rain poured off the roof onto her head, and her jeans dragged in the mud.

"Damn!" She was still zipping her wet jeans when she stumbled back into the cabin. She looked up to see the laughter in Cliff's eyes. "Don't you dare laugh! It's not fair. It's just not fair!"

He handed her a threadbare towel and only half managed to fight back a chuckle before he suggested, "Maybe you should sit by the fire?"

Her clothes were soaked. What she really wanted was to strip them off and hang them by the fire to dry, but that wasn't an option. She took the towel with a grumbled, "Thanks."

She heard Cliff chuckle again before he turned off the kerosene lamp and stretched out on his cot. Cassie sat as close to the fire as she dared. The flames mesmerized her, and she leaned against her own cot and dozed until she felt roasted. Her clothes were still damp when she climbed onto her cot, rolled her jacket up as a pillow, and put her head down to sleep.

~

The scream was only half out of her mouth when the jolt of her body hitting the floor woke her. It had been a long time since she'd had a nightmare. Tonight, there had been whiskey, shared reminisces, and odd sleeping arrangements—fertile ground for a mind prone to terrible imaginings.

Cliff was on his knees at her side. "Cassie? Cassie, are you okay?"

Still half asleep and disoriented, she leaned against him, leaned into him. "I'm okay." She mumbled her response and fought to clear her mind of the remnants of the frightening dream. How could Frank's image still be so real after all this time?

She was shaken and embarrassed. "I'm sorry," she mumbled. "I didn't mean to wake you. How do you big guys manage these cots without falling off?"

She attempted a laugh, but couldn't quite pull it off.

"You were having a nightmare." Cliff said in a low voice.

"It was nothing…must have been the beans…"

She looked up, expecting a reaction to her joke. When she realized how close they were sitting and that he had his arm around her, she froze. Then she exhaled, forcing the fear away. In the three months she'd spent working with this man, he'd never so much as raised his voice or spurred his horse in anger.

Their eyes met and held. In the crisp night air that filled the room from the small open window, she inhaled the scent of pine tempered with the sweat from a long day in the saddle. She smelled the Jack Daniels on Cliff's breath and stared into the depths of sad, gray eyes.

Everything in her past told her to run, to scream, to hit, but when he touched her face with his rough but gentle hand, she cried. She didn't break eye contact as the tears slowly traced their path down her cheeks.

"Cassie?" Her tears obviously confused him, but she said nothing in response.

After a few moments of silence, he wiped her tears away with the pad of his thumb. Then he leaned forward. She closed her eyes and felt the brush of his lips against hers. Her response was tentative, uncertain. She thought to pull away, but couldn't. As he moved his lips against hers and murmured her name, her lips parted just enough to be an invitation, and she reached her arms up to hold him close. The kiss deepened. She felt the scratchiness of his day-old beard as he held her tight and cupped the back of her head with his hand.

Neither of them spoke as they undressed each other in the dark, damp cabin. The fire had burned down to embers while they slept, and the room had a night chill to it, but Cassie barely noticed. Cliff touched her as if she were a fragile flower that would easily bruise. He pulled the blanket off the cot and lifted her hips to slide the blanket under her on the cold hard floor.

He questioned her with his eyes. She answered with a slight nod as she pulled him closer. They had spent weeks together without ever having had a meaningful conversation. They were both loners, and in many ways kindred spirits. Now, they were about to be lovers.

Cassie's body reacted greedily to Cliff's gentle touches, and at first she pegged the unfamiliar sounds she heard to the wind on the now clear, quiet night. Until those moans, her moans, climaxed in a final cry releasing another flood of tears. She held Cliff close and sobbed into his naked, muscled chest as he rocked her back and forth in his arms.

"Are you okay? Did I hurt you?" He asked, concern evident in his tone.

"No. I'm fine." She gazed into his eyes in the dim light. "I'm sorry about the tears," she murmured as she attempted a smile. She thought she saw a glint of moisture in Clint's eyes before he turned his head away.

An awkward silence built. They untangled from each other and began to pull on their clothes in the cold night air.

"Cassie. I'm...I'm sorry. I..." Fully dressed and standing, his discomfort obvious, he reached for her hand to help her up.

She accepted his hand and stood. "There's nothing to be sorry for, Cliff. You didn't hurt me. You comforted me." She swallowed as she searched for her next words. "This doesn't have to change anything."

He nodded and slowly walked toward his cot, before abruptly changing his mind and striding to the door. "Umm…I'll be right back…"

Cassie barely heard him. She sat on her cot with her head in her hands. Her mind was numb, but her body hadn't felt this alive since a naïve young girl gave her heart to her best friend just in time for him to break it. She hadn't thought about Mike in a very long time.

As her brain function returned, she panicked. *Damn! Damn! Damn! How could I let this happen?*

She looked up when she heard the door open.

Cliff glanced in her direction, but didn't meet her eyes. "Horses are doin' fine. They're nose to tail dozin' up against the cabin. We'd best get some sleep. If we don't ride out at first light, they'll be sendin' a search party for us." He stretched out on his cot and tossed the old Army blanket over his legs.

Cassie allowed the silence to build until her inner anger dissipated. Then she exhaled softly and answered him. "You're right. We need to be out of here early. Good night, Cliff."

They were both awake at dawn. Cliff brought in a small stack of wood to replace what they'd burned. He tended the horses while she set the cabin to rights for the next inhabitants. This time, their ride back down the mountain wasn't the comfortable quiet of two solitary people sharing a common space, but the quiet that comes from things left unsaid.

For two days they stiffly acted out their roles as if nothing had changed. Their silences were awkward now, and their attempts at conversation a struggle. What had happened between them in the cold, barren cabin had changed everything, but it was obvious to Cassie that Cliff didn't know how to handle it any more than she did. Their frantic coupling had reminded her both of past pain—and past happiness. This new awareness made a lie of the solitary life she'd chosen.

~

Cliff was waiting for her as she strolled back to the big house after dinner. "Take a walk with me?" he asked.

She nodded and quietly fell into step beside him as they headed out to the corral, away from the prying eyes of the 'kids' as Cassie often thought of the other ranch hands. They stopped at the split rail fence.

Cliff turned to her. "I'm leaving in the morning. I'm gonna' head down to a spread near Cheyenne where I know some folks. I just wanted you to know. Wanted to tell you..."

He hesitated.

Cassie jumped in. "Cliff, please don't leave on my account. I know things have been a little awkward, but we can get through it. I'm sorry if..."

With his lips turned up in a vague approximation of a smile, he held up his hand to stop her. "It's time. Would have been movin' on in a couple weeks anyway now the weather's startin' to change and the cows are down from the hills."

After taking a deep breath, he continued, "I've never been much of a talker so this is hard for me, but I wanted you to know that... that you're a fine woman. I enjoyed workin' with you..."

He took off his hat and smacked it nervously against his leg. "Hell, that's not what I wanted to say at all."

The expression in his usually cool, gray eyes was intense. "Cassie, there's more we don't know about each other than we do, and I think we've both seen more than our share of hurt. The other night..." He smiled. "The other night reminded me that maybe being alone isn't all I've built it up to be. Part of me would rather I didn't know that."

The intensity was gone, replaced by sadness.

Cassie nodded, surprised that Cliff was able to express her own feelings so well. "I think that's what we've both been struggling with. I was so angry that I'd let myself feel again. I swore..."

She shook her head and stared off into the distance before continuing, "I swore I never would. I've reconciled with it now. I'm glad you didn't leave without saying goodbye, Cliff. If you had, I wouldn't have had a chance to thank you for helping me understand that being with someone doesn't always bring pain."

They met each other's eyes with shared expressions of regret.

"Bye, Cass." He bent down and kissed her lightly on the cheek.

"Bye, Cliff."

She turned and headed back to the house and the room where she slept alone.

18

CHEYENNE, WY
2001 – 2 YEARS LATER

Exhausted, Cassie pushed the wet hair away from her sweaty face. The late August Wyoming heat was brutal, and she was looking forward to a desperately needed shower. But before heading back to her cabin, Cassie paused to stare into the distance at the unchanging vista of sagebrush and scrub pine. She wondered, as she always did as yet another season came to an end, where the time had gone.

Another summer, another ranch—soon she'd be heading west to Jackson Hole and another winter of waitressing and bar-tending. These were the times when she became more conscious of the clock ticking away her precious days of freedom. If she was lucky, she had a few more years. Eleven at most. Probably fewer now that Frank had fulfilled enough of his sentence to allow him to apply for parole on a regular basis.

As she stared at the unrelenting landscape, she mused about Frank's second trial, the one that had added five years to his twenty-year sentence for her murder. Over two hundred thousand dollars of untaxed money had been recovered from his home and a variety of safe-deposit boxes. Money, but no paper trail for the criminal activities that had generated it. Tax evasion had been the FBI's fallback charge.

Cassie had no doubt that it was Frank's cohorts, his dirty detectives, who had removed the accounting ledger she'd found nestled in the file cabinet under the stacks of money. She'd often wished she'd taken the ledger with her when she'd run. By pocketing the book with its neat list of accounting details, Frank's men had saved more than just their own asses—and Frank's. The names listed in that document, just on the couple of pages she'd seen, were a 'who's who' of New Jersey's rich and powerful. Frank's goons could easily attempt to blackmail them to gain leverage for Frank.

Still in a reflective mood, Cassie recalled yesterday's unplanned visit to the public library. During a quick trip into town, her truck had seemed almost to turn into the library parking lot of its own accord. As she'd done on her other somewhat irregular visits, she'd slipped into a seat at the nearly empty row of computer terminals and typed, 'Police Chief Frank Peters, New Jersey, murder, parole'.

One mouse click later, Cassie was watching a replay of a TV interview from two days earlier. In a chirpy upbeat tone, the young woman reporter asked Frank, "How do you feel about having your parole application denied?"

Frank's anger at the question was palpable. He leaned forward, his jaw tight and his eyes blazing. The reporter recoiled, sliding back in obvious fear. Seeing her reaction, Frank quickly masked his expression, like a chameleon changing its colors.

His eyes now blank and wearing a tight smile that didn't come close to reaching his eyes, Frank replied in a flat, measured tone, "It's a minor setback. There's always next time." Then he'd stared straight into the camera with an intense, hard-eyed gaze.

This time, it was Cassie who recoiled, the pain in her gut rejecting the logic in her mind.

He can't see me. He doesn't know where I am.

She hadn't paid much attention to the reporter's wrap-up comments, and her hands had been shaking when she'd closed the browser and deleted her search history, the way a young college kid had taught her to do a couple of years earlier. Then Cassie had sat, staring at the blank computer screen, but still seeing Frank's intense, unforgiving gaze.

∼

A loud voice broke into her depressing reverie and refocused her thoughts back to the present, back to a brutally hot afternoon in Wyoming. She shook her head to clear it and turned toward the voice.

"Hey, Mom! It's little Tom's birthday. He's finally legal, and it's our last night here. Come into town tonight and party with us."

Out of the corner of her eye as she turned to respond, Cassie noticed one of the young horses loping around the corral. The beautiful sorrel with the picture perfect star on his face owned a special place in her heart. She would miss his soft, welcoming nickers. She would miss a lot of things, but it was almost time to move on.

Reacting with a ready retort for the sassy ranch hand who had called her 'mom', she said, "You know, kid, I may be an old lady, but I'm not quite old enough to be your mother, and I'll bet I can whup your ass." There was laughter in her voice. Billy was a good kid, and he often came to her for advice, hence her nickname.

"My mother taught me to never hit a woman, so I guess we'll never find out, will we? Come on, Cass. Just this one time? We'll behave. We won't embarrass you…at least not too much…please?"

It was hard to say no to Billy, to the infectious grin, the pleading voice, and the eager look. Whether she'd passed some magic age, or exuded more confidence—or both—the young ranch hands seemed more willing to accept her than in years past. Sometimes, they even asked her advice, like Billy did.

"Well…" she started.

Billy didn't wait for her to finish. "Great! We're leaving at nine. I promise you'll have fun." He pumped his fist in the air. "I told the guys I could get you to come!"

As he strode back toward the bunkhouse, Cassie called after him. "Wait! Billy, I didn't say I would come."

"Sure you did! I heard it in your voice. It's the first time you didn't just say, 'No thanks.'"

Cassie shook her head at the retreating figure of the tall young man whose engaging smile and big brown eyes had all the young girls lusting after him.

"What the hell, why not?" she murmured out loud. "It's not like I've got anything else to do. It's better than moping around here."

A hot shower washed away the day's grime and improved her disposition. She shined her boots, pulled on a clean pair of jeans, and slid her arms into a red checkered, long-sleeved western style shirt with pearl buttons that she saved for special occasions. Leaving her long blonde hair hanging loose, she added a pair of gold hoop earrings, a light application of lipstick and mascara, and with some trepidation met the guys at precisely nine o'clock.

"Cassie?"

There were whistles and whoops all around.

"Wow!"

"You look beautiful!"

"Would you be my date?"

"Hey, I invited her! She's gonna' be my date!"

Cassie curtsied and laughed. God, she was going to miss these guys.

"Thank you! All compliments are gratefully accepted. You guys clean up real good, too!" She looked each of them up and down approvingly.

"There's five of us, so we're going to take two trucks. Do you want to ride with me?" Billy asked in a hopeful tone. "I cleaned out all the fast food wrappers and dirty clothes."

"Thanks, Billy. But I think I'll drive myself. I am, after all, an old lady who needs her beauty sleep, and I wouldn't want to put a crimp in your partying. If you all drive together, which one of you will be the designated driver?" She gazed at them with raised eyebrows, her 'mother' role firmly back in place.

Tom answered. "I will. I promise. I'll just have one beer early on, and then I'll switch to Coke."

Cassie smiled at Tom. She knew his background well enough to know he would keep his word. She had often provided a sounding board for his confidences about his loud and abusive drunk of a father.

"So, what are we waiting for? Let's get this party rolling! There are girls out there just dyin' to dance with me!"

The guys rolled their eyes at Billy's boastful comments and climbed into the truck.

~

Cassie stood near the corner of the bar out of the way of the crowded dance floor of line-dancing, jeans-wearing, boot-stomping party-goers. She nursed a beer as she listened to the band and watched the dancing. Her boys all seemed to be having a good time. After dragging her out on the dance floor for one awkward dance, Billy had fortunately found someone closer to his own age to hold his attention.

The guys nodded at her and waved whenever one of them caught her eye. There was an overwhelming smell of sweat and beer, and the old wooden floor reverberated from the pounding feet of the dancers. Cassie smiled to herself, glad she had come.

At that moment, when she still had a hint of a smile on her face, she had a feeling someone was watching her. She instantly tensed. Turning her head, she met the steely, gray eyes of a cowboy. *What were the odds?* She continued to stare as her mind raced back in time. She could feel her cheeks flush as she remembered the last time she'd seen this particular cowboy.

"Hey," was the only thing he said after he'd worked his way through the crowd to stand in front of her. He had a half smile on his face, and his cowboy hat in his hand.

"Hey, yourself," she responded, gazing up into the handsome, weathered face. "I forgot you'd told me you were heading down this way. How are you, Cliff?"

"Can't complain. You're looking well. Nobody would take you for a cowboy, that's for sure." His expression was approving as his eyes traveled the length of her body in a manner she found complimentary rather than discomforting. Here was a man she trusted. There weren't many of those.

Cassie grinned and nodded her thanks, aware he was purposely reminding her of their friendly argument. How long ago? Two years since...since...She blushed and looked away, embarrassed. When she heard his chuckle, she peeked up at him through the curtain of her hair.

He brushed the hair away from her face and smiled down at her. "Don't think I've ever seen you blush, Cass. Makes you look more like a young girl than a tough horse woman."

His smile faded. They continued to stare into each other's eyes with surprise and disbelief.

"Cassie? Excuse me, Cassie...Umm, can I talk to you for a minute?"

"Hmmm?" Cassie turned at the sound of her name. Billy stood a couple of feet away, his face wreathed with concern.

"Billy? What's wrong? What do you need?"

"Um...I just wanted to see if you needed anything. The guys and I just wanted to make sure you didn't need anything..." He shrugged his shoulder in Cliff's direction as he mumbled.

She smiled at his gesture, and at the recognition that the boys were worried about her. She wanted to kiss him on the cheek in gratitude, but thought better of embarrassing him.

"Billy, I'd like you to meet an old friend of mine. This is Cliff. We used to work together at a ranch in Montana. Cliff, this is Billy. He's the one who talked me into coming into town tonight."

Cliff and Billy shook hands and stood in awkward silence until Billy excused himself and retreated back across the dance floor where Tom stood watching warily. Cassie waved to Tom and smiled.

Cliff's throaty chuckle stirred more memories for her. She turned back to him, the smile still on her face.

He glanced toward the boys and then back to her. "That's nice. They're lookin' out for you. Of course, you probably never told them you could whup most of the guys in here without breakin' a sweat."

She tensed before responding. The smile remained fixed on her face, but it was no longer reflected in her eyes. "Actually, I have said that on occasion, but of course they didn't believe me. And I've been told there's no way they would ever be able to know the truth, because their mothers, bless their hearts, taught them to never hit a woman. I could have been joking..." She glanced up at him, expecting an explanation for his comment.

"How about we take a walk?" he suggested.

"Sure. Let me tell the boys so they don't worry about mom."

"Mom?"

"Don't ask! I'll be right back."

She could feel Cliff's eyes following her as she made her way across the dance floor. "Hey guys, I'm gonna take off. Cliff's going to walk me to my car."

She turned to Tom and gave him a kiss on the cheek. "Happy Birthday! Have a great time, but don't overdo it. Good night, guys. Thanks for inviting me."

An overly exuberant, two-left-footed cowboy, line-danced his way into her as she threaded her way back to Cliff. "Sorry, Ma'am," he said with an embarrassed smile as he grabbed her arm to keep her from falling.

She laughed as she regained her footing and held up her hands to indicate acceptance of his apology. Her muttered, "No problem," seemed to alleviate his concerns. He grinned back at her and stomped his way in the other direction.

Still laughing, she rejoined Cliff, and they headed for the door. He glanced back and nodded as he held the door open for her.

Once outside, they both inhaled a deep breath of the clear night air as they made their way through the crowd on the sidewalk. When they turned the corner, the quiet was a shock after the noise of the bar.

"They like and respect you, you know."

"Hmmm?"

"If they thought of you as one of the guys, they would've made suggestive comments and elbowed one another, or at the very least, rolled their eyes. Instead, they just gave me the eye."

"The eye?"

"Yeah. The eye. The look that told me if you didn't come back in one piece, they'd know who to come after."

"You picked all that up from across a crowded dance floor? Is that why you nodded at them?"

"Yep."

"Wow, I'm impressed. I thought only women were good at subtle cues."

"Well even us Neanderthal men have some of those."

She stifled a laugh, but he heard it and responded.

"What's so funny?'

"Umm, kind of like the way dogs scent-mark trees?" She grinned up at him.

He smiled back at her.

"Women! I pay you a compliment, and what do I get?"

"Sorry." This time she didn't hide her laugh. "Couldn't help it."

She stopped walking. Suddenly serious, she turned to face him. "What did you mean before about me being able to whup all the guys in the bar?"

They were standing under a street light. She stared up at him, waiting for a response.

"Not long after I moved here, I overheard some guys in a bar talkin' about an obnoxious ranch hand who'd gotten his butt kicked for puttin' his hands where they didn't belong. I seem to recall they were pretty impressed with the chick who took him down. Said she had a black belt in judo."

"Why'd you think it was me?"

"Oh, I dunno." He grinned and continued, "Could have been any one of the dozen or so long-legged, sexy, blue-eyed, blonde Montana ranch hands that had a way with horses."

She frowned.

His grin became a slight smile, and he raised his eyebrows in question. "Don't I at least get points for makin' the connection, you know, long-legged, sexy…etc?"

She relaxed and made an attempt to return his smile. "Thank you for the compliment, for 'making the connection' as you say. Did they tell you the guy ended up in the hospital, and that a stupid move on my part almost landed me in jail because some moron wouldn't take no for an answer? I lost control…I forgot…"

She turned and stared into the darkness. "There was no excuse for what I did. I hurt a man, embarrassed him in front of his friends, and made an enemy for life. Not one of my more stellar days. Fortunately, as much as I hated to do it, I was able to use some of those attributes you so nicely pointed out to convince the sheriff I was just a frightened woman trying to protect herself. He convinced the guy that it would be embarrassing for him to press charges and admit to the world that a 'sweet young thing' beat him up."

She sighed, still angry with herself for manipulating the sheriff and for losing control in the first place. She could have lost everything.

"Don't be so hard on yourself. They said he ended up messin' with some young girl whose daddy had him arrested, and now he's doing time—again. Apparently, he really was a bad ass."

"Thanks, that helps a little."

"Doesn't take the fear away though, does it?"

"Fear?"

"Yeah. Fear that the one time you lose control blows away all the effort you put into being anonymous. You don't have to worry, you know. We're a pretty close-mouthed bunch as a rule. I can't see anyone runnin' off their mouths to be on one of those mornin' TV shows. Can't understand why some folks are so anxious for their fifteen minutes of fame. Most of us are like you, Cass. Just tryin' to get by and fly under the radar. You don't have to worry."

He really did understand.

"Thanks, Cliff. I think that's the most I've ever heard you say at one time. I appreciate it. I really do."

She reached up and kissed him on the cheek. "It's karate, though."

"Hmmm?"

"My black belt, it's in karate, not judo. I only have a blue belt in judo, just a little better than a beginner."

"You're not kiddin', are you?"

"No. No, I'm not kidding. I spent the better part of three years living on pain killers. I'm definitely not kidding." There was a steel edge to her voice and a fair degree of buried anger, as well.

They walked in silence, passing other bars with their rowdy patrons carrying the party out into the street.

"So, where're we walking to anyway?" Her tone changed. The subject was closed.

"I live around the corner. I have an apartment over the hardware store. Wanna come up for a beer?"

Cassie nodded, refusing to think beyond the moment and the immediate invitation.

They climbed the stairs. He fumbled for his key and then held the door so she could enter before him. When he flipped on the light switch, she saw a small, tidy apartment. Standing in the entrance to the living room, she viewed a worn, comfortable-looking green sofa, a brown leather recliner, a couple of pine end tables with amber glass lamps, and a portable TV on a stand. Across the living room, she could see a small galley kitchen and a couple of doors which she assumed were to the bedroom and bathroom.

She turned to him with a question in her eyes.

"I got tired of running, Cass. Tired, and too old. I've been here over a year now. I work with the stock at the rodeo and do some other odds and ends. It's not much, but I make ends meet. This place is comfortable, and my old bones have a soft place to rest at night."

She shook her head thoughtfully. "It's nice. I..." She shrugged, not knowing what else to say. She had a long way to go before she could settle down—if she ever could.

"I'll get..." Cliff's words brought her back to the present, to the handsome, sexy man standing next to her. He took a couple of steps past her toward the kitchen where she assumed he planned to retrieve the promised beer.

He stopped and turned to face her. The intensity of his gaze and the desire in his eyes told her all she needed to know. "Oh hell…Cass?" He stepped forward and placed his hands lightly on her shoulders.

When he kissed her, it was like a step back in time. The cool night air from the open window mixed with the scent of his aftershave and the taste of beer, but in that moment, her mind replayed a vivid memory of the sweat and Jack Daniels of that other time—a special time in a small cabin when two lonely people had come together.

He didn't rush her, seeming to understand that she had to lead, that she had to initiate. She wrapped her arms around his neck and leaned into him. He trailed kisses down her neck and tickled her ear with his tongue. She should have been afraid. If this had been any other man, she would have been. But this was Cliff, the man whose face she sometimes saw in dreams that weren't nightmares. She relaxed into his arms as he guided her across the living room and pushed open the bedroom door.

The street light outside his bedroom window provided just enough illumination for her to see. Cliff stepped back and gazed intently into her eyes, wordlessly asking the question, giving her an opportunity to say no.

She nodded and hesitantly, almost shyly, she smiled. Then with an assertiveness that surprised her, she raised her hands and began to unbutton his shirt.

"May I?" he whispered as he reached up to undo her own buttons.

She nodded again and sighed, still gazing with wonder into his eyes.

He slowly pushed the shirt off her shoulders and peeled it from her arms. His kisses nuzzled her neck as he tossed the shirt onto the bed. Moving downward, his mouth found her breast through the thin lace of her bra. She arched toward him wanting more, until his fingers went from stroking her back, to unhooking her bra. Then she panicked. Not from fear, but from shame that he'd see her scars—the daily reminder of her degradation at the hands of Frank Peters.

She stiffened. Cliff froze in response. For a moment, neither of them breathed. He raised his head and murmured in her ear, "I won't hurt you, Cass." He dropped his arms to his sides.

Angry that she'd allowed Frank to intrude on this special moment with Cliff, Cassie shook her head side to side, berating herself. *I escaped. I'm alive. Those scars are part of who I am!* She pushed her embarrassment and shame aside to wrap her arms tightly around Cliff's neck. Just before she kissed him with a passion she didn't think herself capable of, she whispered, "I know. I know you won't hurt me."

They stumbled to the bed. When she reached down to pull off her boots, he stilled her hand and knelt to remove them for her. He stood, and she lifted her hips as he deftly slid her out of her jeans and panties before kicking off his own boots and peeling off his jeans and boxer shorts. Naked and aroused, and with no hint of embarrassment, he gazed down at her with a tenderness that took her breath away.

Through eyes moist with tears, and feeling more than a little overwhelmed, she stared back up at him. Then he reached down, scooped her up with one arm and slid the comforter back before depositing her gently in his bed.

"You're gorgeous, Cass," Cliff whispered, as he slid down next to her and pulled her into his arms.

She mouthed a silent 'thank you'.

He took his time gently stroking and teasing her, and her body greedily responded. He waited until her body had experienced the exhilaration of surfing a long high wave before he lowered himself over her, and when she reached for him, he rode the next wave with her.

When her tears came, he rubbed her back and made soft soothing sounds. She quieted and nuzzled next to him with her head on his bare chest and their bodies still entwined.

With a sigh, she lifted her head. "I'm sorry. I…I never cry—about anything."

She couldn't actually remember the last time she had cried. Tears belonged to her past, to the fragile young woman she'd left in New Jersey.

"Never?" He partially extricated himself from their entangled limbs and reached under the rickety night table for a handful of tissues.

"Thanks." She blew her nose and wiped her eyes. "Well, almost never."

"I guess we're about even then."

"What?"

"I seem to remember the last time…they weren't all your tears. And the tears of a crusty old cowboy have got to carry more weight than those of a soft and sensitive woman, don't you think?"

His wry smile dared her to deny the veracity of his words. She didn't respond. Instead, she continued to stare into his eyes, searching for answers she knew weren't there.

When he spoke, it was obvious he was attempting to answer the question she hadn't been able to put into words. "Trust is never easy, Cass. Take it from someone who long ago forgot the meaning of the word. I think that every now and then we have to let someone else in, if only to prove our own humanity."

With gentle hands, he pushed the hair back from her face and kissed the edges of eyes still wet with tears. Then he wrapped his arms around her and pulled her to him. She relaxed for a long while and dozed against his lean, muscled body.

Before either of them could sink into sleep, she pulled away and sat up, clutching the sheet to her chest. "I have to go. It's late."

"You're welcome to stay."

"I can't...." She started to explain, but it was too hard to put her fears into words. Instead, she took another tack. "What would the kids think if Mom's truck wasn't there when they got back? I have an image to uphold, you know." She laughed, but the tears in her eyes made the laugh a lie.

Cliff just nodded. He sat up and swung his legs over the bed. After retrieving his clothes from the floor, he left the room—allowing her privacy to get dressed.

She found him in the kitchen pulling a steaming cup of instant coffee out of the microwave. "Thought you'd need this to keep awake on the drive back." He handed her the coffee in a covered Cheyenne Frontier Days souvenir cup. "You can keep the cup. Help you to remember Cheyenne." It sounded like a joke, but there was no laughter in his voice.

"Thanks." Her hand lingered on his as she took the cup. She responded to his attempt at humor with a sad smile. "I won't need a souvenir cup to remember Cheyenne."

She watched as he sat to put on his boots. "You don't have to...."

His expression when he turned to her was hard to read. Not anger. Frustration? Exasperation? She couldn't tell.

"I know, but I am anyway. I don't care if you're superwoman. You're not walking back to your truck alone." His look warned her not to challenge his decision.

They walked back to the bar in silence. It was late. The bars were closing. The crowd had dwindled.

There was so much Cassie wanted to say, but nothing that could be said. They were two broken people who for a short time had found a safe canyon where their inner storms could quiet, but there was no permanent refuge, at least for Cassie.

She unlocked the truck door and turned to face him. "You're a good man, Cliff Douglas." She touched his face and reached up to kiss him on the lips with the barest of pressure.

He returned the kiss, then shook his head, his expression grim. "People aren't always what they seem, Cass."

Her laugh, her instinctive reaction to the truth of his statement, made a small hollow sound. "None of us are, Cliff."

He held the truck door open for her. She climbed in, and he pushed it closed behind her. When she opened the window to say goodbye, he handed her a small slip of paper.

"I'll be here, Cass. I know you're self-sufficient and can take care of yourself, but I'm here."

She glanced down at the neatly written address and telephone number and felt the tears bubbling up inside her. "I'm heading to Jackson Hole. Got a job for the winter…"

He nodded his head, acknowledging her good-bye. "Bye, Cass. You take care."

"Bye, Cliff." She put the truck in gear and drove away before he could see the tears that now rolled unchecked down her cheeks.

"Damn it!" She shouted out loud as she smacked her hand on the steering wheel. "Damn it!"

It was better to feel nothing than to feel the pain that came with goodbye, and it would always have to be goodbye. She forced herself to stem the flow of tears and concentrate on the road in front of her, aware of how quickly deer, elk, and a wide variety of other wildlife could materialize in the middle of a dark road. A preventable car accident was not on her list of acceptable ways to die.

She was in full flight mode by the time she got back to the ranch. She had planned to hang around for a few more days to spend time with the green-broke stock horses, especially Clyde, her special project—an incredibly smart horse with a bit of a trust issue. Instead, she was up early and had her truck packed before breakfast. She said goodbye to the boys and settled up with the ranch owner who told her she had a job waiting for her next year, if she wanted it. She made no commitments.

Before she got in the truck, she went out to the corral to say goodbye to Clyde. He nickered a welcome and trotted over as she climbed the fence and perched on the top rail. "Well boy, I guess it's goodbye," she murmured, gently scratching behind his ears and rubbing his face. "You're a smart boy, don't do anything silly and you'll be fine. Hear me?"

She knew most of the guys would think she was crazy, but these were the hardest goodbyes. "I told them about you. I told them you're something special. Don't let me down, okay?" She gazed into Clyde's expressive, brown eyes and smiled as the young gelding gently pulled at her sleeve with his teeth. "No sweetie, I've gotta' go. Go play now."

She swatted him on the rump with a gentle hand, and he trotted off. Sniffling, she wiped away tears as she watched him go. When he playfully nipped at one of his buddies, she laughed, and then watched as the pair of them raced across the corral.

~

With a Reba McEntire tape blaring and the truck windows rolled down, Cassie sped down the highway on her way to Jackson Hole. She wanted to be reveling in the moment and singing along as she drove through the endless miles of open prairie. But she didn't see the landscape, and she barely heard the music. Her heart was bleeding, and her choice to be alone now only meant being lonely.

Unbidden, tears traced their way down her cheeks as she relived the events of the previous night. She swatted at the tears and wiped them on her sleeve.

"Damn you, Cliff! Damn you!"

The slip of paper with Cliff's address and telephone number was sticking out of the ashtray where she'd placed it the night before. With no other outlet for her pain and frustration, she grabbed the paper, crumpled it in her hand, and reached toward the open window. Just as her fingers opened, she saw the expression on Cliff's face when he bent to kiss her goodbye. She closed her fist and caught the edge of the paper before it slipped through her fingers. With a pounding heart, she hit the brakes and pulled over to the side of the road.

Staring down at the neat, precise script of the gentle cowboy who had managed to find the chink in her armor, she smoothed out the wrinkles, folded the paper in half, and placed it carefully back in the ashtray. Then, after taking a deep breath, she gunned the engine, pulled back onto the empty highway, and headed west.

19

JAMESTOWN, COLORADO
2004 - 3 YEARS LATER

"Good morning, ladies!"

Cassie announced her arrival as she pushed open the door to the Jamestown Veterinary Clinic, her place of employment for the last two years.

She hadn't been looking for a job as a vet assistant two summers earlier when she was finishing up her ranch job in Steamboat Springs. Her winter gig had already been lined up. A ski resort in Vail was expecting her, and she'd planned on spending another winter bartending and waitressing. Yet when Will Scott, the ranch vet, mentioned that his friend was looking for a vet assistant, she'd listened. "Connor's a great guy, Cassie. You'd really be helping him out. Besides, wouldn't you rather work with animals than bust your butt waiting tables?"

He'd had a point. She hadn't been looking forward to spending another winter serving demanding customers and fending off drunken lechers. Before she'd had time to list all the reasons why she couldn't do it, Will had made the introductory phone call to his friend. Five days later, she was working for Connor Winston in a small town on the Colorado plains.

She hadn't planned on staying long, just until spring. But when the time came for her to move on to a ranch job near Durango, she couldn't leave. Her years in near perpetual motion had finally caught up with her. She was tired, and her small apartment in this down-on-its-luck town had started to feel like home.

Without planning to, Cassie stopped running. She was pushing forty, and Frank Peters be damned, she had found a home. She hadn't stopped worrying—she could never do that—but she no longer had the energy or desire to keep running.

Her regular trips to the county library kept her apprised of Frank's parole status. So far, so good. He was still locked away, and the trail to find her would be long, circuitous, and hopefully, impossible to follow.

~

Pepper, the effervescent office receptionist, was the first to greet Cassie when she stepped through the door of the clinic. "Hi, Cassie!" Pepper called as she put down the phone.

"Hey, Pepper," Cassie responded with a smile. She was genuinely fond of the young woman, although Pepper's sense of personal style took a bit of getting used to. Her hair color could best be described as an unnatural cross between Cabernet wine and Bazooka bubblegum and was definitely not a color normally found in nature. It was cut in a variety of lengths with the top shooting out in spiky angles. The hair style was an appropriate complement to her two nose piercings, the ring through her eyebrow, and the six earrings in each ear.

Eighteen-year-old Pepper had a heart of gold and a family life from hell—a father in jail, a mother who had yet to meet a truck driver she didn't like, and her own string of rough-around-the-edges boyfriends who invariably broke her heart. Somehow though, she always tried to make lemonade out of the bitter lemon that was her life. Cassie found it easy to forgive Pepper for her constant probing questions. There were even times when Cassie considered sharing something of her own life to help Pepper over a rough patch, but as soon as the thought occurred, she'd push it out of her mind. Her past was dead. It belonged to someone else.

"Mornin', Cassie." Agnes greeted her before adding a motherly scolding. "Where's your sweater? It might be sweltering out there, but it's like a fridge in here!"

Cassie smiled and shrugged in response to the question from the matronly woman who ran the office and mothered everyone. She'd had plenty of practice with her six children and three grandchildren—with two more on the way.

What a pair these two were, Cassie often thought. The conservative Mormon who'd never had so much as a drop of alcohol, and the wild teenager who didn't have much of a family, and was quite willing to share her sexual, alcoholic, and drug exploits with anyone willing to listen. Cassie loved and respected Agnes for the way she took Pepper under her wing. Agnes didn't preach, but rather shared her life by example, and often included young Pepper in her family events.

"Did you have a good weekend, Cassie?" Pepper asked. "Glen and I went dirt biking up in the hills on the way to Estes Park. It was really fun. Then we partied with some of his friends. They're all older than me, and a couple of the guys were a little scary, but it was still fun. What did you do?"

"Just the usual Pepper, nothing fun or exciting." Cassie leaned on the counter to share her story. "I worked with a couple of new horses at the Rescue Ranch. They were saved from a truly awful situation." She shook her head recalling the story Lynne had shared about the pitiful conditions at the abandoned ranch where they'd been found without any food or access to water. "It never ceases to amaze me how some of these rescued horses still have the capacity to trust."

Cassie sighed and continued in a more upbeat tone. "These two, a pretty, sorrel quarter-horse mare with a white snippet on her face, and an older bay gelding with a kind eye, will have a chance now. Hopefully, after some care and feeding, they'll go to a good home." She stepped away from the reception counter. "Well, Doc's not paying me to chat. I'd best get to work."

She opened the door into the examining room, escaping into the world she loved best, then continued on into the kennel area to check on the two dogs that had been recuperating over the weekend.

"Hi guys." She reached into their cages to pet each of them. They wriggled and wagged their tails in response. Cassie's way with animals wasn't exclusive to horses. No matter the species or breed, she had never met one she couldn't get through to—although some took longer than others.

The door opened. A slender man a couple of years older than Cassie, with sand-colored hair, sensitive dark brown eyes, and a thousand-watt smile walked in. He was chuckling. "Mornin', Cassie. You know, you might consider throwing Pepper a bone once in a while about your weekend adventures, even if you have to make something up." His eyes were sparkling as if laughing at some private joke.

"Mornin' Doc." Cassie responded, not bothering to comment on Pepper's musing about her weekend.

When he responded to her greeting with a raised eyebrow, she spoke again. "Mornin' Connor," she said, emphasizing his name. "How many times do I have to explain that it's more professional if I let the world know you're the doctor? You never know, someone might get confused and think it's me!" She laughed.

Connor shook his head. "Don't laugh. You may not have a vet degree, but I swear you know at least as much as I do. And when it comes to understanding our four-legged friends, well, you're way ahead of me in that category."

He rolled his eyes and breathed out a sigh that Cassie recognized as exasperation. "Good job, Cassie. This time you got me to change the subject without a whole lot of effort. I was saying that it might be nice if once in a while you shared just a wee bit of a weekend story with Pepper and Agnes—well, Pepper really. I walked in on her wild musings about how you probably do all kinds of exciting things on the weekend and are afraid to tell us about them."

"Hmmm." Cassie scrunched up her face as if in deep thought. "You think she could handle it if I told her I danced in a strip club in Denver on Saturday nights?" She let loose with a wicked laugh. "Nah, not even Pepper would go for that flight of fancy from an old lady like me. Maybe…how about…roller derby! That's it, I'll regale her with my roller derby stories!"

She'd worked hard to perfect the art of joking to avoid revealing too much of herself. Even after almost two years working with Connor five days a week, plus the occasional evening emergency, she'd shared little about her past beyond idle musings and funny stories about her ranching adventures.

She often assumed the role of mirror, reflecting light back onto the people she spent time with. She asked questions and deftly turned the conversation back around when it turned to her. Since most people liked to talk about themselves, it was actually quite easy to do.

Connor laughed and shook his head in obvious resignation, reminding Cassie of why she was so grateful for his friendship. He never pried. He never pushed beyond the boundaries she'd set for letting people in. Even when he'd witnessed one of her rare flashbacks, he hadn't pushed for answers.

Cassie's mind slipped back in time to an afternoon months earlier when she and Connor were having lunch at the small restaurant a few doors down from the clinic. An obviously drunk man had staggered in and begun shouting and cursing at the woman sitting at the next table. Cassie had watched as the woman shrank back in obvious terror, her haunted expression reflecting both fear and resignation.

Caught up in the woman's fear, feeling it as her own, Cassie had begun to shake, allowing her fork to slip through her fingers. When the fork hit the tiled floor, the sound snapped her back to the present. Embarrassed, she'd shrugged and attempted a quick smile at Connor, but she hadn't fooled him. His concerned expression made it clear that he'd seen the terror on her face.

The uncomfortable silence that followed provided an opportunity for her to explain, but instead, she'd let the silence build. After a long moment, Connor nodded toward the door as his friend Donnie Smith, the burly local police chief, entered. "Donnie's here. He'll take care of that asshole." After glancing down at his watch, he'd added, "We should head back to work. Next appointment's in ten minutes."

He had never asked her to explain.

~

"Cassie?" Connor's voice was a gentle reproach. She'd let her mind wander and had no idea what he'd asked her.

He was examining an energetic, mixed-breed dog, one of the two that had spent the weekend.

"Hmm? I'm sorry, I guess I got lost for a while. What were you saying?"

"Can you have Agnes call Frisky's owners and tell them they can pick him up this afternoon? This big boy is healing well."

"Sure. I'll tell her. Little Davey will be thrilled." She smiled, remembering how inconsolable the child had been when Connor had explained that his dog had to stay in the hospital.

As always, the rest of the day flew by. Cassie and Connor had a comfortable routine that required little conversation. When he needed a needle, she had it ready. When he was looking for a vaccine, she was handing it to him.

They were getting ready to close for the night when Pepper made her surprise announcement.

"Since it's Cassie's birthday in two weeks, why don't we all celebrate at the Frontier Days' rodeo on Friday night?"

Cassie's breath hitched in her throat, and she forced herself to swallow the lump that had lodged there. She fought to keep her voice level and controlled when she responded. "Pepper, how did you know it was my birthday?"

"I'm sorry, Cassie." Pepper answered in a whiny, conciliatory voice. "You had your wallet out the other day to pay for the pizza. It was just lying there with your license showing and everything, and since you've never wanted to tell us your birthday, I just had to look. Please don't be mad. Please?"

Cassie took a deep breath. Pepper was just a kid, a crazy kid with a warm heart. "It's okay, Pepper." She exhaled and shrugged. "I'm not too fond of celebrating birthdays though."

She couldn't explain that Cassie Deahl's birthday—six months later than her actual date of birth—was a fiction supported by a birth certificate created by Doc Waldron's Mafia friends many years earlier.

"Yeah, but you're always a good sport about celebrating the rest of our birthdays. It's about time we did something for you." Pepper turned to the others for support. "Don't you agree, Doc? Agnes?"

When Connor weighed in, Cassie knew she was beat. "You know Cassie, I think there's some kind of law that everyone in this part of Colorado has to go to a Frontier Days rodeo at least once every two years, and your time is almost up. Pepper's only trying to keep you out of trouble with the law."

Cassie shook her head in defeat, taking in the expectant expression on each of their faces. "You're all going to gang up on me aren't you? What about you, Agnes? Are you up for this adventure?"

"I don't remember the last time I went somewhere without the kids or the grandkids. Lord knows I love them to pieces, but it would be fun for

Grandma to kick up her heels a bit. You'd be doing me a favor if you'd agree to let us take you out for your birthday."

Cassie smiled at Agnes's attempt to turn the event into a favor for her. "Okay! Okay, you win. I'll go."

Three grinning faces stared back at her. She fought back the tears. *God, how I love these people.*

"No cakes, no balloons, no telling anyone it's my birthday. Deal, Pepper?"

"Deal, Cassie! Thanks, I love you!"

When Pepper threw her arms around her, Cassie instinctively flinched before she returned the hug. Embarrassed, she glanced over at Connor to see if he'd noticed her response. If he had, he gave no indication. He just smiled, raised his eyebrows, and shrugged. They were all used to Pepper's exuberance.

~

They made their way through a festive crowd on a warm Friday evening, the air redolent with a unique mixture of odors combining animal sweat, manure, fried food, and popcorn. Cassie gestured at the throngs of people surrounding them. "Look at the crowds! I can't believe you guys talked me into coming here on the busiest night."

"We had to do something for your birthday, now that we actually know when it is!" Pepper responded. "Frontier Days is perfect, considering you used to be a cowboy...or is it a cowgirl?"

Cassie laughed at the expression on Pepper's face as her young friend tried to puzzle this out. "That's a question I once debated with someone..." She hesitated, "with a good friend. We never did come to a satisfactory answer. I worked as hard as the cowboys, so if that title comes with more clout, I'll take it."

"Something tells me you probably worked harder. You always work harder," Connor said with a grin.

"Amen to that!" Agnes agreed.

Cassie smiled at the three of them. They were the closest thing to family she'd had in a very long time, since John and Jean had embraced her—and she'd hurt them by disappearing from their lives. "Thanks, guys.

Now before you get me all emotional, are we going to watch some rodeo or what?"

"Looks like there are some good seats over there." Pepper pointed to a small area on the bleachers with just enough open space for the four of them.

Cassie nodded her agreement. "If I'm going to settle in for a while, I've definitely got to hit the ladies room first. How about you grab the seats, and I'll catch up with you?"

Lost in thought, she waited on line for the restroom, remembering that long ago discussion about cowboys and cowgirls. When she'd agreed to come to Frontier Days for her birthday, she hadn't made the connection to Cheyenne. Maybe it was because they hadn't actually focused on the 'Cheyenne' part of Cheyenne Frontier Days when they talked about it. Or, maybe she'd purposely pushed the name of the town out of her mind, like she did so many other things that were too difficult to think about.

Now, here she was, three years later…

"Excuse me, Ma'am. Are you waiting for the toilet?" The woman behind her pointed to the empty stall.

"Oh, yeah. Sorry." She pushed thoughts of the past away.

∼

"Cassie! Over here!"

When Cassie turned to follow Pepper's voice, she caught the eye of a man who had also turned in reaction to Pepper's shouting. Their gazes locked. Then he turned away.

Oh my, God!

Cassie's heart took an extra second to find its rhythm. Everything around her faded into the background. She stared at the cowboy's back startled by the tension she'd seen in his steel gray eyes. Then she saw an earlier version—eyes filled with concern, passion, caring, and sadness. How could it be? It was almost as if by thinking about him, she had conjured Cliff up out of thin air.

She waved to Pepper to indicate that she'd heard her, then she took a deep breath, squared her shoulders, and made her way down the steps and through the crowd. She didn't give herself time to process the surprised and then guarded, almost angry, expression she'd seen on Cliff's face—or to wonder why he had turned away.

"Hi Cliff."

"Cass." His acknowledgment was stiff and abrupt. She could see tightness in his jaw.

"It's been a long time..." The words were lame and cliché, but they were the best she could come up with.

When she touched his arm, he turned with a cool, almost cold, expression and a curt response. "Yes, it has."

Hurt by the tone in his voice, her smile faded. Confused, she stared up at him, hoping for an explanation.

His expression softened. He shook his head, and she thought she saw the trace of a smile. His rugged face was still tanned and handsome, but his skin looked more weathered than she remembered. She fought an urge to brush a strand of his now gray-streaked hair out of his eyes.

"What do you want, Cassie? Small talk?" His voice was soft, but his eyes were watchful and wary.

She turned away from eyes that always saw too much, and now she understood his wariness. She'd hurt him. That slip of paper he'd handed her that night three years earlier contained more than just his name and address. He'd offered her something, or at least the chance at something. She'd known it then, and she'd run from it.

She stared into the empty rodeo arena while she gathered her thoughts and spoke in a measured voice while grasping the fence in front of her for support. "I left the next morning. I wanted to put as much geography between us as possible. I was scared. You got through my armor. No one had ever managed to do that before. I spent more than ten years perfecting that armor and filling in all the chinks, but you got through."

She turned to face him. The wariness was gone from his eyes and in its place was resignation and sadness. She continued. "I wrote you letters."

"Oh?"

"I never mailed them. At first, they were silly, chatty letters about Jackson Hole. They didn't seem worthwhile to send. The ones I wrote after I'd had a couple of drinks were more honest, so I definitely couldn't send those..." She shrugged and half-smiled up at him. "You see my dilemma?"

He nodded, his expression indicating that he actually did understand.

"You look good, Cassie. More settled, less worried." He glanced over at her friends. "Finally stopped runnin'?"

"Yeah, at least for now. You were right about that. You were right about a lot of things, but definitely about that. After a while, I just couldn't do it anymore. I'm still looking over my shoulder, but not as often. I've been in Jamestown, a small town about ninety minutes or so south of here, for the last three years. I work for a vet clinic and volunteer at the local horse rescue."

"Happy?"

"I'm not unhappy. That's something."

She touched his arm again, knowing this time he wouldn't pull away. "What about you, Cliff? How are you doing?"

"About the same."

His gaze shifted, and Cassie turned to see Pepper approaching, her eyes wide and full of questions. Cassie glanced up to their seats. Connor acknowledged her glance by shrugging as if to say, 'I tried.'

Cassie wasn't surprised to see her young friend. She was sure Pepper's fertile mind was reeling with all the possible scenarios involving 'Cassie and the cowboy'.

"Hey Cassie, I'm going to get some snacks. Do you want anything?"

"No thanks, Pepper. I'm fine. This is Cliff, a friend, a good friend, of mine. We used to work together," she smiled back at Cliff, "a long time ago in Montana."

"Cliff, this is Pepper. We work together at the clinic. She keeps the place running and keeps us all on our toes."

"Wow! Cassie, so you really do have a past?" Pepper shook Cliff's hand. He had an amused expression on his face, watching Pepper as she continued on in a rush. "We were just about convinced Cassie either landed from an alien space ship or was in the witness protection program. Did you wish her a Happy Birthday? We came tonight to celebrate. I won't tell you how old she is though. I have *some* manners! Not many, though! Well, I'd better get back before Doc has my head for bothering you. It was nice to meet you!"

Pepper disappeared as quickly as she'd arrived. Cliff chuckled as he watched her walk away. "An interesting girl."

"Yeah." Cassie nodded. "But there's a heart of gold under that 'interesting' exterior."

"Happy Birthday, Cass." He was facing her now. "Can I be rude enough to ask just how many birthdays you've had so far?"

She acknowledged the birthday wishes with a whispered, "Thanks," and then continued, "I made the mistake of leaving my wallet open. The little twerp snuck a look at my license."

Cliff didn't respond, making it clear he was still waiting for an answer to his question.

"Hell, Cliff. Sometimes I feel like I'm eighty, but last time I looked, my license said I was thirty-nine. My turn, what does your license say?"

"Cassie, if you feel like eighty I've got you beat by at least forty years. My license however would tell you I'm forty-eight. Old enough to know where I've made my mistakes, and young enough to know I'll probably make more."

His eyes were serious now, and Cassie didn't know if he considered her to be one of those mistakes. She couldn't ask. "Are you still living here in town?"

"Nope. About a year ago I bought a place about five miles east of here. It's not very big, just a small house on a couple acres. Got a couple horses to keep me company."

"It sounds wonderful, Cliff. Now I'm the one with the apartment over the store. Not sure if I'll ever be able to afford much more. It's nice to have a place to call my own, though. I've even started accumulating stuff. It's amazing how easy that is to do when you have a place to put it."

She laughed, thinking of all the years her belongings fit in the back of her truck, and she lived the life of a gypsy. "Do you still work here?"

"Yeah, especially for big events like this when there's a lot of stock. I also work with some local folks bringing their young horses along."

In acknowledgment of her confused expression, he said, "You're right. Neither of those jobs would pay for a house, but they add up. I do a bit of whittlin', too."

He hesitated for a moment, then continued. "You probably don't remember, but I used to have a work table in the corner of my bedroom..."

Cassie's thoughts took her back to that night. It was an easy trip. She'd replayed it a thousand times in her mind. In the corner of his bedroom, she'd noticed a table that held an array of carving tools. She'd also seen a block of dark wood where a partially completed, incredibly detailed and stunningly realistic head of an Arabian stallion was emerging.

"I remember—the Arabian stallion. At least I assumed it was an Arabian stallion. It was gorgeous. I wanted…I wanted to ask…" She stopped. There were so many things that didn't get said, and so many questions that hadn't gotten asked that night. "That wasn't whittling, Cliff. You're an artist! Are you selling your work?"

His half smile showed his discomfort. "A local place in town sells some of it. The tourists seem to like it. What about you, Cass? What about your drawings?"

How does he know about my drawing?

Although she'd tried to temper her reaction, he reacted to the guarded, almost hostile expression in her eyes. "Whoa! I didn't snoop. You'd go off by yourself when the guys were playin' cards or swappin' stories. You'd sit out by the corral lost in your own world until the light was gone, and you'd sketch. You always seemed to have a 'Do Not Disturb' sign around your neck. It was obviously a private time…"

He paused, waiting for her response.

She relaxed, annoyed with herself for over-reacting. "It's always been my dream, Cliff. I still work at it. For years, I sketched everything I saw. Sometimes in little notebooks, or on scraps of paper if that was all I had. It was like…" She paused, but she knew he'd understand.

She continued softly. "It was like therapy. I still have most of my sketches. I use them to help me remember, to recapture what I saw. It's amazing how quickly I can go back and see the colors in my mind, even though I'm looking at a black and white sketch. I've started painting the scenes. Mostly water color for now. I've thought about trying to sell the pictures, maybe in Boulder. I don't know. Maybe someday." She shrugged.

They had run out of small talk. The PA system crackled, and the announcer welcomed everyone to the night's events.

"Well, I guess I'd better get back to my friends. It was good to see you, Cliff."

"You too, Cass. You take care."

They held each other's gaze for a moment longer, and then Cassie turned and began to walk away. She knew he'd let her go. He wouldn't make the first move. He'd gone out on that limb once, and she had left him hanging there alone.

She stopped. After a moment's hesitation, she rummaged into her purse and found a pen. She ripped her rodeo ticket in half and wrote her phone number on the back.

Cliff was standing along the fence line, his attention focused on the bull rider in the arena. She touched his arm. He swiveled his head to see who was bothering him, his irritable expression changing to one of surprise when he saw her.

Cassie held out the ticket stub. He took it without comment. "I know it's been a long time Cliff, and we can never go back, but you're the only past I've got. If I'm truly going to stop running, it would be nice to have a friend to reminisce with. I'll understand if you don't call, but if you ever…" She shrugged not knowing what else to say. It was up to him now. She turned and once again began to pick her way through the crowd.

"Cass?"

She stopped and turned back.

"I'll call." He held up the ticket and nodded, his facial expression neutral. She was too far away to see his eyes.

She swallowed the lump in her throat and returned his nod. As she walked away, she heard his voice call above the din. "So which is it, anyway?"

She spun back around. "Which what?"

"Alien or witness protection?"

"Alien, of course! If anyone should know that, it's you, Cliff."

The sound of his rich throaty laugh followed her as she joined her friends to celebrate Cassie Deahl's birthday.

20

JAMESTOWN, CO – CHEYENNE, WY

Totally absorbed in a frustrating, and as yet unsuccessful, attempt to recreate her memory of the sun setting over a craggy Montana canyon, Cassie was startled by her ringing phone. The paint brush sailed from her hand. With a muttered curse, she bent down to snatch the brush from the floor, ignoring the smudge of red paint on the wood.

Her phone rarely rang, especially on a Sunday afternoon. A jumble of questions crowded out thoughts about color and sunsets. Was everything okay at the Rescue Ranch? Was one of the horses hurt? Connor had said he didn't need her help with the two new horses, but maybe she should have insisted on helping. What if he'd been hurt?

"Hello?" she answered in a tentative voice, not able to calm the fluttery feeling in the pit of her stomach.

"Cassie?"

The butterflies settled themselves. "Hi Cliff." She grinned, recognizing his voice even from that one word. Leaving the paint brush on the edge of the table, she carried the phone to the couch and sank down onto the cushions. "I'm glad you called. How are you?"

"Fine. I don't much like phones."

"Actually, I'm kind of surprised you even own one." An image came to mind of Cliff perched nervously on the edge of a chair, the phone clutched tightly in his hand while he struggled to figure out what to say.

"I think it's expected. Don't use it much though. Usually don't bother answerin' it."

"I'll have to remember that, if you ever give me your phone number. I didn't do so good with it last time."

"Forget it, Cass. That was a long time ago."

"Thanks," she said, and meant it. "I'm glad you called. I wasn't sure you would. I wouldn't have blamed you."

"I thought about what you said. You're the only past I have, too. Maybe it's not an accident, you know? That we seem to end up in the same place." He paused. There was silence on the line, and then he continued. "It's just…"

She finished the thought for him, certain he shared her own concerns. "I'd be happy if we could just be friends, Cliff."

"I'd like that too." His voice didn't sound as tentative. "This telephone stuff ain't so bad after all."

"Does that mean you'll call me again?" She swallowed back the lump in her throat, surprised at how much she wanted him to say yes.

"I think telephone etiquette requires you call me back first," he answered in a comical attempt at an upper-crust British accent.

Cassie giggled at Cliff's unexpected humor. "For someone who's only recently discovered the wonders of the telephone, you're suddenly an expert on telephone etiquette?" She laughed out loud, happy that Cliff was back in her life. "You haven't even given me your phone number."

"Do you have a pencil? You need to read the number back to me, too. Don't want to take any chances you'll forget it."

Cassie's laughter was gone. "Not to worry, Cliff. I'm not used to getting second chances."

That was the first of what became a cherished weekly event for Cassie. She and Cliff spoke every Sunday evening—a time when she imagined families sat together to enjoy a quiet close to the weekend. Although they never spoke of it, there was a Sunday sadness that Cassie felt, that she was pretty sure Cliff felt as well. An unexplained sadness probably not foreign to other lost and lonely people. Kris Kristofferson had even written a song about it, evoking emotion that never failed to bring tears to eyes when she heard it. When she said good night to Cliff at the end of their calls, Cassie held tight to the emotional connection that helped her deal with her demons. She wondered if it helped Cliff deal with his demons, too.

Young Pepper had started teasing her, especially on Monday mornings. "Wow, Cassie, how come you're so much happier than you used to be?

Why don't you ever tell us about your fun weekends?" Agnes never commented. She always just smiled indulgently, apparently happy for Cassie without needing to know why. Cassie never offered an explanation, certain they'd both be surprised to learn that her weekends hadn't really changed at all—other than for the simple addition of a phone call from a friend.

~

When her phone rang on a Wednesday evening a few weeks later, Cassie's heart skipped a beat. It wasn't Sunday. No one called her just to chat. Her hand shook as she reached for the phone.

"Hello?"

"Cass, it's Cliff."

"Is everything okay? Are you okay?" She didn't bother to hide the concern in her voice.

"I'm fine, Cass. Nothing to worry about," he assured her. "I wanted to ask a favor, and Sunday's too late."

Her interest piqued, Cassie responded without thought. "Sure. Whatever you need."

"It's a big favor, Cass. You may want to hear what it is before you jump in and agree."

Cassie's interest turned to apprehension. "What is it, Cliff? What's wrong?"

"Nothing's wrong." His voice was upbeat. "I wanted to share some good news. You know that horse head I was carvin'—the one you saw in my room?"

"Yes. I remember."

"It's been in a gift shop gallery place for a while. They sold it this week. Cass, I can't believe it. They sold it for thirty five hundred dollars! Seems like a lot of money to me, but I guess some folks are willin' to pay a lot for somethin' pretty."

"Cliff, that's wonderful! Congratulations!"

"Thanks. There's a catch though."

The hesitation in his voice tempered Cassie's enthusiasm. She waited in silence for him to continue.

"The people who bought it want to have dinner with the 'cowboy artist'." He stressed the last two words with a degree of sarcasm. "The shop owner said she'd arrange it."

"Oh." Now, she understood. She would be panicking, too. Strangers, especially tourists, meant questions. Personal questions she was certain Cliff would not want to answer.

"Yeah. Cass, I don't think I can do it."

"Sure you can, Cliff." Cassie responded with an enthusiasm she didn't feel. "It's only dinner. They'll probably do all the talking, and you can be the mysterious cowboy."

Her statement was met with silence.

Finally, Cliff spoke. "I know it's a lot to ask, but do you think…would you come with me?"

Cassie's heart raced. She searched for a reason to say no, but her mind was blank.

He took her prolonged silence as an answer. "I'm sorry, Cass. Forget I asked."

He's the most important person in my life. How can I let him down? Besides, they won't be interested in me, will they?

After lifting the bottom of her tee shirt to wipe the newly beaded sweat off her face, she attempted an upbeat tone in her response. "Of course I'll come with you, Cliff. We'll look at it as a free night out on the town. Kind of like our own masquerade ball."

"Are you sure?" He sounded relieved.

"Sometimes taking a chance is the only way to move forward." Her words were meant to convince herself as much as him.

"They're from out of town. They want to have dinner this Saturday. Can you get away? It'll be a late night. I've got a spare room. You could stay at my place if it's too late to drive back."

Cassie nodded to herself as she worked out the details. "I work until noon this Saturday. If I leave right after work, I can be at your house by mid-afternoon. It will be good to see you again, Cliff. I can't believe it's been almost three months since we saw each other at the rodeo."

The next morning, Cassie woke feeling out of sorts and unrested. After not having had a nightmare in over a year, she recalled bits and pieces of the frightening dream that had ruined her sleep. Her subconscious hadn't been fooled by her upbeat comments to Cliff.

Later that morning, she surprised herself by blurting out one of her simpler concerns to Connor. "My friend Cliff—you remember, the cowboy I ran into at the rodeo?" She didn't wait for his response. "He's having an important dinner with some folks in Cheyenne on Saturday, and he invited me, kind of as moral support. I promised him I'd go." She gestured to the jeans and tee shirt she was wearing under her lab coat. "Connor, this is pretty much it for me. I don't want to embarrass him, and I don't have anything nice to wear."

Connor stepped back, nodding as he took in her outfit. Then he gestured to his own. "Pretty much standard fare for our line of work, but not for a fancy restaurant. Easily fixed though. Take the afternoon off and go to the mall in Longmont. You're sure to find something there."

She opened her mouth, planning to argue, but not actually knowing why.

"No arguing," he announced, seeing the set of her jaw. "You're the one who said you don't want to embarrass him. Go and buy something nice—unless you want to waltz into the restaurant in faded jeans and beat-up cowboy boots."

∼

Four hours later, she was standing in the ladies department in an upscale department store, feeling like a tourist in a foreign country. Her worn jeans, scuffed boots, and battered leather jacket were definitely out of place.

Her frustration mounted as she idly rifled through the dress rack with no idea of what she was looking for. Just as she was about to turn tail and run, a friendly female voice called out to her "You remind me of my daughter. She wouldn't be caught dead shopping for dressy clothes. How can I help?" A silver-haired woman wearing a stylish black dress and a broad welcoming smile walked up to her. "I promise to make it as painless as possible. What do you need?"

True to her word, the saleslady helped her find a beautiful dress—on sale. She even walked her to the shoe department and suggested suitable pumps and a purse.

Cassie, not usually effusive or demonstrative, fought a desire to hug her. "Thank you," she said with sincere appreciation. "You've been a lifesaver. This," she pointed at her jeans and jacket, "is pretty much all I ever wear. I didn't even know where to start."

Feeling proud of herself, Cassie wandered further into the mall, shopping bags in hand. She paused in front of a hair salon and entered on a whim. She'd been cutting her own hair for years, lopping off a couple of inches whenever the length annoyed her. Most of the time, she wore her hair pulled back in a pony-tail. She'd never once thought about having it professionally styled.

The salon staff welcomed her with what seemed like genuine warmth, and Cassie forgot her initial awkwardness. Connie, the young woman who cut her hair, chatted away about her horse and her little girl, in that order. Before Cassie had time to process the idea of it, Connie had cut three inches off the back and layered the front so the hair framed her face and softly flowed from her chin down to just above her breasts.

Cassie shook her head in disbelief when she looked in the mirror and saw the woman staring back at her. Her heart shaped face and deep-set blue eyes were now softly framed by attractively-styled, silky blonde hair. She didn't actually believe the women in the salon when they said she looked like a model, but their comments went a long way toward bolstering her confidence.

On her drive home, she mentally prepared herself for the comments she was sure to hear from the clinic staff—especially Pepper. She fought back a groan, picturing Pepper's face and imagining her reaction. Then she blew out a breath and sighed. *Oh well. Suck it up.*

Pepper's actual reaction was as expected, and then some. "Oh my God! Cassie, you look beautiful! I wish Agnes didn't have off on Saturdays. Wait till I tell her! Wow!" Thoroughly embarrassed, grateful the young woman hadn't seen her in the fancy dress she'd bought, and having no intention of stoking the girl's fertile imagination with information about her planned dinner with Cliff, Cassie thanked her and hurried into the office.

Connor had obviously heard Pepper's effusive comments. He smiled and added his own, more subdued reaction. "I see you did more than just shop for a dress. Pepper's right, Cassie. You look great. You'll impress the hell out of Cliff's friends." That said, he focused on business. "So, who's our first patient?"

Instead of finishing work at noon, a clinic emergency kept Cassie busy until mid-afternoon. She rushed home and dressed quickly, but left time to check herself out in the full-length mirror hanging on her closet door. The scooped neck, long-sleeved, blue dress gathered slightly under her breasts and flowed out in an A-line, ending just below her knees. The black, high-heeled pumps flattered her long legs, although she was still unsure how she was going to actually walk in them.

The friendly salon manager had somehow prized out the reason for Cassie's trip to the mall. With that knowledge, the woman convinced Cassie that even if she didn't want to invest in an array of make-up products, she at least needed a bit of mascara and some lip gloss and blusher. Feeling a bit like Cinderella or, more appropriately, Alice in Wonderland, Cassie had acquiesced. Now, she stared at a woman she truly didn't recognize. Perfectly styled hair framed a face accentuated by a hint of blush. Long dark lashes showed off eyes turned a vivid blue thanks to the color of her dress, and gold hoop earrings and the simple gold choker necklace recommended by the Dillard's saleswoman completed the picture.

Pleased, but more than a little self-conscious about her new look, Cassie stepped away from the mirror for a quick call to tell Cliff she was on her way. Then, with her overnight bag in her hand and a winter coat over her arm, she hustled out to her truck—as best she could in her dressy pumps. On a sunny fall afternoon, she had an easy ninety-minute drive ahead of her, a straight run up I-25 through the outskirts of Fort Collins then over the border into Wyoming. She sang along with the radio, feeling happier than she'd felt in a very long time.

Exactly one hour and fifteen minutes after leaving home, she pulled into the driveway of a tidy, older bungalow with a distinctive field-stone chimney. A couple of rough-hewn rocking chairs sat on a small front porch, overlooking a neatly mowed yard. She stopped the truck next to the house, although the driveway continued, ending at a small barn with brown siding that matched the house. The entire back yard was fenced with split rail and, as if they were assigned welcoming committee duty, two horses stood facing the driveway. The attractive sorrel with an off-center white blaze and an alert-eyed palomino both whinnied as Cassie got out of the truck.

"Hi guys! Aren't you beauties? Thanks for the welcome."

Cassie grabbed her overnight bag and arrived at the front door just as Cliff opened it.

He smiled. "I heard the boys saying hello…" He stopped speaking. He stared, his mouth open and his eyes wide with surprise.

Cassie blushed under his gaze. "Cliff? Umm. Can I come in?"

He blinked a couple of times, whistling under his breath. "Yeah. Sure, of course. I'm sorry. Of course. Come in."

Cassie let out a self-conscious laugh as she followed him into the house and dropped her overnight bag on the floor. "It's me, Cliff. You know, the same ole Cassie who rounded up cows with you, drank your horrible black coffee, and slept on the hard ground."

"I always thought you were beautiful Cass, but …" Cliff shook his head, his expression hard to read, words apparently failing him.

While Cliff shuffled his feet and seemed to search for something to say, Cassie took her own inventory. The man who stood before her bore little resemblance to the rangy cowboy she knew. Gone was the days-old beard, beat-up jeans, scuffed boots, and hair in need of a trim.

The gentleman in front of her wore a crisp, white western shirt with black piping, black dress pants, and fancy, snakeskin cowboy boots. The gray streaks in his brown hair were minimized by a layered, professional cut that left his hair just long enough to run his hands through, while still looking styled. The rugged planes of his smoothly shaved face had softened, and his steel gray eyes were clear and deep.

She let out a low appreciative whistle. "Wow! You clean up pretty good yourself. Aren't you going to give your oldest friend a hug?" She stepped forward.

His hug was tentative at first, as if he was afraid to wrinkle her dress.

"I won't break, Cliff. And hell, it's only a dress."

They both laughed at the sudden awkwardness between them.

"You look great, Cass. It means a lot to me that you agreed to come to the dinner with me tonight."

She kissed him on the cheek in response. "Thanks. Now why don't you show me around and introduce me to the boys?"

Cassie was impressed with the comfortable home Cliff had created. The main room, a combination living room-dining room, took up the entire front of the house. A brown leather sofa and recliner were flanked by rustic end tables, and a matching coffee table was placed on a colorful Navajo area rug in front of a large stone fireplace. A lamp stood behind the recliner to provide light for Cliff to read the books that filled the two floor-to-ceiling bookcases on either side of the fireplace. A portable television was on a stand in a corner.

The small kitchen was simple and utilitarian. Everything was clean and in its place. Across from the kitchen was a small guest bedroom and an immaculate bathroom. The master bedroom ran the length of the back of the house. A noticeable, but not unpleasant, scent of oil permeated the air. A dark pine bedroom set took up half the room, its double bed neatly made and covered with a colorful, old-fashioned crazy quilt.

The other half of the room was devoted to Cliff's tidy studio, which explained the rich scent of oil. On a long wooden work table, Cassie saw a variety of carving tools and small saws. An array of animal figures were arranged on shelves behind the table. Cliff's current work, a mare and foal standing under a tree, looked half finished.

She gazed at his creations in wonder, then turned to face him. "Cliff, how do you do it? It's like you make the wood come alive."

Caught unawares, obviously not paying close attention since he was still staring at her, Cliff responded with a barely audible, "Hmmm?" Then he refocused and turned to face the work table. "Thanks. Like you said about your sketchin', it's good therapy. It's hard to explain, but when I start workin' with a piece of wood, it's like the animals are already in there, and it's my job to help them get out."

He shrugged dismissively. "That must sound crazy."

"No. It doesn't sound crazy at all."

She turned back to examine the carving of a doe with a fawn at her side and marveled at Cliff's ability to somehow show the maternal softness and protective alertness of the doe.

Cliff coughed and shuffled his feet. "We should probably leave. I want to show you the place where they're sellin' my stuff. It's near the restaurant. They close early on Saturday, but you can see a lot through the window. I'll introduce you to the boys in the mornin'. I'd never forgive myself if Clyde snorted all over your pretty dress."

Cassie smiled knowingly at his comment and nodded her assent. She was surprised when he helped her into her coat, held the door open, and then assisted her into his truck. Other than a murmured "thanks", she was too shocked to comment at his unexpected behavior. It seemed that wearing a dress sure changed things.

After settling herself in and putting on her seat belt, she asked, "What do you know about the couple we're having dinner with? I'm terrible at remembering people's names, so I'm hoping I can repeat them in my mind enough times so I won't embarrass you."

Cliff answered as he backed the truck out of the driveway. "I think Anna said they're Doctor Richard Miles and his wife, Dorothy. They're from the East Coast. New York, I think."

Cassie sucked in her breath. A tight vise squeezed her chest, and she recoiled as if she'd been punched in the stomach. New York? She had never stopped to consider where the couple might be from. *How could I be so stupid?* They wanted to meet a real cowboy, for Pete's sake! Of course they'd be from someplace like New York.

"Cass? Cassie?"

The truck stopped. She felt Cliff's hand on her arm. "Cassie, what's wrong?"

She struggled to control her racing heart as an internal argument raged in her mind. There were eight million people in New York City alone. God only knew how many more lived in the suburbs and upstate. Just because it was near New Jersey—besides, it had been more than fifteen years.

She closed her eyes and willed herself to find the warm peaceful center that years of yoga and deep breathing exercises had helped her develop. When she opened her eyes, the frantic out-of-control feeling was gone. Clear-eyed, she turned back to Cliff. "I'm sorry. I'm okay now."

He stroked her hair. "I'm sorry Cass. The name, or the place?"

"How could you know, Cliff? We don't have pasts, remember?" There was a trace of bitterness in her voice as she continued. "The place. A bit too close for comfort, but I'm okay now."

"Are you sure? We don't have to go. I can call and say…"

"Hey," she exclaimed in mock indignation, trying to make light of her initial reaction. "You promised me a dinner, and I got all dressed up and everything!"

He chuckled. "Oh, yeah, that's right, and I forgot you can whup my ass. We'd best get movin' then." He squeezed her hand, put the truck in gear, and drove into town.

The restaurant, appropriately named the Frontier, was the most expensive in Cheyenne. Cliff parked the truck in the lot behind the restaurant and helped Cassie out. "Sorry, never got around to buyin' runnin' boards. Don't get many cowboys with dresses and high-heeled shoes," he teased.

He ducked when she swatted at him.

The gallery that carried Cliff's work was only a short walk from the restaurant. Cassie stumbled—idly wondering how anyone walked on those tall spikey heels if she could barely handle chunky two inch ones—and was grateful for the arm Cliff offered.

"Geez, Cliff!" An impressive array of paintings, sculptures, ceramics, and basketry were within view through the window of Gallery Azteca. "This is a big-time gallery. You made it sound like it was a souvenir shop."

She shook her head as she stared up at him. His humility was one of his many endearing qualities. "There must be a story here. Why do I get the feeling you would gladly have kept creating those incredible works of art and never even attempted to sell them. Unless someone came to you first? But how would they know? How did they find you?"

He had a shy half smile on his face when he answered. "One of the guys I work with saw my stuff when he came by to watch a Broncos game. His aunt, Anna Alvarez, owns the place. He insisted I let her come over and look at my stuff." He shrugged, but she could see a hint of pride in his eyes.

Cassie smiled. "I'm glad she found you, Cliff, and I'm glad people will get to enjoy your sculpture—or 'whittlin' as you so humbly call it."

They arrived at the restaurant promptly at seven, and the maître d' showed them to their table. The doctor, a distinguished looking silver-haired man, stood as they approached. He held out his hand to Cliff.

"Mr. Douglas, I'm glad you could join us this evening. My wife Dorothy and I love your work."

He motioned to a much younger woman who remained seated. Dorothy smiled while her husband continued speaking. "This is a real treat for us."

Cliff shook the doctor's hand. "Thank you, Doctor Miles. You can call me Cliff." He nodded to Mrs. Miles from across the table. "Ma'am."

He turned to Cassie. "This here's my friend, Cassie Deahl."

"It's a pleasure to meet you, Cassie. Please, both of you, call me Richard."

Cassie nodded and smiled at them, amused the doctor didn't offer to shake her hand.

The couple was openly curious about the life of a cowboy artist and even more so about Cassie's life in the saddle. They were noticeably surprised to hear that the woman sitting across from them had spent quite a bit of time chasing cows and training horses. Dorothy peppered Cassie with questions, and Cassie had enough stories to be able to select a few to entertain her.

As the evening progressed, she felt Cliff's leg press more closely against hers in the booth they shared. Perhaps it was the wine, or maybe Cliff's touch, but Cassie wasn't prepared when the questions came. Dorothy Miles' innocent and rapid-fire queries should have been easy to answer.

"So Cassie, did you grow up here in Wyoming, or do I detect a slight accent? I can't place it, though. Is your family in ranching? What does your mother think about your life on the range?"

Cliff squeezed her leg under the table. Cassie knew he wanted to help, that he was silently apologizing, but there didn't seem to be any opening for him.

She had been reaching for her wine glass when the barrage of questions began. Her abrupt reaction knocked over the glass. She stared in horror as the fragile, crystal spine snapped in two. Expensive, red wine splashed across the white table cloth, creating a Rorschach test. Cassie stared. Was it a flower, or a pool of blood?

"I'm...I'm sorry. I..." She stammered, feeling her face grow warm.

The doctor came to her rescue. "It's okay, Cassie. I've spilled more than my share of wine. Haven't I, Dottie?"

Within moments, the waiter had cleaned up the mess and spread a clean napkin over the stain. Dorothy was still waiting for an answer.

Cassie found her voice. She tried to make her words sound more solid than she felt. "No. My family's not in ranching. I just kind of got drawn to the wide open spaces. It doesn't hurt that I love horses either. Have you been to Montana yet? The Montana skies are indescribable. How about Jackson Hole? You wouldn't believe how different it is from Cheyenne. The Teton mountain range is spectacular."

She prattled on until Cliff picked up the thread. God bless you, Cassie thought as he deftly turned the conversation back to how the west was the inspiration for his work. That conversation carried them through dessert and coffee. They said their goodbyes at the front door. Cliff held her arm as they walked through the alley to the back parking lot.

When they were sure they were alone, he stopped and turned to her. "I'm sorry, Cass."

Cassie reached up and touched his face. She smiled in reaction to his concern. "It's okay, Cliff. It really is okay. I'm usually much quicker on the uptake. The wine had me a little off my game. I liked them. They're nice people. I'm glad you invited me."

She reached up and kissed him on the cheek. They walked the rest of the way to the truck in silence. He opened the door for her. She turned to ask him to help her up into the cab and was surprised when he backed away.

His voice was low, strained. "Maybe I should drop you off at a hotel in town." He stood a couple of feet away, his hands stiffly at his side.

"Cliff? Why? What's wrong?"

He stared down at the ground as if looking for inspiration from the pea gravel at his feet. Then he shook his head. When he looked up, his eyes were pained. "We said we'd be friends, Cass. If you come back to my house, I...I can't..."

"Oh, Cliff."

A silent question filled her mind. *Why couldn't I have found this wonderful, sensitive man when I was whole enough to be able to love him?*

"Cliff, look at me, please?" she asked in a soft voice. He gazed into her eyes as she continued. "I'll bet we've both broken a lot of rules over the years, and if there's some stupid rule that says two good friends can't also be lovers, I guess we'll have to break that one, too."

She sighed and continued, her words a whisper, "It's one of the few things I won't have nightmares about." She stepped forward and put her arms around him. "Take me home, Cliff. We are who we are, and if we can enjoy something good in our lives, don't we both deserve it? Tomorrow we can go back to just being friends."

She snuggled next to him on the short drive back to his house, and he took her in his arms as soon as he'd parked the truck. They kissed, each kiss deeper and more passionate than the last. When he banged his elbow on the steering wheel and muttered a curse, she giggled before asking, "You think we'd be more comfortable in the house?"

Moments later, they were in his bedroom. He unzipped her dress, and she let it slide to the floor. Her shoes had been abandoned by the front door, and now she wore just a bra, panties, and a pair of stockings.

Cassie helped him peel off his boots and pants, and they fell together on the bed. With only the light from the half-moon to see by, they gazed into each other's eyes lost for a moment in the wonder of their relationship.

"Cass..." He stroked her face. Until, with mutual urgency, they fumbled to remove the rest of their clothing. She reveled in the feel of his naked, muscled body against her own bare skin and wondered how two broken people could have found each other, could keep finding each other. And even though he'd never shared his past, she knew he was broken too. She could feel his pain—much as she was sure he could feel hers. Maybe they'd never be able to offer each other more than an occasional opportunity to become whole. At least for now, it was enough. This time, she didn't sob after she came back to earth—and she didn't run away. Instead, she sighed deeply, snuggled close, and fell asleep in Cliff's arms.

It was barely dawn when Cassie woke still wrapped in Cliff's arms. Foggy from the remnants of her wine hangover, she felt a moment of panic. Then the fog cleared. A sigh escaped from her throat as she recalled the night's adventures, and she snuggled closer against his warm, naked body.

She lifted her head off his chest when she felt his hand move on her back. "Good morning," she said dreamily when he opened his sleep-filled, dusky gray eyes. "I thought I was dreaming."

He brushed the hair off her face and his mouth found hers. Their lovemaking was lazy and languidly passionate, and when they fell back to sleep, they were still locked in each other's arms.

When next they woke, the sun was streaming in the windows. Through the open slats of the blinds, she could see the horses standing in their corral staring expectantly at the house. Cliff hugged her to him and whispered, "I don't want to let go. Wakin' up alone is going to be harder now." He kissed her, and the sensations he aroused left no room for her to think about his words.

Cliff's lips traveled to her neck. Then he sighed and pulled away. "Don't move," he ordered. "I need to run out and throw the boys some hay and give them their breakfast. I'll be right back."

"Hmmm." Cassie murmured and closed her eyes. She felt the warmth where his body had been and buried her head in his pillow, not wanting to lose him so soon. Moments later, she heard the back door open and close and felt a slight chill as he lifted the covers to rejoin her. They dozed a while longer before Cassie rolled over onto her back.

She breathed out in a long sigh.

"Cass?"

She turned to him.

"This isn't gonna be as easy as we thought, is it?" His gray eyes were a soft, molten silver as they gazed into hers, waiting for her answer.

Shaking her head, she pulled her arm out from under the blanket and gently stroked his cheek. "No," she murmured, her response barely audible.

"Maybe we can... Maybe..." His eyes searched hers, seeking answers she didn't have, a commitment she couldn't make.

She shook her head again and fought back tears, placing two fingers against his lips to keep him from saying more. "You will always be my hero, and my friend. But if we're honest with each other, I think we'd both admit that neither of us is whole enough to ask for more. I can't provide my missing pieces Cliff, and I can't ask you for yours."

He nodded, but he couldn't hide the disappointment she saw in his eyes.

"Okay, Cass. As long as you know the choice is yours. And remember, you're the one who said friends could be lovers." His words were meant to tease, but neither of them smiled.

He tugged her close for a deep, passionate kiss. When he pulled away, he made a brave attempt at a smile that didn't quite reach his eyes. "Okay, you puzzle on that while I take a quick shower and make us breakfast. I don't know about you, but I'm starvin'."

He nuzzled her neck before he got out of bed. "Then we can take the boys out for a ride up in the hills. There are miles of trails right out back."

Her face still flushed from the passion in his kiss, she nodded. Then, after exhaling an uneven breath, she muttered, "Sounds good..." She wanted to say more—needed to say more. "Cliff..." she began, not knowing what she'd say next, even as the words were forming.

He bent down, using the gentle pressure of his lips to quiet her. "Shhh. We have a lot of years to perfect what we have, to figure out what we are to each other. We don't need to do it today."

After he left, and with her arms wrapped around his pillow, she dozed, her mind filled with sensuous dreams. A soft knock on the door brought her back to reality.

"It's your turn for the shower. I'll start breakfast." He glanced at the clock on the night stand and chuckled, "or, maybe I should say lunch."

Freshly showered and dressed, Cassie joined Cliff in the kitchen, just as he was putting platters of food on the table. "Wow, Cliff! I wasn't expecting such a feast." She gestured to the pitcher of fresh orange juice, and the plates of toast, bacon, eggs, and home-fries.

He shrugged and smiled. "I don't often have guests. I usually eat out of the pot when I cook for myself. I may have overdone it a bit. Eat up."

When neither of them could take another bite, Cassie pushed back her chair and began to pick up the plates, insisting on washing the dishes.

"Okay, if you insist." Cliff said, giving in. "I'll go brush the boys and saddle up."

When the dishes had been washed and put away, and the kitchen left spotless, Cassie joined him in the barn.

They mounted, then headed out onto the scrub range and into the hills. In some ways, it felt like old times, only there weren't any cows to chase or fences to mend. They passed a herd of browsing elk, a fox sunning himself on a large rock and a lone coyote picking his way through the brush. A herd of mule deer scattered at their approach.

It was a glorious, sunny day, and when they stopped at the top of a ridge, they saw a bald eagle catch an updraft and soar over their heads, its wings spread wide. When the eagle's flight path finally took him out of sight, Cassie turned to Cliff with a contented smile on her face.

"Thanks."

He smiled back. "Mother Nature put on the show. I'm just along for the ride, same as you."

"That's not what I meant..."

He just nodded in response.

It was late afternoon by the time they returned to the house and finished grooming and feeding the horses. It was time for her to leave, time to say goodbye.

Cliff carried her bag and walked with her to the truck. He stowed the bag on the back seat before turning to her. "Call me when you get home, okay?"

She nodded and wrapped her arms around him. "We've made some wonderful memories together, Cowboy, but this weekend topped them all. Thanks."

They hugged with a fierceness that made a lie of their attempt to keep things light. Then she climbed into her truck and backed out of the driveway, fighting back tears.

21

JAMESTOWN, COLORADO

Cassie had come to appreciate the comfortable daily pattern of what others might consider a boring life. She worked at the clinic, volunteered at the Rescue Ranch, and spent her scarce free time with a paintbrush, attempting to recapture the beauty of the places she'd called home during her wandering years. The highlight of each week, although she tried not to admit that to herself, was hearing Cliff's voice on the phone each Sunday evening.

Entire days went by without thoughts of the past—sometimes weeks went by without a nightmare. Her monthly trips to the Greeley library had yielded nothing new since Frank's last request for parole had been denied over a year earlier. The countdown on her freedom clock didn't frighten her as much as it once had, even though there were less than ten years remaining. She held fast to the hope that Frank's life clock would run out before his sentence did.

As Christmas approached, Cassie's desire to see Cliff trumped her fear of escalating their relationship. When she suggested they meet for a Christmas Eve lunch, he accepted with an eagerness that surprised her. Neither of them had any Christmas traditions—religious or otherwise. They were the folks who worked so others could enjoy the festivities with their families.

Cassie found it difficult to reconcile the events of her life in the context of a greater plan and a loving God. And she preferred not to think about how a righteous and vindictive God would judge her. She found God, or what some might call inner peace, in the quiet majesty of the mountains at sunrise, in watching a hawk soar with effortless grace through the thin mountain air, and in the kind eyes of the horses that enriched her life.

This year though, Christmas would be special, if only because she'd be spending time with Cliff. She invested all her free time working on Cliff's gift. When it was finished and framed, she tried not to focus on its imperfections, and she hoped he would understand its significance.

There was a promise of snow in the crisp air when they met in the parking lot of a restaurant in Fort Collins, a neutral half-way point for each of them. Maybe it was the season that fueled the feelings—or perhaps it was the effect of the Christmas carols playing over the restaurant's tinny outdoor speakers—but they hugged in a tight embrace, kissing more like long-lost lovers than the friends they claimed to be.

"Hi, Cowboy." Cass brushed a lock of hair off Cliff's forehead.

"Hi, yourself. How come you always look so pretty?" He gently stroked her cheek with his rough, calloused hand. "You look younger, happier. I didn't realize just how much I missed you."

He hugged her again. They didn't pull away until falling snow interrupted their embrace. Cliff took her hand, and they began to walk toward the restaurant's entrance.

"Damn! I almost forgot. Be right back." He returned to his truck and removed a beautifully wrapped box from the front seat. When he said, "Merry Christmas, Cassie," his eyes reflected the warmth in his words.

Cassie stared wide-eyed at the impressively wrapped gift. "Wow! Did you wrap this? It's too beautiful to open." The shiny gold paper was wrinkle free, and the green and gold ribbons encircling the box were tied with an impressive bow.

Cliff's face wore a sheepish, apologetic expression when he replied. "Umm, I tried to wrap it, but after I'd made a mess of it, Jenny took over and wrapped it at the gallery."

Cassie quirked an eyebrow in surprise. "I don't get it. You create those incredible sculptures, but you can't wrap a gift?" She grinned. "Well, she did a beautiful job. Hold onto it for a minute while I get your present." Cassie opened the passenger door of the truck and reached into the back seat for the flat, rectangular box that she too had taken pains to wrap. The plaid paper was encircled with green grosgrain ribbon with a small pine cone embedded in the bow.

Her insecurity kicked in as they exchanged their gifts. "I hope you like it."

She shrugged her shoulders to make light of the emotionally-charged moment and was grateful for Cliff's lighthearted response. "The snow's really startin' to come down, you think maybe we should go inside before they stick brooms in our hands and corn cob pipes in our mouths?"

With a slight shake of her head at the thought of such a scene, Cassie met his gaze just long enough to catch the twinkle in his eyes. Then they strode, her long stride matching his own, across the parking lot and into the restaurant's entryway, where the scent of pine competed with the smell of wet, drying wool. As a waitress led them to a quiet corner booth, Cassie noticed the gaily decorated Christmas tree and the festive decorations adorning the walls. Instrumental holiday music played softly in the background. She glanced around at the tables filled with smiling people, and for the first time since—she couldn't actually remember when—she felt the warmth of the holiday season.

Once seated, Cassie was too excited to focus on the menu the waitress handed her. Instead, she ordered the turkey dinner special she'd seen written on the blackboard at the restaurant's entrance. Cliff chose the same.

Once the waitress departed, Cliff gestured to the unopened gift on the table in front of Cassie. "Ladies, first."

She untied the bow and slid her finger under the flap of the paper, careful not to rip it. For just a second, a snapshot memory of an excited little girl opening gifts with her parents on a snowy Christmas morning in Germany, slipped through her mind and was gone.

She lifted the top off the box and pushed the tissue paper aside. "Oh my God," she whispered in a reverential tone before reaching into the box and carefully removing her gift. "It's Dusty!"

She stared in wonder at the slightly dished face, wide expressive eyes, flared nostrils, and cocked head of a horse always alert to every sound. Cliff had captured the attentive expression and dun color of the horse she'd ridden during their time in Montana over six years earlier. Dusty, the rank horse the other ranch hands had thought would teach her a thing or two, had become her willing partner.

"I don't know what to say, Cliff. This is the nicest gift anyone's ever given me." Tears traced a slow trail down her flushed cheeks. "Thank you."

Cliff's smile broadened, his eyes reflecting warmth and caring—and maybe a tinge of relief that she'd understood the significance of his gift.

"Your turn," she said as she wiped her eyes and sniffled into a tissue. "I hope...I hope you like it."

"Do I have to save the paper like you did?" he asked in a cautious tone.

"No, you don't have to save the paper. Just rip it open!" As she gnawed at the side of her mouth, she nervously twisted her fingers in her lap as he pulled off the ribbon, ripped off the paper, and with slow and deliberate movements opened the box. She held her breath as he lifted the cardboard off the glass covering the front of the painting.

She had tried to capture every detail of the tiny refuge nestled in the pine trees where they'd first made love: the rustic cabin, the corral with the two horses—one sorrel and one dun—and the sun rising over the distant snow-capped mountain peaks turning the sky a soft shade of pink.

Cliff said nothing. Cassie waited for his reaction, her stomach in knots. He finally looked up, surprise and disbelief written on his face. "Cassie, it's amazing. It's just as I remember. You didn't miss a detail." He reached across the table and took her hand. "Thank you."

Neither of them spoke, and the emotion-laden silence verged on becoming uncomfortable. When the waitress approached carrying two steaming plates of turkey with all the trimmings, they greeted her with a grateful smile.

Cassie dealt head on with their awkward attempts at conversation. "Look at us. We're like two tongue-tied kids." She took a deep breath and smiled. "This will always be a special Christmas for me, Cliff." She picked up her iced tea for a toast. "Merry Christmas."

He clinked his glass with hers. "Merry Christmas, Cass."

When they left the restaurant an hour later, at least three inches of snow lay on the ground, and more was falling. Cliff held the painting under his coat as he walked with quick strides to his truck to place it on the front seat. Cassie carried the box containing her gift as if it were the most precious of gems. She carefully placed it on the back seat of her truck.

She turned to face Cliff. "You'd think by now it would be easier to say goodbye," she whispered as she hugged him.

"I know, Cass. I know," he answered in low voice, the sound coming from just above her right ear. She felt, rather than heard the sigh that followed.

They held each other as the snow fell, and Bing Crosby's version of "White Christmas" filled the air from the restaurant's outdoor speakers. When icy water began to run down her back from her soaked hair, Cassie finally pulled away.

Cliff held the door as she climbed into her truck and started the engine. "Drive carefully, Cass."

"You too, Cowboy."

She drove out of the parking lot and made a left onto the street that would take her to I-25 South. When she glanced in her rear view mirror, Cliff's truck had made the right-hand turn toward I-25 North. Opposite directions once again.

Cassie drove with care, more concerned about other drivers than the weather. She was used to driving through far worse snow in the mountains. As Christmas carols played on the radio, she tried not to wish for the safe 'feel-nothing' Christmases of years past. Her afternoon with Cliff had made this both the happiest, and the saddest, of Christmases.

She forced herself to smile and wave back to the excited little girls waving to her from the car in the next lane, and she laughed out loud at the Santa with the ugly cotton-ball beard driving in the truck behind her.

The phone was ringing when she unlocked her apartment door. She rushed up the stairs to answer it. "Hello?"

"Hey Cass. It's Cliff. I just wanted to make sure you got home okay."

She shrugged off her wet coat and curled up on the corner of the sofa. "I just walked in the door. Traffic was a little slow, but nothing bad on the roads, considering the weather. How about you, any problems?"

"No. The roads were messy, but no problem. I got home a little while ago. Thanks again for the painting. I hung it in the living room on the wall next to the fireplace. It's right in front of the recliner, where I can always see it."

"Cliff, I still don't understand how you managed to capture Dusty's personality in a piece of wood." She tugged the cover off the box and stroked the smooth grain as she continued, her voice low. "He's the best present anyone's ever given me. Except maybe when I was a little girl, when my Mom..."

She stopped. This wasn't the time for a trip that far down memory lane. "Anyway, you know what I mean. I'll always treasure him, especially since you made him for me."

"Merry Christmas, Cass. I'll call you Sunday."

Cassie hung up the phone, but she made no attempt to move. Her eyes still wet with tears, she stared through the open blinds at a dark sky illuminated by the light of a street lamp. Large lazy snowflakes floated earthward. As she stroked the wooden horse, her loneliness was magnified by the knowledge that she didn't have to be alone. She could be lying in the arms of a man who wasn't interested in pursuing her past, who was willing to accept her for who she was…

The sharp ring of the phone brought her back. She took a moment to compose herself before she answered. "Hello?" she said, her voice husky with tears.

"Merry Christmas, Cassie. It's Connor. Are you okay? It sounds like you have a cold."

Her lips curled into a slight smile at the sound of his voice. It was Connor—her rock, her boss, her friend, her mentor. Of course, it was Connor. He would never let Christmas Eve pass without calling her.

"Hi, Connor. Merry Christmas to you, too. I'm fine, just feeling a little melancholy. You know how it is." He never spoke about his dead wife. What little Cassie knew had come from Lynne at the Rescue Ranch. Connor had his own reasons for being melancholy on Christmas Eve.

"Yeah, yeah I do," he said. He continued in a more upbeat voice, "Just wanted to touch bases and agree on a time for me to pick you up tomorrow night for Mrs. Rollins's annual Christmas party…"

"Connor…"

"Don't 'Connor' me, Cassie. I know you're working at the Ranch tomorrow, but you're off duty at three. I'll pick you up at four-thirty. Then we can head over to pick Pepper up. You have to come. You know how Pepper's mother is. Lord knows what she'll think, let alone what she'll say, if I'm alone when I stop at their house."

"Okay, okay. I'll come. God Bless Mrs. Rollins. Her collection of strays goes way beyond cats and dogs, doesn't it?"

He chuckled. "Yeah, she has an uncanny ability to find the human ones, too."

~

176

Next morning, Cassie was up early for her drive to the Rescue Ranch. She had long ago discovered that keeping busy was the best way to avoid introspection and regret. The smell of fresh hay, and the nickering welcome from the horses when they heard her open the barn door, created the perfect Christmas morning—at least for her.

"Mornin' to you, too. Merry Christmas, guys!" she called out to them as she turned on the lights and the radio, grateful this was the last day for the ever-present Christmas carols. She was sure the horses were as tired as she was of the collection of top-forty Christmas songs and endless oldies. As she threw hay into their stalls, her experienced eye quickly checked each of the horses to make sure they had made it through the night without injury.

They were all awake now. Silence was replaced by a cacophony of sound as the hungry, impatient animals demanded breakfast, some of them convinced they would be forgotten if they didn't call out or kick their stall doors. She didn't blame them. After all, many had been rescued from conditions she chose not to dwell on. They had reason to worry about missing their next meal.

Once they all had their hay, she went outside and traipsed through a foot of snow to feed the hairy, sturdy horses who lived outside in the adjoining pastures with the opportunity to shelter in snug three-sided, run-in sheds as the spirit moved them. She breathed in the frigid air and smiled, watching the sun slowly light up the sky as it made its way fully over the horizon.

Returning to the barn, she mucked out half the stalls before she pushed the feed trolley down the aisle and gave the horses their grain. While she sat on a bale of hay listening to their contented chewing, she drank her coffee and ate her own breakfast. It was a peaceful, soul-quieting time that few would understand. She chuckled to herself thinking how selfless others thought she was for volunteering for Christmas morning duty—not just to feed, but to muck out the stalls and turn out the horses as well. Little did they know she would have gladly paid for the opportunity.

Two by two, she led the horses out of the barn into the snow. With this first heavy snowfall of the season, even the old guys acted like frisky youngsters. They exploded with exuberance as she unhooked their lead lines, and she laughed out loud as they bucked their way across the pastures. Some couldn't resist rolling in the fresh snow, while others raced around and chased one another. They'd settle soon enough and spend much of the day munching on the big round hay bale in the middle of the pasture. For now, she enjoyed watching their energetic expressions of joy.

By midday, other barn volunteers arrived, some to visit and chat, others to work with the horses in the small indoor arena. At three o'clock, Cassie said her goodbyes and left for home, tired but content. Soon she was rushing up the stairs to her apartment to shower and prepare for Mrs. Rollins's Christmas party—the previous night's melancholy and malaise forgotten.

When the doorbell rang at four twenty-five, she ran down the stairs in stockings and slippers to open the door for Connor. He followed her up the stairs, where he then stood staring, wide-eyed and speechless. He finally found his voice. "Cassie, you look beautiful—absolutely beautiful."

Her decision to get some additional wear out of the dress she'd bought for Cliff's dinner suddenly didn't seem so smart. "Maybe it's too much. I should change…" She started to turn away.

Connor caught her arm. "No. No, it isn't too much. It's just that I'm so used to seeing you in jeans. Cassie, you look perfect."

Sensing her continued uncertainty, he added, "Mrs. Rollins will be thrilled that you dressed up. This party means a lot to her, you know." He continued in an obvious further attempt to distract her, "How do I look? Do I look okay?"

She appreciated his transparent attempt to temper her discomfort. Even though he might not understand her sudden mood changes or her need to blend into the background, he always tried to accommodate her.

She looked him up and down. "Hmm. Shined shoes, nicely pressed gray wool slacks, a pretty, red turtleneck sweater, and a very preppy, tweed sport coat. I'd say you look more than okay, Doc. You definitely look more than just okay."

He bowed. "Thank you ma'am, but do you think you can find a different adjective than 'pretty' for my sweater?" He made a face as he looked down in pretend discomfort.

She laughed. "I'm sorry. I should have used a more manly word. It's a very handsome sweater that shows off your masculine physique. Is that better?"

He grimaced, although his eyes sparkled with amusement. "Not really, since now I know you're lying through your teeth." Then he paused, his face taking on a more thoughtful expression. "Seriously Cassie, you do look beautiful. I don't think I've ever seen you in a dress."

"I bought it for the dinner I told you about with Cliff and some art patrons. I didn't know when I'd have another chance to wear it."

"Well, I'm glad you decided to wear it tonight. What do you mean art patrons? You didn't mention that before."

She picked up her Christmas present from the coffee table and handed it to him. "It's Dusty. The horse I rode when Cliff and I worked together in Montana. Cliff gave him to me for Christmas."

She saw the question in his eyes and nodded in response. "Yes. Cliff made it. He's a very accomplished wood sculptor, and a Cheyenne gallery carries his work. A gallery customer wanted to meet the cowboy artist, so the gallery owner arranged dinner at a restaurant in Cheyenne. Cliff invited me to join him. That's why I bought the dress."

"I had no idea." Connor shook his head in obvious surprise at this news. After a long moment, he added, "Artistic talent is one more thing the two of you have in common." His statement contained a question she knew he wouldn't ask. He'd nibbled around the edges of her relationship with Cliff, but he never asked the question. She had no idea how she'd answer it if he did.

Connor placed the carved horse on the table. "Shall we go pick up Miss Pepper? I'm sure she's pacing outside in the snow wondering where we are. With Pepper at the party, you won't have to worry about people noticing you, so there's a comfort!"

They shared a laugh and headed out into the night.

Not surprisingly, Connor's comments both about Mrs. Rollins and Pepper were spot on. As soon as Cassie removed her winter jacket, the elderly Mrs. Rollins, wearing a festive red velvet dress adorned with a sparkly Christmas tree pin and matching earrings, rushed to her side, beaming. "Cassie, dear, you look absolutely gorgeous! You are such a pretty girl, you should show yourself off more often." Smelling like talcum powder and an over-abundance of cologne, the octogenarian wrapped her thin arms around Cassie and squeezed. Discarding her usual reticence, Cassie returned the hug, careful not to squeeze too tight. After that, it was Pepper who garnered the most attention from the party-goers. Wearing a unique Christmas elf outfit, and with her normal effervescence amped up by the excitement of the holiday, she was the life of the party.

Christmas ended on a high note for Cassie. After the party, she climbed into bed, exhausted and content, still bathed in the warmth of the friendships she'd unwittingly made, and too tired to worry about the consequences of letting people get too close.

~

By New Year's Eve, Cassie's holiday glow had been replaced with depression. All the talk about ringing out the old and ringing in the new, made it impossible for her not to reflect on the past. After all these years, the past—the ugly, painful, shameful past she had so carefully tried to bury—was still there.

Cassie spent the day at the Rescue Ranch. She fed the horses and mucked out their stalls. She turned them out in the morning, and then she brought them in for the night and fed them again. In between, she rode the horses she was training.

She shunned company and turned down the party invitations she received. Grateful for the indoor arena, she worked with the horses until much later than normal, and then drove home in the frigid night, hoping she was tired enough to sleep until morning.

At eleven o'clock, physically exhausted but mentally on edge and unable to sleep, she sat in front of the TV staring at the New Year's Eve festivities with the volume muted. She thought about getting drunk, but didn't want to pay the price of the hangover, or at least that was the excuse she gave herself. Deep down, she knew it wasn't the real reason. The real reason was a lifelong fear that alcohol would become a crutch she'd come to depend on—and that would mean Frank had won. She would never let the bastard win.

When her rumbling stomach reminded her it had been a long time since lunch, she heated a piece of left-over pizza and granted herself approval to drink one beer to wash it down. Then, beer in hand, she picked up the phone.

"Hello?" The voice at the other end sounded tired and grumpy, but its familiarity made her smile.

While she was allowing the rich sound of his voice to settle her, he responded again. This time his voice was sharper. "Hello? Who is this?"

"Hey, Cliff. It's Cassie." Her reply was a soft response to his terse tone.

"Hey, Cass." The grumpiness was gone. "Is everything okay?" The sharpness had turned to concern.

"I'm fine, or as fine as I ever am on this night of nights when we're supposed to reflect on our lives…" She paused searching for the words to explain.

She heard him exhale. "I know, Cass. I know. I chopped wood 'til I thought I couldn't lift the ax one more time. I did chores, mucked the barn twice, but still…"

She responded with what was meant as an understanding laugh, but sounded more like a tired snort. "I spent all day at the Rescue Ranch. I fed the horses, turned them out for the day, mucked out the barn, brought them in for the night, and fed them again. I worked with a couple of my project horses until it was way past their bedtime, and my old bones and muscles screamed for warmth and rest. It didn't help. It never does."

It took him a while to respond. Cassie didn't mind the silence as long as the connection was still there. Finally, he spoke. She listened to words she knew were hard for him to share. "Cass, when I finally settled down it was because I figured out that I had been mostly runnin' from myself. I finally realized my demons were gonna be there when I woke in the mornin'—didn't matter where I slept."

He hesitated, and she could hear a deep exhale before he continued speaking. "I'm glad you called. I wish…."

He stopped. He didn't need to go on. She knew what he wanted to say. He'd made the offer before, and she'd rejected it. The silence lengthened as Cassie held the phone to her ear and swiped at the silent tears trickling down her face.

"Thanks, Cliff. Thanks for being there. Good night, Cowboy."

"Night, Cass."

When the nightmares came that night, Cassie fought them away with the happiest memory she could find. She relived her night of passion with Cliff in his cozy bungalow and finally fell into a deep and comforting sleep.

22

JAMESTOWN, CO - CHEYENNE, WY

How was it possible that six months had passed since she'd met Cliff for lunch on Christmas Eve? Cassie stared at the calendar, her fingers toying with the phone cord as she spoke to Cliff on a late June afternoon. They'd never missed their Sunday evening calls, but somehow summer had arrived—and she couldn't figure out where all the time had gone.

"Are you okay, Cliff?" Something was wrong. She could hear it in the raspy tone of his voice and his persistent cough. She asked the same question she'd been asking for at least a month. Once again, he assured her he was fine, although this time he hesitated before he answered. He sounded tired and distant, and he always seemed to be on the verge of saying something that never got said.

A feeling of unease settled over her after they said goodbye. Questions nagged at her. *Is he lying? Would he lie to me?* She tossed and turned in bed, worry keeping her from a restful sleep. In the morning, still bleary-eyed from her restless night, she greeted Conner with a question. "Do you mind if I take the afternoon off?"

His answer was immediate. "No problem. Is everything okay?"

"I don't know. I'm worried about Cliff." The pain in the pit of her stomach wouldn't go away. There was something wrong. She knew it. She felt it.

Traffic was light as she drove north to Cheyenne. Deep in thought, she almost missed the final turn. After checking the street sign, she drove down the quiet country road and pulled into the driveway of Cliff's home. When she noticed his truck wasn't there, she cursed herself for not calling first. Then, as her eyes scanned the yard, she sat back in shock and surprise. The tidy property she remembered was no more. The grass was in need of mowing, and the wood pile was in disarray. The doors to the barn and the gate to the now overgrown paddock were both wide open. *Where are the horses? Where's Cliff?*

Heart pounding, her throat dry, she ran up the walk to the front porch and rapped on the front door. When there was no answer, she knocked more loudly. Frustrated, she turned the door knob. Instead of meeting the resistance of a lock, the door swung open. She hesitated for only a moment before stepping inside. "Cliff? Cliff, its Cassie. Are you home?"

There was no answer. She sucked in her breath as she walked further into the house. A cold shudder ran through her as a stale, musty odor assailed her nose. Her mind registered the layer of dust covering the furniture and the messy stack of books and papers strewn across the kitchen table.

"Cliff? Cliff!" she shouted. Again, there was no answer.

Panicked, she ran toward the closed bedroom door. She took a deep breath and edged the door open, terrified at what she'd find inside. The blinds were shut, and it took a moment for her eyes to adjust to the dim light. The smell penetrated her nostrils while her brain attempted to reject its meaning—it was an odor of antiseptic and sickness she'd only ever associated with a hospital. When her eye caught movement on the bed, she gasped.

"Cliff?" her words were a whisper. Could this wraith of a man, this hollow-cheeked skeleton be Cliff?

"Cass…"

She rushed toward the bed, only to stop a couple of feet away, unable to move, shocked by the sight in front of her. She faced the apparition in the bed, tears blurring her vision.

"Cass…" Cliff whispered her name.

Her words rushed out, unplanned. "You've been sick. You've been sick for months. You lied!" Feeling betrayed, she lashed out at him. "What were you going to do, just not call me one day? Were you never going to tell me you were sick?"

Questions and doubts raced through her mind. *How could he not trust me enough to tell me he was sick?* Tears ran unchecked as she stared at the gaunt face of the man who meant the world to her.

He held up his hand in a pleading gesture. "Cass. Please. Let me explain." His voice was so low she had to step closer to hear him. "I wanted to tell you. I tried." He stopped and fought for a breath. "I tried to tell you... I...I couldn't." His eyes pleaded with her to understand. She took his hand and was reminded of the frail paper-thin skin of Mrs. Allison, her elderly landlady in Wichita—a lifetime ago. Where was the strong, calloused, cowboy's hand she remembered?

Cassie refocused when Cliff continued speaking, "I couldn't find the words. At first, I didn't want to worry you...what if it was nothin'? When I found out..." He choked on his words and swallowed back a cough. Then he closed his eyes, and when he reopened them, Cassie saw his jaw tighten with determination. The words came slowly, forced out between short, shallow breaths. "When the doctor told me...I was afraid...if I told you, it would be real. As long as you didn't know...maybe it wouldn't be true."

He laughed, a dry brittle sound. "I wanted to hear your stories—about the horses, the clinic, Pepper's antics. I didn't want to hear concern and pity. I was selfish. I'm sorry. I'm so sorry..."

Tears welled up in his eyes. He held out his arms, and Cassie moved forward to embrace him.

She held him until her need for answers forced her to pull away. "What is it, Cliff? What's wrong?"

He stared down at his hands on the blanket. She followed his gaze. Hands that had been strong enough to grasp an ax to chop a cord of wood and steady enough to carve the detail in the face of a foal were now veined and fragile, seeming barely strong enough to hold a cup.

"Cancer. Started in my lungs and spread."

"When did you know? Did you know at Christmas? Were you never going to tell me?" She tried hard not to sound combative, tried to keep the accusation out of her voice, but she lost the battle to her feelings of hurt and betrayal. "Was I supposed to just guess at why you didn't call me one Sunday?"

His intense, pained stare begged her to understand, but his voice was barely a whisper when he answered her. "I didn't know at Christmas. I had a cold and a cough that got worse in January. I started losin' weigh, and I was tired all the time." He paused and gulped air in short breaths. "I saw a doctor in March. He sent me for tests. Caught it too late. There was nothin' they could do…nothin' that had more than a twenty-five percent chance of delayin' the inevitable."

His gray eyes were clouded by pain. He paused again to take more shallow breaths. "I wanted to tell you. I tried, but it got harder and harder. I knew I was runnin' out of time. I gave the horses away and donated my truck—and I still couldn't tell you. Forgive me. Please, forgive me?" He gave in to a spasm of coughs that racked his body. Then his imploring gaze returned to Cassie's face.

She sobbed, stretching out next to him on the bed and pulling him to her. "How long, Cliff?"

"I don't know…a couple of weeks, a month. I don't know."

She wrapped her arms around him while her mind raced with conflicting emotions. Part of her wanted to curse and scream. Was she so bad, so evil, that everyone she loved either left her or died?

It isn't fair!

She forced herself to refocus and push the self-pity away. This wasn't about her. Cliff was dying. She clung to him. Finally, she sat up, her decision made. "I'm staying," she announced in a 'don't disagree with me' tone. "Connor can get by without me for a while. I haven't had a chance to cook for anyone in a long time, so I may be a bit rusty…"

"Cass…"

She cut him off before he could continue.

"Don't try to be the tough guy and talk me out of it. I'm doing this as much for me as for you. Why aren't you in the hospital anyway? Not that I want you to be in the hospital, I'd rather be at home if it was me, but…"

His lips curled in a slight smile, and she saw a hint of humor in his pain-filled eyes.

"What? What's funny?" She was still feeling combative, convinced he was going to try to talk her out of staying.

His attempt at a laugh turned into another spasm of coughing. As soon as he caught his breath and relaxed back on the pillows, he reached up to touch her face. "I wasn't gonna try to talk you out of stayin'. I'm too selfish for that. I was just gonna say thank you."

"Oh. Good. Then that's that. Do you have any food in the house? What have you been eating?" She didn't wait for a response. "I'll go to the store and buy what we need." She had to do something, anything. If she couldn't make him well, she'd cook and clean and take care of him. "How does beef and barley soup sound?"

His tear-filled eyes met hers, and he smiled, if a tight compression of the lips with a bare tilt at one end could be considered a smile. Then he nodded and answered in a voice barely above a whisper. "Sounds great, Cass. Sounds great."

~

She called Connor. Telling Connor, saying the words out loud, announcing Cliff's death sentence, somehow made it more final. She fought back another round of tears as she added a request. "Agnes has a key to my apartment. Maybe she can pack some clothes for me?"

"Definitely. Of course she will, and I'll drive them up to you this afternoon."

True to his word, late that afternoon Connor met her in a strip mall on the outskirts of Cheyenne. He handed her the duffle bag Agnes had packed. Then, after exhaling a huge sigh, he placed his hands on her shoulders. She gazed up at him, her focus distorted through a watery filter of tears. The compassion in his eyes was almost too much for her to bear. She sucked in a breath and fought to hold herself together.

"I'm sorry, Cassie," Connor said, his eyes locked on hers. "I can't even imagine how hard this is for you. Promise you'll call me if you need anything—even if you just need someone to talk to. Promise?" Maintaining eye contact, he waited for her response.

Afraid if she opened her mouth, sobs would escape instead of words, Cassie bobbed her head up and down. He hugged her. Then he dropped his arms and stepped back. "Don't forget. Call me," he commanded, his voice stern. Then he got in his car, and she watched him drive away.

Cassie didn't move. She stood alone in a rutted strip-mall parking lot. Competing sounds filled her ears—the wheels of supermarket shopping carts rumbling across the asphalt, a woman reprimanding her child, a crying baby, the shouts of teenagers. Life going on around her while her own world fell apart.

Never one for long pity parties, Cassie let out a long-held breath, climbed into her truck and put it in gear. It was time to return to Cliff, to help him face his death—to help him leave her, too.

The days developed a sad and numbing rhythm. She cleaned, cooked, read to Cliff, listened to his labored breathing when he slept, and talked to the hospice nurses. Occasionally the routine was broken, like when Cliff's lawyer arrived and Cliff insisted she sit with them as the lawyer read over Cliff's will. The lawyer handed her documents. She signed them without question. She did whatever he asked of her, unwilling to focus on the finality of any of it.

One of the hospice nurses helped her drag the recliner from the living room into the bedroom. When Cassie slept, that was her bed. She only left the house if a hospice nurse was there to give Cliff his morphine, or the health aide to wash him and change his catheter bag. Things he wouldn't allow Cassie to do. She allowed him that little bit of dignity. It was the least she could offer him.

When he was no longer able to eat, when he was on intravenous fluids with a morphine drip for pain, Cassie ate crackers and cereal out of the box. She forgot to shower and didn't bother to change her clothes. The hospice nurses explained what was happening, but Cassie barely listened. Words. Just words and none of the words mattered. They couldn't change what was happening.

Although Cliff wasn't always lucid, and he was always in pain, listening to her talk seemed to calm him. She shared stories about her childhood in Germany. She even described her happiest memory of flying a kite in a Swiss meadow and laughing with her mother at the sound of the distant cow bells. She tried to describe the scene the way she remembered it, the way she had shined and embellished it when that memory had been her lifeline to sanity.

Her store of happy memories was limited, and she was unwilling to share the painful ones, so when she ran out of stories, she read to him. Zane Grey novels about the West took them back to their months of riding the range together.

Mostly Cliff slept, and Cassie wandered the house touching his books and his tools. He'd already sold off most of his sculptures. She suppressed her tears—afraid that even in his drugged state he'd hear her if she unleashed the sobs bubbling up in her chest. She was afraid to fall sleep, afraid he'd die while she slept. When she tired, sometimes she lay on top of the blankets next to him, berating herself for holding back, for wasting the months when they could have been together.

Late one evening at the beginning of week three, Cassie had been reading to Cliff when he lifted his hand to stop her. He insisted on talking—in spite of what it cost him. Cassie held his hand, staring into his glazed eyes while he struggled to speak. "Cass…I'm sorry we didn't have enough time…together." His breath came in spurts, and he struggled to continue. "I love you. I'm sorry I never said that before."

Tears ran unchecked down her cheeks, and she was sure her heart would explode, but he wanted to say more, so she just squeezed his hand in response.

"Thirty years, Cass. I ran for thirty years. Until I found you, I never thought…I never thought I could love anyone. Thank you."

He lay back on the pillows, gasping for breath. He'd removed the oxygen mask so he could speak more easily. When she tried to put it back on, he inhaled a couple of deep gulps, then he pushed her hand away, and the mask dropped. "Not done…"

She nodded and continued to squeeze his hand. Knowing what this speech was costing him, she made her own confession. "I love you, too. I'm sorry I was the one to hold back…"

He tried to shake his head and more coughs racked his body. Finally, he found his words. "No…No…not your fault."

She touched his forehead and brushed his hair back. "Okay, okay, it wasn't my fault. Will you put the oxygen mask back on now?"

"I'm scared, Cass."

Again, she nodded, this time in understanding. In their running, they had both turned their backs on a God they felt had betrayed them. Now Cliff was about to face that God. She didn't know how to help him, but the words she said came from her heart. "Cliff, I don't know what you did in that long ago past that you've been running from. I do know you are the kindest, gentlest, most sensitive man I have ever known. You helped a part of me heal, a part I thought died a long time ago. I've never seen you raise a hand to, or speak a word against, another living being. If there is a God worth believing in, when he judges you he will weigh the good against the bad and find infinitely more good. If there is a heaven Cliff, you deserve a place there. You're a good man. Believe that you are a good man!"

With the intensity in her eyes and the fierce tone of her voice, she tried to burn through the drugged haze in Cliff's brain to help him believe. If there was nothing else she could do, she needed to do this one thing to help him die in peace.

"Cliff? Do you understand what I'm saying? Don't be afraid, don't be afraid…" She was sobbing now.

His eyes closed, and he rested, clearly exhausted. She put his oxygen mask back on him, and after a few seconds, he seemed more at peace, and his breathing more even.

That was the last time they spoke. When he again opened his eyes, she could see acceptance. He nodded slightly and reached for her hand. She tried to stay awake, but exhaustion finally claimed her, and she dozed sitting in the recliner next to his bed. In the early morning hours, when silence replaced the sound of his labored breathing, she woke with a start.

He was gone.

She sat for a long time—unable to move, not knowing what to do. So, she waited, holding a silent vigil by his side.

When the hospice nurse arrived at seven, Cassie sat in the living room while the nurse took charge. The woman called for a transport ambulance, then she sat on the couch next to Cassie and asked if there was someone she could call for her.

Cassie stared blankly before she responded with one word. "Connor."

"What's his number, Cassie? Can you give me his number?"

Cassie mumbled the number. She heard the nurse's side of her short conversation with Connor, but her mind was elsewhere.

The ambulance arrived to take Cliff's body to the hospital before final release to the mortuary. He had made his intentions clear, and had already made the arrangements. There would be no viewing or service. He had opted for an immediate cremation. There was nothing left for her to do.

The nurse sat with her until Connor arrived, and the expression of concern on his face brought her back to reality. "I'm sorry, Cassie. I'm so sorry." He hugged her. "I'll take you home. You need some rest and some food."

He held her as she sobbed. She let him lead her out to his car. He put on her seat belt. Then he drove her to his home and helped her up the stairs to his guest room.

When she woke, confused and with a heavy, aching head, Connor was sitting on the edge of the bed. Although her eyes were open, she had trouble focusing.

Connor spoke. "You've been asleep for a while. You needed the rest."

She turned to him, staring with unseeing eyes until the memories found a way through the fog in her mind. "Cliff's dead." Her voice was a monotone. Her eyes focused on something far away.

"Yes, Cassie. Cliff's dead. I'm sorry." Finally able to focus, she watched him take a deep breath and exhale. She felt distant from him, even though he was right there next to her. She only half-listened when he continued speaking. "I took your duffle bag of clothes from Cliff's house when we left. While you were sleeping, I washed them. Why don't you take a hot bath while I make us something to eat? Okay?"

She didn't respond.

Connor got up from the bed. "I'll run the water and lay out some clean clothes for you."

When he returned, he pointed toward the bathroom. "Water's nice and warm. I'll get dinner started. Okay?"

She still didn't respond. The fog in her brain kept getting in the way.

"Cassie? Can you do this?"

She remembered what Cliff had said a few days before he died. "I only saw Connor that one time at the rodeo, Cass, but from everything you've told me, I feel I know him. He's a good man. He'll be there for you."

Cliff had been right. Connor was always there for her. She found some words. "Thanks. I'll be okay." Her words held no conviction, but they seemed to satisfy Connor.

She soaked in the tub and somehow found enough energy to wash her hair. When she climbed out, she dried herself off and pulled on the clothes Connor had laid out. She purposely avoided the mirror.

Dinner was a mostly silent affair. Cassie ate without tasting the food Connor had prepared, although she did remember to thank him. Then she went back to bed. Twelve hours later she got up long enough to share another meal, then once again returned to the refuge of sleep. Most of an entire day passed in the oblivion of sleep.

She woke the next morning, her room bathed in the sunlight streaming through the window. Her eyes were gritty, her nose stuffy, and her pillow wet with tears. After giving herself a stern talking to, she swung her legs out of bed and got up.

She greeted an obviously surprised Connor in the kitchen. "Good morning," she said in a low voice strained from crying. "I'm sorry I've been such a burden. I'm okay now. I need to take care of things in Cheyenne…."

Connor had been reading the newspaper at the kitchen table. Now his eyes met hers, and his worried expression confirmed what the mirror had told her. She was a mess—her face red and blotchy, her eyes swollen from crying. She was barely holding herself together.

"You haven't been a burden Cassie. I want to help. Let me help, okay?"

She nodded and attempted a tight smile. "I…I need to meet with the attorney and clean out the house and…and get…"

Her voice broke. Fresh tears flowed. She shook her head, annoyed with herself. "I need to call the mortician and get Cliff's….ashes. I promised him…."

Remembering the conversation, and the promise, she stopped speaking, forgetting what she'd planned on saying next.

"Cassie?"

When she looked up, Connor continued. "I'll take you. I'd like to go with you, okay? Besides," he added, "we left your truck in Cheyenne."

"Okay, thanks. I forgot." In spite of all the hours of sleep, she was exhausted, her mind still foggy.

During the drive to Cliff's house, Cassie mostly stared out the window without registering the passing scenery. Finally, she turned to Connor and asked, "What day is it?"

Connor took his eyes off the road to glance at her. "It's Thursday."

"You're supposed to be working."

He smiled. "I'm the boss, remember? John Simpson's filling in for me. Lord knows I've filled in enough times for him so he could conquer the mountain peaks of Colorado."

Cassie stared at him, the layers of gauze beginning to peel back from her brain. She remembered the details from the last couple of days more clearly. "What day…what day did Cliff…"

"Tuesday morning, Cassie," he answered, his eyes remaining fixed on the road.

"You've taken care of me since Tuesday." A simple statement of fact, with much left unsaid. It was hard for her to understand why someone would care enough to do that for her.

Connor shook his head and glanced over at her again. He took his right hand off the wheel and squeezed her arm. "That's what friends do, Cassie.

You spend all your time giving. Don't you think you deserve to have the scales balanced just a little?"

He didn't wait for a response.

"By the way, Agnes and Pepper called a bunch of times. They made me promise I would convince you to let them help, too. They love you, Cassie."

She nodded, barely registering his words before retreating back into her fog-filled world where nothing seemed to penetrate, where everything was numb around the edges. When she felt the Explorer slow down and turn, she looked up. Her truck was sitting in Cliff's driveway where she'd left it. For an eighth of a second—for the amount of time for one thought to be replaced by another—she forgot why she was here. The beginning of the idea, the little kernel that would have blossomed into a full-blown thought, was instantly replaced by a deep crushing wave of pain.

Cliff isn't here. Cliff is dead.

They sat in silence until she took a deep breath and lifted her head to glance around. Connor got out of the car. His door closed with a soft thud. He walked around to her side and opened her car door. She sat a moment longer.

"It's just a house…" Where once she had seen a tidy, charming home with a well-tended lawn and two welcoming horses at the gate, now all she saw was an aging bungalow with a patchy, overgrown lawn, and firewood strewn haphazardly across the side yard.

"I know, Cassie. Now, it's just a house."

Together, they boxed Cliff's things, some to give away and some for her to keep. It wasn't a difficult task. Cliff had lived sparingly and hadn't accumulated many possessions. Whatever he could do without, he had disposed of when he understood the finality of his illness. He had wanted to make things as easy as possible for her.

She didn't want to return to the house again, so they left two boxes on the front porch for the Salvation Army to pick up. The furniture could either be sold with the house or given away by the real-estate broker. It didn't matter to her. She carefully packed a few special books, his wood-working tools, the painting she'd made for him, and the already-boxed sculpture he had been working on at the end. He had told her it wasn't quite finished. "You'll see its potential," he'd said. She couldn't bear to open the box. Not now. Not yet.

Connor reluctantly agreed when she insisted on attending her appointments alone. "I'm fine now, Connor. You've done enough. I need to do this alone. I promise I'll be back at your house by five."

She hugged him goodbye and added a whispered, "Thank you." Sitting in her truck, she watched him back out of the driveway, then she backed out behind him, dreading the next few hours.

23

CHEYENNE, WY

An ornate sign in the front yard of a restored Victorian home on the outskirts of Cheyenne announced the law offices of Chad Griffing. Cassie pulled into the gravel parking lot and parked. After dabbing at her eyes with a wadded tissue, she climbed out of the truck and trudged up the front steps.

A middle-aged woman looked up from a typewriter when Cassie pushed open the office door. Her pinched, annoyed expression immediately changed to one of welcoming compassion when she saw Cassie, obviously taking in her disheveled appearance and red-rimmed eyes. "May I help you?" she asked warmly.

Cassie swallowed and licked her lips. Her gaze focused on the rhinestones in the woman's eyeglasses as she answered. "I'm Cassie Deahl. I…" She wanted to announce that she had an appointment, proud that she had actually remembered to call for the appointment from Cliff's house earlier that day. But she couldn't put the words into a sentence. Fortunately, she didn't need to.

A door opened to the right of the secretary's desk and a balding man in a dark suit, sporting suspenders and a bow-tie greeted her with a solemn expression. "Hello Cassie. Come in. Please, come in."

He turned to the secretary as he ushered Cassie into his office. "Hold my calls, Sylvia."

~

Chad Griffing, whom she'd met a few days earlier at Cliff's home, was gracious in his words of condolence. "I'm sorry Cassie," he said, his brow furrowed and his eyes expressing warmth and concern. "I know this is a difficult time for you. I'll try to help as best I can."

Cassie offered him a half smile and a nod. Words were still difficult to form. She remembered Griffing was a long-time neighbor and friend of Anna Alvarez, the owner of the gallery that displayed Cliff's work. Now, the solicitous elderly man gestured for her to sit before he took his own seat behind a large mahogany desk. Stacks of documents lay haphazardly strewn across the desk's top.

In spite of Cassie's initial protests, Cliff had insisted on making her his sole beneficiary. She couldn't deny him after his simple statement, "I have no one else," stole her breath and left a searing pain in her heart.

"Thank you for coming in, Cassie. I promised Cliff I'd make this as easy for you as possible. His estate is pretty straightforward. As you know, he'd already given his stock trailer to the friend who took the horses, and he donated his truck to a local homeless shelter. The house was his only remaining asset. At Cliff's request, a realtor solicited and received offers for the house—including one at slightly over the appraised value. Do you want to accept the offer, or would you prefer to sell the house on your own?"

She shook her head and finally found her voice. "I'll accept the offer." She wouldn't even know where to start to sell a house.

Griffing nodded, then continued "I'll let them know. It's a cash transaction and shouldn't take more than a few weeks to process. The deed has already been changed to reflect both of your names as owners, so there shouldn't be any issues. If you'd like, I can take care of all the paperwork for you. Once the mortgage is cleared, the remaining equity is yours. We can work out the details at another time."

Cassie nodded her assent as he spoke. She didn't want the money, but it would be hers, nonetheless. She felt her anger build at God, or fate, or whatever or whomever pulled the strings and controlled the world. After all his years of rootless wandering, Cliff had barely had a chance to settle in and enjoy the small house that he had made his home. The powerlessness of her anger made her want to scream at the vengeful God who had taken him. Instead, she sat on the edge of her chair, helpless to stop the storm building within her.

When the attorney finished speaking, Cassie rose from her chair, intending to thank him and leave. Griffing held up his hand for her to wait.

He picked up an envelope and shook out a small key which he handed to her along with a business card for a local bank.

She stared in confusion at the proffered offering. "Didn't Cliff explain?" Griffing asked. "This is the key to his safe-deposit box. Making you a signatory for access was one of the cards you signed. His bank account and the safe-deposit box are yours, as well. The bank can help you with the details."

Once again Cassie nodded, having little energy to do more. Feeling unmoored, she grasped the edge of the massive desk to ground herself and focused on the painting behind Griffing's desk. The huge canvas depicted a range of snow-covered mountains with a forest of golden Aspens at their base. The serenity of the scene settled her. She turned her eyes back to Griffing.

He had been watching her. She saw pity and compassion in his eyes, before he averted his gaze. He cleared his throat and this time turned to her with a more neutral expression. "There's one more thing. I know Cliff was adamant about not having a service, and we certainly want to honor his wishes, but Anna thought perhaps he wouldn't mind if she had a quiet dinner party at her home this Saturday for a small group of friends. She's calling it a remembrance dinner.

"Anna wants to invite her staff from the gallery, her nephew—the young man who introduced her to Cliff—and a couple of people Cliff worked with at the show grounds. It would be an opportunity for the people who cared about him to come together and celebrate his life. She was hoping you would come as well, along with anyone you'd like to invite. She didn't know how you'd feel about it. I promised her I'd ask you."

Cassie smiled at the elderly man. Her face might be pale and drawn, and her eyes swollen from crying, but for the first time in days, her smile wasn't forced.

"I'd like that, Mr. Griffing. I think Cliff would like that, too. He deserves it. He deserves to have a remembrance dinner. Please thank Anna and tell her I'll be there. I'd like to bring one guest with me. I've been staying with a friend. I'll leave you his number. Maybe she can call with the address and time?"

She wrote down Connor's name and number and left the paper on the desk.

~

The bank was only a short drive away. The bank manager offered his condolences, verified her signature, and took her to the vault. After he slid the safe-deposit box out of the wall and placed it on the table in the middle of the room, he gestured to a chair and handed her a large manila envelope. "This is to hold whatever you'd like to take with you. I'll leave you now. Please let me know if there's anything you need."

After he'd gone, Cassie stared in confusion at the metal box on the table. Why hadn't Cliff told her about the safe-deposit box? He had gone over everything with her, but not this. Why? With a slight shake of the head and a soft sigh, she pushed the questions aside and lifted the lid.

The box wasn't full, far from it. Inside were two envelopes—one, a standard, legal-sized envelope, the other, a beat-up manila envelope folded in a narrow rectangular shape and wrapped tight with a rubber band. She reached for that one first. Sliding the rubber band off, she slowly unfolded the manila envelope until she could undo the clasp. She glanced inside and gasped.

The stack of money was at least three inches high with a hundred dollar bill on top. Slowly, as if in a dream, she slid the contents onto the table. A rubber band held the bills together. She thumbed the edges and discovered that about halfway down, the hundred dollar bills were replaced by fifties and then twenties. At the bottom was a note: *"$8,000 in blood money. Do something good with it."*

Her hands were shaking when she picked up the other envelope. In it, she found a handwritten letter addressed to her in Cliff's neat, precise handwriting, and a newspaper clipping. The headline caught her attention.

AP News Service. HELL'S ANGEL FOUND STABBED TO DEATH IN POMONA

Police responding to a domestic dispute call in Pomona found the body of Ralph 'Rat' Fairborn, an ex-convict and known member of the Hell's Angels motorcycle gang. Although the coroner's report has not been released, the police stated that it appeared Mr. Fairborn was stabbed to death. The police had been called by a neighbor who reported hearing a woman screaming. They found a woman, presumed to be Mrs.

Fairborn, locked in the basement. She told police her son, James Fairborn, had stabbed his father during an argument before he fled in her car. An all-points bulletin was issued for the eighteen-year-old man who is six-feet tall with short brown hair and a slender build. It is believed he is driving a tan 1973 Ford Mustang with a large dent in the passenger side door.

Neighbors expressed surprise when told the young man was a suspect. One neighbor stated that the deceased Mr. Fairborn had been released from prison about eighteen months ago. His son was described as a good student who at one point had two newspaper routes. The mother, who was on public assistance during the time her husband was in prison, often got into shouting matches with the neighbors over loud music and the revving motorcycle engines of her friends. The police had been called on at least three occasions. No one would speak about Mr. Fairborn, apparently due to fear of retribution from his motorcycle gang.

Cassie exhaled, not even aware she'd been holding her breath. Still processing what she'd read, she stared down at the handwritten pages in front of her.

Dear Cass:

I almost destroyed the newspaper article. I don't know why I've kept it all these years. I certainly didn't need to read it to remember what happened, but even now I can't bring myself to let go of it. Perhaps it's because it's the only tangible link to my past, a past I've tried to bury and to make my peace with in my own way. Please forgive me for leaving it for you to read and for not having the courage to warn you.

The newspaper article only tells part of the story, and they got that part mostly right. I'd like to believe that if we were given the time, someday we would both have trusted enough to be able to share our pasts. I share mine with you now with the hope that it will somehow help you come to peace with your own.

My mother was seventeen when I was born. She lived with her parents in West Covina, Ca. Her father sold insurance and her mother was an artist – a sculptor. I don't remember much about my first four years, just bits and pieces. I think it was a happy, oblivious time for me. My mother had many conflicts with her parents about her lifestyle and the kind of men she was involved with. She finally walked out of their house when she was 21, and she took me with her. Life was a roller coaster of highs and lows from then on. I found my only safe haven when she left me with her parents – often for weeks on end. Sometimes I wished she would never come back, but she always did, and I was always happy to see her. With all her faults, she was still my mother. I never really understood why she kept me. The cynical side of me points to the welfare money she received, but I guess I always wanted to believe it was more than that. I don't think even she knew.

We lived in a variety of places with a bunch of different guys most of whom treated her like dirt, and at best treated me like an annoying pet. Eventually, we moved in with the man she told me was my father. How to describe him? In simple terms, he was a Hell's Angel drug dealer who drank heavily and fought anyone who got in his way. My happiest memory was when he got sent to prison when I was 9. I was pretty much on my own, but a couple of neighbors took me under their wing and saw that I got to school every day. They were my angels, and Lord knows I needed them.

My father was released from prison when I was 16, and the next two years are ones I'd like to forget. Cassie, I hated him with a passion that scared me. It still does when I think about it. He had no use for me. I was a useless sissy piece of trash. I spent all of my time either at school, or at the free afternoon art lessons a caring teacher gave me. I'm not embarrassed to say that when he beat me, I cried. I am embarrassed to say that when he beat my mother, I hated him, but I didn't try to protect her—until that last day.

Something snapped. He was twice my size and had been drinking all day. When she didn't immediately get him another beer, he smacked her so hard she went flying across the room. I yelled at him to stop. I said a lot of things you don't say to a drunken psychopath, not if you want to live. I misjudged him though. I had gotten to the point where I honestly didn't care what he did to me, and he knew it. So he took it out on my mother instead. He hit her harder and harder, and then he took out his knife. He kept taunting me, telling me I wasn't a man. If I was, I wouldn't let him hurt her. She was screaming at me that it was all my fault and that I shouldn't have gotten him upset.

I don't know what happened. I don't honestly remember the details. All those years of repressed rage erupted, and I attacked him. I don't remember anything until I found myself stabbing him over and over again, and I realized he wasn't moving anymore. Through a fog, I heard my mother screaming and telling me she hated me. I guess I had believed she would thank me for ridding her life of the scum who'd abused her.

It's taken most of my life and a lot of research to come to terms with where my mother was psychologically, but it didn't help much then. I killed my father, and I knew then that I had lost my mother, too. I had nothing left but a fierce determination to live. I discovered then that there was more of my father in me than I'd thought. I threatened my mother— told her I'd hurt her if she didn't stop screaming. For the first time in my life, my mother was afraid of me. I later hated myself for that, but not then. I locked her in the basement and told her to keep her mouth shut.

I stole her car and ditched it near a bus station after taking the drug money I'd seen my father tape under the seat. I bleached my hair surfer blonde at a cheap motel. That's where I became Cliff Douglas—from a TV documentary about

Hawaiian cliff divers, and an episode of Streets of San Francisco with Michael Douglas. It was as good a name as any.

I hitched a ride to the beach, figuring it was my best chance to blend in. The next few weeks and months were tough, but I was used to fending for myself, and the beach kids closed ranks around me without knowing why, or caring. I eventually worked my way up the coast and landed in Washington where I spent a few years logging before I moved on to ranching.

Looking back with the perspective of thirty years, it sounds pretty simple, pretty easy, but you'd know better. I'd like to say I never looked back, but you'd know I was lying. I've spent the better part of the last thirty years trying to prove I wasn't my father's son.

I know someone hurt you bad, Cass. I hope our time together helped heal some of those wounds. I want you to know your love and your friendship healed many of mine. I can never fully atone for what I did, but if anyone can understand what drove me, I believe you can. I can honestly say I have no regrets and that I would do the same again. If there is a God, I am about to face his judgment without being able to ask for his forgiveness.

You are the most caring, sensitive, and beautiful woman I have ever known. You deserve happiness, Cassie. You deserve the love of a good man and someone to share your life with. I hope what we had will help you learn to trust again. You've got good instincts, my love, trust yourself to use them.

Thank you for being my lover and my friend.

Cliff

P.S. Over the years I replaced the drug money I'd stolen to help me survive. It's all there. Please give it away for me – maybe to a shelter for battered women, or to the Rescue Ranch. Somewhere it will do some good and help someone else learn to trust.

A steady rapping on the door was followed by the voice of the bank manager. "Miss Deahl? Miss Deahl, are you okay? The bank is ready to close."

Cassie didn't respond. Tears streaming down her face, she sat in the tiny, sterile room clasping Cliff's letter to her chest.

"Miss Deahl?"

When she heard the door open, she slid the money back into the envelope and turned her tear-streaked face toward the bank manager. He greeted her with a relieved expression. "I apologize for bothering you, but it's been two hours. We're about to close." He handed her a box of tissues. "Is there anything I can help you with?"

Cassie checked her watch. It was 4:45. "I'm sorry. I didn't mean to take so long. I'm...I'm just about ready to go."

She slipped the letter and the newspaper clippings back into their envelope and then slid everything into the larger envelope he'd given her. "May I use your phone?"

"Of course," he said, gesturing toward the open door.

She followed him out, leaving the empty safe-deposit box on the table.

When Connor's answering machine announced that he wasn't available to take the call, she left a message telling him she was running late and would be home by seven.

The mortuary was on the other side of town. A dour-faced young man murmured his condolences and handed her an urn. After listening to Cliff speak to her through his letter only moments earlier, she found it difficult to acknowledge the container's contents. Still, when she opened the back door of her truck, she stowed the urn with care.

She drove back to Jamestown as the sun began its slow descent behind the mountains in the western sky and allowed the scene to provide a much needed balm for her bruised heart. When she finally turned her truck into the long track of Connor's driveway, she noticed that the front porch light was on—a welcome home message from Connor.

Cliff's revelations helped clear the fog from Cassie's brain. Now that he'd shared his story, she didn't feel quite so alone, quite so damaged as before. He had known it would help her, providing yet another reason to grieve for the cowboy she had waited too long to admit she loved.

Connor met her at the door. She hugged him on impulse and then laughed at his stunned reaction. "I'm sorry, Connor. I just wanted to show my thanks. I could never have made it through the last few days without you." Having already stepped back from the quick embrace, she then leaned forward and kissed him on the cheek.

He chuckled and shook his head. "No thanks needed. How about some dinner?"

She followed him into the kitchen. "I have some things I need to do tomorrow, but after that I'm ready to come back to work." She sat at the kitchen table, picking at her salad, waiting for his response.

He was silent for a moment, before nodding his agreement. "Okay. How about Saturday morning? It's a half day, a good way to ease back in."

"I also have a favor to ask."

"Sure, Cassie. Anything."

"Do you have plans for Saturday evening? Anna Alvarez, the woman who owns the gallery that sold Cliff's work, wants to have a remembrance dinner. I was hoping..." She hesitated, hating to ask him for another favor. He'd done so much already. "I was hoping you could come with me."

He answered immediately. She heard just a hint of exasperation in his response. "Of course I'll come." He smiled, the warmth returning to his voice. "I think it's a great idea. It'll be a chance for the people who cared about him to come together."

His eyes held hers as he added, "Thank you for including me."

They sat in silence while Cassie framed her next thoughts. "I need to move back home, too. Thanks for taking care of me, though. I've never eaten so good." She grinned, trying to put a light spin on her request, "...but I need to be a big girl and deal with things..."

She stared down at her plate, afraid the uncertainty in her eyes would betray her thoughts. She didn't really want to leave, didn't actually want to face her grief alone, but there was no other realistic option—not for her.

When he didn't respond right away, she looked up. Connor's expression was thoughtful. Finally, he nodded. "How about you do that on Sunday? Give me a couple more days to enjoy your company? I've gotten used to having you around, and it's been a long time since I've had an opportunity to cook for someone." He raised his eyebrows in a question.

Biting her lip, she searched for the words she needed to say. Finally, she blurted out what her heart told her. "Thank you for being here for me, Connor. I've always been able to take care of myself, but not this time."

Her voice broke. She glanced down at her half-eaten salad in an effort to regain some composure.

After taking a deep breath, she looked up and met Connor's eyes. Before he had a chance to speak, she forced a smile and changed the subject. "So where's the main course that's attached to that mouth-watering aroma?"

Connor held her gaze a moment longer before nodding and offering a smile of his own. "Coming right up."

He rose from the table, leaving her to reclaim her strength.

~

The next morning, Cassie strolled into the Jamestown bank at exactly nine o'clock and approached the manager's desk.

"Mornin', Cassie. What can I do for you this morning?"

"Good morning, George," she answered with a smile. "I'd like to access my safe-deposit box, please. How's that cute puppy of yours doing?"

He shared a funny story about the puppy's antics as he took her back to the vault and settled her in a small room by herself. She laughed with him and nodded her thanks.

Like an actress changing scenes, the smile and laughter were gone as soon as he closed the door. She sat for fifteen minutes before moving her hand to lift the lid on the box. Three years. It had been three years since she'd last sat here—three years since she'd last had any reason to open this window to her past. She struggled to breathe in the suddenly stuffy room. Her hand shook as she lifted the lid of the box that contained the secrets of her own past—secrets she had carefully transported from place to place, bank to bank, for eighteen years.

She stared inside the metal box at the three envelopes from her time in hell. It was no surprise to her that Cliff had replaced his father's drug money. She understood why he had repaid every penny and then found himself incapable of giving it away. She laughed, making a hollow, mirthless sound as she picked up a fat creased envelope with two rubber bands around it.

The dirty cop money was all there. The filthy money that had helped her survive, that had kept her alive and one step ahead of her past—it was all there. Like Cliff, she too had replaced it all. It had taken her ten years, but every single dollar of Frank's dirty stash was in that envelope, and she could no more spend it then she could fly. She added Cliff's two envelopes to her three, then closed and locked the box. Perhaps at another time she would confront the rest of it, but not now.

As she stood up from the chair, she reminded herself that it had been over a month since she'd checked on Frank. She needed to fix that. She couldn't afford to get complacent. Not now. Not ever. She amended her mental to-do list, adding a trip to the Greeley library.

24

BITTERROOT RANCH, MT

Once she was settled back home, the seasons marched inexorably forward—summer became fall, fall slid into winter. Cassie's trips to the Greeley library developed a comforting sameness. No news was good news—and there was no news about Frank. She had five more years. Unless Frank died in prison. Then she'd be free.

The bleakness of winter magnified Cassie's grief. She found herself spending more of her free time at the Rescue Ranch—especially on Sunday afternoons when her silent phone became an oppressive reminder of all that she'd lost.

It wasn't human company she sought at the Ranch, though she knew many would gladly offer it. No one said anything outright, but she caught their looks and glances. Connor, Agnes, Lynne—they were all worried about her. She wanted to tell them not to worry. Instead, she soldiered on, hoping the multiplying passage of days would heal her heart.

Spring had always been her favorite season. This year's season of rebirth was no exception. The trees were feathered with buds holding the promise of a leafy canopy, and through an open window Cassie heard her feathered neighbors serenading their mates.

It was time to keep her final promise to Cliff.

She had lain in the dark next to him, knowing he was counting out his life in hours rather than days. When she'd first asked, he told her he didn't care what happened to his ashes. She'd pushed at him, insisting that not caring wasn't an acceptable answer. "If you don't want a cemetery plot,

Cliff, if you don't want a permanent place for your remains, where do you want your ashes to be spread?"

She'd thought his long silence meant he'd fallen asleep, until she'd heard his hoarse whisper. "By our cabin, Cassie. On the ridge, on a gusty spring day when the wind can spread my ashes through the canyon."

"Okay, Cowboy. Okay, that's where you'll go," she'd replied in a calm, measured voice before turning to kiss him. Only when she was sure he was asleep had she allowed herself the release that came with tears.

Now, it was time.

Even though it had been over eight years since she and Cliff had worked at Bitterroot Ranch, Maryann Johnson remembered Cassie when she called. As much as she tried to slide through life leaving the lightest of footprints where she tread, Cassie knew she stood out. She had always played down her looks, wearing her hair pulled back under her hat and outfitting herself in baggy shirts and well-worn work jeans. But there weren't very many tall, slender blondes working the ranches—especially ones who seemed to have a magic way with horses.

Cassie remembered the Johnsons as kind people, and they didn't disappoint her. After she'd explained the purpose of her planned trip, the elderly matriarch invited her to spend the night in their home and offered a horse for her trip into the mountains to fulfill Cliff's request.

Cassie splurged and hired a small private plane to fly her to Bozeman, Montana, allowing her to avoid a twelve hour drive. She'd already ruled out flying out of DIA where cameras and security abounded—and her identity would be scrutinized. However, when she saw how small the single-engine plane actually was, she questioned the wisdom of her plan. The pilot joked her out of her apprehension, and she was rewarded with breathtaking aerial views of the rugged land she had once called home.

They landed in Bozeman in the early evening of a sun-filled, late spring day. Not wanting to waste the time required for a sit-down meal, Cassie's first stop was Taco Bell, fortifying herself with a burrito and a large Coke. Then, with the windows of her rental car rolled down, she headed north, immersing herself in the sights, sounds, and scents of the Gallatin Valley. She reveled in the miles of prairie and grasslands, now blanketed with delicate wildflowers, the Blacktail Mountains a not-so-distant beacon drawing ever closer.

Not quite two hours later, she turned off the highway and started the drive down the long winding road to Bitterroot Ranch, one of the largest horse and cattle ranches in southwest Montana. She surprised herself by eagerly gazing ahead, searching for remembered landmarks. She wasn't used to such nostalgia. Her years on the run had always meant never looking back. A grin turned into a broad smile when she saw the herd of Quarter Horses grazing along the side of the road. The smile turned reflective and her stomach tightened when the handsome, stone-faced ranch house came into view.

She had a lump in her throat when she parked the rental car in the driveway next to the house. It was all just as she remembered. She took a deep breath to steady herself, to remind herself that it wasn't the same. Eight years had passed. Nothing was the same, except the simple things, like getting up before the sun when you worked on a ranch. She grabbed her overnight bag from the back seat and headed toward the house.

Carl Johnson answered the door at her first knock. "Hello, Cassie." He shook her hand, his expression solemn. "We're sorry to hear about Cliff. We didn't know him well, but we both remember him as a quiet, hard-working man. We're honored you reached out to us and that this is the place he'd asked to have his ashes spread."

As she started to respond to Carl, his wife joined them and offered her own condolences. Cassie thanked them both, not only for their words of sympathy, but for their gracious offer of a place to stay. Expecting to be shown to the bedroom off the kitchen that she'd called home when she worked for them, she was both surprised and humbled when Maryann led the way up the stairs to a second-floor bedroom.

"Wow," Cassie murmured, glancing appreciatively at the tasteful furnishings and oak-beamed ceiling. "The room off the kitchen would have been more than enough." As she spoke, she experienced a quick flashback, recalling the high-priced resort hotel she'd worked at many years earlier. The rooms there had been impressive, but this room was both impressive and inviting.

After placing her bag on an upholstered chair near the bed, she walked to the window. Wide-eyed at the expansive view of snow-covered mountain peaks, she added in a near reverential tone, "This is a gorgeous room with an incredible view. Thank you."

"It's one of my favorites," the diminutive, elderly woman said, pride evident in her response. "I love the view. Make yourself at home, Cassie. If there's anything you need, just let me know. You said you wanted an early start, so you're welcome to have breakfast with the guys. You know where the bunkhouse kitchen is. As you'd remember, the fare is hearty, if not all that healthy. Luke will have a horse ready for you."

She chuckled and gave Cassie an appreciative glance. "I wish I had your genes. You certainly don't look like you've aged any since we last saw you, and I'm guessing weight gain has never been an issue. Not like some of us!" The older woman looked down at herself and shrugged. "Fortunately, my husband doesn't seem to care that I've put on a few pounds over the years." Without waiting for a comment, she patted Cassie on the shoulder and left, pulling the bedroom door closed behind her.

Cassie slept fitfully that night in spite of the comfortable accommodations. She was awake early. After a quick shower, she dressed, wearing a long-sleeve shirt and heavy jacket, aware that spring in the mountains often felt more like winter. The bunkhouse kitchen brought back bittersweet memories, but she didn't linger to embrace them. Instead, she selected a couple of slices of toast and washed them down with a cup of strong black coffee, grateful that the ranch hands had already eaten and she had the place to herself.

Warmed by the coffee, she headed to the barn. Luke was there, watching a group of young horses frolicking in the corral. He'd obviously been waiting for her.

As she approached, he smiled and reached out his hand, shaking hers firmly as he spoke. "Good to see you again, Cassie. I'm real sorry about Cliff." He didn't wait for a response before turning toward a pretty, chestnut mare, already saddled. "It's been a while, and not many of the same stock are around, but this here's Sky. I think she was one of the youngsters you worked with. She's a fine working horse now. All the stock you started turned out to be fine working horses."

"Thanks, Luke. I'm glad. It's hard to believe it's been eight years." She raised her arm, gesturing to the barn and the overall property. "Everything around here looks the same. Although, we're all a little older now."

He snorted and nodded his agreement. "Don't I know it? Well, I'll let you get on with it. Take your time. The barn'll be here when you get back." He left her then.

With a slight shake of her head to clear the memories, she placed the canvas bag containing Cliff's urn in the saddle bag. Then she mounted and followed the sun's rise. No grand Gothic cathedral had the power to evoke the sense of spirituality that Cassie felt as she watched Mother Nature paint the sky with a palette of salmon and gold as the sun rose fully above the horizon.

Even though eight years had passed since she'd been in these mountains, she had no trouble finding the way. The trail was imprinted on her brain. She reined her horse in at the top of a ridge, breathed the thin, clear, woodsy air deep into her lungs, and watched as the sky finished its slow metamorphosis, erasing the subtle pink and finishing with a bright, cloudless blue.

She passed herds of elk and mule deer, a stealthy fox on the trail of breakfast, a lone coyote, and of course, cattle. They all peacefully co-existed, at least for this moment, in the picture postcard scene she imprinted in her mind. She took her time, feeling Cliff's presence beside her, feeling she was sharing it all with him—that he was seeing it with her one final time.

When at last the little cabin in the pine-filled canyon came into view, the eight years disappeared.

"Oh Cliff…"

She spoke the words out loud and lost her battle with the tears she'd been fighting to hold back. She rubbed her eyes to clear them, kicked her feet out of the stirrups, and then slid off her horse, leading the mare beside her down the mountainside. Had the building always been this shabby? How could this simple, Spartan cabin—barely more than a shack—be the place where she had learned to trust again?

After staring in disbelief at the sad little structure, she peered into the lone, dirt-stained window to see the cots and the rough-hewn table and benches. As she gazed into the cabin and back into the past, an errant ray of sunlight filtered through the tiny window and bathed the humble room in light. She wanted to believe it was a sign from Cliff, and she smiled a thank-you. She leaned her head against the rough siding, wanting to hold on to the memories, not willing to admit that it was all gone, that Cliff was dead—that she was standing in front of an old shack.

She stepped away, shook her head, and tried to laugh off her uncharacteristic behavior, but the sound stuck in her throat. She remounted and rode to the top of the ridge overlooking the flower-filled meadow surrounding the cabin. Dismounting again, she opened the saddlebag and removed Cliff's ashes.

She opened the urn, holding it up high on the windy ridge. As she turned it upside down, she whispered her final farewell. "Goodbye Cowboy. You'll always be alive in my heart."

The wind took the ashes and in an instant, they were gone. Cassie stood in silent tribute, sensing the presence of a greater being. It was in these unspoiled places surrounded by the majesty of the earth—the snow-capped mountain peaks and undulating valleys cut through with narrow ribbons of water where great rivers once flowed—that she came closest to believing in God. Her doubts would return. They always did.

She laughed when her horse nudged her in the back.

"Okay, girl. Thanks for being so patient. Let's go home."

She rode back to the ranch in a contemplative mood. After again thanking the Johnsons for their hospitality, she drove to the airport for her flight back home to Colorado. The pilot was waiting. "We're in luck, Ms. Deahl. It's a clear day with very little wind. It'll be a smooth ride."

They landed at a small private airport outside Boulder. Cassie thanked the pilot and walked to her car, a smile on her face. The short trip had been cathartic. Cliff was at peace. She could finally let him go. She slept better that night than she'd slept in a very long time.

The next morning, she greeted Agnes and Pepper with an enthusiastic "Good morning!" and a grin which broadened when she saw Connor. She'd shared her plans with him, and she knew that he'd worried about her. He hadn't said much, but his expression had been easy enough to read when he'd wished her a safe trip. Now, she saw relief, and something else—something she still wasn't ready to acknowledge. He was a good friend. At least for now, she wanted to keep it that way.

25

JAMESTOWN, CO

Cassie yawned and stretched before pouring a cup of coffee and glancing at the calendar on the wall next to the refrigerator. It was Friday, July fourteenth, and the heat wave that held the Colorado Front Range in its grip showed no signs of breaking. It was only eight-thirty, but the air conditioner Connor had surprised her with a week earlier was already straining to cool her small apartment.

She shook her head, smiling in remembrance and gratitude. Connor had used the emergency key she'd given him and had installed the air conditioner while she was at the Rescue Ranch. She'd unlocked the street-level door and trudged up the stairs covered with sweat and grime anticipating a stifling apartment only to be happily surprised. Blissfully cool temperatures greeted her when she'd opened the upstairs door.

Still dressed in the oversized Rescue Ranch tee shirt she wore as a nightgown, Cassie turned on the TV and half-watched the Today show while she sipped her coffee. With one leg tucked comfortably under her on the couch, she mentally worked through a training plan for the young mare that was her latest project at the Ranch.

Her mind elsewhere, Cassie wasn't focused on Matt Lauer when he explained the show's next segment—something about an update on a murder case. The TV screen flashed to a picture of a young woman with teased blonde hair, heavy eye make-up, and bright red lipstick. The skimpy black dress she wore threatened to release her breasts—and the smile on her face didn't quite reach her eyes. A tough-looking, middle-aged man with a short military haircut, an arrogant expression, and a proud, self-satisfied smirk on his face, stood with his arm draped in a proprietary manner around the young woman's shoulders.

Cassie gasped, sucking coffee into her windpipe. She choked and coughed, coffee spewing out of her mouth and splattering the front of her tee shirt. She fought to clear her lungs and still focus on the reporter's words.

"Former Pine View, New Jersey, Police Chief Frank Peters will soon be released from prison—five years early—although an actual date has not yet been announced. Peters was convicted nearly twenty years ago for the murder of his young wife, Catherine, who is standing next to him in this photo. Her body was never found, and he has consistently maintained his innocence.

"This move by the parole board, is, we've been told, the result of lengthy behind-the-scenes negotiations with his legal team. The board announced that their decision was based on Peters' deteriorating health and his exemplary behavior in prison. Since previous requests to the parole board had been denied, this decision caught everyone by surprise.

"Matt, you may remember that the circumstances surrounding Peters' arrest and subsequent trial were pretty bizarre."

When a picture of a familiar two-story, colonial-style house replaced the reporter's face, Cassie shuddered.

The reporter continued speaking. "The police were called to Peters' home by a neighbor who found the Chief's police car partially blocking the road in the quiet neighborhood of well-kept, middle-class homes. When they arrived on the scene, the police found Peters unconscious in the living room with his service revolver on the couch next to him and illegal drugs on the table in front of him.

"It was eventually determined that he had overdosed on a legal prescription drug, although it had not been prescribed for him, and no other trace of the drug could be found in the house. There was no sign of his wife. When the FBI took over the investigation, they discovered fresh blood on the mattress, a bloody woman's shirt under the front seat of his car, and a blood-spattered and ripped nightgown in the garbage.

"Although Peters never testified at his trial, his attorney maintained that Peters knew nothing about his wife's disappearance and repeatedly asserted that he had been framed. The government built a case on circumstantial evidence which the jury found convincing. Based on that evidence, Peters was convicted and sentenced to twenty years in prison for his wife's murder.

"In a separate trial, based partially on evidence obtained from off-shore bank account records, and the almost $200,000 in cash the police recovered from his home and in a variety of safe-deposit boxes, Peters was also convicted of tax evasion. That conviction added another five years to his sentence. No one, either in Pine View or on the police force, would testify against him, so although rumors flourished about drug sales and involvement with organized crime, the government had to settle on the lone tax evasion charge.

"An attack in prison a few years ago left Peters in a wheelchair. The sixty-five year old senior citizen is leaving prison a mere shadow of the angry—some would say psychopathic and violent—man who was sentenced twenty years ago."

They flashed to a picture of an elderly, balding man sitting in a wheelchair, staring fixedly into the camera.

"Regardless of the shape he's in, the folks in Pine View aren't throwing any welcome-home parties. Off the record, I've been told that Peters acted as his own judge and jury during his long reign as the Pine View Police Chief. Though no one would comment on camera, the people I spoke to expressed shock at his pending release. They definitely do not want him back in their town. Some have even questioned whether his health issues are real."

Cassie slid off the sofa onto the floor, her eyes locked on the TV screen. She didn't see a crippled old man in a wheelchair. She focused on the eyes. They were the cold, calculating eyes of the man who had raped and tortured her—the man who wanted her dead. There was no question that he would hunt her down, no question that he wouldn't rest until he watched her die.

She had spent the last twenty years anticipating the inevitability of this day. Every year on the anniversary of Frank's conviction, Cassie heard the ticking of her mental countdown clock grow louder—even though it was no longer the focus of her daily life.

She'd thought she had five more years of freedom, five more years to prepare, five more years clicking down on Frank's life clock, and the death she would have prayed for—if she prayed.

Long after the Today show moved on to another story, she sat, not moving, still seeing the eyes of the insane man who wanted her dead. Her mind was caught in a loop repeating the same thought over and over.

He's going to kill me. He's going to kill me. . .

Trapped in a near catatonic state, she forgot about work. Forgot about everything, until she heard the hammering of a fist on the street-level door to her apartment, followed by the pounding of footsteps on the stairs. Even then, she didn't move. She sat on the floor, staring blankly into space, rocking slowly back and forth.

"Cassie! Cassie!" Connor's voice grew louder. Cassie heard the upstairs door hit the wall with force as Connor pushed it open. His hurried footsteps approached.

Still, she didn't move.

"Cassie, what's wrong? When you didn't show up this morning..." His words trailed off.

She felt him shaking her. "Cassie! What happened? Did someone hurt you? Cassie, look at me!"

He held her face in his hands, forcing her to look at him. "Do you want me to call a doctor? Take you to the hospital? Please, talk to me!"

The frantic, demanding tone in his voice finally reached her. She tried to focus on Connor's face, but she flashed back to another man, another time. "No...no...no...please...no," she whimpered and began to shake, slipping back into a past she couldn't outrun.

She felt arms wrap around her, someone rubbing her back, and she slowly returned to the present, to an understanding of where she was—but she still couldn't control her shaking. She tried to focus, to breathe, and slowly, very slowly, she began to reclaim herself.

Connor was speaking. "It's okay, Cassie. I'm here to help. It's okay."

He stroked her back, but she couldn't accept his offer of solace. She pulled away, pushed herself up, and began to pace. Ignoring Connor's presence, she ran her fingers through her hair, and barefoot, wearing only a stained old tee shirt, she paced back and forth across the room like a caged animal.

She looked beyond Connor and spoke her thoughts out loud. "I should never have stayed. As long as I was moving, he couldn't find me. I gotta go..."

"Cass? Cassie, look at me, please?" Connor spoke slowly, insistently.

She glanced down, surprised to see Connor still sitting on the floor, a wary and concerned expression on his face. He pushed himself up and walked towards her. "Let me help, Cassie. Tell me what's wrong. Let me help."

As he approached her and held out his arms, she stopped pacing. Her panic subsided, but when she spoke, the resignation in her mind came through in her words. "You can't, Connor. You can't help me, and you shouldn't. You don't know…"

She raised her hands in a helpless gesture and turned to face the window, allowing her mind to float untethered through a morass of terrifying thoughts.

"Stop!" Connor's voice was loud in her ears. It wasn't like him to raise his voice. She refocused and turned to face him.

His gaze was intense, his jaw tight with tension, his words pleading. "Do you think there is anything you can tell me, anything at all, that would cause me to change the way I feel about you? Cassie, I've spent some part of almost every day of the last five years with you. Whoever you were before, whatever you've been through, whatever you're running from—it won't change anything. Can't you trust me enough to finally let me in?"

The silence built. His words hung in the air. Her voice was flat when she spoke. "You may regret that offer, Connor. You may regret you ever knew me."

"Not a chance." He repeated the words as he put his arms around her. "Not a chance."

Drained now that her terror-fueled adrenaline spike had dissipated, she stepped back and gazed up at him. "Give me some time, okay? I need some time. I've got some things I need to do. Can I…can I stay with you for a couple of days? I don't want to be alone."

"Of course you can stay with me. While you get your things together, I'll go back to the office and cancel the rest of the day."

Reading the concern in her face, he continued, "Don't worry. I won't tell them anything. How about we take Quincy and Belle for a ride in the foothills? It's been a while since they've had a good outing. We'll get away from civilization for a few hours."

She nodded her acceptance, compressing her lips in a small tight line as he turned away and started for the stairs. She called after him. "Wait.

Don't cancel the whole day. I'll meet you at your house in a couple of hours. I have some things I need to do first. Okay?"

When he turned back to face her, she could sense his uncertainty.

"I promise. Connor, I promise. I'll be there before noon."

It was his turn to nod. She listened to his heavy steps on the stairs and waited until she heard the downstairs door close before she moved. She trotted down the stairs to lock the door behind him. Then, her mind now on overdrive, she took a quick shower and dressed, pulling her wet hair back into a ponytail.

After throwing a couple days' worth of clothes in her overnight bag, she sat at the kitchen table and forced herself to concentrate, to think things through, to remember life before she settled in Jamestown—to remember how she needed to live again.

Thirty minutes later, she left the small apartment over the lawyer's office on Main Street, the place she'd called home for the last five years. She had an overnight bag clutched in one hand and a backpack slung over her shoulder. She placed both on the front seat of her truck. As she strode down Main Street on her way to the bank, she was already feeling nostalgic for the little town that had embraced her. She was already separating herself, already saying her mental goodbyes. This time it wouldn't be easy to leave. She had tied up tight here, with more than just the quick-release knot she had used in the past. This time her leaving would be painful—and not just for her.

As she strode along the cracked sidewalk, she passed the barber shop with its old-fashioned, candy-striped barber pole. She glanced at the hair salon with the faded pictures in the window and the elderly clientele who remembered when those pictures were new—women who showed up weekly to have their hair washed and set while they gossiped about their friends and family. It was a snapshot in time frozen thirty years ago, but the sameness was comforting. She passed the empty stores that had been home to a variety of short-lived tenants, and the stationery store that sold odds and ends and probably made most of its money from the sale of lottery tickets.

Most of the townspeople had pets. Cassie knew their pets and she knew them—some she even thought of as friends, or at least something beyond acquaintances. A couple of people waved and called out to her as she passed, and she nodded in response. She had become part of the fabric of the town. Somehow, without even trying, she had been woven into its pattern. No, this time leaving would not be easy.

She squared her shoulders and opened the door to the bank. After greeting the manager with a forced smile, she asked for access to her safe-deposit box. She knew exactly what she was looking for. She removed an envelope, closed and locked the box, and returned it to its place. This was her trump card. If her plan failed, she would be running for the rest of her life. She shuddered and amended her thought—if her plan failed, the rest of her life would be short, and the end painful.

~

She was sitting in one of the comfortable, old rocking chairs on Connor's porch when his truck turned down the driveway. She smiled and waved. He tooted the horn in acknowledgment. He was her friend—her best friend, her only real friend. She couldn't allow him to be more than that. It didn't matter that she wanted him to be more, that she knew he wanted to be more. There was no place in her life for permanence—or for love. Leaving Connor would mean leaving the best part of herself. Her smile faded, and she fought back tears. She had no choice.

Cassie followed Connor's truck down the driveway and watched as he expertly backed it up to the horse trailer. When he climbed out and smiled down at her, the relief in his expression was apparent.

"I'm glad to see you," was all that he said, but she could sense a much deeper emotion before he turned away and began to hitch up the trailer

Cassie stowed the saddles and bridles. Connor loaded the horses. She was calmer now and was breathing more deeply, but the worry and fear hadn't left her, and her mind was elsewhere. They drove to the trailhead and saddled the horses, mostly in silence. She was grateful Connor didn't press her for conversation, and they exchanged only a few words about the scenery during their ride through the foothills.

It wasn't until they were driving home that she finally said, "Connor, I have to take a short trip tomorrow. I need to leave early. I'll be back tomorrow night, though. Don't worry about me, okay? I promise you, I'll be back. I'll explain then. Please don't tell anyone I'm not here. I won't ask you to lie for me, but…"

He sighed, his frustration evident when he answered her. "I won't tell anyone Cassie, but don't ask me not to worry about you. It's too late for that."

Pulling the truck into the driveway of his home, he parked by the barn before turning to her. "Cassie, it's not just you anymore. Like it or not, I care about you—a lot of people care about you. If you plan to leave, if you plan to run away, just think about how much you're leaving behind."

He didn't say any more. He unloaded the horses, fed them, and stomped back to the house, alone. Cassie didn't follow him. She sat on a hay bale, ignoring the brilliant sunset as the sun disappeared from the sky. She was fighting an internal battle between her younger self—a woman who had survived hell by battling the devil—and her current self, older by twenty years, a woman who didn't know if she had the energy or the will for another battle. She was sure no bookmaker would take the odds. Success was less than a long shot.

She pushed herself up and trudged across the backyard to where the brightly lit kitchen drew her like a welcoming beacon. When she opened the back door and entered the kitchen, Connor was rinsing lettuce for a dinner salad. He turned to her. When their eyes met, he held her gaze, refusing to break eye contact.

She acknowledged the commitment in his eyes with a small nod before she shrugged her shoulders and spoke. "I'm tired Connor. I've been running for twenty years, and I'm tired." She laughed, although the sound held no humor. "I need to amend that. I think I'm tired because I stopped running a few years ago when I settled in here. Before that, I had a routine, a regimen, a formula—always moving on, always moving forward, and never looking back. I broke all the rules when I stayed here, and now I don't know what to do. I'm not sure I even know how to run anymore."

She sat at the kitchen table and stared down at her hands. When she raised her head, she saw that he was focused on her with an intense, pained expression. She hated herself for hurting him.

"Okay," she said, hoping she wouldn't regret the words even as she spoke them, "I promise you this. When I come back tomorrow night, I'll try. I'll try to find a way to explain, to share my past with you." She wondered if her words sounded as anguished as she felt saying them. "You may regret asking. People aren't always what they seem, Connor."

He shook his head. His voice was clear and firm when he spoke. "No matter what you tell me, I'll have no regrets, Cassie. I've been alone for a long time. I've been running from my own demons, mentally if not physically. I'm ready to share my past, too. But let me help you deal with yours first. I want..."

He looked away. When he looked back at her, his expression left little doubt about his feelings. "I need you in my life."

Cassie's vision blurred as tears filled her eyes. She broke eye contact and stared down at the table. She needed to be strong. When she again glanced up, there was no more talk of running or of shared confidences. She gestured to the steaks on the counter. "Want some help grilling those? I grill a mean steak."

He nodded. The subject was closed—at least for the moment.

After dinner, they sat in the living room, an old Alfred Hitchcock movie playing on the TV, but Cassie had no idea what the story was about. As the credits rolled on the screen, she gave Connor a quick hug and said good night before heading to her bedroom to face what she knew would be a mostly sleepless night.

26

SAN DIEGO, CA

Awake before dawn, Cassie was on the road a few minutes later for the ninety-minute drive to Denver International Airport. Although post-9/11 security requirements complicated things, she tried to minimize her profile by tucking her hair under a baseball cap and avoiding eye contact.

The two-hour flight to San Diego landed on time. Based on all the business suits she saw, Cassie assumed most of her fellow passengers were business travelers. They stared at their laptops and phones, paying little attention to their surroundings—or to her.

Grateful for the anonymity, Cassie made her way to the rental car counter. With a contract in hand for a small economy car, she entered the ladies room as an unassuming blonde-haired, jean-clad woman in a baseball cap and long-sleeved chambray shirt. A different woman—one with short, curly brown hair, wearing a white tee shirt and black cropped pants—sauntered out a few minutes later. Her look was accessorized with oversized tortoise shell sunglasses and bright pink lipstick. This new version of Cassie Deahl strode to her rental car, tossed her backpack on the passenger seat, and drove away.

A chain drug store provided needed supplies. A few minutes later, Cassie parked at the public library and approached the circulation desk with a pocketful of change for the copy machine and a borrowed name from the local telephone directory—just in case. The kindly old woman managing the desk pointed her toward the computers, no library card or other identification required.

So far, so good.

Cassie's nervousness abated slightly as she approached the mostly empty computer room. She chose a computer close to the door and far away from the only other occupant, a young man so engrossed in his online research he didn't even glance up at her arrival. It didn't take her long to prepare the letter she'd written out on the plane—one that purposely included a variety of misspellings and grammatical errors. She then typed out three names and addresses. Finally, she printed it all, including a fictitious Chula Vista return address for the envelopes. Grateful for the early hour and the resultant lack of library patrons who might think her behavior odd, she pulled on latex gloves, picked up the printed sheets and slipped them into a manila folder.

Hands shaking, she took a dingy envelope from her backpack, an envelope she'd stored in a variety of safe-deposit boxes for twenty years. She removed the worn, wrinkled pages covered with a young woman's girlish script. After smoothing the wrinkles with a loving hand, she placed each of the pages on the glass of the printer and pressed the copy button. Copies and originals safely in hand, she gathered her belongings, stored the gloves in her purse, and strolled out of the library.

The most difficult part of her task accomplished, Cassie tried to relax during the twenty-minute drive south to Chula Vista, a town a few minutes from the Mexican border. Country music played on the radio as the scenery sped by. She barely noticed the music—or the scenery.

Turning off the freeway, she parked in a small strip mall and once again pulled on the latex gloves. She prepared three identical mailings, all addressed to news media—TV and newspaper—and applied a liberal amount of postage to each envelope. Hands trembling, she deposited the manila envelopes in a mailbox in front of the Chula Vista post office a short walk away.

Once she'd returned to her car, Cassie finally allowed herself to fully breathe. She drove back to the airport, trying not to second guess her plan. It was too late for that. Instead, she turned the radio up loud and sang along to country music classics—but even her favorite music couldn't quell her uneasiness.

She changed out of her disguise in an out-of-the-way airport restroom, and once again Cassie Deahl was an unassuming blonde in jeans and a chambray shirt. With three hours to kill before her flight home, she secreted herself in a booth in an airport bar. Beer and a slice of pizza filled her stomach, but did little to settle her mind. She didn't absorb a word in the paperback book she'd tossed into her backpack for the trip. The book became little more than a prop. Her mind was in turmoil. Every thought, no matter how mundane, ended with an echo of the reporter's words as he announced Frank's imminent release from prison.

Her plane landed late at DIA after a delayed take-off due to local thunderstorms. Knowing Connor would be worried, Cassie reclaimed her truck and sped down the dark back roads toward Jamestown. She berated herself for not having called him from the airport, but she hadn't been ready to talk. She still wasn't. Her mind searched for what to say, for how to explain her trip—and came up empty.

Exhausted and emotionally overwhelmed, Cassie hiked up the front porch steps of Connor's home slightly before eleven o'clock. Before she had a chance to use the key, the door opened. Connor stood there, concern and worry etched on his face.

A chastened Cassie apologized. "I'm sorry, Connor. I would have been here an hour ago, except—I had a flat tire." She hated herself for lying, but she wasn't ready to explain her trip to San Diego.

She nodded at the exasperation she saw in his eyes. "I know, it's 2007, I should have a cell phone. If I had a cell phone, I could have called you." For some reason, she continued to expand on her lie. "I was doing quite a good job of getting the spare out to change the flat before the State Trooper showed up. He insisted on calling the roadside assistance truck. I had to let them help." She shrugged, raising her eyebrows in resignation before walking past him, collapsing on the couch and dropping her backpack on the floor beside her.

He followed her into the living room and stood in front of her, hands on his hips. "Tomorrow," he announced in a determined voice. "I'm buying you a cell phone, and I want you to promise to use it."

"I can buy my own..." she began, until she saw the expression on his face. Before he could say another word, she nodded. "Okay, I promise. Thank you, Connor."

He bent down and placed his hand on her arm, leaving it there as he spoke. "You look exhausted. How about we both get some sleep and in the morning we head up to the cabin with the horses for the next couple of days? We can drive back early Monday in time for work. I've got the truck packed, and the horses are raring to go. What do you say?"

The expression in his eyes told her he was going to hold her to her earlier promise. He wanted answers.

"Okay." She nodded and laughed. "I think you were stretching the truth just a wee bit though. Belle may be raring to go, but Quincy would be just as happy to stay home."

He smiled, matching her attempt to keep things light. "Okay, I may have taken a bit of liberty there. But Quincy will follow Belle anywhere, so he'll be happy enough."

She pushed herself up from the comfortable couch, kissed Connor on the cheek, and headed off to bed—where, in spite of her exhaustion, she was unable to fall asleep. She had taken her one shot, her only shot. If it didn't hit its mark, she couldn't run far enough—or fast enough. It had to work. It had to be enough. With that thought as her mantra, she finally fell asleep.

~

Cassie opened her eyes to a sun-filled room. After glancing at the clock, she propelled herself out of bed with a muttered curse. Still tying her bathrobe, she stumbled down the stairs.

Connor glanced up from the newspaper with a smile. "Good morning!"

She stammered an apology. "Connor, I'm sorry. I know you wanted to get an early start. I…"

He offered an indulgent smile. "We have all day, Cassie. There's no hurry. You get the full bed and breakfast treatment when you stay at my house. So, while you get showered and dressed, I'll make good on the breakfast part." He glanced at the clock and chuckled. "We'll call it brunch."

Ninety minutes later, they were in the foot hills of the Rocky Mountains, driving under a brilliant blue sky sprinkled with fluffy cumulus clouds. Connor rolled the window down, and they both inhaled the fresh clean scent of the air, but neither of them spoke. An Alan Jackson CD provided background music for their separate thoughts.

Connor drove down a hard-packed, rutted dirt road past small cottages and A-frames on the edge of Rocky Mountain National Park. He'd never shared much about his dead wife or his marriage, but Cassie knew this had been their special place. She also knew it was the place where he most often ran when he needed to escape. She was humbled by his offer to share it.

After they'd unloaded the horses and turned them out in the fenced paddock attached to the small A-frame, they unpacked the truck and lugged the rustic porch furniture out of the house and onto the front porch. Chores completed, they saddled up and followed the trail into the park.

Cassie wasn't quite ready to share her thoughts, and it seemed Connor was reticent about sharing his as well. So instead of talking, they rode in companionable silence, occasionally laughing at the antics of the local wildlife. They rode single file as the horses picked their way across the clear gurgling streams that wound down the rock-strewn mountainside. Wider trails allowed them to ride together, their horses matching stride for stride. Neither of them commented on the natural beauty surrounding them.

Just as the sun was setting behind the line of imposing pine trees surrounding the cabin, they returned from their ride. Still in a reflective and mostly silent mood, Cassie fed the horses, and then set the porch table with paper plates and plastic cutlery. Connor added the supermarket fried chicken, potato salad, and coleslaw. As they pulled the pine-wood chairs up to the table, Connor handed Cassie a beer.

After they sat down, he broke the silence. "I have a confession to make."

She turned to him in surprise, a forkful of potato salad almost to her mouth. "Confession? I thought that was supposed to be my line, Connor. What could you possibly have to confess?"

She watched him pick at his food and swallow a sip of beer. The only light came from the half-moon and the Coleman lamp. The intimacy of the darkness should have made it easier to share, but she could sense it still wasn't easy for Connor to divulge whatever it was he believed required confession.

"I was worried about you. I wanted to find out what had upset you so much." He hesitated a moment before continuing. "I noticed the Today show was on when I found you. I wondered if that was what had upset you. It was a long shot, but I had plenty of time, so I watched a rerun of the show on the NBC website."

She held his gaze in the dim light trying to gauge his reaction. She thought she saw compassion—and questions he was afraid to ask.

"Oh," was all she could manage.

"It explained a lot, but I have more questions than answers. Cassie, you were barely more than a girl. How did you manage? How did you get away? What about your family?"

She sighed before replying in a low voice. "Connor, if anyone deserves answers, you do. I've never told another living soul though. I'm not even sure I know how."

"Cliff?"

"No. Not even Cliff. He and I were kindred spirits, reflections of each other in so many ways. Somehow two damaged people who spent their lives running from their pasts magically found one another. I still don't understand how. I think that through each other we learned to trust again, but no, I never told him. Perhaps, if he'd lived…"

She shrugged and stared into the darkness before continuing. "It's a long story, Connor."

"I've got all night."

She started at the beginning with her happiest memory, smiling as she recounted the tale of a little girl holding her daddy's hand as she skipped across an alpine meadow with a bright yellow kite soaring above her head. Her voice turned somber as she explained how her ten-year-old world fell apart when her mother committed suicide.

She told him about moving from Germany to New Jersey with her father when she was fourteen, and about knowing she was an American, but always feeling more like an immigrant. It surprised her that after all these years, she could still feel the sting of the loneliness and isolation of her adolescence.

She smiled again when she told him about her art teachers, about a special girlfriend in high school who helped the shy outsider fit in, and just a bit about Mike, her best friend and first love. The boy who broke her heart.

She stopped every few minutes to take another bite of food. It gave her time to gather her thoughts. When she got closer to the painful parts, she wasn't sure she was ready, or able, to put some of it into words. The silence grew as she sorted things out in her mind.

Connor handed her another beer and peered into her face. "Are you okay?"

She nodded. "Yeah. I'm fine. I told you, I've never done this before, and now I'm getting to the hard parts."

"I want to help Cassie, but I don't want to pressure you. I don't want you to tell me anything you don't want..."

"I need to Connor. It's time."

She searched his eyes for some idea of what he was thinking. "When you hear the whole story, you'll understand why I may need to run again. Why I can't take the chance to stay."

She got up from the table. "I'll be right back."

She went into the cabin to use the rudimentary toilet facilities. When she returned, Connor had cleared the table and retrieved their jackets. The temperature had dropped at least twenty degrees since the sun had set. He was standing by the porch railing and held her jacket while she slid her arms into the sleeves.

When she turned to thank him, his expression was both loving and concerned. She hugged him in gratitude.

He returned the hug. Then he dropped his arms and stepped back. "You still feel up to talking?"

"Now that I've started, I don't think I can stop. The genie is out of the bottle, and I don't think I can get it back in. I don't think I even want to try." Her final words were barely audible. She held his gaze when she continued. "Like I said, you may regret you ever asked."

She swallowed and turned away, finding the words difficult to find. "I'm scared, Connor. I want to tell you, but I've never exposed this much of myself to anyone. I've never let anyone get this close..."

His voice was gentle. "Look at me, Cassie."

She turned to him.

"There is nothing you can tell me—nothing—that will make me turn away from you, or judge you. Do you understand that?"

She nodded, and, with a resigned sigh placed her chair at an angle to his without the table to separate them. She sat. Her voice took on a casual, matter-of-fact tone she was sure he could tell was forced.

"My father left the day I graduated from high school. He was an Army communications specialist, and the Army had reassigned him to the Mid-East. He kissed me and left. I don't think he actually did it, but I could swear I heard him breathe a sigh of relief when he said goodbye. He was never comfortable being the single parent of a teen-aged girl, but he did his duty like the good soldier he was."

There was no bitterness in her voice, just a hint of sorrow for the relationship she'd never had. She had long ago forgiven her father for his abandonment. It had been a very long time since she'd fought back tears after witnessing loving embraces between the fathers and daughters that had crossed her path.

"A wonderful woman who owned an Arabian horse farm in the small Jersey shore town where we lived became like a mother to me—or maybe more like an aunt, or an older sister. She invited me to live with her and John, her husband. They made me a part of their family. Their home became mine, even after I went away to college.

"I still remember the day they came to my apartment in Pine View— the town where I was going to college—to tell me my father was dead. I couldn't believe it at first. It didn't seem possible. He was the only real family I had. Even though we were never close, I think he loved me, in his own way. Then he died—and it was too late for us to ever really get to know one another."

Her voice broke. Connor put a consoling hand on her arm. She nodded her thanks.

"I had trouble focusing on school after that. I couldn't really focus on much of anything. Fortunately, John and Jean were there for me. They took me back to the farm and found a psychologist to help me. Then I moved back to Pine View and went on with my life—back to school and work."

Her lips pulled up in an unplanned smile when she thought about Doc Waldron and his wife, Betty. "I lived in an apartment over the vet's office where I worked part-time. Doc Waldron was my hero. He helped me in more ways than I could ever explain." She made eye contact with Connor and attempted a lighthearted comment. "You're not the first vet I worked for, you know."

He grinned and nodded. "I'm not surprised. He taught you well."

Cassie stood and walked over to stare at the sky above the porch railing. The night air was crisp and cool, heavy with the scent of pine. Thousands of stars were strewn in haphazard array across the night sky and, other than the occasional sound of the sleeping horses as they shifted their weight, there was total silence. She inhaled a deep breath of the clear, thin air before continuing in a slow, measured monotone while she stared out into the night.

"I met Frank at the diner where I waitressed. He was a regular—and the local police chief. Although he never paid for anything, he left big tips. It seemed like everyone respected him. I was shy and self-conscious, and I appreciated the interest he showed in me."

Her voice took on a slightly bitter edge. She gripped the porch railing and continued speaking. "He brought me presents, always told me someone gave him the stuff. He drove me home in bad weather. Somehow, he always just seemed to be there. When people made cautious comments about him, and about the difference in our ages, I thought they were jealous. Besides, I saw him as a kind of father figure. He was middle-aged, for God's sake. I was just a kid. A naïve, stupid kid!"

She couldn't hide her anger. Even after all this time, she still couldn't understand how she could have been so freaking stupid.

"In their own way, everyone tried to warn me, but I was young, innocent—and alone. Exactly what a predator hunts for in his prey. No one dared say anything straight out. Frank was a vindictive psychopath who had the power to make people suffer if they got in his way. They all knew that. I didn't.

"When he handed me plane tickets and said he was taking me to Las Vegas, I went. I didn't know how to say no. When he bought me clothes only a hooker would wear, I wore them. When we ended up in a wedding chapel, I was too drunk to know what was happening." She stopped speaking, reliving the horror of the morning when she woke up a married woman. Her tone changed when she continued, "When we flew home to New Jersey, I was Mrs. Frank Peters. Cathy Dial was gone."

She stared out into the darkness and continued speaking, suppressing the emotion she wouldn't allow to surface. "I was allowed to continue my art courses at college and to work two days a week with Doc Waldron— as long as it didn't interfere with my wifely duties. There was no honeymoon, no idyllic period of bliss. No hunter had ever bagged an easier prey."

She laughed, emitting a sharp, brittle sound with no mirth in it, but she didn't turn around to face Connor. Staring out into the night, she continued to recite the story of her life in as dispassionate a manner as she could manage—telling her story to a mute audience of stately pine trees.

"The abuse started right after I had the ring on my finger— after he had the papers that said he owned me. It didn't take much to displease him. Within a few months, I was convinced I was a worthless piece of trash, deserving of his abuse. He'd tell me stories about the horrible things he did in Vietnam, and he'd brag about what he got away with on the job. At first, I was shocked, but after a while I didn't care what he said. As long as he was talking, he wasn't finding new ways to hurt me."

She may have been standing on a rustic porch in Colorado, but her mind was two thousand miles and twenty years away.

"He treated people with contempt, and they kowtowed to him in fear. He'd laugh at what stupid assholes they were, and he'd brag about how afraid they all were of him. He'd remind me that if I didn't toe the line, there would always other girls dying to take my place. Then he'd laugh at his sick joke."

She was silent for a long time as she searched for the courage to continue. Finally, she took a deep breath and once again spoke, staring out at the majestic pines and the star-filled sky.

"He killed my baby."

It was a simple statement filled with raw pain. She touched her stomach in an unconscious gesture.

"I was afraid at first, afraid of what he'd do when he found out I was pregnant. He would never have shared me—he'd never have put up with that. I couldn't even imagine bringing a baby into that house. I was considering an abortion, but as it turns out, Frank took care of it for me." She spit out the words, her anger and bitterness spilling out.

Her voice sank to barely more than a whisper when she continued. "One day in an alcoholic frenzy, he knocked me down and kicked me in the stomach before I could do anything to protect myself. Then he hit me in the face, something he'd never done before. He'd always been careful— to protect himself, not me. He didn't want to take a chance anyone would suspect him of being the brute that he was. He couldn't let anyone see my damaged face, so he locked me in the bedroom whenever he was out of the house.

"The next day when I started bleeding and cramping, I just dealt with it—alone. I couldn't call Jean. He'd already warned me about that, about what he would do to her and John if I told them anything.

She stopped speaking, lifted her head, and turned to face Connor. His shocked expression told her that he had expected to see sadness and tears. Instead, he saw rage.

"I sank deeper and deeper into depression. I wanted to kill myself—like my mother...."

She stared back out into the night and fought for control. Then she spoke in a more moderated tone. "I spent a lot of time locked in that bedroom."

When she once again turned to face Connor, her anger was gone. "One day when I was cleaning the closet as a way to stay busy, I found some paper jammed behind a shelf, a few handwritten pages. They were written by his wife, Connor. Amy, his second wife, the woman everyone thought had lost her balance and fallen down the stairs—a young woman with a story like mine who had lived through her own hell locked in that bedroom. She'd written it all down, chronicling her pain, her fear, her degradation, and her certainty that he was going to kill her—like he did his first wife."

Cassie's voice sped up as she relived the adrenaline high of the discovery. "I think there are four things that saved me—a cherished memory of a kite-flying child playing in a sun-filled Alpine meadow, Doc Waldron's support, my all-consuming desire for revenge, and Amy. It was mostly Amy.

"She was there, Connor. Amy was in that damned bedroom with me, and she pushed me to fight. She showed me where her story was, and in the middle of the night she'd wake me up with ideas. I never believed in spirits or angels before that, but it's the only answer. How else could I have gone from a naïve young girl planning ways to kill herself to someone able to develop and carry out an elaborate plan to survive? Amy gave me the strength, and together we did it. We did it. We made him pay!"

Cassie took a deep breath, trying to control her rising hysteria as she continued in an even more brittle voice. "And now it's my turn. I'm going to pay for my hatred, and my need for revenge. I could have made sure his drug overdose was fatal, but I didn't want it to be that easy for him. I purposely rolled his truck down the driveway so that someone would find him. Part of me believed I did it because I was a better person than he was—that I wasn't a killer. But the real truth, a truth I didn't ever want to acknowledge, is that I wanted him to be alive when everyone found out he was a dirty cop. I wanted him to feel the shame, to know what it was like to be powerless, and I wanted the world to believe he'd killed me, so he could pay for my murder, even if he'd never had to pay for killing Amy and his first wife."

She once more faced Connor.

"I wanted to have the last laugh, Connor. I figured if I ran, I'd be fine. I'd stay ahead of anyone he'd send to find me. Maybe he'd die in jail. I never planned this far ahead, and now I'm going to pay the price for letting him live. I'm going to pay for the price of my revenge."

Tear-filled eyes distorted her vision and prevented her from seeing Connor's reaction. How could he understand? She couldn't find words to describe the things Frank had done to her, and even if she could, she would never speak of them. No one would ever hear about the depth of her degradation and shame. She'd willingly die first.

Connor was the kindest, most sensitive man she had ever met. How could he ever accept what she had done? How could he comprehend that, even after all these years, her only regret was that she didn't kill her husband?

She stumbled down the porch steps and forced one foot in front of the other down the rutted dirt road and into darkness lit only by the light of a half moon. She wanted to be alone, to think, to compose herself—to deal with the rejection and condemnation she knew she would see in his eyes.

When she heard Connor's voice, she jumped in surprise. She hadn't expected him to follow her.

"Cassie, please wait. Please stop." His tone was low and gentle, but insistent.

She stopped walking.

"Please, look at me."

She turned. He held out his arms. She stared, confused, refusing to believe he wouldn't reject her, refusing at first to acknowledge the compassion in his eyes. She didn't feel her feet move, didn't consciously take a step forward, but somehow she was in his arms. Sobs racked her body as he held her.

When her sobs finally slowed, he kept his arm around her as they walked back to his welcoming little house. She curled up on the old sofa, wrapped in a colorful Navajo blanket, while he added kindling to the wood in the fireplace and struck a match. They didn't speak as the flames devoured the kindling and the warmth permeated the room.

She stared into the hypnotizing flames, allowing the heat to seep into her bones. She turned as Connor put a steaming cup of coffee and a paper plate with a piece of apple pie on the table next to her.

"You didn't eat much for dinner." He smiled and held her gaze as he sat down next to her on the couch. "I'm not going to judge you, Cassie. I thank God you survived. I wasn't there to help you then, but I can help now. I promise I won't walk away."

She shook her head. "Before Cliff, I was afraid to trust. I'm still not sure I know how."

"It's okay. Take your time. Take however long you need. I'm not going anywhere." He hesitated for a moment. "Can I ask you a question?"

She nodded.

"Where did you go yesterday?"

She turned back to stare into the fire. "I kept Amy's hand-written story, her pain-driven tale of degradation. I never really knew why, but for some reason, I didn't leave it for the police to find. I think she understood, maybe she was even the one who influenced me. The other day, when I saw the news about Frank's release, all the pieces came together."

Her lips curved into a smile of their own accord when she thought about Amy. She again faced Connor. "I suddenly realized why I had kept those pages safely locked away all these years. They were always going to be my last chance, my trump card, my 'put him back in jail' card. Or, at least I hope so.

"I flew out to San Diego and drove to a little town near the Mexican border. I hope I disguised myself and my trail well enough so that when the reporters get the letters I sent, they'll focus more on the information than on the fake identity of the sender."

She sighed. It was difficult not to feel a sense of hopelessness, no matter how hard she tried to be upbeat. The weary resignation in her voice betrayed her feelings. "Connor, if it doesn't work and they still let him out of jail, I've got to disappear again. He won't stop until he finds me, until he makes me pay—until he kills me."

"There has to be another way."

"There isn't. It's twisted poetic justice. I wanted him to live so he'd suffer. He did. Now it's my turn."

"You've already suffered."

"I said it was twisted justice. I never said it was fair."

He looked so sad, so powerless, this man who had suffered his own pain and loss and who now wanted to stand and be her defender. She made a joke as she reached up to tussle his hair. "No matter how fertile Pepper's imagination, I'll bet she never came close to the truth."

He didn't even smile.

"Okay, so that wasn't funny. Let's wait and see what happens. I refuse to let him control me. It's one more way that he wins."

She forced a smile. "I'll bet I can beat the pants off you at seven card stud. There wasn't much else to do hanging out with the boys, and I'm quite the card sharp. I might even have to allow you a handicap. What do you say? Are you game?"

He played along. "What do you think we did in vet school, study? I'll show you a thing or two about cards, my friend."

After they'd each won two hands, they called it a draw and succumbed to exhaustion. Connor threw more logs on the fire and refused to discuss who was going to sleep on the sofa bed—the only bed in the cabin. As Cassie reluctantly crawled under the covers, Connor pumped air into a blow-up mattress and stretched out on his impromptu bed. When Cassie heard his even breathing, she allowed the warmth of the cozy cabin to relax her, and she slept.

The cabin was cool when Cassie bolted upright in bed, the sound of a half-strangled scream still sounding in her ears. She gasped for air and fought back against the memory of her nightmare. Connor stumbled from his bed and came to her.

As her eyes focused on him, she quieted. "I'm...sorry." She stammered, embarrassed that he had been a witness to her nightmare.

"Are you okay?" He sat and stroked her hair.

"I'm fine." She tried to laugh, but couldn't quite pull it off. "I'd...I'd like to get some air. Could you...would you sit outside with me for a couple of minutes?"

"Of course. Stay bundled up though. It's pretty frigid out there."

Wrapped in their blankets, they opened the door and stepped out onto the small front porch. Cassie inhaled huge gulps of the crisp night air and stared up into the inky blackness. The brilliant, countless stars seemed so close she was sure that with just a little effort she could touch them. The setting humbled and calmed her.

After a few minutes, she took another deep breath and turned to him. "I think I'm okay now."

Connor hugged her before they went back to their separate beds and their separate thoughts. There were no more nightmares.

When Cassie woke again, Connor had breakfast waiting. There was no more talk of the past. They spent the day exploring mountain trails Connor knew well. The spectacular scenery and the companionable ride provided some respite, but panic was filling the spaces in her brain—pushing her to action, urging her to run.

~

They returned to Connor's house in Jamestown, but not to the same routine. Cassie's obsession with all things news—network, cable TV, and internet—consumed her free moments, leaving eating and sleeping as optional behaviors. When Pepper and Agnes asked if she was sick, she cracked a joke about dieting, but a quick glance in the mirror at her increasingly gaunt face and haunted eyes told her she wasn't fooling anyone.

As part of her new regimen, she was up early every morning, already dressed for work and watching the TV news at a time she normally would have been hitting the alarm's snooze button. Then, almost a full week after she'd mailed the letters, an NBC news reporter announced that there was another chapter in the bizarre case of Frank Peters, the former New Jersey Police Chief.

Cassie screamed for Connor. As the reporter gave the background story about the man who was convicted twenty years earlier for murdering his wife, Cassie bit her lip and bounced on her feet, unable to contain her nervousness.

She heard Connor approach. He reached for her hand. They both stood frozen in place as the reporter announced he had received an envelope post marked from Chula Vista, California that contained a document allegedly written by Frank Peters' second wife, Amy.

The reporter explained that the handwritten document, not yet authenticated, went into graphic detail about the physical and mental abuse Amy Peters had suffered, how Frank Peters had kept her locked in the house, how she was certain he was going to kill her—and how he had bragged that he'd killed his first wife.

Cassie felt light-headed and realized she had been holding her breath. She exhaled slowly and forced herself to breathe as the reporter continued.

"Included in the envelope was a short, type-written letter from someone self-identified as a recovered drug addict. This individual, who did not sign his name, stated that he found the hand-written document over twenty years ago when he broke into Peters' home looking for drugs. The letter explains that he had kept the pages as insurance, a kind of 'get out of jail free' card if he ever got in trouble with the police. The document had been all but forgotten—until he heard that Peters was going to be released from jail. Having now found God, this man determined it was his duty to make sure the world knew what happened to Peters' other wives.

"There is no proof these documents are authentic. However, at least one New Jersey newspaper reported receiving a similar letter. Both packages have been turned over to the FBI for investigation.

"There is speculation that Amy Peters' body may be exhumed to determine if any forensic evidence was overlooked when she died. An autopsy on the pregnant woman was not performed at the time. The FBI would neither confirm nor deny the exhumation rumor."

The reporter concluded: "The authorities are not ruling out the possibility of a hoax. Anything is possible since Mr. Peters was known to have a number of enemies."

As the reporter finished, and the news anchor picked up the commentary, they flashed a recent picture of Frank Peters on the screen along with a picture of his second wife, Amy.

Cassie gasped. She stared at the picture of a woman with long blonde hair and a slightly lopsided smile gazing dreamily into the camera with a happy, hopeful look—a beautiful young woman who had her youth, her innocence, her baby, and, ultimately, her life stolen from her.

"Hi, Amy," Cassie whispered. She shivered and felt the bumps rise on her bare arms—she was finally meeting her angel.

I'm sorry I waited this long. I promise you he'll pay.

Silent tears fell as she communed through the years with the only other person who would ever truly understand her life and her actions.

When she looked up, Connor was watching her, his face a map of compassion. He offered her a tight smile and squeezed her hand before releasing it. She returned the smile—grateful there was finally someone she could trust.

27

LEAVING JAMESTOWN

Cassie moved back to her apartment the next day. She'd foolishly hoped the government would react quickly to either postpone or cancel Frank's parole. They didn't do either.

As the announced date for Frank's prison release drew closer, Cassie's nerves stretched to their breaking point. She jumped at sounds only she heard and woke in the middle of the night drenched in sweat from half-remembered nightmares. Sensing her nervousness, the horses at the Rescue Ranch became restive and agitated. Her training magic gone, the Ranch no longer offered a place of solace and refuge.

Two weeks after she'd returned home, and four days before Frank's scheduled release from prison, Cassie woke from yet another disturbing dream. She shuddered involuntarily as her mind fought its way back to reality. Then she opened her eyes to a daylight-filled room—and cursed when she saw the time.

Late for work, with dark circles under her blood-shot eyes and her hair still wet from a hurried shower, she jogged the short distance to the clinic and rushed in with no more than a nod for Pepper and Agnes. She was as taut as a rubber band stretched beyond its limit. The question wasn't if she would snap—but when.

"Connor said he'd be back from the conference around two," Agnes called out as Cassie passed her.

"Okay." Cassie answered without stopping. She had no desire to chat. Instead, she rushed into Connor's empty office and reached for a pad of note paper to make a list of needed supplies. She had to keep busy, had to keep her mind active—had to focus on something other than Frank Peters.

As her fingers grabbed the notepad, she glanced over the telephone messages on Connor's desk. The top message, written in Pepper's childish scrawl, stopped her cold.

To: Doc

From: Carolyn Andrews

Msg: Help - Frank Peters

Tel: 201-999-3099

Sucking in her breath, Cassie snatched her hand back—as if a flame had seared her fingers. Her body began to shake.

There had been too many nights without sleep, too many nightmares when she did sleep—and too many years convinced there was no one she could trust. The frayed, strained rubber band that was holding her together, that was keeping her sane—snapped. She stumbled from the office and brushed passed Pepper as the young woman reached out to her. In her rush toward the door, she ignored Agnes's frantic questions and pleas for her to stop.

She ran blindly down the sidewalk—not seeing or caring where her feet landed until a searing pain forced her to stop. Hopping on one foot, she grabbed the trunk of a nearby tree for support while she rubbed her twisted ankle and cursed the uneven concrete. Finally, as the pain subsided to a slight twinge, she resumed her travel, this time at a walk.

As she turned the corner on Main Street and approached the remaining half-block to her apartment, she anxiously searched the sidewalk in front of her, hoping her landlord's busybody secretary wouldn't be standing outside taking a cigarette break. *Not now. Please, not now.* She exhaled in relief when she saw an empty stretch of concrete where the woman usually stood.

Cassie pulled out her key and unlocked the street-level door to her apartment. After carefully pulling the door closed behind her and reengaging the lock, she staggered up the stairs and pushed open her apartment door. Fear clawed at her. As uncontrolled shaking began to claim her, she stumbled to her bedroom and sank to the floor in the corner, hopelessness clouding out rational thought.

Nothing made sense. Nothing.

Why would someone call Connor about helping Frank? Why?

Even if she was wrong, even if she'd misunderstood the note, the fact that someone was calling Connor about Frank meant that her twenty years of running had been wasted. All the moving, all the rootless years—all wasted. Cassie Deahl, aka Cathy Dial Peters, could now be traced through Connor Winston.

Frank knows where I am.

A loud, insistent ringing penetrated the fog in her mind. She heard the sound without any conscious recognition of what it was, or what she was supposed to do to make it stop. *Is it the telephone?* Suddenly, there was quiet. The sound and its silent aftermath freed her, like a startled deer held captive by a car's headlights is finally freed when the vehicle passes.

Still shaking, but now mentally alert, she checked her watch. It was 10:45. Connor was due back by 2:00. She grabbed the battered suitcase that had been her constant companion—until she'd run out of energy and forgotten how to run. She scanned the apartment, the place she'd called home for almost six years. The TV, the cheap furniture, the pictures and recognition plaques from her work at the Rescue Ranch, none of it mattered. She would take none of it.

When her eyes landed on Dusty, standing in his place of honor next to Cliff's exquisite but not-quite-finished carving of a mare and foal, the tears started. Brushing them away with impatience, she reached for the wooden likeness of the horse that had played such an important part in her life. Holding the warm wood brought back memories that once again sent her to her knees. She hugged the little horse to her chest and sobbed.

Her whispered words to Cliff were an indictment. "You told me I could trust him!"

Annoyed, she pushed herself up from the floor. This was no time for self-pity. There would be plenty of time for that later, years and years of time. Dusty, the mare and foal, and the picture she'd painted for Cliff, were the only things she couldn't live without. She wrapped them in towels before placing them in a small cardboard box along with a much-used

Cheyenne Frontier Days cup. She left the box at the head of the stairs, next to the suitcase stuffed with items from her bureau drawers, and a small pile of clothes still on their hangers. Then she picked up her purse, put on her sunglasses, and marched down the stairs.

It was a short walk along Main Street to the bank. She responded with a halfhearted smile to the bank teller's cheerful comments as she cashed a check for most of the money in her account. The bank manager's comment about the weather went unnoticed, and Cassie barely nodded her thanks when he granted her access to the vault where she emptied the contents of her safe-deposit box into a large purse. With the straps over her shoulder and the purse clasped tightly against her side, she tried to appear nonchalant as she strode out of the bank without a backward glance.

During the short walk back to her apartment, her mind was focused on ticking off details of the emergency plan she'd drafted over the past few days as she'd searched the internet for news of Frank's release. The spare ID in her purse had never been tested, never vetted. She had to use it now.

This time when she disappeared, it would have to be out of the country. In an age of instantaneous information and heightened security, it would be impossible to surface with a new identity in the United States. This time, she would be running from her country—as well as her past.

She could make the plan work—*no, I WILL make it work*—her mind shouted at her when a hint of indecisiveness crept in. Her Spanish was reasonably fluent, thanks to the years she'd spent working at ranches and restaurants across a variety of western states. She had money—two bundles of cash lay nestled in her purse. *Maybe this was why I never spent Frank's money, or Cliff's. Maybe I always knew it would come to this.* The money would go a long way toward creating a comfortable life in the Mexican countryside.

With her mind occupied creating reassurances about the future, Cassie didn't question why the deadbolt on her apartment door refused to unlock when she turned the key. Without thought, she turned it again, pushed the door open, and trudged up the stairs, slowing as she neared the top.

Had she left the upstairs door open? Uncertain, she stepped forward, past her box of memories and her clothes. Mid-stride, she stopped, finally understanding why she'd struggled with the door lock. Her first turn of the key had locked the door— because Connor had already unlocked it. He was standing in the living room, not more than five feet away.

They faced each other, Connor's gaze alternating between her and the luggage at her feet. Even in her frantic state, Cassie could read the mix of emotions in his eyes—surprise, hurt, confusion, and anger. She reacted only to the anger. She knew how to handle anger, knew better than most what happened when a man got angry. Memories of the years she'd spent with the man she was finally beginning to acknowledge as more than a friend evaporated like fog under a bright sun. In front of her stood the angry man who had betrayed her.

She steadied herself. He was the enemy now. Reaching into her bag, she hesitated for a long moment before pressing her lips together and making a decision. Her fingers clamped around the cold steel of the unregistered pistol she'd stored in a safe-deposit box for years. The feel of it in her hand gave her courage, her mind flashing back to a long-ago time when that gun had saved her life. She'd never killed anyone, never even wounded the guy who'd tried to rape her, but she'd scared the hell out of him and took a chunk out of the wall only inches from his head. She had never felt so powerful.

Connor's expression changed when he saw the gun. Fear and confusion replaced some of the anger and hurt. "Cassie? Why are you looking at me like that? Put the gun away. Cassie, for God's sake, put the gun away!"

She focused on his anger and raised voice. She spared little time to acknowledge the concern and hurt that came through in his words.

"Cassie, please. Please tell me what's wrong. Agnes called me. She was worried about you. She told me you were upset. I drove back as fast as I could." His tone became pleading as he crossed the room, ignoring the gun in her hand, oblivious to the danger.

"Stay there, Connor." She fought to keep the emotion from her voice. "I don't want to hurt you. I didn't expect to see you. I'm leaving."

"No explanation? No goodbye? I don't get it, Cassie. I thought, I thought we were...friends." He'd hesitated before adding the last word as if he was unsure how to define what they were to each other.

Connor's words and the expression on his face would have broken her heart had she allowed herself to believe the emotion was real.

I almost fell in love with him.

She was grateful for the sunglasses that hid her eyes. He couldn't see her own hurt and confusion—he couldn't see the tears she was fighting to hold back.

"I told you I might have to go. It's time. I'm leaving. I'm sorry if you don't understand." Her words were purposeful and deliberate. She couldn't let him know she was screaming inside and that it was taking every ounce of self-control to stand there, to will her hand not to shake as it held the gun.

Connor turned away to stare out the window. She watched him take a couple of deep breaths. When he once again faced her, he wore a mask—a neutral expression hiding his emotions. She backed away as he approached.

"Put the damn gun away, Cassie. I'm the last person who would ever hurt you. If you haven't figured that out yet, I feel sorry for you." He pushed past her and was gone.

She listened, the sound of each step taking Connor down the stairs and out of her life. She was alone. That was what she'd wanted, wasn't it? She fought back the tsunami of tears and the sense of loss threatening to overwhelm her. After inhaling a deep breath to settle herself, she returned the gun to her bag. Then she grabbed her suitcase and stumbled down the stairs.

A quick check of the sidewalk assured her Connor was gone. She ran the short distance to her truck and deposited the suitcase on the back seat. One more trip for her extra clothes, and her single box of memories, and she would be on the road, leaving behind her apartment, her friends—and her life as Cassie Deahl.

28

PHOENIX, AZ

By the time Cassie saw the sign for the Days Inn on the outskirts of Phoenix, her truck had wandered over the rumble strips twice. She'd driven all afternoon and half the night before she felt safe enough to acknowledge her exhaustion. She took the next exit on the interstate.

Once parked in the motel parking lot, she struggled to clear the fatigue from her mind, so she could think straight. It was time to use her new identity, to be Callie Denton, a name appearing on a birth certificate and social security card that had spent the last twenty years buried at the bottom of a variety of safe-deposit boxes. The second false identity had been the added insurance her younger, paranoid self had insisted on—just in case. Now, her worst case scenario was playing itself out, proving her paranoia had indeed been justified.

A quick glance in the mirror at her haggard face and weary eyes reassured her that she'd have little trouble convincing the motel clerk her credit cards and ID had been stolen, especially if she had cash in hand. She was right. The clerk barely listened to her sad story. He took her money with a disinterested nod and handed her a key card. A simple transaction.

After she unlocked the door and stumbled wearily into the room, the basic, no-frills space felt as inviting as a suite in the most expensive resort. Without bothering to unpack or even brush her teeth, she stripped off most of her clothes and crawled onto the bed where she fell into a deep, dreamless sleep.

She opened her eyes to a room immersed in semi-darkness, bright stripes of sunlight leaking in around the edges of the drapes. Confused by the strange surroundings, her heart beat double-time, and she bolted upright in bed swiveling her head in panic. Then she remembered. Her situation came crashing down around her, the knowledge draining her. She was alone—again. She had to start a new life—again. The task seemed too overwhelming, too daunting. She lay back down and buried her head in the pillows.

It was eleven o'clock before she finally found the energy to drag herself out of bed. Her head hurt, and her stomach grumbled. She couldn't recall the last time she had eaten. After a quick shower, she dressed and headed out. She needed food, something to restore her energy before she could begin the monumental task of creating Callie Denton.

Fortified by two cups of coffee, a stack of pancakes with blueberry syrup, and a few strips of crispy bacon, Cassie was ready to attack her challenging task. Callie Denton had to be unique, bearing nothing in common with Cassie Deahl. Her long, very identifiable, blonde hair had to go. As the blonde strands piled up on the floor around her chair in the hair salon, Cassie was overwhelmed by the memories of the last time she'd shed her identity—and the twenty-year odyssey that had brought her full circle. Lost in her memories, she ignored the stylist's comments and questions. Soon the chatty girl got the message and styled her hair in silence.

Cassie left the salon in a daze and headed to a drug store for a box of hair dye to continue the transformation into someone she didn't want to be. One final stop at a giant discount store netted clothes and eyeglasses to complete the disguise—or more accurately, the metamorphosis. She was going backward though, from a butterfly to a drab caterpillar.

Returning to her hotel room, she applied the hair dye, waited the requisite time, and then showered, watching her past swirl down the drain with the residue of the dye. Finally, she stared into the bathroom mirror at a pallid-skinned woman with short, wavy brown hair and sad, haunted eyes. There was no time for regrets, so she took a deep breath and turned away.

Callie Denton had a short time frame to accomplish the items on her to-do list. First item—proof of a Phoenix address to establish Arizona residency for a driver's license. A quick check of a local phone book provided the information she needed for her visit to a local cable TV office. Fifteen minutes after walking through the doors of Arizona Cable, she walked out with a receipt for installation of cable service at an address Callie Denton would ostensibly, but not actually, call home.

At four o'clock that afternoon, wearing scholarly, black-framed glasses and a loose-fitting, flowered print shirt over black polyester pants, she stepped hesitantly into the Department of Motor Vehicles. She rifled in feigned confusion through a variety of forms while she observed the clerks. Once she recognized an older woman with a world-weary demeanor as a potential kindred spirit, she readily gave up her place in line, until she was certain to be helped by the woman who looked like she had endured more than her own share of pain.

In a halting voice, Callie Denton told her story. She was used to telling stories, and she found a receptive audience for her latest tale. The story was partially true—or at least it had been. In halting words she explained to the clerk that after many years of abuse, she had finally built up the courage to leave her alcoholic husband and move to Phoenix to be near friends. "I found an apartment. It's not much, just a basement in someone's house, but it'll be all mine—no one to tell me what to do anymore.

She shared a hesitant smile with the clerk. As proof of her Phoenix address, she presented the wrinkled receipt she'd obtained at the cable TV office earlier in the day. The people at 63 Alameda Street would certainly be surprised when the cable company knocked on their door, but she didn't feel bad for borrowing their address. She presented her birth certificate and social security card as her only other forms of ID.

She'd chosen her mark well. Hearing her story, the clerk's gruff demeanor disappeared, replaced by genuine sympathy. She went out of her way to help the wretched woman in front of her. She scheduled Callie's written and eye tests for that same afternoon.

After acing the simple tests, she was happily surprised to find an opening for a driving test at ten the following morning. As she checked off more items on her to-do list, she grew more confident about her decision to run. Now, all she needed was a car for her road test. A quick call to a driving school and an offer to pay for lessons she wasn't planning on taking, netted her a car and an instructor who would pick her up at her hotel and take her to the motor vehicle office.

Next, she needed to find a car—one Callie Denton could purchase after she passed her road test and acquired her license. Cassie had more than cut her hair and shed her jeans, she'd also added a few years to her age. She was now a frumpy, if youngish looking, forty-six-year-old retired elementary school teacher from a small town in Kansas. Her car choice needed to match her new persona.

After a nearby used car lot closed for the day, Callie parked her truck at a fast food restaurant across the street and wandered through the lot in search of a low-key used car, one a shy school teacher on a tight budget might own. She found the perfect candidate squeezed between a red Suburban and a green Jeep. The six-year-old, white Honda Civic with only 50,000 miles on the odometer met her exact specifications.

Dinner was a Burger King Whopper and fries consumed in her motel room while she perused the travel guides purchased at a Border's book store. They were her research materials and her introduction to the Mexican city she would call home. Once she got to Mexico, it wouldn't matter what happened to Frank. Even if he was released, even after he tracked Cassie Deahl's trail to its end—and she was certain he would—Cassie would be long gone. He'd never find Callie Denton.

As she prepared for bed, she reflected on her life. Twenty years ago, a young woman named Cathy had put all her energy into creating a new identity—a woman named Cassie Deahl. Cassie had put down roots and created a life filled with people she cared about, people who loved her. Now it was all gone. She'd thrown it all away to become a timid, middle-aged school teacher—a painful, gut-wrenching transformation she had never planned to make.

She didn't remember turning off the light, but the motel room was dark when she woke. The travel guides slid noisily to the floor when she sat up, gasping. She had a fleeting memory of a dream about a tall, sandy-haired man standing alone, staring into the night. She wiped her eyes, took a deep breath, and tried to focus on her driving test, her car purchase, and the route she would take to the small city on the central Mexican coast that Callie Denton would call home.

Awake again by dawn, she reread the travel guides, re-plotted her southward route, and gazed at the sunrise as it turned the sky amber, pink, and soft shades of turquoise before becoming a cobalt blue. The spectacle of the new day's dawning failed to provide the sense of peace and wonder she had come to expect from nature's big show. Her mind was too filled with plans she didn't want to make.

Later that day, with her new driver's license in hand, she attacked her car purchase with an Oscar-winning performance. The salesman was happily counting the stack of bills from the unexpected all-cash sale when she drove her Honda Civic off the lot. She parked the car at a Hilton Hotel by the airport and took a taxi back to the Days Inn to pick up the truck that had played such an important role in Cassie Deahl's life. Cassie was gone. Soon her truck would be, too.

It was Callie who drove the truck to the long-term parking lot at the airport and replaced the license plate with one borrowed from a car a few rows over—a trick she'd remembered from a book read years earlier. The truck's license plate, wrapped in the plastic bag from her discount store purchases, found its way into a half-full dumpster. As long as there was a license plate on the truck, even if it was the wrong one, it would take some time before anyone realized the truck had been abandoned.

When she took the Hilton shuttle bus back to the hotel parking lot where she'd left her car, Cassie's beloved truck began its sad and lonely demise. She fought back tears as she drove her new vehicle back to the Days Inn, grieving for the life she left behind in an old truck in an airport parking lot.

She'd checked off all the items on her to-do list, yet she felt no sense of accomplishment, no sense of pride. Tomorrow morning she'd head south, leaving her home and the country she loved. Once she left, she wouldn't be returning, except for one final visit to empty the safe-deposit box she planned to establish in Tucson before she crossed the border.

She'd spent her entire childhood in Europe, but hadn't left the States since she'd arrived in New Jersey as a fourteen-year-old, over thirty years earlier. Now, she had less than twenty-four hours to spend in the never-never land between her old and new lives—between the life of the woman who had foolishly planted roots that went too deep, and one who would now build a higher and stronger wall around her heart.

There would be horses in her future, and as soon as she was settled, she'd get a dog and a cat as well. She wouldn't be alone, not if she was surrounded by the four-legged creatures whose needs were so easy to understand, who so readily and freely loved without guile or betrayal.

Eager for distraction, she turned on the TV to watch CNN's update of the national news. A reporter was standing in front of a familiar building—

the Pine View New Jersey police station. She sucked in her breath and turned up the volume as the TV anchor introduced the reporter.

"Here's Chuck Smith reporting from Pine View, New Jersey with the latest news in the story of Frank Peters, the former Pine View Police Chief who was convicted—twenty years ago now—for the 1987 murder of his young wife. Her body was never found and Peters has steadfastly proclaimed his innocence. Chief Peters was due to be released from prison on Monday. I understand there's some breaking news, Chuck."

"Yes, Scott. Peters' second wife, Amy, died tragically in what, at the time, was deemed to be an accidental fall down a flight of stairs. She was six months pregnant when she died. Last week, a document alleged to have been written by Amy Peters was received by at least three media outlets. The pages provided details of a life of mental and physical abuse and included a statement that Amy Peters believed her husband was planning to kill her. The police had refused to comment on the validity of this new information, until today.

"This afternoon, New Jersey Attorney General Anthony Richmond issued an official statement suspending Peters' pending release and announcing that Peters will be charged for the murder of his second wife, Amy. Prosecutors have been unusually tight-lipped about the case. An unnamed source in the prosecutor's office has however indicated that they will be petitioning the judge to deny bail while they build this new murder case against Peters."

Cassie stared at the TV in stunned silence. She wanted to be happy, wanted to believe she had a reprieve and that Frank would stay in jail—but she was too afraid. She dared not allow herself to do more than hope.

"The Attorney General's statement noted that a family member had come forward with letters from Amy Peters which a hand-writing expert used to prove the hand-written document was not a hoax. With her permission, the police identified the family member as Carolyn Andrews, the woman who raised Amy Peters after her parents' death.

"Earlier this afternoon, we interviewed Mrs. Andrews. Here are the highlights of our interview."

The face of a frail, elderly woman appeared on the screen. Cassie heard only a part of the reporter's question. Shocked, she focused on the woman who spoke in a shaky voice full of emotion.

"Amy was my niece, my sister's daughter. She moved in with us when she was twelve, when her parents died in a car accident. I loved her like my own daughter." She swiped at her eyes with a tissue before continuing. "I wish I had had the courage to come forward twenty-five years ago. Maybe I could have saved that other beautiful young woman. I've had to live with that guilt every day."

Obviously distraught, she stopped speaking and gazed down at her lap. When she looked up, she stared directly into the camera. "My family kept telling me we didn't have any proof, and we couldn't make allegations without proof, but the truth was that everyone was afraid of Frank Peters, including me. He never let Amy visit us. After a while, she didn't even call. My husband and I stopped at their house one day, and he wouldn't let us in. When I think of what that poor girl was going through…I've blamed myself all these years…"

Her voice broke. She dabbed at the tears in her eyes with a balled up tissue held in a veined and shaking hand.

The reporter waited for her to regain her composure before he asked his next question. "I know this is hard for you, but I have to ask, why did you come forward now? You could have given the information to the police and asked not to be identified, but I understand you wanted to speak to the media."

She hesitated a moment before she answered. Anger and defiance came through in her words when she did. "My husband passed away five years ago. I'm on my own now. I was never one to stand up for myself, but this was my one chance to make things right. It's too late to save Amy, but it's not too late to make that monster pay for killing her. She was a wonderful young woman, and he…he…no one has the right to do what he did to her."

She was openly crying now, but the defiant expression remained on her face. The reporter thanked her as the tape ended and the station went back to the live feed.

Cassie didn't move.

Carolyn Andrews. That was the name of the woman who had called Connor. How did he know her? Why hadn't he explained? Why…? Her mind raced in a million directions. None of it made sense. He'd had a chance to tell her. Why hadn't he…?

She closed her eyes and forced herself to replay the memories of that day. *Was it only three days ago?* So much had changed in so short a time.

She recalled how upset she'd been when she'd rushed out of the clinic without stopping to talk to Agnes and Pepper. The note that made her run, what had it actually said?

"Damn!"

She slammed her fist on the bureau as the realization hit her. Connor probably hadn't even known about the note. He hadn't known Carolyn Andrews had called him. Agnes must have called Connor to tell him Cassie was acting strangely. He'd rushed back to see if she was okay, and what did he find? The woman he'd come back to rescue, threatening him with a gun!

How Connor knew Carolyn Andrews—and why he hadn't shared that information—still bothered her. It still created a link to her that Frank could follow, but that wasn't important right now.

Cassie wandered over to the window. She stared out at the interstate and the ribbon of car lights moving steadily up and down the highway—some heading north and some heading south. She was stuck in the middle. Cassie wasn't officially gone, and Callie had only a tentative hold on life. Who was she? More importantly, who did she want to be?

Did she have a life to go back to? Would Connor forgive her rush to judgment? Or, was it too late? Knowing Frank could trace her now, did it make more sense to just move on and not look back? Everything was in place. She could get on the highway in the morning and head south to a new life, a safe life. No one would ever find her. No one.

She glanced down at the cardboard box on the floor next to the desk—the small box containing the important memories of her life. A sad smile played on her lips as she knelt to pull open the battered cardboard top. She unwrapped the beautiful dun horse. Once again, she marveled at Cliff's ability to recreate the spirit of the little gelding.

Holding Dusty always brought Cliff close to her, and if ever she needed him, it was now. She spoke to him in her heart. *You were right, Cliff. You were always right—about everything. I don't think I really understood that until now. I don't know what to do. I'm stuck in limbo, and I don't know what to do.*

She gently stroked the warm wood of the horse that was carved out of love. Cliff's presence filled her heart, and she didn't feel quite as alone. She stifled a yawn, her overwhelmed mind refusing to process any more thoughts. When the fatigue hit her, she crawled into bed and surrendered to her exhaustion.

Her restless slumber was punctuated by vivid and disturbing dreams. A kaleidoscope of her life, fractured memories and relationships, all intermingled. When at last she woke to a room bathed in early morning light, she realized that as disturbing as the dreams had been, they weren't the horrific nightmares that had plagued her for the last twenty years. Instead, she'd dreamt of her mother and father, of Jean and John, even of Agnes and Pepper. Somehow, they were all intertwined. Except the last dream, the one she'd had just before she'd opened her eyes, that dream had been erotic. She'd been in bed with Cliff, or at least she thought it was Cliff, except he had Connor's sandy hair.

As she put her feet on the floor and climbed out of bed, she thought of an incredibly appropriate cliché. She laughed before addressing the dark-haired stranger staring back at her from the dresser mirror: "Today is the first day of the rest of my life." She nodded and smiled, no longer feeling quite as confused or depressed. When she turned her car onto the interstate that morning, she knew the direction she would be heading. That was something. That was a start.

29

ESTES PARK, CO

The years spent behind the wheel of her sturdy Chevy Silverado left Cassie ill-prepared for driving a light economy car, especially when buffeted about by speeding eighteen wheelers. At least three hours passed before she was comfortable enough to relax her death grip on the steering wheel, though the infrequent stops for gas were a welcome tradeoff.

Twelve hours after making her commitment to head north, an exhausted Cassie pulled into the driveway of Connor's home in Jamestown, Colorado. She assumed he'd be home on a mid-week evening, but the house was dark, and his truck and horse trailer were both missing. Disappointed, Cassie dragged herself out of the car to check the barn. Both horses were gone. Too tired to handle the hour plus drive to his house in the mountains, she was faced with a dilemma she hadn't considered.

A blonde, jean-clad Cassie Deahl left her apartment four days earlier with no plans to return. She was Callie Denton now, a frumpy woman with short, dark hair wearing polyester pants and over-sized glasses, driving a Honda Civic with Arizona tags. The future was still uncertain, and her drive north might be only a side trip on the way to Mexico. Returning to her apartment wasn't an option. She sighed and closed her eyes for a long moment before she rolled down the window, backed the car out of the driveway, and headed for the highway.

The first motel she saw became her home for the night. She checked into the Super 8, then headed to the Waffle House next door to satisfy her hunger pangs. In the morning, she'd head west to Estes Park to apologize to Connor. If that didn't go well, tomorrow night she'd be back on the road, heading south to Mexico.

When she glanced out the window the next morning, she groaned. Her little car was no match for Rocky Mountain snow—even if it was only a September snow squall. She breathed a sigh of relief after the weatherman on the radio promised the skies would clear by early afternoon.

She considered dawdling over breakfast to wait out the snow, but that thought was overruled by her desire to see Connor. By ten-thirty she was back on the road, driving through a light snow on her trip toward Estes Park. The little town that swelled with Rocky Mountain National Park tourists in the summer would be comfortably returned to its small, year-round population by now, but Cassie wasn't driving quite that far. The turn off to Connor's cabin was a little east of town.

As she drove down the rutted, dirt road just before noon, the snow stopped, and the sun came out. Desperate for something positive to cling to, Cassie chose to see the weather change as a good omen, and the thin wisp of smoke rising from the chimney of Connor's cabin as a welcoming sign. She fought back tears as she pulled up in front of the rustic porch and parked.

After opening her car door and stepping out onto the snow-covered ground, she inhaled the familiar, acrid scent of recently burned wood on the crisp, clear air. Quincy stood alone in the small corral. Belle was gone, meaning Connor was too. Shaking her head in disappointment, Cassie reconciled herself to a long wait. Depending on when they left, it could be hours before they returned from their trek through the wilds of the park.

"Hi, Sweetie." She called to Quincy as she approached the fence. Recognizing her voice, he nickered. It didn't matter that her hair was different or that she had on clunky glasses. He reached his head over the fence, so she could pet him and scratch behind his ears.

"I've missed you, buddy—and Belle, and your dad. I messed things up real bad though...real bad."

He nudged her with his head when she stopped scratching him, and he focused on her with his wise brown eyes when she spoke.

"Any idea when they'll be back? You want some company while we both wait?"

Not expecting an answer, she maneuvered a bale of hay off the porch and partially wedged it under the corral fence. Then she climbed over the fence and sat on the bale. Quincy nibbled on the edges while she petted him and occasionally shared a thought or two. They both half dozed in the brilliant midday sunshine until Quincy pricked up his ears and released a throaty welcoming nicker. He'd picked up Belle's scent.

Cassie watched their approach. It was too late to run, but her heart raced in panic anyway. Maybe Connor wouldn't want to see her—maybe this was a mistake.

Connor dismounted a few yards away. Even from that distance, she could see the anger in his eyes, and when he spoke, his tone was anything but friendly. "Excuse me, Miss." He gestured toward her and spoke in a clipped tone. "Please get out of my horse's corral. Is there something I can help you with?"

Cassie took a deep breath, stood, and slid between the rails of the fence, so she was once again outside the corral. She was about ten feet away from Connor when she got a good look at him. She tried not to gasp in reaction. He hadn't shaved in days, or combed his hair for that matter. His face was haggard, and his eyes bloodshot.

"Hi, Connor."

She registered his confusion and, realizing that the clunky, school-teacher glasses were making it difficult for him to see through her disguise, she removed the glasses and forced a smile.

"It's me, Connor....It's Cassie."

"Cassie? I...thought...I never thought..." He shook his head, confused.

Cassie watched as Belle nudged him to get his attention. As if snapping out of a trance, and without further acknowledging Cassie's presence, Connor unsaddled his horse and turned her out in the corral. After nuzzling Quincy, Belle pulled a mouthful of hay from the edge of the bale. Seeming to sense the emotional undercurrents, the horses stood together, their attention focused on the human drama unfolding just outside their corral.

Connor turned back to face Cassie. Although he didn't speak, she could easily read the hurt and confusion in his eyes.

Cassie had had hours to plan her words, but she couldn't find any good ones. "I was going...." She corrected herself. This may be just an out-of-the-way stop on a circuitous route south. "I'm...I'm on my way to Mexico to start my life over...again. I'm..." She owed him honesty, some olive branch of trust. "I'm Callie Denton now."

She reached into her pocket, pulled out her Arizona driver's license and handed it to him. Connor glanced down at the picture and then back at her. Confusion, mingled with pain, was etched in the haggard lines of his face and in his tired, bloodshot eyes.

"I came to apologize, Connor. You've always been there for me. I should have trusted you. You deserved to have me trust you." She took a deep breath. This was harder than she'd imagined it would be. "I saw the note on your desk. I panicked. I still don't understand how you knew about Carolyn Andrews, and I need you to explain that—but that's not important right now. I jumped to conclusions that were horrible and unfair, and I'm truly sorry."

She pressed her lips into a tight line and swallowed the lump in her throat. She needed to finish before the tears overwhelmed her. "But, regardless of your intentions, you left a trail that Frank can use to find me. I can't stay here, but I shouldn't have accused you...I shouldn't have run the way I did."

Connor didn't respond. He stared at her with an expression she couldn't read. The silence built between them until it became a solid presence—a wall Cassie didn't know how to scale. She reached forward and slid her license out of his hand.

Once again she murmured her apology. "I'm sorry, Connor."

She moved past him, and although her eyes were focused on the ground, she still stumbled in a rut behind his truck. She grabbed the tailgate for balance and then hurried to her car, tears nearly blinding her. Her fingers were on the door latch when she felt a hand on her arm. She looked up. Connor's eyes met hers for a long moment before he turned his head and looked away.

His intense, pained expression surprised her, made her wonder if she was missing something, if there was more going on than just what had happened between the two of them.

When he again faced her and began to speak, his eyes were reflective and sad. "We had a fight that morning. A fight about something stupid, and I lost my temper and made Tracy cry. She was crying when she left for work. It bothered me all day, but I knew I couldn't call her when she was teaching, and it was way before cell phones existed. I left the clinic early and picked up flowers. I was going to make dinner to show her I was sorry..."

His gaze shifted away, and when he again faced Cassie, his eyes glistened with unshed tears. He continued in a small flat voice. "I never got the chance. The police came to our house and told me she was dead. Her car hit a pole after a reckless driver swerved in front of her." The tears streamed down his face. "Don't you see? We argued, and then she was gone. I never saw her again. I never had a chance to say I'm sorry. She died, and it's all my fault. I never even had a chance to say goodbye."

Cassie was too stunned to speak. The pain on Connor's face wasn't caused by the death of the wife he'd buried more than ten years ago. There was an admission in his words, an admission that defined a relationship between the two of them that they had never openly admitted. She'd put him through hell. They'd argued, and she'd disappeared from his life, just like Tracy had. The past repeating itself.

Cassie struggled to find words. She thought about the good times they'd had together and how she had come to depend on his unwavering dependability and friendship. Was that all it was, or had it always been something more? Her relationship with Cliff confused things. She had never quite sorted that out, didn't know what would have happened if Cliff had lived. They had been two kindred spirits, two damaged people without pasts who had found in each other a friend and a lover who didn't need answers—who wouldn't ask questions. Their passionate coupling had filled a need, and they'd helped each other heal. Could it ever have been more than that? Or would they have settled into a warm and comfortable friendship based on a shared past, the only past either of them would ever acknowledge? She'd never know.

The snow started falling again while Cassie and Connor stood next to her car gazing into each other's eyes. Big, fluffy flakes fell around them, and their cheeks were wet from more than the silent tears they were both shedding. Still, neither of them spoke.

Finally, Connor broke the silence. "Don't go, Cassie. Please. Don't go."

She reached out and touched his face. Then she stepped forward into his arms. She'd been in his arms before. This time was different. This time was new. These weren't the arms of a friend telling her everything was going to be okay. The man who held her stirred feelings she'd thought were dead, feelings she'd thought she had been willing to live without.

The sound of Quincy's snorting broke the spell. They watched as he stomped his foot and shook like a wet dog after rolling in the fresh snow.

He shook off the snow and snorted again to clear his nose. Belle remained on the ground rolling in the ever-deepening white powder with her four feet in the air.

They laughed out loud when Belle sat up like a dog, and with what seemed like an embarrassed expression, dug her front feet into the ground and pushed herself up. She shook daintily before trotting over to Quincy and playfully nipping his neck. They chased each other around the small corral.

Connor smiled. Before letting Cassie go, he kissed the tip of her nose and brushed the snow out of the wet hair hanging in her eyes. "I think I should give the critters their dinner and throw them some hay, so they can settle down for the night in their shed. Why don't you go inside and get warm?"

Cassie nodded. While he fed the horses, she retrieved her suitcase from the trunk of her car and carried it inside. After she hung her wet coat on a peg by the door and shook the worst of the snow from her hair, she gazed with wonder around the cozy room with the knotty pine walls, the big stone fireplace, and the tidy, efficient kitchen and dining area. A place she'd thought she'd never see again. The wide-plank pine flooring was covered with colorful Navajo Indian rugs, and the curtains were a deep forest green that matched the place mats on the drop-leaf pine table and the cushions on the chairs. It was a comfortable space put together with care and love. She whispered a thank you to Tracy, the woman who had loved Connor and built a life and a home with him before her own life was so tragically cut short.

The fire was down to embers. The room was almost, but not quite, cold enough for the back-up electric heater to kick in. Cassie added more logs and kindling and soon the fingers of the newly stoked flames wrapped around the dry wood and spread warmth throughout the room. She turned on the antique western lamps, and the room was suffused with a soft warm light—a cozy refuge from the storm raging outside. She turned when she heard the door open. Connor stomped the snow off his boots, his arms filled with logs that he piled on the hearth. Then he returned to the door to hang up his wet coat and pull off his boots.

"I guess you're stuck here. It's pretty wild out there."

Cassie glanced through the window into the darkening afternoon sky. The snow was no longer falling at a leisurely pace. This was snow heavy with purpose. She turned to him with a shy smile. "It's a good thing I wasn't planning on going anywhere."

He straightened up from pulling off his boots, and this time when they faced each other, they communicated without the wall they usually kept between them. Connor grinned. The haggardness was gone, replaced by an impish expression in eyes that held a challenge, and a promise that made Cassie giggle. He raised a finger to ask her to wait. Then he strode to one of the kitchen cupboards, rummaged inside and produced a bottle of red wine and a corkscrew. It didn't matter that there were no wine glasses. The basic utility of red plastic cups suited them both.

"To staying." Connor's grin faded when he offered the toast.

"To staying." Cassie answered with the same serious tone. They touched their cups, and Cassie focused on the moment, pushing aside the painful truth that made her words a lie—just for now, she'd live in the moment.

Connor's eyes didn't leave hers as he took the cup from her hand and placed it on the table next to his own. He gently touched her face with one hand as he pulled her close with his free arm. When their lips met, they hungrily made up for the lost days and the pain of futures that might have been spent alone.

Their kisses ignited passion they had both denied. They were two good friends who had shared thousands of hours, hundreds of meals, too many tears, and not enough laughter, but who were only now discovering each other. Connor stroked her face and ran his hands through her damp hair. Cassie moaned in response when he buried his face in her neck kissing and nibbling lightly as he unbuttoned her shirt.

He pulled the blanket off the couch to cover the rug in front of the fireplace. When he tugged her gently down to the floor beside him, she inhaled the smoky scent embedded in the weave. She saw the fire reflected in Connor's eyes as they wordlessly undressed each other. Cassie shrugged out of her unbuttoned shirt. Connor kissed her neck and began to nudge her bra strap off her shoulder while he reached his arm behind her to unhook the clasp.

She suddenly stiffened and held her breath.

"Cassie? Honey, what's wrong?"

She didn't respond.

"What's wrong? Please tell me. It's okay. We don't have to do anything if you don't want to. I would never…"

She shook her head and fought back tears as she whispered. "It's not that. It's just…I…have scars…Frank…" Tears of shame and embarrassment silently traced a path down her cheeks as she buried her face in his chest.

He lifted her face and held her gaze as if to emphasize the sincerity in his words. "Cassie, I think you're the most beautiful woman in the world. Do you think I'd love you less, want you less, because you have scars?"

He brushed the tears away and kissed her cheeks. Cassie took a deep breath, then reached behind her back, unhooked her bra, and shrugged the straps off her shoulders.

She heard Connor suck in his breath. "Oh, Cassie. My beautiful, brave Cassie."

Then he leaned down to kiss her before he gently slid his mouth down her neck, nibbling and kissing as he went. He kissed each scar before his lips tugged gently on the nipple of her left breast. She gasped and arched her back toward him not expecting the electric current that ran through her. As he stroked her skin, she reveled in the feel of his hands on her.

He fumbled with her belt and the zipper on her jeans. He tugged them down, and she lifted her hips to help him slide them off. He quickly discarded his own jeans, never taking his eyes from hers.

As she gazed at him, she marveled at the sexy, athletic body of the small town vet who had started as her boss and become her best friend. He lay on the blanket next to her propped up on his elbow as he gently traced the shape of her mouth with his finger before leaning over to kiss her and pull her into his arms.

"I love you, Cassie. I've loved you for a long time. I almost didn't get the chance to tell you that." He seemed to tense a little, as if afraid he'd said too much. "Of course, that could just be a line," he added. "I could just be lusting after that incredible body of yours and not be thinking straight."

She smiled lazily at him as she ran her finger along his jaw, all thoughts of danger and running gone—for the moment. "Hmmm. Maybe. Did you really think you needed a line?" She leaned forward to kiss him and slid her arms around his neck. The teasing and conversation were over.

They fell asleep in front of the fire still wrapped in each other's arms. The room was dark when Cassie woke, and she felt cool air on her back. She glanced toward the fire and noticed the flames were just beginning to come back to life. Since Connor was no longer beside her, she assumed he'd gotten up to replenish the wood. Her gaze traveled around the room until she located him. He was sitting in the rocking chair wrapped in an afghan, deep in thought.

"A penny for your thoughts?" Cassie asked softly.

He turned to meet her quizzical gaze. She scooted back to lean against the couch with the blanket wrapped tight around her.

"I was thinking about my mother." He glanced down at the green and white afghan with the rows of snowflakes around the border. "She made this for us, right before she died from breast cancer." Even in the dimly lit room, Cassie could see the deep sadness in his eyes. She fought back tears as Connor continued, "I wish you could have met her, Cass. I think you would have been good friends."

He got up from the chair and bent down to kiss her on the tip of her nose before sliding under the blanket next to her, facing the now roaring fire.

Snuggled next to him, Cassie whispered, "I would like to have known her. I'll bet she was very proud of you."

"I hope so. She had a hard time of it, but she never complained. Her glass was always at least half full, no matter how bad things got."

They went back to staring into the fire, dozing from the warmth and the mesmerizing flames.

Connor nudged her. "Do you think we have enough energy to stand up and open the bed? I bet it would be a lot more comfortable to cuddle under the blankets on a soft mattress."

Cassie murmured a soft laugh in agreement, surprising herself with the happiness in the sound. As she stood, a movement outside of the window caught her eye.

"Connor, look!"

Together, they stared out the window at the winter nightscape illuminated by an almost full moon. A massive bull elk, his head crowned with an impressive rack of antlers, stood just a few feet from the house. As if he sensed their presence, he turned to face the window. He stood proudly, head held high, before he picked his way through the snow and back into the woods.

Connor squeezed her hand, acknowledging the special moment. Then, with that picture postcard scene in her mind, Cassie helped him open the sofa bed. She climbed into the warm nest of blankets and fell asleep with her naked body comfortably intertwined with his.

She woke to a room filled with the soft light of an early sun. The fire was down to embers, and she rubbed her cold nose and cheeks to warm them. She raised herself up on one elbow to watch Connor sleep. Not wanting to wake him, she restrained her desire to touch his perfect nose and dimpled chin. He might not be movie-star handsome, but it wasn't just veterinary skill that kept the appointment calendar full. His easy smile and caring personality had most of the local women pining over him.

Is this just a dream, Connor? Will we wake up and find out that this was just a dream? She spoke the words only in her mind, but her heart was heavy with uncertainty as she slid out of bed and pulled his sweater over her head. She shivered when her bare feet touched the cold floor on the way to the bathroom. Instead of returning to bed, she slipped into her jeans and pulled on her coat and boots before stepping outside in the frigid morning air to check on the horses and throw them some hay. On her way back into the house, she grabbed a few pieces of dry firewood from the porch.

A burst of frigid air forced its way into the house when she opened the door. She was greeted by Connor's sleepy, questioning gaze as he pulled the blankets more tightly around him. After securing the door and dumping the wood on the floor, she responded to Connor's unasked question. "The kids were hungry."

He smiled and shook his head. She grinned back at him before adding more logs to the fire and efficiently stirring it back to life. When the flames were once again crackling and sending warmth into the room, she kicked off her boots and rehung her coat by the door. With quick motions, she shed her clothes and slid back into bed, and into his arms.

"I could get used to this you know," he murmured in her ear.

Cassie said nothing. She relaxed in his embrace as their tangled bodies found a rhythm. It was so easy, so right—yet so scary to love someone this much. *What if…* She pushed the thought out of her mind and gave in to the passion.

This time when she woke, it was to the smell of coffee and frying bacon. Connor, wearing jeans and a bulky sweater, was standing at the gas stove, a coffee cup in his hand.

"Good morning." She said through a sleepy smile.

"Hey, beautiful. Good morning to you, too. How about some breakfast, or..." He glanced at the clock over the sink, "...maybe lunch?"

She laughed. "Call it what you will. It smells wonderful, and I'm starving!"

They ate in companionable silence with the bright Colorado sun shining through the windows.

"You think we're too old to have kids?" Connor's question hit her like a ballistic missile to the gut.

Cassie choked on her toast. "What?"

"I came up here to be alone. Condoms were the last thing on my mind. When I woke this morning, I felt guilty about that." He made a face, his discomfort obvious. "Then I thought maybe it wouldn't be so bad. I mean, having a baby. Unless...well, we're both in our forties, and I don't know how you feel about it." He eyed her questioningly, a hesitant, half smile on his lips.

Cassie remained silent, still searching for a response.

Connor's earlier tentative smile faded, and his expression changed to one of shocked realization. "I forgot. Cassie, I'm sorry. That was insensitive. I'm sorry. I forgot...you lost a baby."

She shook her head and immediately responded. "No, that's not it, Connor. It's okay. I got over that a long time ago."

How to explain? She got up from her chair and walked to the window. "I didn't tell you the whole story about my miscarriage, Connor. I didn't go to the doctor right away. I had so many bruises, I knew Frank would never have let me see a doctor. There would have been too many questions. I had some cramping and bleeding and then things seemed okay." She snorted out a bitter laugh. "Or, maybe I couldn't tell the difference. Pain is pain, after all.

"I was so busy planning my escape, I didn't pay attention to anything else. By the time I got to Kansas, I knew something wasn't right."

She turned to face him. "I spent a night in the hospital. The doctor did a procedure that helped, but she said I had scarring and damage from..." She took a deep breath. It was still hard too hard to talk about the abuse. It would always be too hard. "It doesn't matter. Anyway, I can't get pregnant." She tried for a light, conversational tone, but even she could tell that some pain leaked through in her words.

Connor's expression held no pity, only caring and love. With his eyes locked on hers, he walked the few steps across the room to join her at the window. His strong, gentle hands cupped her face as he spoke. "You know, it's funny how things turn out. Sometimes I wonder what it would be like to be a father, but I've never really felt the loss. I only thought of it today because I realized how much I love you, and if it turned out you were pregnant, I wouldn't be unhappy."

He hugged her.

"I'm sorry you never had the choice, Cassie. I can't think of a better mother for my child, but all I want is to know that I get to hold you in my arms every day for the rest of my life."

Her body tensed.

He stepped back. "Cassie?"

She walked away and held on to the back of the kitchen chair for support as she spoke. "I'm not sure there's such a thing as forever, Connor. I hope so. I'd willingly give up a long life to know I can spend whatever time I've got left waking up in your arms."

He was obviously confused by her words. "But?"

"But there are only three people in the world who know Cathy Dial Peters didn't die twenty years ago: me, you, and the psychopath who spent twenty years in prison for my murder. I ran for over fourteen years, Connor. I always covered my tracks and was careful to tread lightly and never retrace my steps. When Cliff first told me he'd finally settled down because he'd gotten tired of running, I didn't understand. I was still running then.

"By the time I met Cliff again in Cheyenne, I understood. By then, I'd stopped running. I'd made a life for myself with you, Agnes, Pepper, and the Rescue Ranch. I had a life and a home. And every day that I stayed, I made it easier for Frank to find me. And now…" She sighed. "I'm sure you were just trying to help, but now he won't have to try very hard."

She squared her shoulders and asked the question she should have asked him days ago—instead of pointing a gun at him and running away. "How do you know Carolyn Andrews, Connor? How did you know about her connection to Frank?"

Connor took her hand and led her back to the kitchen table. He poured them both another cup of coffee. She held the steamy cup in her hand and inhaled the rich aroma while she waited for him to speak.

He sat and faced her. "I didn't know, not really, and I'm sorry, Cass. I shouldn't have gone behind your back. I didn't want to say anything to you because I wasn't sure if I was right. And by the time I was sure, you were gone."

He snorted a laugh. "I guess I need to start at the beginning, huh? As you already know, I grew up in Pennsylvania and went to Penn State for my undergraduate degree. My roommate was from New Jersey. One summer I lived with his family and worked for his father's construction company. Drew's next door neighbors were a family named Andrews. He called the woman, Aunt Carolyn."

He paused then, letting his words sink in. Cassie nodded at him to continue. "Mrs. Andrews was more of a family member than a neighbor. She and her husband had lived next to Drew's parents forever. I remembered there was a pretty girl living with them. She was a couple of years older than me. Drew used to tease me about her. We only spoke a couple of times, but I guess I had a bit of a crush on her. "Her name was Amy. Her parents died when she was twelve. That's when she went to live with the Andrews."

His eyes bored into hers. "When you told me Amy Peters' story, there were so many similarities to the girl who lived next door to Drew. It nagged at me, so I called Drew. We're still good friends, although life's gotten in the way of our getting together much anymore. We chatted for a bit and caught up on things. I reminisced about the summer I spent with his family, and I asked him what happened to the girl who used to live next door. He told me she'd married an older guy, a cop, and that she'd died young—a long time ago."

Cassie didn't know what to say. What were the odds? Incredulous, she shook her head as she tried to process everything Connor had told her.

He nodded. "I know. Pretty strange, huh? Drew told me Mrs. Andrews still lived next door, so I looked up her number and called her. I wasn't sure why I called, or what I wanted from her. I just thought maybe there was some way she might be able to help. I didn't tell her about you, Cass, just told her I'd been following the news stories about Frank Peters. We talked a bit. She said the police had contacted her about Amy. She wasn't sure why, and she hadn't gotten back to them. Since she seemed unsure about what to do, I encouraged her to call them."

He shrugged. "That was it. I would have told you, but you were gone by the time I saw her note and called her back. That's when she told me she'd spoken to the police. You know the rest."

He seemed to be struggling, wanting to say something more. Cassie waited. Finally, he asked in a tentative voice, "Do you really think he'll be able to trace you through my calls to Mrs. Andrews, Cassie? Isn't that a bit of a stretch?"

She tried to quell the anger that bubbled up and threatened to spill out. She reminded herself that Connor didn't know, couldn't know, what a monster Frank Peters was. After taking a deep breath, she glanced out the window at the snow-covered trees and the idyllic winter scene.

When she was calm again, she met his eyes. "I know you think I'm paranoid, Connor, but you need to believe me about this. I destroyed Frank's life. He's vengeful and vindictive, and he's made people suffer for much less. He may have been in jail for twenty years, but I'm absolutely sure he still has connections."

Her voice turned low and harsh. "There is only one truth of which I am certain. If Frank isn't in prison, or dead, he will spend the rest of his life searching for me. If he finds me alone, he'll make me suffer before he, or more likely one of his henchman, kills me. If he finds me with you, he'll have you tortured and killed—then he'll kill me. I know it sounds crazy, but it's true, Connor. He's a psychopath. He killed his first two wives for no reason other than he was tired of them, and he thought he could get away with it. I humiliated him and stole his freedom—he's got plenty of motive to make me pay."

She grasped his arms and stared up at him with a fierce intensity. "I won't let that happen, even if it means I have to spend the rest of my life alone." She blew out a breath before continuing, "Connor, I had no idea I could ever be this happy, that I deserved this much happiness." She knew her words sounded anything but happy. Even she could hear the anguish coming through. When next she spoke, her words were resolute. "I promise you this, Connor. Even though I have to leave, you'll always know where I am. Maybe we can eventually find a way to be together."

The warmth had gone out of their perfect day even though the sun was still bright and the sky clear. Connor stood in silence—perhaps in shock.

Finally, he took a deep breath and said, "We'll find a way, Cassie. Last night will be just one of the thousands we'll have together. I can't believe they'll ever let him go—not with the new evidence of Amy's murder. For now though, let's just enjoy the time we have. Okay?"

He wrapped his arms around her, tightening his hug before stepping back. He grinned down at her. She could tell he was trying just a little too hard.

His forced grin turned into a mysterious, maybe even mischievous expression. "How about you do the dishes while I go rummage around out back for a minute?"

Cassie nodded, grateful and willing to postpone more talk of leaving. She'd finished washing the dishes and was wiping the table when she heard the door open.

"Found them! I knew they were in the back of the shed somewhere."

He held up two pairs of snowshoes as if they were trophies. "I have a treat in store for you. Traipsing around these mountains on snowshoes is second only to doing it on the back of a horse. Grab your coat girl, and let's go."

They spent the next two days exploring the mountains on snowshoes and horseback, and they spent the evenings creating passionate memories. On Saturday night, they drove into Estes Park for an early dinner in the cozy, paneled bar of the elegant Stanley Hotel. Neither of them cared that their lack of appropriate attire banned them from the formal dining room. They were happier in the bar.

"To us." Connor tapped her beer glass with his and reached over to kiss her.

"To us." Cassie smiled at the man who was her best friend, her boss, her lover, and the person with whom she–without a doubt–wanted to spend the rest of her life. Her tone was wistful as she added, "Back to reality tomorrow."

Connor frowned and nodded.

The next day, after a relaxing ride through the park, they cleaned the house, mucked out the corral, left a stack of firewood by the front door for an uncertain future visit, and loaded the horses for the trip home. Before Connor locked the door, they stood together and took one last look at their refuge, the magical place where they'd finally admitted their love. As they turned to go, Connor pulled Cassie to him and held her close. When he kissed her, their passion was tinged with the fear that their future might not be the happily-ever-after they both so desperately wanted.

30

JAMESTOWN, CO

Cassie followed Connor's truck and horse trailer on the drive back to Jamestown, but she paid little attention to the road. Cementing her relationship with Connor further complicated her life at the same time that it made it worth living. She needed the drive time to emotionally distance herself. Otherwise, she would never survive the pain of her pending goodbye.

She parked her car behind Connor's house where the densely treed property would keep it from the view of Connor's neighbors. For additional insurance, she scooped a handful of mud out of the melting snow and spread it over the distinctive Arizona license plate. While a muddy, nondescript Honda Civic might be easily forgotten, not so an out-of-state plate.

An uneasy silence prevailed when Cassie joined Connor in the house. There was little left to say that hadn't already been said, yet she sensed that Connor still wasn't convinced about the danger Frank presented. So they sat in the living room, each in their separate silences. As Connor flicked through the TV news shows, she searched the internet to find any news updates on Frank Peters. There was nothing.

With her mind too unsettled to relax, she paced between the living room and kitchen, trying to think of a way to make Connor understand. She needed him to accept her certainty that Frank would find her—that she had no choice but to leave. Finally, she plopped down on the sofa next to him and after taking his hand in hers, attempted to explain the unexplainable. "He owns a lot of people, Connor. He never worried about

271

what he said in front of me. I guess he figured I couldn't testify against him. I'd be his happy little mute wife, or I'd be dead. Pretty safe bet."

She continued, this time making eye contact, desperately hoping she could make Connor understand. "It doesn't matter that it's been twenty years. He owned judges, an assistant DA, a couple of state legislators, and God only knows who else. I can't believe he hasn't been pulling strings while he's been in prison. He was always the master puppeteer. He could have taken a lot of people down with him when the feds got him for tax evasion, but he didn't. For years there's been a conspiracy of silence all around. A lot of people still owe him—big time."

Then she sighed and looked away, shaking her head. "I should have taken the ledger I found in his locked file cabinet—the details of his drug, blackmail, and bribery empire. I thought the FBI would find the book, so I left it. I should have known his crooked cops would get there first. The two detectives who were part of his crew were much younger than Frank. They're probably still on the force. He definitely still owns them."

She squeezed Connor's hand. She wanted—no, she needed—him to understand. Her voice became strident and her gaze intense when she again locked eyes with him. "He's going to walk, Connor. Even if they indict him for Amy's death, he'll find a way to get out on bail while they build their case. I know it. I feel it in my gut. Just like I know that if they make him pay a bond, he'll forfeit it. The money's not important to him.

"He ran Pine View. Hell, he ran the entire township. He had power, money—and control. I took that away, at least some of it. He still has a lot of power, and I'm sure he's got most of the money squirreled away somewhere, probably in some numbered account out of the country. I humiliated him, Connor. I proved he wasn't all-powerful. A mere woman he'd thought was disposable took him down. He's spent the last twenty years figuring out how he's going to make me pay for daring to do that."

She searched Connor's eyes as she spoke. She saw concern, and something else, something she couldn't quite define, vulnerability, maybe. It left her wanting to reach out and hold him. So she did. She knew he wanted to protect her—wanted to make all the bad stuff go away, so they could live their happily-ever-after life together. Maybe that was why he didn't want to believe her. Or maybe it was because someone as good as Connor Winston couldn't even begin to comprehend the evil that was Frank Peters.

She was used to being a chameleon, used to changing, used to being whomever she needed to be in order to survive, and so she'd created yet another persona. Connor's role would be a much harder one to play. He'd have to go into the clinic and face each day as if nothing had changed. He would have to stand on the sidelines—totally on the sidelines—while the drama unfolded outside of his view.

When they went to bed that night there was a desperation to their love-making, an intensity much different from their magical time in the mountains. There was only now, this moment. They fell asleep wrapped in each other's arms with their bodies tightly entwined as if by sheer will they could merge into one.

Cassie kissed Connor goodbye the next morning, waiting until his truck backed out of the driveway before she broke down and sobbed. It was up to him to explain her absence, to tell Agnes and Pepper the story they'd concocted together, the same story he would share with the folks at the Rescue Ranch and others who might ask.

He'd tell them Cassie had left a message on his voicemail over the weekend, explaining that she'd received news about a close family member who had been in a serious accident in Oregon. She'd taken the next flight out to Portland. Since Cassie had never shared any stories about her past, a fictitious family in Oregon was as good a choice as any—and Oregon was a long way from Mexico.

After a lifetime of lying, deception came easy to Cassie. Not so for Connor. She hated that he had to lie for her, but she pushed aside the guilt while she searched the internet and cleaned the house. Physical activity was the only thing that kept her from breaking down—or from just jumping in her car and heading south. She could feel the impending danger in every fiber of her being. She could practically taste it. But she'd promised Connor she'd stay one more night.

Meanwhile, he had a special job to perform. She'd asked him to clean out her apartment, to depersonalize it and remove all traces of Cassie Deahl. At lunchtime, he'd slip as unobtrusively as possible into her apartment to bag up the clothes she'd left, collect her mementos and awards, and clean out the refrigerator. After work, when the businesses on Main Street had closed for the evening, he'd retrieve the bags and boxes, discarding them either in anonymous garbage dumpsters or in the donation boxes in the strip mall outside of town. Cassie Deahl's imprint on

Jamestown would be no more. Frank's trackers, men who wouldn't hesitate to break into her apartment in search of clues to her whereabouts, would find nothing.

She wrote out a check and mailing envelope for the next and final month's rent, planning to drop it in the mail from an out-of-town mailbox, leaving Connor to explain to her landlord that she was in Oregon and wasn't planning on returning to Jamestown.

As the day wore on and her nervousness grew, Cassie cleaned the horses' stalls and brushed yet more mud from their coats. Anything to help fill the hours until Connor returned home. At four o'clock, at least two hours earlier than expected, she heard Connor's truck barreling down the driveway at a much faster speed than normal. Leaving her dinner preparations, she raced to the backdoor. Instead of driving toward the barn where he usually parked, she heard the gravel spray as Connor braked just outside the back door. Moments later, the truck door slammed. He rushed through the back door just as she opened it.

"Connor?" Alarmed, Cassie didn't get a chance to say more.

His words spilled out in a rush. "Pepper got a call this afternoon while I was out at the Rescue Ranch. Some guy told her that he was from American Veterinary Magazine. He said they were looking for a small Midwest practice to spotlight. He asked her a lot of questions about who worked at the practice, and what they did."

Connor ran his hands through his hair and shook his head, apparently still in disbelief. "Pepper told him all about you. She said he was really interested and asked a lot of questions. He wanted to know how long you'd worked at the clinic and what you looked like." He hesitated, then his eyes locked on hers when he added, "Cassie, I've never heard of American Veterinary Magazine."

As her legs gave out, Cassie collapsed onto the kitchen chair. The hair on her neck felt prickly and goosebumps rose on her arms. *I knew it. He's found me.*

Still distraught, Connor slid down on the chair across from her. He continued speaking. "Pepper was so excited. She thought she'd done something good. I lost my temper and yelled at her. I don't even remember what I said. I've never raised my voice to her before. She's just a kid. She didn't know any better."

He buried his face in his hands. When he removed them and looked up, even with her own mind racing, Cassie could read the remorse and pain in his eyes. "I felt terrible. I apologized. Told her I had a lot on my mind. I tried to explain that she shouldn't give out information on the phone—that sometimes people lie to get information."

He sighed. "It gets worse. I went into my office to collect my thoughts and calm down. Agnes followed me in." He made eye contact with Cassie and his expression changed. "She didn't ask any questions. She said she just wanted to tell me that before she could intervene, Pepper—who as you know worships the ground you walk on—told the man all about you, including her oft-repeated joke that you have a mysterious past."

Cassie groaned, unable to find any words.

Connor nodded in understanding. "Agnes also said…" He smiled and continued, "and I quote, 'I might be an uneducated housewife who's never seen much of the world, but I know pain when I see it, and in Cassie, I've always sensed a deep well of pain.'" He reached across the table and took Cassie's hand. "She wanted you to know that she loves you, she's on your side, and she'll pray for you."

Thinking about Agnes, her friend, the older woman who had taken young Pepper under her wing and who'd always had a ready word of support, Cassie broke down and sobbed.

When she regained her composure enough to speak, she faced Connor. "I knew he'd find me. I just didn't think it would be so soon. I thought I had a few more days." She pushed herself up from the chair, squared her shoulders and let out a deep sigh. "I can't wait, Connor. Someone could be on a plane tonight. I can't wait."

The anguish on Connor's face broke her heart. *I have to be strong. I have to leave.* She reached for him and pulled him close, forcing out the words she needed to say. "We've discussed everything. We've made our plans. I need to leave now, not tomorrow morning."

Connor nodded, his eyes filled with tears. His words were barely a whisper when he answered her. "I understand. I'll take care of everything here."

~

One hour later, Cassie left Connor's home—for good. As agreed, his computer workstation, minus the hard drive that included a record of every internet search they'd both made over the last weeks, was on her back seat. With the hard drive carefully wedged behind the wheel of her car, she backed up. Then she rolled forward again, got out of the car, picked up the pieces, bagged them, and placed them on the passenger seat. She was taking no chances.

Connor wrapped his arms around her. "I love you, Cassie. We'll be together again. We'll find a way to be together." His frantic embrace belied the certainty in his words.

Unable to speak, Cassie sniffled, brushed away her tears and climbed into her car. She didn't have the courage to look in the rearview mirror as she drove away.

When she passed the long dirt road leading to the Rescue Ranch, she fought the urge to turn the wheel. She wanted to see Lynne, to say goodbye, to explain—but she couldn't. Instead, with tears silently tracing their way down her cheeks, she drove on.

Like all prey, she had long ago learned that survival meant staying one step ahead of the predators—and leaving nothing to chance. The remnants of the hard drive were discarded south of Denver, the rest of the computer shared the bottom of a dumpster lined with Egg McMuffin and Quarter Pounder wrappers at a McDonald's in southern Colorado. She used the rest of her coffee, and some napkins, to rinse the mud off the license plate.

Then, Callie Denton, a retired school teacher from a small town in Kansas, put on her glasses, carefully reapplied her apple red lipstick, smoothed her conservative navy slacks and matching print blouse, and climbed back in the car. She had a long drive ahead of her.

31

ALBUQUERQUE, NM

Cassie pulled her car into a nearly empty parking lot at the Canyon Motor Inn just as the first rays of the rising sun appeared in the early September sky. She'd chosen a different route south this time, heading to Albuquerque instead of Phoenix. Exhausted, she'd given little thought to her choice of motels, selecting the first one she passed after exiting the interstate on the outskirts of the city. She regretted not having been more selective as soon as she opened the door to her room and was accosted by warring odors of stale cigarette smoke and cloying room deodorizer. Too weary to do more than sigh, she tossed her overnight bag on the bed and locked the door. She needed sleep.

At two in the afternoon, she woke, headachy and depressed. A lukewarm shower in the stained bathroom tub did little to improve her mood. Re-donning her Callie Denton attire, she went in search of food. With nearly four hours to fill before she could call Connor, she resigned herself to the frustrating afternoon in front of her—not even the best fast food would take that much time to eat.

She people-watched while consuming a hamburger platter and two cups of not bad coffee at the truck stop restaurant next to her motel. Unfortunately, there weren't that many interesting people to watch. So, after finishing her lunch, she wandered through the gift shop until she couldn't bear to look at one more plastic tourist trinket or collectible spoon.

Returning to her room at five o'clock, she was too wired to focus on the array of reading material she'd purchased about Mexico. Instead, she slumped in a chair, put her sock-clad feed on the bed, and gazed around the room. The cheap prints of the Grand Canyon failed to hold her attention, so she walked over to the window and stared out at the parking lot and the cars speeding by on the highway.

She constantly checked the time as she paced the small room—wondering how sixty seconds could somehow feel like sixty minutes. Finally, when the digital clock on the night stand clicked over to 6:00, she sank down on the bed and unfolded the slip of paper clutched in her hand. She carefully dialed the telephone number Connor had given her—a hopefully untraceable number.

"Tommy's Bar," a gravelly male voice answered.

Flustered, Cassie stuttered a response. "Hi…ahh…I'm looking for Con…"

"Sure, sure, just having a little fun," he said with a laugh.

Cassie heard muffled voices and then, "Hello?"

She exhaled with relief. "Hey, Connor. It's me. I wasn't sure what to say when that guy answered."

"Sorry. Tommy's an old hunting buddy with a strange sense of humor. His is the number I gave you to call. We can talk now. He took off to find some dinner and knowing him, probably a few beers as well." He cleared his throat. "How was the drive? Where are you?"

Did she imagine the edge that had crept into his voice? She quickly filled him in on the details of her uneventful, but sometimes white-knuckled drive. She still missed her truck, especially those times on the highway when her little car was buffeted about by growly eighteen wheelers. When she finished speaking, there was a long silence on the other end of the line.

"Connor? Are you still there?"

"Yeah. Yeah, I'm here." He hesitated, and she sensed he was struggling with what to say next. "I need to tell you something."

She swallowed, but the lump in her throat didn't move. Her breathing felt constricted like a band was tightening around her chest. "What?" was the only word she could manage to squeak out.

"Cassie, I, uhh…" He stumbled, words apparently failing him.

Cassie's already frayed nerves were thrumming with so much excess energy she felt like she was main-lining caffeine. She fought back the urge to scream at him.

Finally, after sighing audibly, Connor spoke in a low voice. "Hell, there's no easy way to say this. Some men came to see me this afternoon. They said they were detectives from Pine View, New Jersey."

If Cassie hadn't already been sitting on the bed, she would have collapsed to the floor. As it was, her vision blurred along with the once-bold stripes of the bedspread she'd been staring at. The receiver of the motel phone fell from her hand.

What if I had stayed just one more day?

"Cassie? Cassie, honey, are you there? Cassie talk to me."

She heard Connor's muffled voice coming from the phone receiver lying on the bed in front of her. For a long moment, her mind blank, she stared at the curious beige plastic item with the long curly cord.

"Cassie!"

The frantic sound of Connor's voice snapped her out of her shock. She picked up the phone. "I'm here. I'm here, Connor." Her voice was low, barely a whisper. "I knew they'd find me. I just didn't think they'd get to Jamestown so soon."

She glanced around the drab motel room, at the drapes she'd pulled closed over the windows, and at the locked motel door. She was safe now, and as long as she managed to stay one step ahead, she'd stay safe. But what about Connor? What if they figured out that he was more than her boss? She shook her head, pushing that fear away—at least for the moment. She needed to hear more.

"Tell me exactly what happened, Connor," she said, forcing a more confident tone into her voice. "Who were they, and when did they get there?" She got up from the bed, too nervous to stay still.

"Thank God for Agnes," he began. "Around three o'clock she came into my office and told me two tough-looking guys had just marched in, flashed a badge, and said they wanted to talk to me. They wouldn't explain why.

"I'm glad I had the presence of mind to tell her to give me a minute before she brought them in. I called Donnie. Thankfully, he wasn't out on a call. I didn't tell him much, just that there were two guys in my waiting room who said they were out-of-town police wanting to talk to me. You know Donnie," Connor chuckled as he spoke. "He's a pit bull when a friend's in trouble. By the time the two guys had muscled their way past Agnes, Donnie was on his way."

Cassie's breathing settled. Donnie Smith was Connor's closest friend—and the local Jamestown police chief. A formidable man who had spent ten years as a detective with the Denver police department. "I'm glad you thought to call Donnie," Cassie said. "He can be pretty intimidating."

"Definitely! Once the goons had pushed past Agnes, I was even happier that I'd called Donnie. They looked and sounded like they were from central casting for a role on the *Sopranos*, rumpled suits, 'Joisey' accents and all. While I waited for Donnie, I stalled and acted like the country bumpkin I assume they thought I was. When Donnie walked in, he was definitely in grizzly mode."

Cassie interrupted, "Did the guys give you their names?"

"Yes—Turner and D'Alonzo."

She gasped. The hair raised on her arms as a vivid memory of Frank and his thugs invaded her mind. She'd hoped she was wrong about Frank's control, that his men were long gone—or dead. Once again, her fears had been realized, instead of her hopes.

When at last she found her voice, she found her anger, too. Venom spewed forth with every syllable. "All brawn. No brains. I'm sure they haven't aged well. Detective D'Alonzo is the sleazy bastard who used to hit on me while his psycho boss was in the next room. He's probably the one who stole the ledger. Twenty years, and they're still doing Frank's bidding. I'm not surprised. What happened when Donnie confronted them?"

Connor continued. "Just as they were flashing their badges and getting overbearing with me, Donnie walked in, all official-looking, with his holstered gun displayed on his belt. When I introduced him as Chief of Police Donald Smith, they about pissed their pants. I almost wanted to laugh.

"Donnie sized them up and said in his most authoritative voice, 'Did I see one of you with a badge? You'd like to show that to me, wouldn't you? After all, I believe it's common courtesy to check in with the local police when you're out of your own jurisdiction. Actually, it's more than just common courtesy, but we won't go there for now.'

"He was brilliant, Cass. I actually started to breathe again, knowing he was in control. They told him they wanted to speak to one of my staff about what they called a 'cold case' in New Jersey from twenty years ago. Donnie made quick work of naming my staff, and explaining why they couldn't possibly have been in New Jersey twenty years ago. He started with Pepper and Agnes. When he got to your name, they immediately perked up.

"Cassie, I've never shared any of your past with Donnie, but you'd never know it from the way he acted. It was as if he knew they were there for you and it was his job to point out the error in their thinking. He informed them that you'd worked for me for six or seven years and had spent your entire adult life working on ranches in Colorado and Wyoming. Then he said that as far as he knew you'd never even been to New Jersey, and if they had called him before coming, they wouldn't have wasted a trip.

"Unfortunately, they totally ignored what he said. They made it clear that, in spite of what Donnie might believe, they still had to talk to you. Fortunately, I'd seen Donnie at the Rescue Ranch yesterday. I told both him and Lynne about your rushing off to Oregon to take care of family, so that's what he told the goons. They weren't happy. Actually, their expressions immediately changed to something that looked a lot like panic—kind of like kids who failed an important test at school and were afraid of being punished by their parents."

Cassie snorted in agreement. "Frank's wrath is a whole lot worse to deal with, but you're on the right track. He sent them out there to pick me up. He must have been salivating with glee, so sure they'd find me at the clinic." She caught her breath as the full impact of her statement hit home. They'd been so close. She forced herself to exhale and remember that she was in control. She had a foolproof plan. "They're going home empty handed. It won't be pretty."

"Yeah, I could sense that," Connor said. "They were pretty aggressive about getting your contact information. I told them that you'd been too distraught to leave any forwarding information in your message. They accused me of lying and got pretty obnoxious. But, so did we. I showed them the door and Donnie ushered them through it.

"Before they left, Turner gave me his card. He got in my face, beer gut, rotting teeth and all. He insisted that if I didn't call him as soon as I heard from you, there'd be hell to pay. That's when I thought Donnie was going to lose it. When hefty, six-foot-four Donnie Smith got all up in their faces, I almost felt sorry for them. He told them they had two choices—come to his office and establish an official line of inquiry, or head back to New

Jersey. He made it clear that if they chose any other option, he'd throw their asses in jail and call their superiors to lodge a formal complaint. They left, but from what you've told me, they're probably more afraid of going back empty-handed than of getting arrested. I doubt they headed to the airport."

Connor, usually a man who measured his words and spoke calmly, had raced through the telling of his story. Now, Cassie heard him take a deep breath and exhale. After his frenetic words, the ensuing silence felt almost like a solid presence. She wanted to believe Connor was safe, and that by leaving she'd secured his safety. She wanted to believe it, but she wasn't sure, and the uncertainty was eating at her.

She stood at the window next to the bed, the telephone receiver still in her hand. After pushing the drapes aside, she stared out into the darkness at the ribbon of highway and the steady stream of lights heading south. The sight calmed her. Finally, she spoke, asking the question that had been forming in her mind, scarcely allowing her to focus on the rest of what Connor had been saying. "What did you mean when you said Donnie seemed to know about my past?"

This time when Connor spoke, his tone was more measured. "After the detectives left, and after Donnie told me I needed to sit down before I fell down, he explained that he'd figured out a while ago that you were running from your past.

"He paid you a compliment, Cass. Donnie said you could earn a damned good living teaching people how to hold lengthy conversations without sharing the slightest bit of information about themselves. He said he'd been concerned when young Sara started coming home from the Rescue Ranch extolling the virtues of, as he called you, 'the sainted Cassie'. He needed to figure out if you were someone his young, motherless daughter should trust."

Connor laughed as he continued, "Donnie said, with obvious respect, that you really knew how to play him, and you probably now know more about Sara as a baby than even I do, and I'm her godfather!" The laughter gone, Connor continued. "He also said he noticed how you reacted when some jerk yelled at his wife in the restaurant where he'd invited you to share Sara's birthday dinner a couple of years ago."

Cassie smiled, remembering how Donnie had tried to grill her about her past. "He's right. His questions were way too easy to deflect, even if he is a seasoned detective." She continued in a more somber voice, "I didn't mind his grilling though, even if I couldn't share much more than my memories as a Montana ranch hand. He's a good dad. It can't be easy for him to raise Sara on his own. I always felt a kinship with her. We both lost our mothers when we were little girls."

Connor's voice intruded before her thoughts could stray too far into the past—to her own motherless childhood. "Donnie's in your corner, Cass. He said he'll do what he can to help. He didn't ask me any questions, but he said, and I think I can quote him pretty accurately, 'She saved my little girl. She took a shy child who had lost her mommy, and turned her into a caring, confident teenager with a wall full of horse show ribbons who can hold her own in the world.'"

Silent tears traced their way down Cassie's cheeks as she thought about the special moments she'd shared with the sweet, freckle-faced girl, starting with riding lessons and ending with blue ribbons and tears of joy as Sara wrapped her arms around the neck of her Rescue Ranch pony. Cassie would probably never see her young friend again—or Pepper, or Agnes, or Lynne at the Rescue Ranch. People she cared about, people she loved.

She sniffled and wiped her nose with the back of her hand, too overwhelmed to care about finding a tissue. The silence grew, but Cassie didn't attempt to fill it. She was seeing the faces of her friends, the streets of the little town she'd called home, and the horses at the Rescue Ranch. They were all an important part of the life she'd created and foolishly hoped she'd be able to keep.

"Cassie?" Connor's concerned tone conjured an image of the warm, expressive eyes of the man she loved. Eyes that had been filled with tears when they'd said goodbye. She thought about the plans and promises they'd made. Had she been kidding herself? Was she being selfish and putting his life in danger by just staying in contact with him—even with all the safeguards they'd planned?

"Cassie, we'll get through this. I know it's a shock that they found you so quickly, but the important thing is that you got away. It'll all work out. You'll see."

Was he trying to convince her, or himself? She didn't ask the question out loud. There wasn't an easy answer, and she knew it. Just like she now knew with startling clarity that the only chance she had of keeping him safe was to sever all ties and walk away.

"Connor..." She felt the very real pain of her heart breaking as she struggled with how to back away, how to say a final goodbye. "He won't give up. You're not safe. No one is safe. I need to disappear—to actually disappear. I know we said..."

"No!" All warmth gone from his voice, Connor continued in a steel-edged tone, "No, Cassie. That is not going to happen!" She had never heard him sound so angry. "You are not walking out of my life. You don't get to decide. I'm a big boy. I can take care of myself."

"You don't know...." Cassie started to say.

"I didn't know. I admit it. But I do now. I am truly sorry for ever doubting you. I'm in this for the long haul, Cassie. I love you. I understand the risks, and I'm going to hold you to the promises you made to me."

At a loss for words, warring emotions battled within Cassie—relief that Connor was willing to fight for their love, and terror that she was possibly signing his death warrant if she didn't walk away.

"Cassie? Don't get all quiet on me." His voice was stern. "This isn't a decision you get to make on your own."

"But..." she started.

"Listen to me," his voice dropped to almost a whisper. "You're all I have. When you left...when you left and I thought I'd never see you again, I lost it just like I did when Tracy died. Cassie, I'm willing to go down fighting, but I'm not willing to let you walk out of my life again."

She fought back the sobs, so she could get out the words she desperately wanted to say. "Okay, Connor. I promise." Her chest heaved, and she gasped out the remaining words, "I'm afraid for you, but I don't want to let you go. I won't walk away. I should, but I won't."

"We'll find a way, Cass. Someday we'll find a way to be together." His voice broke. "You'll see."

Cassie pulled a tissue from her pocket. She blew her nose and wiped her eyes. When she spoke, the fierce determination that had kept her alive for twenty years was back. "Connor, just promise me you'll be careful. It'll make things a little easier for me knowing that Donnie is there for you."

"I promise. You be careful, too. You're the one who'll be hiding out in a foreign country."

Cassie's answer was dismissive. "I'll be fine. I'm used to being on my own. I speak fairly good Spanish, and I'm going to an area that's pretty safe. Don't worry."

She blew out a breath as she mentally made a change in her plans. "Listen, can I call you again tomorrow at this number? I think I'm going to hang out another day in the states. I want to get a better idea of what's going on there in Jamestown before I leave. Once I'm in Mexico, it'll be too risky to call and our internet contact will be too sporadic."

"Sure. Tommy owes me, and he isn't a guy who'll ask questions. Same time?"

"Yeah. Same time."

"I love you, Cass."

"I love you, too. 'Night, Connor."

She hung up the phone and collapsed onto the bed. She never prayed. Hadn't even thought about praying since she'd tried to bargain with God when Cliff was dying. Now though, at the risk of further alienating a supreme being she had never been on the best of terms with, she offered up this entreaty: *Please God, please don't let Connor suffer for my mistakes.*

285

32

ALBUQUERQUE, NM TO EL PASO, TX

Cassie remained on the bed, too emotionally drained to move. She wasn't hungry, and her desire for a glass of wine, or something stronger, fell victim to her malaise. Though it was only seven o'clock, she climbed under the covers and clicked on the TV. The antics of the game show contestants provided amiable company while she perused the road atlas and updated her to-do list. In spite of the too-soft bed and scratchy sheets, she was soon asleep.

She woke just before dawn. Anxious to leave the Canyon Motor Inn behind, she was out the door a few minutes later. After stopping at a nearby fast-food restaurant for a breakfast burrito and a cup of black coffee, and desperate to put more miles between herself and Frank's men, she filled her car with gas and pulled onto the highway to begin the four-hour drive to El Paso.

She had little need for the road atlas on the seat next to her. Interstate I-25 was nearly a straight run, taking her practically the entire six hundred and fifty miles from Jamestown to El Paso. The atlas was insurance, just in case.

As she drove, she mentally ran through her to-do list, or at least she tried. Too often, her apprehension intruded. She'd stomp on the gas pedal and push the little car beyond its limits—and too far above the speed limit. Then, she'd lose focus and slow down. More than once, annoyed drivers flashed their lights and tailgated her in the left lane.

Finally, acknowledging the danger created by her erratic driving, she pulled into a rest area to take a break—and get her act together. When she got back on the highway, she stayed in the middle lane and tuned into a country western station on the radio. Expanding her gaze to encompass more than just a narrow stretch of highway, she regularly took full deep breaths to center and calm herself.

As the outskirts of El Paso came into view, she exited the highway to drive through the city. Her first goal was to find a bank. She needed to establish a bank account and set up another safe-deposit box, knowing she'd breathe easier once she was able to offload the stacks of cash she'd been carrying. Eventually, she'd be back to pick up the money, but until she was settled, she was afraid to carry too much money across the border.

She was soon parked at a local branch of a large international bank. After an application of Callie Denton's signature red lipstick, she was once again a timid, retired school teacher. Just inside the door of the bank, she hesitated, unsure if she should approach the teller windows or go directly to one of the people sitting in the small side offices.

Apparently sensing her confusion, a young, dark-haired woman rose from a desk to greet her. "Good morning," she said with just a hint of a Spanish accent. "How can we help you?"

Thirty minutes later, Cassie left the bank with a lighter hand bag, pleased to have checked more than one item off her to-do list. In addition to renting a safe-deposit box, Callie Denton now had a bank account. The $9,800 in the account, carefully kept below the $10,000 reporting limit, was tied to a debit card that would be available for pick up at the bank's branch in Mazatlán, Mexico—her planned new home.

To counter the depression threatening to claim her on her last night in the United States, she decided to splurge on a hotel, choosing the picturesque Casa Martina in the historic district. The desk clerk, a distinguished looking Hispanic gentleman, welcomed her with a smile. "Good afternoon. Welcome to Casa Martina. How may I help you?"

Cassie returned his smile. She almost relaxed, allowing his warm demeanor to help calm her nerves. After confirming that a room was available, the clerk showed only the slightest hint of surprise when she counted out cash for her night's stay. If he thought the middle-aged woman with the oversized glasses and frumpy clothes a bit eccentric, he kept his thoughts to himself. Her payment was accepted with a smile and a deferential nod. The clerk handed her a key card folder, pointed toward the elevators and announced, "If you have any room-service charges, we'll settle them in the morning when you check out. If there's anything we can do to make your stay a more pleasant one, please don't hesitate to let us know."

When she pushed open the door to her room, any concerns she'd had about her decision to splurge disappeared. The large, tastefully appointed room exuded a calm, peaceful ambiance. The king-sized bed looked welcoming, and she was certain there would be an adequate supply of hot water in the spacious shower. She exhaled, feeling some of her mental heaviness disappear. Although she'd have to manage her money carefully, this hotel had been a worthwhile expense.

After dropping her overnight bag on the plush carpet next to the bed, Cassie went in search of lunch, and to begin the process of checking off items on her lengthy shopping list. She wandered the downtown area, and when she finally sat down at an outdoor café surrounded by her purchases, she was sure the chatty young waitress took her for a tourist. She played along, but in truth, she'd barely registered the historic sites she'd passed, nor had she purchased any trinkets or souvenirs. All her purchases were items needed to start her new life. All had been paid for in cash.

While waiting for her quesadilla, she sipped her coffee and enjoyed the ambience of the café with its overflowing flower baskets and cascading trellises of bougainvillea. Her mind strayed to memories of Anna Alvarez, the woman who'd owned the gallery where Cliff had sold his carvings. Even in death, Cliff had come to her aid. At his memorial dinner in Anna's home, the woman had mentioned that her older brother was a police captain in Mazatlán, Mexico. Cassie had listened politely, never believing the information would someday be important.

Mateo Alvarez was still the captain of police in Mazatlán, or so her internet research had revealed. And since she had never been to Mexico, the resort area on Mexico's Pacific Coast seemed as good a choice as any for her new home. With a large ex-pat community, it might even be a better choice than most. Besides, it felt right—as if Cliff was directing her there.

After settling in, she planned to search out Captain Alvarez. She'd explain that a friend suggested she move to Mazatlán based on the glowing description provided by his sister, Anna. Not quite a first-hand introduction, but more of a half-truth than a lie. If the captain was anything like his sister—and she was counting on it—Alvarez would be a good ally to have in her corner.

After a satisfying lunch, and energized from the caffeine hit provided by two cups of coffee, she attacked the rest of her shopping with renewed energy. At four o'clock, she returned to her hotel dragging two newly purchased suitcases stuffed with her acquisitions, including a wardrobe of new clothes and a laptop computer.

While focused on her shopping, she'd had little time to think about what might be happening in Jamestown. But once inside her room, there was nothing for her to do but wait and worry. At exactly 6:00, and nervously gnawing on her lower lip, she dialed the now familiar phone number—her apprehension growing with each unanswered ring.

When Connor finally picked up the phone on the fourth ring, he didn't bother with hello, and the frantic tone of the one syllable he uttered had her heart pounding with fear.

"Cass?"

"Yes, it's me." Reacting to the tone of his voice, she didn't bother with chit-chat. "What happened, Connor?"

"I've got more bad news," he said, before letting out a heavy breath.

"What happened? Tell me what happened."

"I'm still trying to wrap my head around it. Someone broke into my house."

Cassie let out a low moan and clutched the phone tighter in her hand. Pulling in great gulps of air, she fought back the panic. *Was Connor hurt? It's all my fault...*

"Cassie? Honey, it's okay. I wasn't home at the time. I called Donnie. It's okay." His voice lost the frantic quality and became soothing. "I didn't mean to scare you. I should have said it differently."

"What happened, Connor?" She tried to pull herself together and respond rationally. "What did they do? What did they take?"

"They didn't take anything, at least not that I could see. I thought maybe I was getting too paranoid, but when I left this morning, I set up little booby traps. Things I'd learned from reading espionage novels over the years. I jammed a small piece of paper in the door. I put the phone down on a specific line on a note pad. I wedged some paper under the wheel of my desk chair. A bunch of things like that, and when I got home—Cassie, even before I noticed that every single one of my traps had been sprung, I felt it. I knew it. I could sense it, like when the hair stands up on the back of your neck and you're not quite sure why."

Cassie heard him take another breath and exhale before he continued. "There's more. D'Alonzo and Turner went out to the Rescue Ranch." He snorted, making a derisive sound. "Lynne called me. She was livid. She said these, as she called them, 'cartoon-character buffoons' came racing down the driveway, totally ignoring the ten-mile-an-hour sign and oblivious to the horses, including poor old Rocky who she was hand-walking at the time. When they got out of the car, they glanced around like it was beneath them to even be there, and then managed to further piss her off when they totally disregarded her and said they needed to talk to the man who ran the place."

Connor let out a short laugh. "You know Lynne. She doesn't take crap from anyone. She's put her heart and soul into that place. She figured they were up to no good, so she excused herself to put Rocky in his stall and used that time to call Donnie."

Cassie shook her head, imagining the scene. Lynne was one tough lady. She was also Donnie's aunt and Cassie's closest friend, one she'd almost shared her past with. Now, she was glad she hadn't. In the twenty years she'd been on the run, Connor was the only person she'd come clean with, and now his life was in danger.

She refocused as Connor continued speaking. "Lynne said they about turned green when Donnie drove up a few minutes later. He apparently ripped them a new one. This time, I think they might have actually headed straight back to the airport."

"What does Lynne know, Connor?" Cassie's voice trembled. Lynne was nobody's fool.

"Nothing of substance—but maybe everything that's important. She's a smart lady, Cass, and she thinks of you as the daughter she never had. Donnie told her the guys were looking for you. When I talked to her, she told me, just like Agnes had, that she'd figured out a long time ago that you were hiding from something or someone. In classic Lynne speak, she told me she'd 'cut off the balls' of anyone who tried to hurt you."

Cassie was tired of the emotional roller coaster she'd been on, especially lately, but hearing how her friend was willing to protect her, without even knowing why or from what, was too much. She couldn't hold back the tears. She pictured Lynne's face, imagined her confronting D'Alonzo and Turner, and through her tears, she smiled.

"Cassie?"

"I'm here." She sniffled and wiped her eyes. "Lynne's a good friend."

"So is Donnie, Cass. Pepper and Agnes, too. Probably more people than you realize count you as a friend, as someone they'd protect. They don't need to know why."

He cleared his throat and continued, "I'm glad you insisted on taking my computer, and although I hated parting with all of your awards and recognition plaques, you were right about that, too. There was nothing in the house for them to find, nothing at all to tie me to you—except the answering machine tape where you say you're on your way to Oregon."

"Well, at least something worked out as planned," Cassie offered with a sigh.

"It's a hollow victory though, Cass. I have no pictures of you. I'm angry and frustrated, and I want to lash out at someone—and yet, nothing really happened. I wasn't hurt, my house wasn't damaged. I guess I just feel powerless, and I don't like feeling that way."

Cassie imagined him sitting alone in his friend's house, maybe in the dark, tapping his fingers on the table as he often did when he was nervous. She'd brought all this down on him. Because of her, he didn't even feel safe in his own home. He'd be better off if he'd never met her. "I'm sorry, Connor. This is all my fault…"

He interrupted before she could continue. The upset and pain she'd heard earlier were gone. "No. Don't say that. None of it is your fault. Hell, Cass, I don't know how you did it. The more I understand what you've been running from, the more respect and love I have for you. I'm the one who's sorry. I'm whining, and you're all alone, still having to run…I wish I were there with you."

"Me too, Connor. But you have a life and a job. People need you—and what would their four-legged critters do without their favorite vet?" She asked, attempting to lighten the conversation. She didn't want their last conversation to end on a depressing note.

He chuckled, taking the bait. "Don't know how much the critters like being jabbed and poked, but I think their families appreciate it at least." His voice was serious when he continued. "Are you nervous about tomorrow?"

"Yeah, a little. I have everything I need, though. I did some shopping today to fit my 'Callie' persona. The retired teacher is well-outfitted now. I don't expect any issue with the border crossing, and I'll stay on major roads, so it should be a safe trip. It's about a sixteen-hour drive, so I'll need to make it a two-day trip. I studied the road map and found a major tourist town about midway where I can stop for the night. I'll be fine."

She hoped her voice sounded more upbeat than she felt. Truth was, she was scared—scared and angry. She wasn't sure she could pull it off. She wasn't even sure she wanted to, but it wasn't as if she had a choice.

"I'll be thinking about you, and praying for your safe arrival. I wish there was some way…"

This time it was her turn to interrupt. "We talked about that, Connor. Once I cross the border, I can't call. How many international calls do you think Jamestown, Colorado receives in a day? A week? Not many, I'm sure. I don't understand the technicalities, but if there's even the slightest chance the call can be traced…"

"I know. I understand. You can't take that chance. I'll be looking for your messages though. I think we did a good job working out our internet messaging. At least we'll have some way to stay in touch."

For the second time in as many days, their call ended with professions of love.

"I love you, Cass. I'll miss you. Be safe."

"I love you, too, Connor. You be safe, too. I'm glad Donnie's there to help."

After hanging up, Cassie felt more alone and adrift than she'd felt since she'd climbed out of that eighteen-wheeler truck in Wichita twenty years earlier. All those years on the run, of being alone and of painful goodbyes—as hard as it had been, none of it had hurt like this. She'd left a full life with a man who loved her for a lonely future in a foreign country.

She was angry, and she was tired of running. There had to be another way. She made herself a promise. Once she got to Mazatlán, she'd find a way to stop running—even if it meant confronting her past.

33

MAZATLÁN, MEXICO
CALLIE DENTON – OCTOBER, 2007

Two days later, just as the sun was setting, Cassie Deahl—no, *Callie Denton*—passed the signs welcoming her to Mazatlán, the Mexican Riviera. She breathed a sigh of relief, but was too exhausted to spend time gawking at the luxurious oceanfront hotels along the Zona Dorado—the Golden Zone. In spite of her fatigue, she couldn't resist pulling off the road just long enough to inhale the scent of the ocean and allow the sound of the breakers to roll over her. She'd never been this far west, and the Pacific Ocean was new to her. Yet the scents and sounds reminded her of her childhood, of the Atlantic Ocean, of memories she couldn't afford to dwell on.

As she faced the ocean and witnessed the last rays of sun dip below the horizon, the palette of colors chasing themselves across the cloudless sky gave her a sense of peace she hadn't felt in weeks. The trip was behind her. Her fears about the border crossing had proved unwarranted. The Mexican border guard had waved her through without question, barely glancing at her driver's license.

Still imbued with the unfamiliar sense of peace, she drove to her hotel on the edge of the historic district. The previous evening, when she'd mentioned her final destination to an accommodating desk clerk at her hotel in Torreon, the young man had recommended the Mazatlán Centro. He'd even made the reservation for her. The charming-looking hotel had a classic stucco exterior, red tile roof, and cascading arches of magenta bougainvillea. For Callie, its charm was further enhanced by the knowledge that it was significantly less expensive than a hotel with an ocean view.

As the bellhop helped her unload her luggage, she realized she no longer missed her truck. Her no-frills economy car, already a basic and pedestrian vehicle, had been further humbled by a layer of road grime and a liberal spattering of dead bugs. Although she'd spent eight hours a day driving on poorly maintained roads with more than a few potholes, her little car had performed admirably. Its efficiency and uncomplaining attitude were growing on her. At the very least, she owed it a trip to a car wash.

After checking in, she followed the bellhop to her room on the second floor, wanting nothing more than a comfortable bed to collapse onto. She was pleased to see that the hotel's charm was not restricted to the exterior. Her small room was colorfully and comfortably furnished and had French doors opening onto a small balcony overlooking a courtyard with a tiled water fountain. Tomorrow, she'd start looking for an apartment. Meanwhile, this picturesque old-world hotel would be her home.

The following morning she woke refreshed in a sun-filled room. She pulled open the balcony doors and breathed in the salty ocean air. For a long moment, she allowed herself to relax and enjoy the scent of the air and the sound of the water bubbling in the courtyard fountain. The moment passed, but enough of it lingered to leave her in a positive frame of mind.

After a light breakfast in the hotel restaurant, she ambled along the cracked sidewalk in search of an internet café. She found one two blocks from the hotel, just as the waitress had promised. Although it had been only forty-eight hours since she'd spoken to Connor, fear nagged at her. She repeated the mantra that guarded her sanity. *Connor is safe. Donnie will keep Connor safe.*

Once seated at a computer workstation, she hesitated. After inhaling a deep breath made ragged by her fear, she typed "Frank Peters" into the search bar of the internet browser. The short wait for the news pages to open seemed interminable. As she waited, she mentally reviewed the news she'd received just before leaving Jamestown. Frank had been indicted for Amy's murder. His parole had been revoked. Citing his 'fragile health', Frank's lawyers had been fighting to get the parole reinstated, so he could be released on bail while the prosecution built their case.

Callie opened every referenced news story. There was nothing new. In Frank's case, no news wasn't good news. No news meant more nightmares and more worry. She leaned back in the chair and stared at the most recent news article, one she had already read. The face of an elderly, blank-eyed man stared back at her.

"Bullshit!"

She smacked her hand on the computer table in anger. Her unplanned outburst surprised her at least as much as it surprised the young man sitting at the computer next to her. Glancing up, she met his wide-eyed stare. Embarrassed, she murmured, "*Perdone*," before turning back to the computer screen.

It was all bullshit. She knew it. She felt it in every fiber of her being. If Frank was ill, if he was in 'fragile health' as the article had stated, D'Alonzo and Turner wouldn't be in Jamestown tracking her down. Conner's home wouldn't have been broken into. No, the bastard was playing a role, taking a page from that mobster she'd read about. What was his name? She nodded to herself when she remembered—Crazy Joe Gallo. Frank was creating his own version of the 'crazy' mobster. She considered the idea that maybe people wouldn't buy his act. Then she shook her head in disgust, astonished at her naivety in even entertaining the thought.

She pushed away from the workstation, knowing it would be fruitless to search for a message from Connor. Yesterday was Sunday, his day at the Rescue Ranch. There was no way he could have made it to the local library to use their computers—especially not with their limited Sunday hours. She paid for her computer usage and left the café. It was time to check out the town and look for an apartment. She planned to do some people hunting, as well. She'd begin her search for Captain Alvarez.

~

Late that afternoon, Callie again sat in front of a computer at the internet café. This time she did so with a feeling of accomplishment and a better understanding of her new hometown. She'd spent the afternoon wandering through the resort hotels, asking questions and reading tourist literature. She'd even gotten a glimpse of Captain Alvarez leaving a café near police headquarters. A chatty waitress had confirmed that the man she'd seen was indeed Captain Alvarez. She'd even proudly announced that he often frequented the café.

Callie logged onto the computer with anticipation—and more than a little apprehension. As she and Connor had lain in bed on their last night together, they'd finalized an elaborate scheme to stay in contact. They'd chosen two internet chat groups: one focused on travel and the other on cooking. Connor would log in at the public library as Don from San Francisco, looking for information about Costa Rica, or as Friendly Chef from New York, interested in chatting about campfire cooking. In the travel group, Callie would be Sara living in Costa Rica. On the cooking site, which they'd added as an emergency back-up, she'd be Dusty from California.

She nervously nibbled her lower lip. Their plan was untested. So many things could go wrong. What if—? She didn't allow herself to pursue that line of thinking, to consider all the 'what ifs'. She couldn't accept a life without a connection to Connor, without a way of knowing he was safe.

Her anxiety mounting, she scrolled through the entries on the travel site. When she found his message, a huge grin creased her face, and she fought back tears of joy. Don from San Francisco had posted a message. She beamed down at the screen with pride and satisfaction. Even if their connection had to be coded and obtuse, it was still a connection.

His message, left an hour earlier, was short: "Someday I want to travel, especially to Costa Rica. It's peaceful but lonely here at home. What's it like there?"

She'd been perched on the edge of the chair with her shoulders tight and hunched as she scrolled through the site. As she reread his words, she relaxed against the back of the chair. Connor was safe.

Her response was immediate. "Hi, Don. I think you'd like Costa Rica. It's beautiful and peaceful. I just moved here and I'm settling in. Looking forward to sharing more info with you."

That was all. Tomorrow, she'd check in again. Leave another short message. It wasn't much. It would have to be enough.

Back at the hotel, she slept better than she'd slept in weeks. She was safe, at least for now. More importantly, Connor was safe, and she had a lifeline, a way to stay in touch with the man she loved.

~

Even though she occasionally got doused with a blast of cold water in the shower, Callie quickly settled into a comfortable routine in the old hotel. The staff was friendly and the area safe, but she couldn't afford to stay forever. She needed to find an apartment.

By the end of day four, after again poring over the classified ads without any luck, she shared her dilemma with one of the friendly desk clerks. "You are looking for an apartment?" the young woman asked in English.

Callie smiled. Knowing she was from the States, the hotel staff, at least the front desk staff, answered her in English even when she spoke to them in Spanish. She assumed they were trying to be helpful.

"Yes, I am. Do you know of a place?"

As it turned out, the young woman did. The pretty desk clerk's parents owned a small apartment building a couple of blocks from the hotel—with an apartment for rent. It was a tiny apartment in an old building, and the odor of fried food lingered in the air from the small restaurant across the street. But the price was right, the area safe, and the colorful, eclectic furnishings suited her. She rented it on the spot.

34

MAZATLÁN MEXICO

Callie checked out of the hotel the following morning. Having now found a place to call home, she focused her energy on a plan to meet Captain Alvarez. Marching into the bustling Mazatlán police headquarters wasn't an option. The very thought made her heart race. Not even the passage of twenty years had diminished her distrust, bordering on outright fear of the police. Besides, she hoped the captain would be more open to her third-hand introduction in an informal setting.

She couldn't admit to knowing his sister Anna—that would be too easy to check. Anna might remember Cliff's good friend, Cassie Deahl. She would never have heard of someone named Callie Denton. Instead of claiming a direct tie to his sister, Callie planned to tell the captain a friend recommended she move to Mazatlán based on hearing his sister speak warmly both of the location and her brother, the local police captain. She hoped she'd be able to pull it off, to flatter but not overplay her hand.

Every day for a week, Callie ate lunch at the café near police headquarters where she'd glimpsed the captain on her first day in Mazatlán. She dawdled over her meals, varied her arrival times, and asked an occasional question, hoping her queries came across as friendly rather than suspicious.

Finally, on the afternoon of day five, she overheard the name "Alvarez" in a conversation between two waitresses. Callie stopped chewing mid-bite to hear the response. "Oh, the captain is away. I heard him tell Marco on Friday that he was going to Mexico City for a couple of weeks on some police business." Callie went back to chewing, grateful to hear that the captain's absence was temporary.

With her opportunity to meet Captain Alvarez delayed, Callie focused her attention on finding a way to earn a living. If she lived frugally, she could survive a few months on the money she'd brought with her. And if she made the drive back to El Paso to access the remaining funds in her safe-deposit box, she'd be able to eke out another few months. After that, she'd be broke.

She was still mulling over job possibilities one afternoon while she was shopping for sandals in a small, out-of-the-way shop usually frequented by locals. The prices and often the quality of the goods, were better in such shops than in the stores that catered to tourists. On this particular afternoon, Callie encountered an elderly American woman struggling to buy a gift for her grandchild. The store owner, a middle-aged woman who spoke no English, was rapidly losing her patience. Tempers flared, and voices were raised.

"Can I help?" Callie was usually reticent about becoming embroiled in other people's arguments. However, since the issue seemed simple enough to resolve, she hadn't hesitated. She listened as the frustrated customer explained what she wanted, and she relayed that request in calm and apologetic Spanish to the store owner.

"Thank you! Thank you so much." The elderly woman was effusive with her gratitude as she paid for her purchase. She turned to Callie. "I know I should learn the language. After all, it is their country. I just get so flustered. Can you tell her I'm sorry? I didn't mean to lose my temper. I hate to be an ugly American." She glanced between Callie and the store owner. "Can you please tell her I'm sorry?"

Callie nodded, and as she relayed the woman's apology, she had an epiphany. *Maybe this is how I can earn some money! How hard could it be to teach basic Spanish to the elderly American women who winter here?*

As they left the store together, the contented customer insisted on treating Callie to coffee and pastries at a nearby café. Callie accepted, grateful for an opportunity to discuss her idea with a potential student. As soon as they were settled at a small table near the window, the woman introduced herself as Hannah Goldsmith and explained that this was the second year she and her husband were wintering in Mazatlán. She also peppered Callie with questions about her life.

Deflecting the questions was easy enough, but Callie did tell the well-dressed woman with the impeccable manicure and well-coifed hair that she'd recently moved to Mazatlán and was looking for a job. "Mrs. Goldsmith, I'd like your advice. Do you think some of the Americans who live here would be interested in learning basic Spanish?"

The woman nodded vigorously in response, her dangling gold earrings bouncing with each shake of her head. "Definitely, Callie. Definitely. If you were the teacher, I'd be your first student! Are you free tomorrow? If you'd like me to, I can introduce you to some of my friends."

Callie Denton had a business.

The following week, as Callie was walking to her car after teaching her first class for Mrs. Goldsmith and a small group of her friends, she passed a café nestled between a dress shop and a high-end jewelry store. The name caught her attention: Café Alvarez. *What were the odds?* A thrum of expectation ran through her. In addition to coffee and a variety of lunch-type items and pastries, a sign in the window noted that the cafe offered Wi-Fi.

Callie pushed the door open and stepped inside. The welcoming aroma of roasted coffee encouraged her forward. As she ordered a coffee and chocolate pastry from the harried clerk, she glanced around the attractive, busy café. A framed picture on the wall behind the counter caught her attention. The uniformed officer standing to the left of a smiling young man and a *Gran inauguración* sign looked just like the picture of Captain Alvarez that she'd found on the internet. Finding it difficult to suppress a broad grin, she covered her mouth, concerned that a sudden smile for no apparent reason would make her look like the village idiot, or more likely, a crazy *gringa*.

She couldn't believe her good fortune. She had an apartment and a job, and now she'd found a charming café with a link to the man she needed to meet. The café became a daily stop, even on the days when she wasn't teaching her enthusiastic, if frustratingly slow learning, language students.

It didn't take long for the friendly proprietor to introduce himself. When she gestured to the photo on the wall, Juan Alvarez proudly announced that the smiling, uniformed man in the picture was the captain of the police, Mateo Alvarez, his uncle. Callie feigned surprise, but confessed it was the name of the café that had drawn her to the place. "A friend of mine knows someone in Colorado by the name of Anna Alvarez. She's the reason I decided to come to Mazatlán. Is she a relative?"

"*Tia Anna*! *Si…Si.* " Juan enthusiastically confirmed that Anna was his aunt. At that moment, Callie realized her introduction to the captain would be easier, and less awkward, if made through his nephew. As her conversation with Juan continued, she explained that when she was considering places to retire in Mexico, she recalled all the good things her friend had told her about Mazatlán, based on conversations with his *Tia Anna.*

Juan grinned. His eyes sparkling with obvious excitement, he explained that his uncle Mateo, the police captain, would be home from Mexico City in a couple of days. "He will be very pleased to hear that your friend knows his sister. I will introduce you to him." Callie wanted to hug the young man. Instead, she just smiled and said, "I look forward to meeting your uncle."

~

One week later, and three weeks after beginning her new life in Mazatlán, Callie was sitting at her favorite table in the back corner of Café Alvarez. Between her laptop and the piles of worksheets for her students, there was barely room for her coffee. Engrossed in her work, it wasn't until she heard someone clearing his throat that she glanced up.

A handsome, uniformed man with a military bearing stood a few feet away, waiting for her acknowledgment. She recognized him immediately. Once they made eye contact, he approached with an open and cordial expression. "Senora Denton?"

She stood. "*Si. Captain Alvarez?*"

He smiled and nodded, answering her in English. "Yes. My nephew tells me that you are here in our city because of my sister?"

"Yes, I am." She explained, just as she had with his nephew. This time, adding a bit more embellishment, and ending with, "So, you see, I have your sister to thank for introducing me to…" she opened her arms in a gesture to encompass the café, and by extension, the city, "this beautiful place."

After giving an exaggerated glance to the over-burdened table and the chair stacked with books, she shrugged in apology. "I'd offer you a seat, but…I'm afraid I've taken up all the space."

He laughed. "No worries." He pointed to the Spanish/English dictionary and the worksheets she'd prepared for her students, "Are you a teacher?"

She nodded and gestured to the papers in front of her. "I'm giving elementary Spanish lessons to some of the American women who live here in the winter."

"Ahh, I see. And how is that going?"

It was her turn to laugh, acknowledging the raised eyebrows and head tilt that accompanied his question. "Much as you might imagine, I'm afraid. But, they try."

They shared a conspiratorial chuckle. The captain continued, "Is it only elderly American women that you teach?"

"So far. They're the only ones who have expressed an interest."

His expression turned pensive. "I am wondering, and I would need to discuss this further with my wife, but our daughter Mariana is in need of some assistance with her English. Mariana is twelve. She is very bright." He chuckled. "But of course as her father I would think this. She does not always," he hesitated as if searching for the correct English word, "apply herself. Have I said this right?"

"Yes, I understand. Perhaps being twelve is the problem? There are many things more interesting than learning English when you're twelve."

He laughed out loud and nodded his head. "Yes, that is true."

"If your wife and Mariana agree, I'd certainly be willing to help."

They made plans for her to meet his wife and daughter. "I'm happy for the success of my nephew." The captain gestured to the crowded café. "But perhaps a quieter location would be best. I know of just the place."

Callie didn't sleep much on the night before their planned meeting at a restaurant not far from her apartment. This time, it wasn't nightmares about Frank that kept her wide-eyed and staring at the ceiling fan as it quietly rotated above her head. It was the questions the captain and his wife might ask—and all the ways she could trip herself up.

She turned on the light and wrote the questions down. She polished her answers, reminding herself that her retired Kansas school-teacher persona existed only in her mind and in vague references made to a group of elderly women. Since her bland appearance could serve as a canvas for a variety of other past lives, she decided now might be the time to modify her background to one less easy to check.

~

The next evening, Callie dressed in a modest, but stylish black dress. For good luck, she wore the simple gold choker and hoop earrings she'd purchased for her night out with Cliff's art patrons—a lifetime ago. She'd chosen the dress with care, for once allowing her ego to overrule her frumpy persona. She needed the courage and self-confidence that looking good gave her—especially since she was meeting the captain's wife.

The upscale seafood restaurant in the historic district where she was to meet the Alvarez family was only a short walk from her apartment. When the restaurant's proprietor showed her to the white-clothed table and she saw the stunning woman seated next to the captain, she was glad for the care she'd taken with her appearance.

Elena Alvarez greeted Callie with a warm handshake and a friendly smile. As the dinner progressed, Callie decided that she liked this woman with the quick wit and pleasant demeanor. Mariana sat on the other side of her mother, dressed in a demure blouse and skirt, her long dark hair neatly combed. After a respectful hello, she had remained silent, but exuded energy and curiosity as she actively followed the adults' conversation in English.

Pleasantries were exchanged, dinner recommendations offered, and meals selected before the gentle interrogation began. Callie was prepared with the latest version of her life story. "Since I never married, and my parents died when I was young, it made sense for me to be the one to take care of my aging aunt. Before I moved in with Aunt Florence, I'd done some part-time teaching, and in my younger days I'd traveled a bit and held a variety of unimpressive jobs. That's actually how I learned Spanish. I later took some formal language classes while I was living with my aunt.

"I guess you could say" Callie gave a slight shrug of her shoulders, aware of the absurdity of her next words, "my life has not had much excitement. When my aunt passed away and left me a small inheritance, I decided to take a leap of faith outside of my comfort zone." She laughed and shook her head. "Of course, the brutal Kansas winters might have had something to do with my decision to move south, but it was a remembered conversation with an old friend that sent me here to Mazatlán."

Hoping to move the focus away from herself and the past she'd thinly constructed to replace the truth, Callie turned to Mariana. The child was too well-mannered to interrupt the adults, but Callie could sense that she wanted to speak. The conversation between the adults had proceeded in English. Callie switched to Spanish when she addressed Mariana. "You are very lucky to live in such a beautiful place. Do you enjoy the water? Or, do you have other interests that are more fun?"

Once given an opportunity to speak, Mariana chatted away about how much she loved reading and art, especially water-color painting. She shared stories about her terrier puppy, and confessed that she'd always wanted a horse, "but Mama says there's no place to keep him." Before she could continue, her mother interrupted with a laugh.

"Mariana," she addressed her daughter in English, "perhaps Senora Denton would like to hear you tell her all of that in English?"

Mariana frowned and sighed. "*Si, Mama*" She turned to face Callie. "I study English since I am a little girl, but…" She shrugged. "It is not easy."

Callie nodded. The child's exuberance, and that hint of insecurity, brought back bittersweet memories of her young friend Sara, Donnie's daughter. Her mind wandered to a vision of the pretty, blonde-haired girl laughingly hugging her pony. *Stop it!* She admonished herself. *This isn't the time for a trip down memory lane.*

Callie refocused with a small intake of breath and smiled at Mariana. "I understand. English isn't easy, but if you'd like, and if your parents agree," she turned to the captain and his wife, "I'd like to help. Maybe we can even make it fun."

By the end of the dinner, Callie was Mariana's English tutor.

~

The month of November came and went. Thanks to Callie's efforts, her elderly American students were gaining confidence and could manage a smattering of Spanish phrases. More important were the twice weekly tutoring sessions with young Mariana, through which Callie had developed a friendly relationship with the child's parents. Her busy schedule, including her twice weekly message-board chats with Connor, kept her sane. Otherwise, worry over the lack of news from New Jersey would have consumed her days—and nights. She tried to temper her concern by reminding herself that the extended time allowed her to strengthen the bridge she was building between herself and Captain Alvarez.

In early December, after finishing a class with one of her senior-citizen groups, Callie retired to her favorite table in the back corner of Café Alvarez to check on news from New Jersey. Engrossed in her computer search, she didn't notice anyone approach.

"Good afternoon, Senora Denton."

Callie recognized the warm voice and the inflected accent. She closed her laptop and glanced up with a smile, *"Buenos días, Captain Alvarez. ¿Cómo está?"*

"I'm fine. Thank you. You're looking well as always. I thought I'd find you here." He always spoke to her in English, either for practice, or in deference to her native tongue. At first she hadn't been sure. She'd finally decided it was the latter, since his proficiency in the language denied any need for practice.

"Uh oh! I guess I'm too predictable. I'll have to make sure I don't do anything I'd want to hide from you." Callie laughed at her own joke, an actress playing a role. "Were you looking for me for any particular reason?" Her question appeared merely curious, but her heart beat a little faster while she waited for his answer.

"Yes. Since it is but three weeks away, my daughter insists I invite you to our Christmas celebration before you make other plans." He laughed and grinned. "Of course, she is the child, and I am the parent, and I am in charge. So, it is my decision. Mariana's mother and I would very much like for you to join us at our Noche Buena celebration—after our Las Posadas procession on Christmas Eve."

He responded to her quizzical expression before she had an opportunity to ask the question. "The posada is a local tradition. It is a parade through the village where Mary and Joseph search for a place to stay. This is your first Christmas in Mexico, is it not?"

Callie nodded and smiled. She genuinely liked the police chief and his wife. They'd made her feel welcome in their home, and a shared love of horses created a bond with Mariana that greatly assisted in the young girl's English lessons.

"Yes. I'm looking forward to it. I'd love to join in your celebration. Are you sure I won't be intruding? Isn't Noche Buena a family time?"

"It is a big fiesta, a party that includes all our family and friends. You will come?"

"Yes, *gracias*. I'll look forward to it."

"Good. I will tell Mariana. She will be happy with her papa. Good day, Senora."

"Good day, Captain."

Callie held her smile as the captain maneuvered his way through the tables and away from where she sat in the back corner of the noisy café. As always, the café was filled with a mixed group—those who came for coffee and conversation, and those, like Callie, who drank their coffee and communed in silence with their laptops. She waved when the captain turned and glanced back at her before he opened the door and exited into the brilliant morning sunshine.

Only a camera with a fast shutter speed would have caught the change. One second a smile, the next a troubled, pensive expression. As she stared down at her laptop, Callie bit her lip in thought. Then she slipped her laptop into her oversized handbag and pasted the ingratiating smile of her Kansas schoolteacher persona on a face fast becoming lined and aged with worry. After a quick smile and a mumbled *"Gracias"* for Juan Alvarez, she donned her sunglasses and slipped out of the café.

It had been almost three months since she'd left Colorado to begin life as Callie Denton, a frumpy, middle-aged woman hovering on the edges of the ex-pat community on the Mexican Riviera. Only Mariana occasionally caught a glimpse of her real self. Sometimes Callie let down her guard when she was with her friendly and engaging student. She was initially confused by the puzzled expression on the young girl's face when she shared stories about ranching in Montana. Then, she'd remember. Mariana was looking at a dowdy, middle-aged school teacher, not the athletic horsewoman who had honed her riding skills ranching in the mountainous states of the American west.

Unfortunately, Cassie Deahl didn't much like Callie Denton. In her panic to create an unrecognizable new identity, one far removed from that of Cassie Deahl, she had gone too far. She found Callie Denton to be stifling, boring, and somewhat pitiable. She despised the unattractive short brown hair that made her skin appear sallow, the heavy glasses that hurt her nose, and the polyester pant suits that defined a person she never wanted to be.

She had buried Cathy Dial. She didn't pine for the young woman whose desperate need for love had almost cost her life, but she did miss the woman who had become Cassie Deahl—the woman who, after a twenty-year odyssey, had abandoned happiness in order to survive. Yet even as these thoughts played out, she pushed them aside. There was too much at stake to dwell on the minor annoyances of her new life, and she couldn't afford long pity parties.

~

Callie's internet searches for what she mentally referred to as 'the news from New Jersey' had become somewhat routine. Every day, she logged on, checked a selection of news sites, and, finding nothing new, logged off to go about her day. She thought she'd be prepared for the moment when her internet search bore fruit. She wasn't.

Two days after the captain's gracious invitation to spend Christmas Eve with his family, she logged on at the café and read the words she'd been dreading—

Disgraced Police Chief Granted Parole

Even though she had been expecting it, the news hit her like a punch to the gut. Her hands exploded off the keyboard as if scalded by hot grease, and her nearly full cup of coffee splattered across the table and onto the floor.

"Senora?" Juan Alvarez called out to her as he rushed across the café to her table. His face wreathed in concern, he quizzed her in English, "Are you ill?"

Shaken, but also embarrassed by the scene she'd caused, Callie shook her head. "I'm sorry. I...I just received some disturbing news." She dabbed at the keyboard with her napkin, grateful the spilled coffee had barely touched it. She quickly closed the laptop and looked up. "I'm truly sorry, Senor Alvarez." Still shaky, she gestured to the pooled coffee on the floor and across the table. "I'm afraid I've made quite a mess."

"Do not worry. It is only coffee." The proprietor smiled as he gestured to the young woman behind the counter. Moments later, he had a towel in his hand. He wiped up the table and the floor. "See. Good as new." He grinned and then quickly turned serious. "I am sorry that you've had bad news. If there is anything…" His words trailed off.

"Thank you. You're very kind. I'm fine now. I apologize."

"There is no problem." With a smile and a nod, he returned to the counter at the front of the café.

Even though her bare, sandaled toes were wet with coffee, Callie didn't move. Her mind shouted at her to open her laptop and read the rest of the article, but her hands were frozen, her fingers balled into fists.

A woman's loud laughter followed by a man's hardy guffaw shocked her back to reality. She looked up to see a young couple approaching the counter. Their exuberant happiness was infectious. People glanced up from their laptops or turned away from their conversations to share their joy. Callie couldn't even fake a smile. She idly wondered if or when she'd been that carefree. She didn't have the time or the desire to probe her past for an answer. Besides, she already knew what that answer would be—at least twenty years ago, before she met Frank Peters.

She sighed and opened her computer, nodding to herself in grim understanding as she read the news articles. As much as she'd hoped otherwise, she had never actually doubted Frank would manage to get paroled. It proved that the powerful men in his debt feared Frank Peters more than they feared public sentiment.

Being granted parole for his original imprisonment would not result in Frank's automatic release from jail. Bail for his current indictment for Amy's murder had been set at two million dollars. Not surprisingly, Frank's attorneys were pursuing a bail reduction claiming the amount was unnecessarily excessive and that Frank wasn't a flight risk. Callie knew better—on both counts.

Frank was definitely a flight risk, and she was sure he had more than enough money hidden away, probably in a number of offshore accounts, to cover the ten percent needed for a bond. But he'd already been convicted of tax evasion, and Callie assumed he'd depleted his legitimate savings paying the legal fees for his first trial. She doubted he had two hundred thousand dollars in accessible funds. What she didn't doubt was that someone would post the bail for him.

Her mind on overload, Callie left the café in a daze. She was tired of running, tired of looking over her shoulder, tired of nightmares—and tired of having to keep her lies straight. If she didn't want to live the rest of her life in fear and exile, she needed to face the monster head on—on her turf—on her terms. She had been toying with this idea for some time, both terrified and exhilarated by the thought of forcing a confrontation with Frank—before he found her on his own.

She fought an internal battle between her two selves: The woman whose vivid recollections of cowering on the floor at Frank's feet turned her blood cold and made her want to run to Captain Alvarez and beg him to protect her. And her other self, the woman who had made Frank pay for what he'd done but who had never foreseen what it would cost her. That woman, whose survival had been based on a long series of complicated lies, knew that running to the captain wasn't an option—at least not yet.

If she went to him now, her house-of-cards life would tumble in a heap. As the head of the police department, Alvarez would have no choice but to contact the American authorities. Her passport was fraudulent. Even her last identity was a lie. They'd arrest her. Frank would find her—she would die.

That wasn't an option.

But if she played her cards right. If she planned things out just so, she could be free, and Captain Alvarez would be the one to make it happen. Everything she'd learned about the captain in the previous weeks convinced her he was a good man, a fair man. He would help her. She would finally be able to stop running, stop hiding. She and Connor could plan a future. With those heady thoughts filling her mind, she pushed any remaining doubts aside. She would do it. She'd take the chance.

On her way to teach a class at the Mexicana Sunrise Community Center on December 10th, Callie put the first piece of her plan in place. Her landlady's nephew, the doorman at the Tropic Palace Resort Beach Hotel, grinned and nodded when she pulled up and asked in a meek voice if she could park her car by the door for "*tan sólo un minuto diminuto*".

The glitzy ten-story hotel lobby was usually packed with tourists during check-in time, and with laughing party-goers during happy hour at the bar. This time of day, it was empty. A hurried purchase at the gift shop garnered a postcard with a photo of the hotel emblazoned with the words *WELCOME TO MAZATLÁN* across the front. She added a stamp, a short note, "*Miss you. Can't wait to see you. Love, C*," and Connor's address. As the card slid through the outgoing mail slot, she pursed her lips and exhaled. Tomorrow, she'd mail a second card—as insurance.

There was a resolute bounce in her step, and a broad smile and *"Gracias"* for Antonio when she returned to her car. As she pulled away from the hotel, she rolled down the car window, inhaled a warm sea breeze that held the scent of freedom, and tilted her head back against the seat so the sun could caress her face. Humming along to the Spanish version of Jingle Bell Rock playing on the radio, she drove down the street lined with stately palm trees and expensive hotels.

The post card to Connor was the first in a line of poisoned bread crumbs that the vultures would swallow on their way to find her. She'd lure Frank to Mexico, and with the help of Captain Alvarez, she'd have the trap ready to spring when he arrived. She'd finally taken control of her future. No more running away.

35

MAZATLÁN, MEXICO

Thirteen days later, at exactly 8:50 a.m. on the 23rd of December, Callie sat in a small phone booth, one of only two in the Tropic Palace Resort Beach Hotel. After dialing the number, she waited, nervously drumming her fingers on the booth's Formica ledge. With each ring, her apprehension grew. *Agnes and Pepper always arrive at the vet clinic at least fifteen minutes before Connor. Why aren't they answering the phone?*

"Jamestown Animal Hospital!"

Callie sucked in her breath at the sound of Pepper's energetic, welcoming greeting. She could picture the vivacious young girl with the multi-colored hair and various body piercings. She hadn't allowed herself to think about how much she missed Pepper, or Agnes, or any of the other people who had graced Cassie's Deahl's life. Hearing Pepper's voice created an unexpected wave of grief that stole her voice.

"Hello? Is anyone there?"

Callie inhaled a gulp of stuffy phone-booth air and tried to speak. All she managed was a strangled "hello". She cleared her throat and tried again. This time, she released four words in a breathy voice, hardly more than a whisper. "Hey, Pepper. It's Cassie."

"Cassie!!!" Pepper shrieked. "Agnes, it's Cassie!" Her questions came in a rush. "Where are you? Are you coming home? When are you coming home? We miss you! Doc really misses you! Even the animals miss you."

Callie smiled through her tears. She had forgotten…no, not really forgotten. She had forced herself not to remember how much she'd loved the life she'd had to abandon. As she waited in silence, Pepper chattered on.

Finally, she heard another voice—the mature, caring voice of a good friend. "Pepper, come up for breath. Is it really Cassie? You haven't given her a chance to say a word." A moment of silence was followed by, "Hello? Is it you, Cassie?"

"Yes. Hi Agnes. It's me. I only have a couple of minutes. I just wanted to wish you all a Merry Christmas. Please tell everyone I wish them a Merry Christmas. I don't have time to talk. I just wanted you to know that I love you all."

"We love you, too, Cassie. You're always in my prayers. And Merry Christmas to you, too. I'm sorry Connor isn't here to talk to you."

"That's all right. Bye, Agnes. Be well." Emotion choking her words, she was barely able to add, "Merry Christmas."

Callie Denton hung up the phone and exhaled the shaky breath she'd been holding. Revisiting her life as Cassie Deahl, if only for a few moments, was harder than she'd imagined it would be. She allowed herself a moment to mourn, but only a moment.

She'd calculated the timing of her call. Knew that she wouldn't have to say much, that Pepper would ask a million questions. She'd also planned to finish the call before Connor arrived. She couldn't speak to him, wasn't ready to answer his questions, couldn't explain why she'd broken all the rules they'd established about their contact. It was part of her plan, a plan she hadn't shared with Connor.

She could picture the scene at the clinic, probably occurring at that very moment. Connor, walking through the door with a "Good Morning" greeting, and Pepper pouncing on him with news that "Cassie just called!" He'd hide his confusion and hurt, at least from Pepper. Agnes would pick up on it. Then he'd retreat to his office. She hated herself for hurting him, for holding back, for keeping him in the dark, but she had no choice. It was the only way she could hope to keep him safe.

At least twice a week, they connected via coded conversations in the online chat group. Somehow, and against her better judgment, he'd managed to convince her it would be safe for him to visit her—after Christmas, on New Year's Day. He was going to tell everyone he was heading south to meet an old college roommate for a couple of days. Then he'd fly to Durango and drive the remaining 150 miles to Mazatlán.

All his plans were arranged to protect her, and yet here she was on the phone and sending postcards. He wasn't stupid. He'd figure it out, figure out that she was purposely leaving a trail. And when he did? When he finally figured it out, what would he do then?

Please God, don't let him get here too soon! She shook her head in annoyance. If there was a God, he'd given up on her a long time ago. Now wasn't the time for prayerful entreaties. She needed to make her own luck and do her best to ensure Connor stayed safe, even as she felt guilty for using him to get to Frank. *As long as he stays away, as long as he waits until the New Year, he'll be fine.* She repeated that thought to herself whenever the guilt overwhelmed her.

~

Callie wasn't in the mood for the festive atmosphere and the warm Feliz Navidad wishes that enveloped her when she left her apartment on Christmas Eve. After a quick trip to the store for milk, she spent the rest of the day finishing her Christmas gifts for the Alvarez family: a small matted and framed water color portrait of a laughing Mariana for her parents, and a peaceful scene of grazing horses framed by a Montana sunset for Mariana.

For the Noche Buena celebration that evening, she wore a festive, but conservative, calf-length wine-colored dress with a black lace shawl over her shoulders. Her outfit was accented with faux pearl stud earrings, a matching necklace, and sensible black pumps.

"Buenas Noches! Feliz Navidad, Callie!" Elena Alvarez, greeted her with a warm smile and a hug when Callie arrived at their home. An elegant red dress swirled around her calves as she stepped away and ushered Callie into a home already crowded with noisy guests. She switched to English as they walked. "I'm so glad you could join us for our Noche Buena festivities. Let me introduce you to the rest of my family, and our other guests."

After numerous introductions, most of which Callie was sure she wouldn't remember, an excited Mariana rushed over. "Senora Denton! Feliz Navidad!" She turned back to her mother with a sheepish grin. "I'm sorry, Mama. I meant to say, Merry Christmas!" Elena Alvarez laughed and patted her daughter's cheek. "Feliz Navidad is fine for tonight, Mariana."

"Mama, may I show Senora Denton all the food?" Mariana's eyes were wide and her excitement contagious. Callie smiled at the young girl she'd grown fond of.

"Yes, Mariana. That's a wonderful idea. Perhaps you can help her select some that are your favorites." Elena turned back to Callie. "There are many traditional foods you may not be familiar with. Mariana will enjoy playing the role of teacher this time."

When Callie bade goodnight to the Alvarez family around midnight, their joyful Feliz Navidad wishes were accompanied by the distant sound of church bells welcoming parishioners to midnight mass. She smiled as she reflected on the evening's festivities. The extended Alvarez family had embraced her—welcomed the shy, unassuming school teacher who studied their culture and flattered without embarrassing them. She'd been humbled by their praise of her paintings and by the family's gratitude for the gifts she'd created for them.

She needed the Alvarez family—more specifically, the captain—to care about her, believe in her, or she would be cornered in her own trap. When her calculating appraisal of the captain and his family provoked feelings of guilt, she pushed the feelings aside. She genuinely cared for them. She just needed the captain to do his job.

~

Mid-day on the 26th of December, Callie drove to police headquarters to put phase two of her plan in place. It was finally time to get Captain Alvarez on board. As she parked her car, she struggled to catch her breath and fight off an anxiety attack. The imposing building terrified her, but she needed to meet the captain in his official capacity, leaving no question regarding the seriousness of her situation.

With shaky steps, she entered the building and stopped at the front desk where she stammered out her request to see Captain Alvarez. After a phone call ascertained the captain's willingness to see her, Callie was directed to his office. *You can do this...you can do this.* She repeated the words over and over in her mind as she marched down the hall, eyes downcast, afraid to make contact with the uniformed men who seemed to be coming at her from all directions. She directed herself forward—each step more difficult than the last.

The captain glanced up from his desk when he saw her approach the open door to his office. "Senora Denton! To what do I owe the pleasure of your visit?" His smile faded when he noticed her pained expression. He stood and stepped away from his desk. "Is there something wrong? Something I can help you with?"

This meeting was a calculated risk. There were still at least a couple of days before she needed to share her story with the captain, but she'd decided it was too risky to wait. What if he decided to take some time off? What if he got called away on a big case? There were too many 'what ifs'. Yet in spite of her determination, now that she was in his office, she was suddenly mute.

Finally, she squared her shoulders and blurted out the lines she'd memorized. "I didn't want to bother you. I thought I could handle it myself." As she stared into the captain's intense, concerned brown eyes, she let him see the emotion in her own eyes, emotion she normally kept well hidden.

Compassion came through in the tone of his words. "Please, please sit. Tell me what is wrong."

She sat. He returned to his own chair, placing his folded hands on the desk, his demeanor and expression an encouragement for her to speak. She began with an apology. "I'm a fraud, Captain Alvarez. I apologize for not having been truthful with you. I'm...I'm not here in Mazatlán as just another retired ex-pat. I'm here because I'm afraid for my life."

She cried, not manufactured tears to gain sympathy, but tears of genuine fear and terror as she came to terms with the magnitude of the risk she was taking. After all her years of running, she had invited Frank to find her. The postcards emblazoned with the hotel's name provided the place. The phone call to Connor's clinic placed from a phone booth in that same hotel, provided confirmation that she was the one who'd sent them.

She was absolutely certain that Frank had someone watching and listening. There were plenty of people willing to break the laws needing to be broken, and it would be easy enough to trace the calls to Connor's office and to monitor his mail.

"I'm sorry," she said as she wiped her eyes. "I pride myself on not being overly emotional, but it's hard for me to talk about all of this."

She took a deep breath and continued. "Twenty years ago, a man was sent to prison for murder—because of me. He's free now. He was released on parole." She gulped in air and swiped at her tears. "I thought I could hide from him, but I was wrong. He knows where I am." She sat up straight and forced herself to stare directly into the Captain's eyes. "He's coming here to kill me."

She couldn't tell him more, not yet. It was too soon to share Frank's name. If the captain contacted the American authorities now, they'd have too many questions for her, and too much time to pursue the answers. She had to wait. Once she knew Frank was on his way, she'd tell the captain his name, but not that she was his wife. She was Callie Denton now.

"You and your family have been so kind to me, I'm sorry that I misled you about why I was here."

She watched as the captain processed the information, his expression a mixture of confusion, compassion, and concern. Hoping to allay at least part of the concern, she said, "I'm here in Mexico legally." Yet one more lie in a string of lies she had gotten too used to telling.

He visibly relaxed, but his expression remained troubled. She was manipulating him, as she had manipulated so many others over the years. She struggled with her duplicity, but accepted that she had no choice.

Now, she sat, awaiting the captain's judgment. Her life depended on whether or not he believed her story. Would he be willing to help her, or would he throw up his hands and tell her to call the American authorities—a certain death sentence?

While she waited, the interminable silence weighed on Callie's remaining composure. She tried to maintain eye contact, but tears blurred her vision. As she fumbled for a tissue to wipe her nose, her purse fell from her lap. She retrieved it with trembling hands.

Finally, the captain seemed to come a decision. He nodded. "Tell me more, Senora Denton. Please, tell me more. What is this man's name?"

"I can't tell you that right now." Her eyes pleaded with him to understand. "I trust you. I truly do, but if you contact the FBI, or the other U.S. authorities, he'll find out, and he'll have more time to plan his revenge. He's well connected—and he has plenty of money. I'm afraid, not only for me, but for my friends and family. I promise you, in a couple of days I'll give you his name. It won't matter then because he'll already be on his way here to find me. My family will be safe. Please understand…"

His troubled expression returned. Then, he nodded.

Since there was still much she hadn't shared, the captain made no specific promises. Yet when Callie walked out of his office a few minutes later, she believed he would be there for her when she needed him...he had to be. She had no other options.

If her calculations were correct, by the time she shared his name with Captain Alvarez, Frank would be on a plane to Mazatlán. He'd know about the postcards and Connor's planned trip. He would be on his way to find her—and he'd be breaking the law. Legally, he couldn't leave New Jersey, let alone the country, but that wouldn't stop him. He could buy a new identity and a fake passport without breaking a sweat.

A less arrogant man would send someone else to kill her, or to kidnap her and bring her back to the States. Not Frank Peters. Frank wouldn't do that. He wouldn't trust anyone else. Only he was smart enough, only he hated her enough. She could hear his words: "Those wetbacks won't have a fucking clue. We'll be in and out of there before they know it." Shuddering, she felt the hate and saw the madness in his eyes.

As she walked to her car, a myriad of "what-if's" cartwheeled through her mind. *What if I've made a mistake in my planning? What if I've misjudged the timing?* She pushed the doubts aside. If she focused on all the things that could go wrong, she'd be paralyzed with fear. Frank would win—and she would die. That was not an option. If someone was going to die, it would not be her.

36

MAZATLÁN, MEXICO

There wasn't much work for a language teacher during the Christmas holidays. Grateful for the respite, Callie focused her attention on cultivating the friendships she'd made at the Tropic Palace Beach Hotel over the previous weeks. As the kindly American who was always willing to lend a helping hand, she'd befriended the harried reservations clerks, helping them with their English and explaining various American accents and attitudes. The staff was used to seeing her. On occasion, they'd even allowed her behind the reception desk.

Now, though, when Callie most needed access, it wasn't coming easy. Time was running out. Since it was high season in Mazatlán, Frank and his thugs would need a reservation, assuming rooms were still available. That additional complication caused further worry. The only way to allay her concerns would be to find their reservation—one that would definitely not be booked under Frank's name.

In spite of the pressure she was under, Callie couldn't help smiling as she remembered how she and Connor had initially cemented the details for his trip. As her Costa Rican persona, Callie posted that she'd recommended the Tropic Palace Beach Hotel to a friend planning a trip to Costa Rica. She ended the post with "fortunately she was able to make reservations. It's high season here, and very busy."

In confirmation of his trip, Connor had posted that he'd made reservations to visit a friend on New Year's Day. "Someone I can't wait to see."

Callie's smile faded as she recalled a more recent chat—the one resulting from her call to the clinic on Christmas Eve. After she'd said goodbye to Agnes, Callie had used the hotel's Wi-Fi to log on to the chat group and leave a happy Christmas message for Connor. She'd spent the rest of that day, and all of the next, worried about his reaction to her call.

On the morning of the 26th, she entered Café Alvarez, purchased her coffee, placed her laptop on the table—and then taken a deep breath and logged on. Connor's message was exactly what she'd feared it would be. Instead of a short, concise chat message, he'd laid it all out. "A friend I care deeply about did something very dangerous. I think I understand why, and I'm not happy. I've changed my New Year's plans, but I'm having trouble getting earlier airline reservations. Unless the airline finds an open seat for me, I won't be able to see her before the 30th."

Heart pounding, Callie hadn't known how to respond. She struggled with a variety of responses and rejected them all. Finally, she wrote, "Maybe you've misunderstood things? Perhaps it's not as bad as you think. I'm sure she'll be happy to see you on the 30th though." Then, overwhelmed with all the new 'what-if's', she'd slumped back in her chair and allowed the doubt and worry to wash over her.

She had planned for Connor's January 1st hotel reservation to be one more in the line of breadcrumbs leading Frank to her. She was sure he would want to arrive before Connor. He'd salivate over the idea of killing them both. Two for the price of one—the worthless slut who'd cost him twenty years of his life, and the man who dared to care about her.

But if Frank wanted them both, he would need to plan carefully. As a parolee, with a high profile murder case pending, he couldn't disappear from New Jersey for more than a couple of days without risking a manhunt by the authorities. Assuming the holidays gave him some breathing room, Callie doubted he'd arrive before the 29th. December 30th made the most sense, allowing him just enough time to get the lay of the land. Just like she needed just enough time to set the trap that would finally end her nightmares and allow her to welcome Connor and embrace the New Year.

But after reading Connor's message, Callie had new worries. What if he arrived too soon? What would happen then? Callie pushed those thoughts aside. She couldn't afford to waste time worrying about things over which she had no control. She needed to focus on the final and most crucial parts of her plan.

It wasn't until late afternoon on December 27th that Callie was finally able to review the hotel's reservation listings. The Tropic Palace was short-staffed, and the harried reservation clerk was grateful for the bathroom break. Finally alone with the computer, Callie tried to focus, to steady herself as she ran down the list of reservations. She checked the 28th. There was nothing.

Her mouth dry, she reviewed reservations for the 29th. Could she have been wrong? Had she misjudged Frank's determination? No. That was impossible. She continued her search. Then she saw it—two small suites booked under the name of Patrick Turner for late arrival on December 29th.

Suddenly dizzy and light-headed, she lowered her head and pulled air into her lungs. Turner was a common name. There could be other Patrick Turners, but the pain in her gut and the dryness in her throat told her it was him, the corrupt detective who'd always done Frank's bidding. Just as she had expected, they were coming to kill her.

She didn't sleep much that night—or the next. The nightmares were vivid. Twenty years disappeared. The pain, the hate, the fear—it was all there. She'd awake in the dark, shaking and covered with sweat, afraid to close her eyes. Daylight didn't bring relief. She couldn't eat, couldn't stay still. She worked on her deep breathing to stay focused, reminding herself that this was what she had wanted, what she had planned. One way or the other, she would never have to run again.

~

On the morning of the 29th, Callie drove to police headquarters under a stormy sky, not the usual brilliant sunshine of the Mexican Riviera. As she hurried across the parking lot through the rain, she couldn't decide if the weather was a good or bad omen. She decided not to dwell on it.

When Captain Alvarez greeted her in his office, his manner was distant and abrupt, his expression wary. She understood the reason for the change in his demeanor, but it left her with a twinge of sadness at the loss of the friendly relationship they'd had.

Callie approached him as a supplicant, not a friend. "Thank you for meeting with me, and thank you for your patience, Captain Alvarez." She reached across the desk to hand him two sheets of paper. One contained a list of names: Frank Peters, Patrick Turner, Tony D'Alonzo. The other was a screenshot photo of an elderly man.

She nodded toward the picture as she explained the documents. "Frank Peters is the man I told you about. Don't be fooled by the picture. He'll be traveling under an alias with those other two men. They'll all be armed. They're booked for late arrival at the Tropic Palace Resort Beach Hotel under the name Patrick Turner."

"How do you know this?" the captain asked, his expression troubled, bordering on angry—but still a bit unsure.

With an appropriately shamed demeanor, she explained. "I took advantage of a friendship I'd made with the reservation clerk. She let me see the reservations." Callie took a deep breath and continued. "I also checked the possible flights they could take. There's only one that fits. I believe they'll be on a flight from New Jersey that arrives at five o'clock this evening."

"You are sure about this, Senora Denton? This is a very serious accusation you are making."

She couldn't afford not to be sure. She couldn't afford for the captain to see uncertainty in her eyes. "Yes. Yes, I'm sure. Frank Peters had to forfeit his passport. He'll be traveling under a false identity. But yes, I'm sure."

She held his gaze, addressing the hesitation in his eyes with the terror in her own. She stepped forward and clutched his arm. "Please, help me. He's had twenty years to plan his revenge. He's coming here to kill me!"

"All right." The captain's eyes flashed in anger. He rose from behind his desk. Gone was the demeanor of the amiable man, the loving, doting father she'd come to know. In the rigid stance and penetrating eyes of the man in front of her, she saw someone who had witnessed the worst in humanity. "I will meet with my superiors and speak to the U.S. officials this morning. If you are correct about this, these men will be stopped."

A few minutes later, Callie left the captain's office, knowing she'd done everything she could do. She was sure the U.S. authorities would have questions, but it was too late for that. She wouldn't be home if they came to find her—and the clock was ticking.

~

At four-thirty that afternoon, Callie slipped into the hotel lobby from the side entrance. The usually quiet lobby bar was crowded, filled with restless, impatient tourists who were losing an expensive day of sun worshipping because of the rain. Once again she wondered if the stormy day was a bad omen, or a good one. She tried to remind herself that she wasn't superstitious.

Nerves taut, stomach churning, she bounced from one foot to the other as she assessed the crowd. The drunken revelers were an added complication, but maybe one she could use to her advantage—if she could get an empty table, a specific table, the one behind the column next to a big potted palm.

The two middle-aged guys sitting at that table didn't seem to be in any hurry. She nervously tapped her foot while she waited. Flirting to get the table was out of the question. They'd laugh at the schoolmarm with the unflattering glasses and frumpy clothes.

"There you are!" Callie turned as two overweight women wearing tight slacks and carrying large woven handbags rushed over to the men's table. "We've been looking all over for you. If we can't go to the beach, we might as well get some souvenirs. Come on. Let's go. You'll both be skunk-faced before dinner at the rate you're going."

Callie smiled in gratitude as the two men were hustled off by their wives. She slid into one of the newly emptied chairs, pushed their empty glasses aside, and buried her face in a fashion magazine before anyone noticed the table had been vacated. As the afternoon turned into evening, she sipped a glass of Chardonnay, picked at nachos and salsa, and periodically turned a page in her magazine.

The wait was interminable. She gnawed on her lip and constantly checked her watch, always surprised at how little time had passed since the last time she'd checked.

Then everything changed.

She glanced up from her magazine as two burly men wearing loose-fitting sport coats over khaki pants and gaudy Hawaiian print shirts approached the registration desk. Holding her breath, she edged forward on her seat, her gaze darting from face to face in the crowded lobby. It took her a minute to locate the third man—the man who had been the focus of her nightmares for over twenty years. He was standing off to the side, attempting to blend in with a family group registering with the next desk clerk.

It was Frank.

Callie stifled a gasp. Every nerve ending fired, and she understood the equine fight or flight response on a visceral level better than she'd ever understood it before. She covered her mouth with her hand to keep from crying out. It took all her focus to force her hand down to clasp the other one in her lap. Quick glances to either side confirmed no one had noticed her reaction. The people at the table to her right were sharing stories about their last vacation. The couple to her left only had eyes for each other. She exhaled slowly.

The man responsible for destroying her life—for all her years of running, for all her pain—was standing not more than fifty yards away. The elderly white-haired man leaning on a cane may have fooled the others. They likely wouldn't waste a glance on the frail senior citizen. But Callie didn't see the feeble guy with a cane. She saw the strong body and hard cruel eyes of the man who had stolen her innocence, tortured and degraded her, and made her wish for death—until she'd found the strength to fight back.

She'd beaten him once. She could do it again. Closing her eyes, she drew on her years of yoga and martial arts training—all the learned focus techniques. She breathed in and exhaled slowly, finding her center, her core. When she reopened her eyes, the scene hadn't changed, but she had. This was her fight now. He was on her turf and her timetable. Only one of them was going to survive. Whatever the outcome, it was better than running. She was done with running.

She reached into her purse, reassured when she touched cold, hard steel. Her lips curled in a small smile as her hand found its place, and her finger rested on the trigger of the gun that had been hers for almost twenty years. In the early years, she'd carried it with her and spent long hours at the shooting range, learning its secrets. Eventually, it had found its way into a series of safe-deposit boxes. The gun was an old friend.

She had taken a calculated risk when she'd smuggled the gun over the border taped under the passenger seat of her car. She had risked the chance of discovery confident that Callie Denton, the dowdy, middle-aged school teacher, could exhibit believable shock if they discovered a hidden weapon in her recently purchased used car. She felt certain she would have been convincing, but was glad she hadn't been tested.

THE PRICE OF REVENGE

Hatred filled the spaces where fear had been. She stood and hit speed dial on her cell phone, leaving it where it lay on the table. Standing at the back of the lobby, Captain Alvarez glanced down at his phone and then across the lobby at her. When their eyes met, she inclined her head toward Frank and then gestured toward the two men standing together in front of the reception counter. After acknowledging her with a nod, the captain gestured to his men, and they moved forward. Her plan was coming together.

But she had a fallback plan, too—one she hadn't shared. The gun was just for protection. She wouldn't take the first shot—or at least that's what she kept telling herself.

As she stepped forward and began to inch the gun out of the purse hanging on straps from her shoulder, a movement caught her eye. There was something familiar about the man who was walking briskly toward the reception desk, head down, totally unaware he was about to walk into the middle of a shoot-out.

Callie whispered his name. "Connor."

He wasn't supposed to be here now. She was counting on him not arriving until tomorrow. She'd taken a risk in sending him the cards and making the call, but she'd never believed Frank would go after Connor. She thought he'd be safe, as long as he stayed in Colorado.

As she stared at the man she loved, a thought came to her. Maybe there had been another reason for not wanting Connor here, a reason she hadn't wanted to acknowledge. Maybe she hadn't wanted to take the chance he'd see her die.

Confusion began to cloud her brain. Then she pressed her lips into a tight line. It was too late for self-analysis. Her right hand was on the gun in her purse. The captain and his men had split up, silently approaching Frank and his goons. She forced one foot in front of the other and walked out from behind the palm. She focused on Frank, but kept Connor in view.

As if sensing her presence, Connor turned. Their eyes met for the briefest of seconds. "Cassie!" He called out to her—his excited voice echoing across the lobby.

Time stopped. The background sound of the mariachi band disappeared. The conversations of the lounge revelers faded.

Frank turned to face her. At first, there was no recognition. The mousey brown hair, the glasses, the frumpy clothes, she wasn't the woman he remembered—the dolled-up caricature he'd created. As she stepped forward and closed the distance between them, she reached up with her free hand to remove her glasses.

Frank's response was immediate. His eyes widened in recognition, and he emitted a guttural, inhuman sound. Hard, cold eyes locked on hers. Hatred sparked between them, the electricity so real she could feel it in the air. He raised his arm.

She saw the gun.

Her right hand clutched her own gun. She began to raise it from her purse.

Then she heard the deafening crack of a gunshot and a man's high pitched laugh. Both sounds reverberated through the luxurious hotel lobby. Screams...more shots...more screaming. Cassie had only a fleeting moment to take in the scene, to watch as dream vacations turned into nightmares for the tourists unexpectedly involved in the carnage.

She staggered back as a speeding freight train slammed into her chest. A searing pain ripped through her head. She collapsed in a heap to the floor.

"Cassie!"

Through vision becoming cloudy and unfocused, she saw Connor bend over and reach for her.

"Connor..." she whispered.

As the pain stole her breath, she struggled for more words. She had to know. If she was going to die, she had to know.

"Cassie, honey, don't talk."

She hovered on the edge of consciousness, watching as Connor tore off his shirt and pressed it against her chest.

"Hold on Cassie. Hold on!"

The pressure was unbearable. As she slipped into unconsciousness, she managed one more word. A question. "Frank?"

Connor's answer was the last thing she heard. "He's gone, Cassie. He's dead."

37

DENVER, COLORADO

Beep…beep…beep…

A peaceful repetitious sound played to the accompaniment of voices, soft voices that made their own peaceful repetitious sounds. A haze blanketed everything, a deep cottony haze where there was no pain.

Words came to her in muted tones—a girl's voice she couldn't quite place, "Doc, look…" She sank back into the peaceful quiet until she felt a touch on her face. This time, a man's voice intruded through the haze. She knew this voice…

"Cassie….please…"

Her eyelids fluttered and opened, greeting a world of vague shapes and colors. The effort too much, she allowed the fog to once again claim her.

A voice, insistent and demanding, penetrated her mental fog.

"Cassie…please don't leave me."

A choking sound. *Crying?* A warm hand on her face.

She wanted to respond—but the effort was beyond her. Instead, she relaxed into the fog until she felt warm calloused fingers squeezing her hand. The voice was closer now. "Don't give up, Cassie. You can do it. You can come back to me."

The desperation in the voice pierced the oppressive darkness that held her hostage. She struggled to move her fingers, reacting to the warmth and strength of the hand holding hers. She blinked, finally finding definition in the shapes and colors. Her vision shifted to locate the source of the words. Although still out of focus, she recognized the man and tried to smile.

Then the haze once again claimed her.

Sometime later—she didn't know how long—the fog finally lifted. The shapes and colors were fully defined now. She slowly shifted her gaze, taking in the details of what her mind told her was a hospital room. When she moved her head slightly to the right, she saw a machine next to her bed and as more sensation returned to her body, she realized that tubes were connected to her arm.

With a slow turn of her head, she glanced to the left. A man with a few days growth of beard and shaggy, sandy-colored hair was sitting in a chair next to her bed, his head tilted back. He appeared to be sleeping.

She opened her mouth and found her voice. "Connor?" The word came out as a raspy whisper. She swallowed. Although her throat was dry and her mouth parched, she tried again. "Connor?"

He opened his eyes and turned to face her. Jumping up, his chair rocketed back against the wall. "Cassie? Cassie!" Tears streamed down his face into the overgrown stubble on his cheeks. He grabbed her hand. "I knew you'd make it. I told them. I knew it."

She heard murmured words, "…find the doctor." Connor turned away, as if searching for something.

Afraid she'd float away again if he let go of her hand, she whispered a frantic plea. "Don't leave me."

"I won't leave, honey. I'll never leave. I just need…okay, here it is."

He fumbled through the coverings on her bed and picked up something with a long cord. A buzzer?

Moments later, a young woman in a light blue top rushed in. "Is everything…" She stopped mid-stride, her assessing gaze meeting Cassie's eyes. Then she shook her head and smiled. "Welcome back, Cassie. How do you feel?"

"Tired," was the only word she could manage.

The nurse nodded. Her smile still firmly in place, she approached the bed and glanced at the machines. Cassie felt a cool hand on her forehead. Then, stepping away from the bed, the woman turned to Connor. "I'll tell Doctor Reynolds. He's on rounds. He should be here in a few minutes."

Cassie closed her eyes and drifted away.

∿

When next she woke, the room was in shadows. It was obvious some time had passed. This time, she felt more awake and alert.

"Connor?"

She heard the sound of a chair scraping against the floor. "I'm here, Cass. I'm still here." He took her hand "You fell back to sleep for a while."

Her voice low, almost a whisper, she asked, "How long?" She didn't have the energy to finish the thought, but his answer told her he'd understood the question.

"Two weeks. You gave us quite a scare..." He stopped and took a deep breath. His furrowed brow softened, and he smiled. "You're back now. That's all that matters."

She tried to match his smile, but her lips were too dry to allow more than a tiny effort. She had more questions, a lot of questions, but didn't have the energy to ask them.

"What happened?" was all she could manage.

When her question seemed to confuse him, she struggled to find more words. It took a while to get them all out. "I know... I remember what happened. I think...." She still wasn't sure if she'd dreamt those final moments, or if they were real. Had Connor told her Frank was dead, or had she just wanted to believe that he had? "I mean, after...?"

Connor seemed distressed by her question. She wanted to reach out to touch him, but couldn't. So she just squeezed his hand. "Tell me."

"He's gone, Cassie. He'll never bother you again. Frank Peters is dead."

She relaxed back into the pillow and closed her eyes. *Was it finally over?* When she again opened her eyes, tears clouded her vision.

"Cassie, I'm sorry. I didn't mean to upset you."

She pulled Connor's hand to her dry, chapped lips and kissed his palm. She spoke slowly and so softly that he bent close to hear her. "It's..." She searched for a word. "...over. I'm free."

There were so many things she didn't understand. "How?"

"The Mexican police captain grabbed Frank's arm just as he began shooting. The bullet missed your heart by a few centimeters."

She heard Connor take a deep breath. He squeezed her hand and continued. "You went through a difficult operation to repair significant internal damage. A second bullet grazed the side of your head causing brain swelling."

She watched Connor's eyes cloud over as he relived the painful events.

"I almost lost you."

"Captain Alvarez saved my life?"

He nodded.

"Then what happened?"

Connor looked away. She squeezed his hand to regain his attention. "Connor?"

He stroked the side of her face with his free hand. Obviously troubled by what he was about to say, he compressed his lips. The lines in his forehead deepened. Finally, he stared directly into her eyes and answered her question. "While Frank and Captain Alvarez fought for the gun, it went off again. The captain was shot…"

"No!" The word came out as a shriek.

Connor's voice rose above hers. "Cassie, listen. Let me finish. He wasn't killed. He was wounded, but he'll survive."

He stopped speaking. Cassie closed her eyes. *It's not fair. He was only trying to help.* She pulled her hand away from Connor's so she could swipe at the tears.

"Here." She felt the soft edge of a tissue dabbing at her eyes. "He's going to be fine, Cass. He and his men were heroes. The other police officers shot Frank. His two henchmen surrendered without a fight. They were arrested. They'll be doing time in a Mexican jail on weapons charges, maybe even attempted murder —unless they're extradited. I doubt they'll say much if they are."

Cassie kept her eyes closed as she tried to process the information. She kept coming back to Captain Alvarez. He was a good man. Young Mariana worshipped her father.

Finally, she spoke. "It's my fault. He has a family. It's all my fault."

"No, Cassie. He was doing his job. It isn't your fault. No one blames you. He's expected to make a full recovery."

He smiled. "I've spoken to his wife Elena a couple of times. She's been concerned about you. She made me promise to call her if…" He stopped and shook his head. "*when* you came out of your coma. She'll be thrilled to hear the good news."

Connor let go of her hand just long enough to point at an array of cards and flowers covering the window sill and every other horizontal surface. A drawing of a horse was taped to the wall. "Mariana drew you a picture. There's a card from her over there as well. Her mother wanted you to know that you are in their prayers."

Cassie stared in amazement at the colorful cards and flower arrangements. Now that her senses were returning, she became aware of a pleasant floral scent warring with the omnipresent disinfectant smell she always associated with hospitals.

Do I even know this many people?

Connor laughed when she turned her confused gaze back to meet his eyes. "A lot of people were praying for you, Cass. You have a lot of friends. One of them is a young woman who rarely left your bedside these last two weeks. Pepper will be sorry she missed your awakening." He glanced at his watch. "She should be here soon, though. When she gets here, I'll step outside for a little while to make some calls. Agnes will spread the word."

Too overwhelmed and exhausted to react, Cassie once again closed her eyes. Then she forced herself to reopen them. Two more questions needed to be answered before she could rest.

Connor was still standing by her bed, gazing down at her. "I know this is all a bit overwhelming Get some rest. I'll be here when you wake up."

She shook her head. Her gaze took in the hospital room and then focused back on Connor. "Where am I?"

"Denver. University Hospital."

"Who am I?" The question was mumbled as if she was wondering out loud rather than asking a question of Connor.

He chuckled. "Now that's an interesting story. Once you were stabilized, I arranged for medical air transport to fly Callie Denton out of Mexico. The tricky part was that I needed them to deliver Cassie Deahl to the hospital in Denver. Things would have been way too complicated otherwise.

"Donnie and a friend helped. It pays to have friends in high places, and fortunately, Donnie has some very good friends. It helps that he comes from a law enforcement family. Sometime I'll fill you in on the details. Rest now. You're home, and you're safe."

He bent down and kissed her.

Cassie closed her eyes, but she didn't fall asleep, at least not right away. Instead, she spent a few minutes processing everything Connor had told her. She was Cassie Deahl again. She was back in Colorado. Connor was with her—and Frank was dead.

When she finally drifted into sleep, for the first time in more years than she could remember, she slept without fear.

EPILOGUE

JAMESTOWN, CO

"You look beautiful." The warmth in Connor's eyes showed he meant every word of his simple declaration.

"Thank you." Cassie squeezed his hand and smiled. "You make me feel beautiful."

She coughed self-consciously and tried to hide her tears. The doctors had explained that emotional excesses were common with head trauma. They'd promised that the ever-ready tears would stop once she had her strength back and was home following a daily routine. She hoped so. Everything from a blue sky to the kind words of a stranger made her cry. Now, though, all dressed up and ready to go home, she didn't want to ruin the moment with tears.

Her three weeks at the rehabilitation center were finally over. She still had work to do, and weeks, maybe months before she was truly well. But none of that mattered. The hard part was over. She was going home.

Earlier that morning, Pepper had taken her to a beauty salon. Her hair had been cut, styled, and dyed a golden-blonde shade that suited her. She'd been thrilled to see her ugly brown locks and blonde roots disappear, hating her Callie persona less from vanity than because it reminded her of the recent past.

She loved the short, fluffy, pixie style the stylist had recommended. It was sexy and feminine, but very different from the long blonde mane Cassie Deahl had worn. She hadn't planned on making a statement with her new hair style, but that's exactly what she'd done—declaring her freedom from the past, from the fear that had ruled her life.

"Are you ready to go home?" Connor asked, breaking into her thoughts.

She laughed. "Does a horse whinny? Does a dog bark? Hell, yeah, I'm ready to go home!"

This time it was his turn to laugh. She loved hearing the sound of his laughter. They'd been through a tough few weeks, and it felt good to laugh. She had made his life hell, and now she would try to make it up to him.

As an attendant pushed her in the rehab center's wheelchair to Connor's Explorer, Cassie glanced down at the manila envelope in her lap—an envelope that contained what she would always think of as her freedom papers.

Thank God for Donnie Smith.

Connor's best friend had not only been there for Connor when he'd most needed help, he'd also been there for her. Donnie had been the one who'd insisted she hire a good attorney before she talked to the FBI agents who had haunted her hospital room while Connor played guard dog. Once she was out of danger, the agents had insisted on speaking with her—and on getting answers.

The attorney had represented her well. He'd listened to her story, asked myriad questions, and brokered a deal. The government would forgive her many legal transgressions—after she told them everything she knew about Frank Peters and his dirty dealings. Fortunately, during her long trip west to freedom in Pete Connelly's truck over twenty years earlier, she'd had the presence of mind to jot down the information she'd read in Frank's ledger. She'd stored her notes away—just in case. Even though her information was more than twenty years old, it still had value. Many of the men Frank owned remained in positions of power. In exchange for the information, Cathy Dial Peters could stay buried. Callie Denton, having existed for only a few weeks, would be allowed to fade away. And Cassie Deahl could continue life as a small town veterinary assistant.

Her identity resolved and her future secure, Cassie was able to focus her attention on getting well. She'd worked hard to make her therapists happy, and her effort had paid off. However, when her doctor had announced in a stern voice that she couldn't go near a horse—let alone get on one—until the dizzy spells stopped, she'd nodded dutifully, but she had no intention of following his orders. Horses, and riding, were as necessary to her as breathing, and she had spent far too long out of the saddle. Quincy would take care of her, and Connor would make sure she didn't overdo it.

As soon as she could convince Lynne she was strong enough, she'd reclaim her role with the Rescue Ranch horses.

She stared out the partially open window as Connor drove the thirty miles back to Jamestown. The flat, mostly brown landscape included the occasional farm building, small herds of cattle, some newly plowed fields, and a few houses—none of it impressive. Yet as she breathed in the rich ripe scent of earth and cow dung, she smiled. She was going home.

Even though the bright Colorado sun made her squint, she didn't reach for her sunglasses. She wanted to see everything without a filter, everything she'd almost lost for good. Connor drove past a small state park where she'd once seen a bald eagle's nest. She strained to find it and was rewarded for her effort by the sight of a white-capped head. Her vision blurred. She sniffled and rummaged in her pocket for a tissue.

"Cassie? Honey, is something wrong?"

How to explain? The simplest things brought feelings of overwhelming sadness. She went from joy to malaise, experiencing a depression she didn't understand. After spending so many years hiding, so many years on the run, how could she learn to live differently?

The car slowed. Connor pulled over to the shoulder and braked to a stop. She turned to face him when he touched her arm.

"It's okay, Cassie. It's really okay. You'll see. You just need some time."

She nodded, forcing a smile in response to the hopeful expression on his face. He had aged in the last few weeks. There was gray in his sandy hair and deeply etched lines in his face.

"I love you," she murmured, staring into his concern-filled eyes.

When she saw Connor's tears in response to her words, she offered teasing words to make him smile. "Uh-oh. I didn't realize what I had was catching. We can't both cry. Someone has to get us home."

He hugged her and whispered, "I love you, too, my beautiful Cassie." Then he sat back and wiped his eyes with the back of his hand. "Pepper and Agnes will skin me alive if we don't get home soon. They made me promise you'd be there by three o'clock. They're making a big welcome-home dinner."

"Let's go home then." She turned back to the window and glanced up just in time to see the eagle leave the nest and soar up into the clear, blue Colorado sky.

~

A few minutes later, Connor turned the car down the long driveway and parked close to the house.

Cassie pointed excitedly at the huge 'Welcome Home Cassie' banner hanging over the front door. "Look, Connor!"

Connor laughed and nodded. "Pepper wanted balloons as well, but I told her we should keep it low key. Seeing the joy on your face, I'm thinking maybe I should have let her have her way."

"No. This is just right."

A wide grin creased her face. She didn't need a banner, or balloons. Being alive and coming home on a beautiful spring day—that's all she needed. But she had to admit the banner was pretty cool, too.

She heard Connor's car door slam, and then there he was, beside her, holding her own car door open. "Are you okay to walk, or do you want me to help you?"

"If I can lean on you, I can make it." When she met his eyes, letting him know she wasn't just talking about the short walk to the house, she saw an acknowledgment of her broader message.

She climbed out of the car. Connor put his arm around her waist. "Here goes."

Pepper opened the front door as they approached. When she stepped back, a chorus of voices shouted, "Welcome home, Cassie!"

Her body trembled.

Connor tightened his arm around her waist. "Are you okay? Is it too soon for a party? Should we have waited?"

The concern in his voice gave her strength. "No, Connor. It's not too soon." She took a deep breath and stood up straight, taking in the room full of smiling, happy people.

Agnes and Pepper were standing closest to her. Agnes, her eyes filled with tears, mouthed the words, "Welcome home," when their eyes met. Just beyond them, Donnie and his daughter Sara stood next to his Aunt Lynne from the Rescue Ranch.

As a smiling Sara raised her hand in a shy wave, Cassie marveled at how the girl had grown in the few months she'd been away. The child she

THE PRICE OF REVENGE

remembered had grown into a beautiful young woman. Next to Sara, the unflappable Lynne had tears in her eyes.

Cassie's vision blurred. Those damned tears again. She sniffled. Pepper handed her a tissue. In the last few weeks, it seemed like no matter what she needed, the indomitable Pepper was there to hand it to her.

"Thank you, Pepper. Thank you..."

Pepper hugged her and stepped away. "You have friends who came to see you."

Cassie expanded her gaze. Her eyes rested on a group of people she didn't recognize. She looked up at Connor in confusion as he led her to an elderly woman sitting on a straight-backed chair. The woman looked vaguely familiar.

"Cassie, I'd like you to meet Carolyn Andrews from New Jersey."

Cassie's hand flew to her mouth in surprise. Connor nodded and added quietly. "She insisted on coming."

The old woman stood and hugged Cassie. "Welcome home, dear. Thank you for what you did for my Amy."

Overwhelmed, Cassie could find no words. She just nodded. More tears fell. She wiped her eyes with the remnants of the tissue Pepper had given her. As she did so, she caught the eye of a tall, familiar-looking woman standing across the room. The slender woman with silver hair and warm brown eyes strode toward her. It had been so long—over twenty years. Could it really be her?

"Jean?" Cassie asked, her voice overcome with emotion.

"I've missed you, Cathy." The woman made a slight grimace and covered her mouth. "Sorry, I mean, Cassie. Welcome home."

Still in shock, Cassie looked beyond Jean to the couple she had been standing next to. She saw a frail, elderly man sitting in a wheelchair. Tears ran unchecked down his cheeks and, sitting next to him, Cassie saw the kindly face of a tiny, white-haired woman whose own tear-filled eyes shone with warmth and happiness.

It couldn't be.

"Doc? Betty?" Cassie shook her head in disbelief. She was shaking now. She turned to Connor. He hadn't left her side. He hadn't let go of her. Now he helped her into a chair and knelt beside her.

Jean spoke first. "Connor invited us. He tracked me down from some of the stories you'd told him. Of course, it was a bit of a shock for me. Not for Doc and Betty."

Jean smiled as she glanced over at the elderly couple. She continued in a low voice. "They kept your secret well, as we all will now. I love them for it. They knew that John would have had a problem…."

Jean stopped and sighed. "I wish he were here."

She responded to Cassie's shocked and questioning look. "Heart attack, two years ago. He went quickly. It was what he would have wanted. To the very end though, he told me he hoped you were alive, hoped you had gotten away. He'd be so happy for you. He loved you like a daughter."

Speechless, and overcome by emotion, Cassie experienced a sudden flashback to a long-ago conversation with Mike, her once best friend and first love. Sitting on a hay bale in Jean's horse barn on a hot, summer day, she'd grown tired of listening to Mike complain about the demands of his large family. She'd blurted out, "You're lucky to have those roots you complain so much about. If it wasn't for Jean, I'd have no one, and she's your family, not mine." She'd been sixteen then, and her mostly-absent father had left her feeling abandoned and alone long before his death three years later.

Her childhood had been defined by loss, her early adult life by pain, and the last twenty years by fear. Always on the run, she'd seen herself as a tumbleweed controlled by the vagaries of the wind or as a seed buffeted about and never allowed to alight long enough to root. She'd been wrong. Gazing around at this roomful of people who loved her, she realized that the elusive roots she'd long ago given up on had been growing all along.

She laughed out loud through tears of joy. She was home.

*****

Acknowledgements

Writing is a solitary endeavor, but an author cannot be successful without the support of others. I am indebted to my critique partners for soldiering on with me during the creation of THE PRICE OF REVENGE, a rewrite and restructure of CASSIE'S JOURNEY, a novel originally published in 2015—at the beginning of my writing career.

I thank Brenda Hiatt Barber, Leigh Court, and Shirley Jones—all talented authors in their own right—for their insights and suggestions throughout the two-year rewriting process. Cassie's story has been made all the richer as a result.

Kosi, my equine partner, is truly 'My Therapist Who Eats Hay' as I described in an article published in EQUUS Magazine (Winter, 2022). My lifelong love of horses is something I shared with Cassie.

My husband Bob, and Smokey, my gray tabby cat, round out my family and provide the solid and entertaining base from which I write. I have much to be grateful for – including you, my readers. Thank you.

Rita M. Boehm

The Villages, Florida

www.ritamboehm.com

ABOUT THE AUTHOR

Rita M. Boehm spent over forty years toiling in the world of contract management for various defense electronics companies, retiring in 2014 as Director of Contracts and Compliance. Retirement provided an opportunity to rekindle her childhood dreams of being a writer.

Her first book, SECOND CHANCES, was published in 2015. Later that year, she published CASSIE'S JOURNEY, a novel partially triggered by headlines about an Illinois police officer convicted of killing his third wife. The disappearance of his fourth wife, a young woman twenty-four years his junior, remains unsolved.

After publishing two more books in the Second Chances romantic suspense trilogy, Rita switched genres and delved into the world of cozy mysteries. In MISSING ON MAPLE STREET, history repeats itself—a young girl goes missing in a once grand old Victorian mansion that four disparate families now call home.

A bluebird family provided Rita with an opportunity to combine her love of photography with her love of storytelling. BLUEBIRDS IN THE GARDEN was awarded Best Children's Book honors by the Florida Writers Association in 2019.

In yet another genre switch, Rita was compelled to share her father-in-law's WWII story after reading the journals he wrote while serving in North Africa and Europe from 1942 through 1945. ONE SOLDIER'S WAR – IN HIS OWN WORDS is dedicated to all those unsung heroes who tirelessly serve and protect our country.

When she's not writing, Rita enjoys riding her dressage horse, Kosi, playing with her hefty tabby cat, Smokey, and golfing with her husband, Bob.

Reviews are the life blood of independent authors. If you enjoyed THE PRICE OF REVENGE, or any of Rita's other books, please leave a review on Amazon.com. You can visit Rita's website at www.ritamboehm.com or contact her via Facebook at Author Rita Boehm.

Made in the USA
Columbia, SC
04 April 2023

14332594R00193